About the Author

Mark Hayden is the nom de guerre of Adrian Attwood. He lives in Westmorland with his wife, Anne.

He has had a varied career working for a brewery, teaching English and being the Town Clerk in Carnforth, Lancs. He is now a part-time writer and part-time assistant in Anne's craft projects.

EIGHT KINGS

The Sixth Book of the King's Watch

MARK HAYDEN

www.pawpress.co.uk

First Published Worldwide in 2019 by Paw Press
Paperback Edition Published 2019
Reprinted June 2020 (7) with minor corrections.

Cover Design – Rachel Lawston
Design Copyright © 2019 Lawston Design
www.lawstondesign.com
Cover images © Shutterstock

Paw Press – Independent publishing in Westmorland, UK.
www.pawpress.co.uk

ISBN: 1-9998212-6-2
ISBN-13: 978-1-9998212-6-5

For the original

Maggie Pearce

The one inside this book is only a pale imitation

EIGHT KINGS

Dramatis Personae (at end)

After much nagging from Mr Hayden, I have put some notes here about the characters who appear in this book. I hope you find them useful.

Mr Hayden has put them right at the back of the book (apart from the Mowbray family tree).

I recommend that you glance at them and then refer back to them if you need to. As ever, there are full lists and a glossary of magickal terms on the Paw Press website:

www.pawpress.co.uk

I hope you enjoy the book,
Thanks,
Conrad.

The Mowbrays of Cornwall

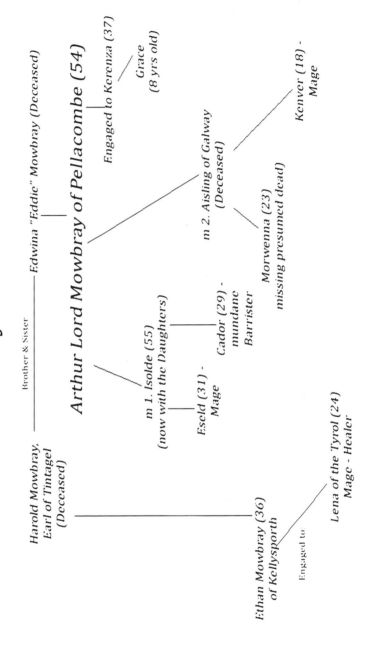

Harold Mowbray, Earl of Tintagel (Deceased) — *Brother & Sister* — Edwina "Eddie" Mowbray (Deceased)

Arthur Lord Mowbray of Pellacombe (54)

Engaged to Kerenza (37)

Grace (8 yrs old)

m 1. Isolde (55) (now with the Daughters)

m 2. Aisling of Galway (Deceased)

Eseld (31) - Mage

Cador (29) - mundane Barrister

Morwenna (23) missing presumed dead

Kenver (18) - Mage

Ethan Mowbray (36) of Kellysporth

Engaged to

Lena of the Tyrol (24) Mage - Healer

Part One — Dog Days

1 – How do you Solve a Problem like Sofía?

'I love what you've done with the place,' said Mother.

She pivoted on one foot, staring around the sitting room of Elvenham, the house she'd come to as a young bride and which she'd handed over to me last Christmas.

'It's exactly the bloody same,' said my father. 'We haven't come in here to see whether Mina's turned the old place into the Taj Mahal.'

Mother fixed him with one of her hard stares. 'The Taj Mahal is a tomb, and a Muslim one at that. Mina is both alive and a Hindu, Alfred. The television is new, and your old armchair has been relegated to the far corner. Shall we sit down?' We made a triangle around the coffee table, each to a different chair.

My parents were giving each other some space, for good reason. A few minutes ago, outside in the glorious July sunshine, a whole bunch of friends, colleagues and various relatives had witnessed the surprise appearance of a young Spanish woman. Sofía. Then they had heard Vicky Robson pronounce that Sofía was my half-sister.

Vicky is a Mage. Her special skill is looking at people's Imprints and spotting things. Things like the fact that Sofía and I share a father, something that was news to both of us. That news had shocked me; to Sofía it had looked nigh-on traumatic.

Mum, Dad and I had sought sanctuary inside the house, and so had Sofía. We were in the sitting room, and Sofía was somewhere else, with Mina.

It clearly hadn't been news to my parents. Dad was looking angry, and his eyes kept flicking to the door: he wanted to see her and to introduce himself properly. Dad is a good dad, and his concern was for Sofía's welfare. For now he was restrained by forty years of marriage and by obligation to me, his firstborn.

Mother looked as if she were rising above it. Being six foot tall, she rises above most things, including Dad and his enthusiasms, but this was different. Trust me, I know that look: she was as close to a breakdown as Dad was close to an explosion.

'There's one thing you needn't worry about, Conrad,' said Mother. 'The Clarke bond still holds: A Clarke's Word is still Binding.'

'I'm more worried about Sofía, Mum.'

She held my gaze. 'And so am I, dear, but you need to know what happened.'

'Don't, Mary,' said Dad. 'This is down to me, not you.'

She turned to him. 'If you mean that you had sex with Mercedes and I didn't, then yes, it is down to you. But I started it.' She turned back to me. 'When you toddled off to primary school, I went back to work full time.' She glanced at the family photos in a corner. 'Do the 1980s count as history, now? No matter. I was promoted to section leader, and they sent me into the field.'

'I never knew.'

Mother was a cryptanalyst for GCHQ, and a very good one, too. Apparently. On certain occasions she's allowed to wear her CBE.

'The Cold War was hotting up,' she continued. 'Just before the Soviet Union imploded, everything went a bit crazy. The director called me into his office and told me to go to Berlin and evaluate a potential asset.'

Asset. They still use that word to talk about agents. Makes it less personal if they're uncovered and tortured, I suppose. 'Why you?' I said. 'I thought you never saw the light of day at GCHQ.'

'The prospect's price was very high. MI6 would only meet his price if his product was genuine, and I was the only one who could both evaluate the product and get into West Berlin undercover at short notice. There was a bridge tournament on, and Six asked a retired diplomat to pull out. I replaced him.'

Dad gave a humourless smile. 'I thought she was in Brighton, until she got back.'

Mother ignored him. 'The secrecy, the deception, the adrenaline. It was all quite … stimulating. Intoxicating. After I'd pronounced the prospect genuine, the MI6 handler won his bet.'

'Sorry?'

She dropped her eyes and pulled at the knees of her lightweight floral trousers. 'I found out later that he'd bet the residency chief that he could get the freaky geek into bed. I'd never heard the word *geek* before.'

There was an awkward silence. My skin felt so itchy that I expected dancing cockroaches to crawl up the table legs and put on a show. Hearing about your parents' sex life is bad enough; listening to your mother confess to being someone else's casual conquest is infinitely worse, believe me. I shuddered and tried to be a grownup.

I crossed my legs and said, 'Sounds like #MeToo. Was reporting him an option back then?'

She snorted and looked out of the window at the drive. The taxi that had brought Sofía to blow up the party had left deep ruts in the gravel. She frowned. 'It was a mistake, not an assault. We'd both have been forcibly retired for jeopardising the operation if I'd said anything.' She turned to Dad. 'Your father could tell the moment I got back. The guilt was all over me like a rash, and I lasted five minutes before I confessed. He told me not to mind, but I'd broken our vows, hadn't I?'

'And you took that as carte blanche, did you, Dad?'

He looked sheepish.

As a young man, I'd once asked him if he'd always been faithful, and he'd put on his trust-me-I'm-serious face. 'I've never loved any woman but your mother,' he'd said.

I'd been naive enough not to realise that he'd answered a different question, and I never had the courage to ask again. Scared of the answer, I think. With good reason.

'He was very careful,' said Mother, with a mixture of gratitude and loathing.

'And then I went to Spain,' said Dad.

I clicked my fingers. 'Of course. Cranwell. I'd just enrolled for officer training and you went to try your luck on the Costa del Crime.' I'd been eighteen, my full sister a decade younger.

'It was worth it,' he said. 'Financially. And then I met Mercedes.'

He opened his mouth to continue the story, until a polite knock on the door stopped him. He started to get up, and Mother reached out a hand. 'Leave it to Conrad. This is his house now.'

Dad subsided, and I got up and limped to the door. I opened it a crack and found Myfanwy, our resident Welsh Druid, housekeeper, Herbalist and romantic. She was holding three glasses and a bottle of the best brandy.

'You're a lifesaver,' I said, taking the goods. 'How's it going out there in the garden?'

She grinned. 'They talked about the food for all of ten seconds, then Vicky's Dad had a go at her for spilling the beans. Furious, he was. Miss Parkes stepped in, and it all kicked off big time. They're loving it.'

As was Myfanwy. Still, she doesn't get out much: she's under a Confinement Order and can't leave the village of Clerkswell, but that's another story. 'I'm glad to hear it,' I said. 'I hadn't planned any entertainment, so this is a bonus, isn't it?'

'Sorry, Conrad, it's a shame an' all that, but you should have seen the look on your face. I so wish we had CCTV here. Maybe a Necromancer could...'

'...Shh! Any sign of Mina and Sofía?'

Mum and Dad had got up to join us, and Myfanwy tilted her head to look at my father. I think she was wondering what Mercedes had seen in him. Satisfied, she gave a small nod. 'They're in the library. I don't speak a word of Spanish, but I'm sure Sofía's on the phone to her mother. She's doing that shouting and crying at the same time thing. Poor kid.'

Dad couldn't contain himself. He pulled the door open and marched across the hall. As he did so, a tiny black and white bullet shot into the sitting room – my dog and Familiar Spirit, Scout. He did not look happy.

'I'll leave you to it' said Myfanwy. 'I'd better serve desserts.' She grinned. 'The audience will be getting restless.' She placed her hand on my arm and whispered, 'Keep going, Conrad,' before bouncing off down the passage to the kitchen.

'Pour me a large one and sit down,' said Mother. 'And what's got into that dog?'

'He's very sensitive.' I reached down and gave him a scratch. Scout is the result of a roaming Spirit (origin unknown) merging with a new-born border collie pup. He really doesn't like it when the humans fight.

Mother settled back on to the couch and accepted a brandy. 'To family,' she said, before knocking back a double.

I topped up her glass. Not too much. 'I think it may be my fault,' I said.

She drank more brandy. 'You've always been precocious, Conrad, but even you would have struggled to impregnate Sofía's mother from another country.'

'But I did meet them.'

She sat up. 'How? When?'

'Last month. When Mina was getting her nails done.'

'Of course. Mercedes' house is opposite the salon. But why did you go knocking on their door?'

Mina slipped into the sitting room, a vivid splash of red against the pale walls. She'd decided on Indian dress for the party.

'How is it?' I asked.

She leaned against the door, closed her eyes and breathed out. 'Sofía is off the phone. Alfred is comforting her. I'd give them some space.' She stood up and spotted the third brandy glass. 'I need that.' I poured for her and she curled up on the couch, next to Mother.

'You were saying?' said Mother, not one to be distracted by news from elsewhere.

'It has to do with magick, I'm afraid.'

Mother closed her eyes. 'Dear God, no. Please tell me that Mercedes' tarot readings don't really tell the future.'

'They do. Sort of. Her home is full of magick, and I leaned against the wall. They knew I was there immediately, and I knew it was a house of magick. Sofía came to see who it was and invited me in. They only discovered that I was a Clarke later, and now I know why Mercedes wasn't very happy.'

Mother shook her head. She'd joined the world of magick recently, but refuses to engage with it. Dad is different: he can't see it at all, and never will. It's a defence mechanism. 'So why is Sofía here now?' she asked.

'I left Mercedes my card. She will have been on the phone and found out that I'm connected, in a modest way. I'm betting that she wants me to get Sofía into Salomon's House.'

'That's the Invisible College isn't it?'

'It is. Sofía doesn't have Mercedes' gift, but she does have talent. She needs to develop it before it fades.'

'No surprise there. This is the second time it's happened.'

'You've lost me,' said Mina.

Mother turned to Mina as a relief from the doings of the male Clarkes. 'Mercedes didn't tell Alfred about his daughter until the child was thirteen. She said she needed money for a private school'. Mother frowned at me. 'Your father insisted on a DNA test first, and insisted that Mercedes tell her the truth eventually. Of course, he told me straight away.'

Mina did the maths. 'Six years ago, Mary?'

'Yes, dear. You're quite right, as usual. When Alfred told me, I said that he could – should – pay the woman, but only if he sold Elvenham and agreed to live in Spain.' Aah. That explained a lot. Dad had sold Elvenham to me and used the money to buy their villa. The deal had been done five years ago, and they'd divided their time between Clerkswell and San Vicente, the small town near Valencia. That was partly because they couldn't let go of life here and partly because I was in Afghanistan most of the time.

Mother does have an evil side. She mostly reserves it for games of bridge, and she has a special grin she uses when she is pulling out the winning trump. She used it now. 'I made Alfred tell you he'd lost money on a *Spanish venture*.'

Ouch. Dad spent his life trying to convince people that being an antique dealer is a steady job. It must have hurt deeply to pretend that he'd lost all that money in business, not in bed.

'And now Mercedes wants you to put Sofía through university,' said Mother, shaking her head.

'I don't think it's that,' said Mina. 'There's no tuition fees at Salomon's House. Not as such, I don't think.' She reached under her kurta and pulled out a tissue.

She passed it to Mother, and to my amazement, Mother gathered Mina into her arm and kissed her head. Perhaps it was the emotion; perhaps it was the brandy.

Mina looked bewildered. She is tiny, compared to Mother, and extricated herself with some difficulty. Mother realised that she'd inadvertently shown affection to someone and hastily moved a few inches away, a red glow appearing over her cheeks. She cleared her throat and said, 'If it's not money, then what?'

Mina was trying to compose herself, and I stepped in. 'I think Mercedes wants her daughter to study somewhere that won't draw attention to Mercedes' illegal activities.'

'Hmph,' said Mother. 'You know about her weed empire, then. Did Alfred tell you, or did she try to sell you some to go with the tarot reading?'

Mina smoothed her kurta. 'Sorry. You've lost me. Us.'

Mother shook her head impatiently. It was her *keep up* look, the one she'd used when trying to help me with my A level maths homework. 'Mercedes sells very high grade marijuana. If you have arthritis in San Vicente, all the doctors send you to Casa Conventa. She only sells to customers over forty, so that's probably why you escaped.'

'Erm, that's interesting,' I said, 'but not her real crime. She does tarot readings for mundane clients and uses an enchanted deck. That's a big no-no.'

'Really?'

'Yes. I've arrested Mages for far less.'

'I'm sure you have, dear. I meant, can she *really* use magick like that.'

'Yes, but you'll have to ask Vicky or Francesca for details.'

The door clicked open and Sofía entered. My father – our father – had his hand protectively on her shoulder. You wouldn't think that Sofía was half English at first. She has black hair, olive skin and the mixture of grace and awkwardness that marks late adolescence. Her left hip was leaning into Dad for support at the same time as her right shoulder drew away from his touch.

She'd made some effort to clear the smudged makeup off her face, but the tears had left her eyes swollen, and that's where you could see her dual genetic heritage. It wasn't in the dark hazel of her pupils but in the wide spacing and openness of her eyes below a high forehead. She hitched up her jeans with a wiggle that could have been our sister Rachael at nineteen and moved away from Dad. Towards me.

'You really are my brother?' she said. 'You? The Dragonslayer?'

What do you say to that? I had nothing, so I stepped forward and opened my arms.

2 – Eight Card Trick

When we broke apart, I noticed that Mother had disappeared.

'She's gone to make the ultimate sacrifice,' said Dad. 'She's going to call Rachael.'

Now that was brave. Very brave. Even braver than what Sofía said next.

'Can I join the party? Is that okay?' Scout emerged from his hiding place and lolloped up to Sofía with a small bark. 'He is gorgeous. Hello.'

She bent down to stroke him, and both of them jumped back when the spark of Lux lit up.

Sofía said something in Spanish and put her hand to her mouth. Scout's ears flattened and he shook himself. He looked at me.

'Scout, this is my long-lost sister,' I said. 'She's part of the family.'

He crouched and licked her toes. Sofía flinched, but held still. With a bark, Scout pulled back his gums in a doggy grin and dashed out of the room.

'Bloody strange dog, that,' said Dad.

Mina took Sofía's arm. 'If you're serious about making an appearance, we need to do some work, starting with your hair and working down. Conrad, go and prepare the way.' Easier said than done.

I left the house and went into the new gardens, designed by Myfanwy and being celebrated with a bit of a do. Almost all the people I love and trust were there, barring my sister Rachael and my boss in Merlyn's Tower. I limped across the much reduced lawn and it went very quiet.

'Can we break this up a bit?' I said. 'The poor girl actually wants to come out, and if we're all in a group, she'll run a mile. I'm only going to say one thing and it's this: can we pretend she was always coming and that her flight was delayed?'

'That's one way of putting it,' said Myfanwy. She took charge immediately, breaking up the group, settling me on the well with a bucket of beers and commanding a couple of the younger Mages to help her clear plates into the kitchen.

I lit a cigarette and opened a beer. The stone wall of the well rim was warm with both heat and magick. That well is the reason the Clarkes are here. It used to be a door into the realm of Fae, and it still has residual magick. During the Black Death, William the Clerk used the magick and Clarkes have lived here ever since, father to son, with only a change of spelling in six hundred years.

Vicky emerged from the kitchen and walked slowly across the lawn. She's convalescing from a badly punctured lung, a stab wound inflicted on my last mission. I was thrilled when she was promoted to Captain of the King's Watch rather than Officer, but very sorry to lose her. Vicky was my first magickal partner, and we have a bond that goes beyond being comrades in arms.

She carried her plate over to the well and sat next to me with a huff. 'Gateau and cheese,' she said. 'A peace offering for blurting out that that lass is your sister. I'm sorry about that.'

I accepted the plate. 'It's a start. I'll get over it, and the look of horror on your face when you realised what you'd done was priceless, but it's not me who's had their entire world upended, is it?' I took a large bite of gateau and waited for the sugar rush.

'Nah. You're right, Uncle C. How can I make it up to her?'

'Take her under your wing. Find out if she's cut out for the Invisible College. I know she's not a Diviner like her mother, beyond that, I can't tell.'

'Aye. Right you are. Before I forget, what are your plans?'

The garden party and the cricket matches yesterday had been a moment of escape from the day job of keeping the peace in the world of magick with the King's Watch. 'No idea. We've got an appointment to Skype the Boss tomorrow afternoon, so we'll find out then.'

Vicky took some of the cheese. 'This is good. Hang on, here they come.'

I'd seen a flash of red in the kitchen as Mina introduced Sofía to Myfanwy and Erin. They emerged into the garden and moved quickly across the open space.

'Isn't that one of Mina's dresses?' said Vicky.

'Mmm.'

Sofía's jeans were gone, replaced by a blue and green print dress. Mina buys from the petite ranges, so this one was a lot shorter on Sofía, something that immediately drew the attention of Vicky's new magickal partner, Xavi Metcalfe.

'Aren't you gonna do the introductions?' said Vicky.

'No. Mina needs to do this.'

'Stamping her authority as lady of the manor, eh?'

Only Vicky could – or would – say something like that and get away with it. There was too much truth in what she said for me to argue, so I lit a cigarette and watched the show.

'...And this is Victoria Robson. Vicky,' said Mina when she'd dragged a slightly dazed Sofía over to the well. 'She's a Watch Captain – *Inquisidor* – as well, but more than that, she's family.'

'You too?' said Sofía after an embrace.

'Aye, pet,' said Vicky, 'and this is me Uncle Conrad.'

We're not really related, but I helped re-start Vicky's heart when she was dead. You could call me her blood-uncle, like a blood-brother but with embarrassing dance moves.

'I'll explain later,' said Vicky. 'Excuse me, I need to sit on a chair with a back.'

'And I need a drink,' said Mina. She walked off with Vicky, leaving Sofía and me alone at the well.

'Welcome to Elvenham,' I said. 'Do you want a beer? It's San Miguel.'

She managed a smile. 'The best. I went to school in Barcelona. We drank it all the time.'

I passed her the bottle. 'Are you okay?'

'Can you give me a cigarette? Please?' Another thing she and I both inherited from Dad. He smokes cigars these days. I passed her the packet and my lighter.

'Thank you.' She turned her head slowly, looking from the house to the gardens, to the party, to me. 'I have met more Magos, no *Mages*, more Mages today than in my whole life. I think perhaps Mamá was right to keep me away from them. They are all so … powerful. I will never fit in here.'

'Ben has no magick at all. Neither do Vicky's parents. Nor does Mina, really. You'll find your own place, Sofía. Besides, when it comes to fitting in, magick is not the most important factor.'

'Eh?'

'The biggest question is whether you can play cricket.'

'Cricket?' She thought that was hilarious. She'll learn.

'Do you want to stay here – in Clerkswell – for a few days, or do you want to go?'

'Can I stay?'

'Of course. You are as much of a Clarke as I am, and this is Clerkswell.'

'I have so much to learn. I remembered how you smoked at Casa Convente, and how you liked the manzanilla sherry. I have brought both. As a gift.' She shook her head. 'When I bought them, I didn't know I was buying a gift for my brother. Drink and cigarettes. Not a good first gift, no? But please take them.'

'I will. Everyone likes the sherry, so I'll open a bottle later, when everyone's gone and you've been grilled.'

'Grilled?'

'Questioned. When the place has been cleared up, Mina and I are going to take Scout for a walk. Vicky and the girls are going to find out what sort of Mage you are.' I paused. 'That's why you've come to England, isn't it? To study?'

'Yes. Mamá said you would help. She lied and lied, you know. She said that you knew I was coming when you did not, and on the phone just now she said that she did not know that Alfredo and Maria would be here. I think she lied about that as well.'

'Perhaps.'

Our eyes flicked to the lawn. Mother was on her way, bypassing the party and heading for the well.

Sofía's hand flew to her mouth. 'What should I call her?'

'Señora Clarke. Until she says otherwise.'

Mother looked tired. Very tired. Strangely, she had Scout with her. I'd been wondering where the mad mutt had got to. She opened her arms and gave Sofía an embrace. I wouldn't call it a hug. She stepped back and said, 'I want you to know that the door is always open to you at Villa Verde. I don't blame you.'

Sofía balked. The idea of being blamed for being born had never crossed her mind. She stammered out a *gracias* and bobbed her head.

'Could you give us a minute, Sofía?'

'Of course.'

Scout detached himself and followed Sofía to the main group, no doubt in search of food.

'That was truly awful,' said Mother.

'Rachael?'

She nodded. 'Much worse than when Alfred told her that we – he – had sold Elvenham to you.'

I sighed and squeezed her hand, quickly letting go before she could flinch. 'I wish Rachael would grow up.'

Mother did what she does best when faced with a challenging conversational gambit: she ignored it. 'We won't stay long, dear. We're seeing the Thewlises later, and I need a lie down, but you and Mina must drag Sofía along to the Inkwell tomorrow morning for a farewell breakfast.'

'Will do.'

She stood up and bent down to kiss me. 'Do you remember your eighteenth birthday? Grandma Enderby baked you a cake with RAF wings on it. You'd just passed your board. When you picked up the knife to cut the cake, Rachael said, "I can't wait until he flies away and leaves us alone." Do you remember what you said back to her?'

'I honestly don't remember. I made my first legal trip to the Inkwell later, so most of the family party is a bit of a blur.'

'Hmm. You said, "If you're not careful, I'll wish for a better sister." I think you must have made that wish, because Sofía was conceived less than a year later.'

It was a beautiful late evening. Bees were buzzing lazily round people's gardens as we left the village on the little lane that leads to Clerkswell Station. We passed the last house and I slipped Scout off the lead. We only use it for the sake of propriety.

'When are you going to take me on the train?' said Mina as I took her hand.

'We've been on loads of trains. Birmingham, London, Valencia, Madrid...'

'In my whole life, I have never been on a steam train, and you have the Gloucester-Worcester Steam Railway running by the village.'

The station was shut up but the yard gate was still open. I steered Mina towards the buildings and Scout ran happily round the compound sniffing out new smells. 'There,' I said, pointing to the noticeboard. 'How about a dinner special on your birthday in September?'

She pushed back her hair and stared up at the poster. Her eyes lit up when she read the small print. 'Can we? It's a Downton Abbey Special! I get to dress up!' Her face fell. 'Will there still be tickets?'

'Ben's cousin is a volunteer. We'll get Myfanwy on it in the morning.'

She looked at the date again. 'The next night is when Carole should have got married.'

'We should throw a costume party. Take everyone's minds off it.'

'Really?'

'Ask the Coven. Get Myfanwy to ask Carole. If they're up for it, why not?'

'That would be the best present I've had since I was fourteen. I will be twenty-eight in September, so that makes it half a lifetime ago.'

We left the station and continued up the lane, over the bridge and into open country. Just ahead was a field I knew to be empty. 'What happened on your fourteenth birthday?'

'Papaji got tickets to a red carpet screening of *Parineeta*. In London. He got Sunil to stand there for two hours to keep our places. I got Vidya Balan's autograph. It was before selfies became a thing.'

I could see tears forming. Sunil was her eldest brother. He looked out for Mina at school and she idolised both him and her father. When she was twenty-two, Sunil had been murdered in front of her and Papaji had died shortly after.

We arrived at the field in silence. Scout had already slipped between the bars and was racing around like a lunatic. By the way, I do not recommend this for dogs who aren't magickal.

Mina dried her eyes and smiled. 'Thank you, Conrad. A costume party would be brilliant.'

'I can't think of a better setting for a Downton dress-up than Elvenham.'

'Oh no.' Her eyes glinted in the setting sun. 'I'm looking forward to trying on a corset for the train, don't get me wrong, but for my birthday party, we're going Bollywood. My cousin, Anika Ben, the one who helped me in India. Do you remember me telling you?'

'I look forward to meeting her one day and thanking her for what she did.'

'And you will, one day. You know she's standing for election, on a women's rights platform?'

'I do.'

'She supports a charity, and the charity has a fundraising section in the UK. We could dedicate the evening to them. We could sell outfits made by their clients. We could have fittings in the afternoon. Show films. And dancing, of course.'

'Of course. I can't wait.'

She pulled me down for a kiss. 'And neither can your Familiar.'

Inside the field, Scout was parked in front of the gate, tongue hanging out and eyes full of mischief. I pushed the gate open and took the tennis ball out of my pocket. 'Ready, boy?'

'Arff!'

'If my grandma could see me now, she'd go mental,' said Vicky. She raised her glass of Manzanilla and admired the delicate, pale golden colour before sticking her nose in and sniffing. 'I'd swear I can smell the sea.'

'You can,' said Sofía. 'Why would your grandmother be a mental case?'

'It means getting angry. *Loco*. If she could see me sitting with me feet up in a house like this, sipping sherry on a Sunday night, she'd say I was a class traitor.'

Sofía's English is excellent. Mercedes chose a school that specialised in my mother tongue, because she knew this day would come. Having said that, the rather academic course in Barcelona focused more on BBC English and Shakespeare than Geordie accents and Marxist ideology.

Wisely, Vicky let the concept of *class traitor* slide and focused on magick.

Mina and I had found the coven slouched around the drawing room, with Vicky in the chair. Literally. Because of her lung, she has to sit up most of the time. Sofía jumped up, eager to please and eager to get out of the spotlight. While Sofía put the sherry bottle back, Vicky gave us the verdict.

'Sofía can get in to Salomon's House, nay bother, but none of us has a clue where her real talents are.'

'I want to work with Myvvy in the garden,' said Sofía.

I nearly choked on my sherry, and not because Sofía struggles with Welsh. 'No hemp plants, please,' I said. 'Not here.'

'Hemp?' said Saffron, my current partner in the King's Watch.

'Sí. I grow amazing cannabis. Everyone says it is very good. I have brought seeds.'

Myfanwy is a clever woman. She can also be very naive. That's why she's Confined to the village: she trusted the wrong people. If she hadn't helped me save Vicky's life, she'd be locked up in Blackfriars Undercroft. Myfanwy waved her glass. 'Miss Parkes' arthritis is terrible. It could really help.'

Erin looked at me over Myfanwy's head and mouthed *I'll sort it.* To change the subject, Erin said, 'I still can't believe you can't read tarot, Sofía. Surely with an enchanted deck...?'

The shrug is an under-documented area of body language, in my opinion, and I'm something of a connoisseur. In Spain, the shrug is more a hand gesture, an open palm, than a shoulder movement. Sofía shrugged. 'It is easier if I show you. Mina, you play bridge, no?'

'I am only learning.'

'You have new decks of cards?'

'Yes. I'll get one. Let's go to the kitchen.'

We installed ourselves in the kitchen. I could see from Sofía's face that she much preferred it to the sitting room. It is lovely, with an antique farmhouse table in the middle and an Aga to keep us warm in the winter. I topped up the Manzanilla, and when Mina got back, Sofía took the deck from her and broke the seal.

She quickly discarded the Jokers and fanned the cards out to show that they were in order. 'Before I could read books, Mamá taught me to shuffle. Watch.'

She riffled the cards with a lightning speed and professionalism that would get her a job in any casino. While she shuffled, she said, 'To read tarot, you need two things. You have to put magick in your fingers, and you have to have the Sight. I have the fingers, but not the Sight.' She plonked the deck in front of Mina. 'Cut. Please.'

Mina lifted a quarter of the cards and put them underneath. Sofía handed the deck to Saffron. 'You deal, please … Mmm … Deal to Conrad first, then Mina, then Erin, then yourself. Six cards each should do it.'

Saffron held the deck in her open palm and closed her eyes. 'No residual Lux. I couldn't perform magick and leave no trace like that. You did perform magick, didn't you?'

Sofía pinned back her hair again. 'Deal the cards and we shall see,' she said with a smile that was pure Mercedes. If she used that smile on Xavi, she'd have a slave for life. Saffron swiftly dealt the cards. I picked up my hand and scanned it.

Sofía said to me, 'There is no Knight of Swords in this deck. I gave you the Jack of Spades. Same thing.'

And there he was.

When Mercedes had read the tarot for me, I'd drawn the Knight of Swords as a symbol of myself. I turned the Jack of Spades to show the group. Everyone looked impressed, except Mina, who looked alarmed as she scanned her cards.

She slowly laid down the four kings. 'How in Ganesh's name did you do that?'

'And the other one,' said Sofía. Mina laid down the Queen of Hearts. Sofía tapped it with her finger. 'Queen of Hearts outranks the Jack of Spades. As it should be.'

'Wow, Sofía,' said Myfanwy. 'That's amazing. Well done.'

'Now you know why I cannot read Tarot. Without the Sight, all the cards would come from my fingers.'

Erin gave a dramatic sigh. She's a Witch, and learnt her magick with the Brotherhood of Arden rather than at Salomon's House. I met her on a mission, and she turned up here one day, curious to meet Myfanwy. They are now firm friends, and Erin rents one of my empty stables as a studio. Erin is an Enscriber – she can put Lux into words, signs, runes and images. More than that, she is an excellent slip fielder and useful Number Four bat.

Now, I don't obsess about women's appearances, but bear with me for a moment. Myfanwy's hair is a honey-blonde that matches her cornflower blue eyes. Saffron has the biggest mane of white-blonde hair in Clerkswell and keeps it well pinned up most of the time, like a barely restrained polar bear. Myfanwy and Saffron are naturally blonde; Erin is not, but her dyed, curled halo suits her.

She has an open, simple face with a dimple, and when Mother gets back to San Vicente, she will probably describe Erin as a girl-next-door type, which she is, if your neighbours go in for firearms and obsessional violence.

Erin threatened Vicky with a shotgun not so long ago, and despite Erin being one of the Elvenham Coven, I'm not sure that Vicky trusts her any more than I do.

We all stared at Erin, and Erin stared at Sofía. 'I thought it was me you loved,' said Erin. She laid down another four kings and two more queens – Hearts and Diamonds. She grinned and sat back with her glass of sherry.

'*Madre de Dio,*' said Sofía. 'May I see?'

Erin slid the cards over to Sofía, who picked them up and stroked them. She passed them to Vicky and said, 'I can feel the magick in them. It is not an illusion – they are fixed, but how did you do it? A Transformation?'

'She's not that good,' said Vicky. 'Clever, though. Very clever.'

Erin grinned. 'While Mina went for the new deck, I nipped out to my workshop. I've got quite a few blank playing cards and I brought them in. When everyone was looking at Mina's hand, I swapped them, then imprinted something dramatic. If you look closely, you'll see that the backs aren't quite right.'

She picked her original six, random cards from her lap and returned them to Sofía. 'Sorry. I didn't mean to steal your thunder. No way could I do what you did with the shuffle. That was awesome. How did you fix the cut? Mina could have cut the deck anywhere.'

Neatly done. Erin *had* stolen Sofía's thunder, and now she was graciously handing it back.

'That is my secret,' said Sofía. Her lips curled and I could see that she was thinking fondly of her mother, perhaps for the first time since she'd arrived here. If a Mage says that something is their secret, you have to change the subject. It's very rude to probe any further.

Mina picked up the baton. 'Why do you have blank playing cards, Erin?'

'There's always money in vanity. You can have a personalised deck for fifty pounds a card. Here. Watch.' She took more blanks out of the pouch in her phone case and took some of the original cards from the table. She pressed two blanks to the back of the mundane cards, creating perfect copies of the cross-hatching. Then she looked at the other sides and stared in concentration for a second. 'There. To celebrate your engagement.'

She laid down yet another Queen of Hearts and a King of Spades. The cards had Myfanwy's and Ben's faces, grinning and smiling. They were very good.

'Aww, Erin, that's ...Thank you.' Myfanwy leaned over and gave Erin a hug.

'You are engaged?' said Sofía. 'Where is the ring?'

'Long story,' said Myfanwy. 'Conrad tells it best. I'm gonna be a party pooper, I'm afraid. See you all tomorrow. Mina? Can you put Vicky to bed for me?'

'Howay, I'm not five,' said Vicky.

'No, but you do need your dressing changed and your blood pressure taken.'

We all got up. It had been a very long day. 'Come on, Sofía,' I said. 'I'll tell you that story over a last cigarette in the garden.'

3 – Back in the Field

When we got back to Elvenham after breakfast the next day, the Elvenham Coven was waiting for us in the kitchen: Myfanwy, Vicky, Erin and Saffron. After yesterday, no one had any particular appetite for hard work this morning.

Mina slumped into the nearest seat, and Myfanwy jumped up. 'What's wrong, precious? And where's Sofía?'

'Dad's taking Sofía for a walk round the village,' I said. 'Showing her the ancestral lands and all that.'

Mina looked up. 'Do you know what Mary said when he suggested it? She said, "Alfred, are you really going to show off that girl like a prize pig?"'

'Ouch,' said Myfanwy.

'That's harsh,' said Saffron.

'Harsh, but a bit too close for comfort, I reckon,' added Vicky. 'What did Sofía say?'

'She didn't understand, thank the gods,' said Mina. 'But that is not the worst thing. Oh no.'

'Coffee?' said Myfanwy. 'Cake?'

Mina shook her head. 'I am awash with coffee and protein. Those breakfasts are designed for people twice my size.' She gave me an accusing look.

'Rosie was serving,' I said.

'Oh, no,' said Myfanwy. 'All three counties will know about Sofía by now.'

'Still not the worst,' said Mina. 'When Alfred and Sofía went for their parade, Mary fixed me with one of her looks. You know, Conrad, I swear that your mother is part serpent. I am rethinking whether I adopt her, you know.'

Saffron was struggling to keep up. 'How can you adopt Conrad's mother?'

Mina swept her hand round the table. 'You all have mothers. Why should I be left out? Sofía even has two mothers if she wants them. Do any of you have aunties with no children that I could borrow?'

Myfanwy grinned. 'I've got Auntie Bethan, but she's more Welsh than the Archdruid. Might be a bit of a communication problem there. Anyway, what did Mary say to you? Was it about your past? I've avoided being alone with Ben's Mam for exactly that reason.'

'She asked me if I was ready. Ready to be her bridge partner *on a cruise next week.*'

'No!'

'I'm afraid so,' I said. 'Mother asked me if I had any leave owing yesterday, and I foolishly said yes. It's a twelve night cruise round the Baltic, leaving Liverpool next Monday.'

'You haven't agreed, have you?' said Saffron. 'You're only twenty-seven, Mina. Even Conrad's too young to go on a cruise.'

'Oy, Hawkins,' I said. 'Watch it. As it happens, we did agree, didn't we love?'

Mina threw her hands in the air. 'Mary said we shouldn't go if I wasn't up to it. The Clarkes have their motto, and so do I: *no one pushes a Desai*. Of course I had to accept. And they're paying.' She planted her elbows on the table and jammed her chin in her fists. 'I have so much to do. Mary said I only need three ballgowns. *Three!* I didn't even wear a ballgown for my school prom.'

Vicky (whose parents have cruised a few times) gave Mina a sly smile. 'You know what, pet, you should wear Indian dress on the ship. You don't want any of the passengers to mistake you for a waitress do you?'

'Vicky! How can you say that?' said Myfanwy.

Mina pushed her nose up. 'That will not be a problem. I am a princess, remember?'

When the Clerskswell Coven had stopped laughing, Saffron said, 'Will the Boss let you go?'

'We'll see this afternoon, won't we?'

I arranged the chairs in the library around the desk and lined up the video camera on the tripod behind my laptop. Mina and Saffron appeared with the coffee and Vicky brought up the rear, closing the doors behind them. This was a strictly King's Watch meeting, so Erin had disappeared to the stables and Myfanwy was off digging somewhere with Sofía. If you're wondering why Mina was present, she has a post with the Cloister Court, and I wasn't going to say no, was I?

At two o'clock precisely, the screen pinged with an incoming call. Saffron leaned over and clicked Accept.

The first shock was that the Boss was wearing her wig. Hannah Rothman, Peculier Constable of the King's Watch, normally wears a headscarf over the titanium plate in her head. For some unknown reason, she also has a big, bright red curly wig that she wears for visitors. I don't know about them, but it scares the living daylights out of me.

The second surprise was the man to her left, Deputy Constable Iain Drummond. I don't particularly like the man, but I do respect him. He did his time in the field, and then became the Watch's prosecutor and attorney. He wasn't the important visitor, so I wondered who'd been calling.

'Pack your bags,' said Hannah. 'You're coming to town. Well, some of you are.'

'The Cloister Court is sitting on Thursday,' added Drummond helpfully. 'Judge Bracewell has been to see us.' Aah. So the Honourable Mrs Justice

Bracewell was the important visitor. Strange for her to trek out to Merlyn's Tower.

Drummond continued, 'She wants to tie up all the loose ends before she goes away.' He picked up a paper and his eyes flicked to where Mina would be sitting on their screen. 'She asked me to tell you to be ready, Ms Desai. She's going to open the hearing into the Flint Hoard.' Mina grabbed my hand out of sight of the camera. I predict another *what-do-I-wear* crisis before we get out of the room.

He wasn't finished yet. 'And this Wessex business has come to the boil much faster than we thought. The poor Earl of Tintagel is barely cold and Mowbray is already up to his tricks. As are the Daughters of the Goddess.' He frowned. 'Hannah?'

The Boss tapped the end of her pen in a nervous gesture. 'Saffron, you and Conrad need to change places.'

Saff and I looked at each other and stood up.

'Sit down,' said Hannah. 'I didn't mean it literally. Saffron, you need to be the teacher. You have to brief him on the magickal aristocracy.' She grinned. 'As you're such an expert, it should be a doddle.'

Saffron went bright red. 'Yes, ma'am.'

'Excuse me,' said Drummond. 'Nine o'clock sharp in the Old Temple on Thursday for Ms Desai and Watch Captain Clarke. Got that? Good.'

He stood up and left our field of vision. Hannah moved the camera to centre it on herself and looked to her right until we heard the great oak doors close. She grinned at the screen and rubbed her hands. 'Well? What's she like, then?'

I groaned inwardly.

Vicky flashed me an evil grin. 'Who would that be, ma'am?'

Hannah blinked, then shot up and disappeared from the screen. We heard an *ow!* and a curse in Yiddish. When she reappeared, the scary wig had been replaced by a hastily tied green headscarf and the small part of every adult that is afraid of clowns breathed a sigh of relief.

The Boss glanced at her desk. 'Sofía Elizabetta Torres entered the country at Birmingham International Airport on Sunday morning. She was flagged as being registered with the College of St Raphael as a Mage. They do like their bureaucracy in Europe.'

'Who snitched?' I said.

Hannah wagged a finger. 'Like you, Conrad, I protect my sources. Now I really do wish I'd gone to your party. That must have been a sight.'

Mina answers to Mrs Bracewell, not Hannah. It means she can occasionally say things I can't, and she did so now. 'Sofía is still a child, Hannah. She has enough to deal with right now and needs our support.' She paused. 'So long as she takes after her father, I'm sure she'll be an asset.'

Vicky chipped in. 'But hopefully a less annoying asset than her brother.'

Hannah held up her hands. 'Enough already. I get the message: the Elvenham Coven have taken her under their wing. Moving on.' She checked her phone. 'Yes, Conrad, you can have two weeks off, and to save Mina the trouble, I asked Marcia on her behalf. No problem there either. Enjoy your holiday. You both deserve it after the Triangle business.'

'*Who's Marcia?*' whispered Vicky, forgetting how sensitive the microphone is, and that there's nothing wrong with Hannah's hearing.

'Marcia is the Honourable Mrs Justice Bracewell,' said Hannah. 'No one except her husband knows her real name, and I'm not sure about him. Saffron? You can cover the Mercian Watch, can't you?'

My young partner nodded enthusiastically. 'Yes, ma'am. I'll do my best, and I'm going to base myself here. Vicky is going to mentor me.'

'Good,' said Hannah. 'Vicky, you are not to go into the field under any circumstances while you're convalescing. That's an order. Understood?'

'Ma'am.'

'Anything else?'

'Can I have a word?' I said.

'Of course.'

It was my turn to wait for the room to clear. On the screen, Hannah pulled at the straps of her bra, totally unconcerned that I might still be watching her. I'm not sure, but I think she's had a double mastectomy, as well as the head trauma and other injuries. When the library was empty, I coughed discreetly.

Hannah zoned back in, and couldn't resist another dig at my family. 'Does Sofía look like her passport photo?'

'How should I know? I didn't check her passport when she turned up here, did I?'

'Never mind. I'll order Saffron to message me a picture.' She folded her hands on the desk. 'Are you taking this leave on her behalf?'

It was an honest question. Hannah cares about all her team, and what affects us affects her. 'No, Boss. Sofía's going home, and we're taking a proper holiday, but I did want to call in a favour on Sofía's behalf. Is Dean Cora still in town?'

'The Invisible College shuts down at the end of the week. I'm seeing her tomorrow. Leave it with me, Conrad. I'll set something up.' She nodded to herself, making a mental note. 'I'm glad you asked for a private word. The judge has given me a deeply unpleasant job, one that I legally can't delegate to you.'

'Oh?'

'Yes. I have to make a report on Myfanwy. Marcia even gave me a court order requiring it. Don't worry, I know you wouldn't let her break Confinement, but it has to be done.'

A mad thought struck me. 'Is there a deadline?'

'End of September. Why?'

'Put it in your diary for Friday the twenty-fifth. Vicky can bring you.'

Her eyes narrowed. 'That sounds horribly ominous, and you know I have to get back by sundown.'

'No you don't. You carry out the inspection, then we'll have a proper kosher Shabbos dinner. I shall drive you to the Cheltenham synagogue on Saturday and bring you back here in time for the fitting.'

She was already shaking her head. 'Whatever it is, I say no. Big no.'

'It's for charity.'

'I don't care if *it* will feed every starving child in the world. I am not going to *it.*'

'Bollywood not your thing, Boss?'

She was actually speechless. For half a second, her synapses seized up and no words came out of her mouth. I dived right in. 'Good. Formal invitations in a couple of weeks. You know you want to really.'

'I do not.'

I stared at her. Just for a second. 'You're coming, Hannah, or I'll tell Ruth.'

Hannah is a twin. They are utterly devoted to each other, so much so that Ruth invited me, a Goy, to Friday night dinner for the sole purpose of checking me out properly and letting me know that I was expected to look out for Hannah. All unspoken, of course, but true.

'You wouldn't,' said Hannah. 'No, hang on, you would. You'd do anything for Mina, wouldn't you?'

'Yes. Absolutely. But this is for you, not her.'

The internal struggle played out on her face as her right eye blinked and her nose twitched. She rubbed her cheek, and some of the freckles that lurk underneath her foundation surfaced. Finally, she spoke. 'I have come *this* close to regretting that I ever met you so many times that I've lost count, but every time that lives were at stake, you've come through for me. Don't let a social occasion break the mould.'

I nodded mutely. Why the seriousness? It was only a party, after all.

'See you in court on Thursday,' she said. 'Safe journey.'

We disconnected, and I wandered through to the kitchen. Vicky was alone at the table.

'Where's Mina?' I said.

'She dragged Saffron upstairs to try on outfits for the Cloister Court. I said I was too tired. What did you want with the Boss?'

'I was asking about Cora. Oh, and I've got her to come to the Bollywood party.'

Vicky dropped her phone. 'You did what? How? Why?'

I heard the sound of heels, distantly on the hall floor. Mina was approaching. 'I'll tell you everything in a minute. When we've both made positive noises about her outfit.'

'It's gonna rain,' said Ben. 'Probably not on Saturday though. That's the main thing.'

Cricket pitches need to be rolled. Clerkswell Cricket Club has a selection of rollers, one of which is motorised and replaced a huge monster roller that needed four men to pull it. The old roller was too big to scrap, so it was parked near the nets and left to quietly rust. It has an excellent view of the pitch, and is our favourite place to talk tactics and generally put the world to rights, especially before a game or like tonight, after training. The last of the men shouldered his bag and walked off into the village. We'd be following shortly.

'No Bloxhams this weekend,' said Ben, looking over the ground to the trees that screened us from Clerkswell Manor, home of Stephen and Juliet Bloxham. 'What do you reckon the chances are?'

'We can do without Stephen,' I said, 'but the Coven...'

The women's team is officially Clerkswell Ladies; unofficially it's the Clerkswell Coven and includes three of the Elvenham Coven as members – Mina, Erin and Myfanwy, who's also vice-captain. I should point out that both uses of "Coven" are strictly informal. There are rules for magickal covens, but we'll come to them later.

'They're going to struggle without Juliet,' said Ben.

Juliet Bloxham is their captain and opening bat. She's very good, and I reckon she only got involved so that she could be more successful than her husband. So far, she's doing a great job. I even like her. Up to a point.

'That's not all,' I added. 'With Emily gone too, they've got no pace bowler at all. It's a shame about Sofía.'

'Which bit?' said Ben with a snort. 'The part where she laughed at the pads and gloves or the part where she used magick to bat?'

'Both. I should have known – there's so much magick in her fingers that she can't help it. As soon as I bowled at her properly, instinct took over. Did Myfanwy tell you about the eight card trick?'

'She did. She even tried it herself a couple of times. Ready for a pint?'

'Absolutely.'

We headed down to the Inkwell, discussing whether it would be better to bat or field if we won the toss on Saturday. Before the men's practice, the Elvenham coven had tried to get my new half-sister interested in cricket, with dismal results. They'd abandoned the experiment and gone for a drink when the rest of the men had turned up, including Ross Miller. I'd noticed before they left that he and Sofía had been talking, and when Ben and I approached the pub, Sofía looked over our shoulders with disappointment.

'Ross?' she said. 'He is not coming?'

Ben and I glanced at each other. 'Sorry, no,' I said. 'He's too young.'

Her brow furrowed.

'He's only sixteen,' added Ben.

'Ptchoof.'

That's the closest I can get to transcribing the sound she made. I'm not sure what it meant, but I detected regret, disappointment and a lingering whiff of desire. Ross is a strapping lad. Or so I'm told.

Not all of the coven had made it to the Inkwell. Vicky had gone back to rest, and Erin had gone home to Stratford on Avon. Two more stood up to leave: Myfanwy to join Ben at a table of their own, and Sofía to go and call her mother. They still had a lot to talk about.

Sofía drained her glass and gave me a kiss. 'Your beer is strange, but good. A bit like my new family. See you later.'

Saffron was getting up, too, for the noble reason of giving Mina and me some quality time. 'Not so fast, Saff,' I said. 'I'll get you another drink.'

She sat down and looked uncomfortable. After I'd kissed Mina and been to the bar, I took a long swig from my Inkwell Bitter and said, 'So … we all know you're properly posh. Not like us country yokels.'

Mina slapped my hand. 'Speak for yourself. I am an Anavil Brahmin.' She grinned. 'Or I would be if I weren't a woman and hadn't married out. Go on, Saffron, I'm all ears.'

Saffron took a deep breath. 'How much do you want to know, and how far back do you want to go?'

'Enough not to look like an idiot in the Cloister Court on Thursday.'

'Right. Well. This is a northern European thing. And a Celtic thing, but with unpronounceable names. It goes right back to pre-Christian times. In every political unit – village, tribe, kingdom, whatever, there was always a mundane leader and a magickal leader. A king of the sword and a king of the staff. A warrior and a Mage. You'd have to ask Francesca if you're interested in more details.'

'Keep going,' I replied. I glanced at Mina, who nodded. 'We've got you so far.'

'So, we fast-forward to the Anglo-Saxons. You're a history nerd, Conrad, so you've heard of the English Heptarchy, yeah?'

I decided to let the use of *nerd* go past me. 'The Heptarchy was the seven kingdoms of Anglo-Saxon England. It gave a certain Mr Martin the idea for the Seven Kingdoms and an Iron Throne, if I'm not mistaken.'

'It did. Of course, there were non-Anglo kingdoms, too, still speaking Brythonic or Gaelic, but I'll come back to them. In the English kingdoms, the sword kings are all part of mundane history and boring. The staff kings were elected in different ways, but that all changed with Alfred the Great.'

'Have I heard of him?' said Mina. 'Was he a real person?' She looked at me. 'OK, OK. I'll Google him later. Carry on, Saffron.'

'Alfred converted a lot of the seven kingdoms to Christianity, and he said that magick was the preserve of the Church, and justice could only be dispensed by the sword king or the bishop.' She smiled. 'You won't find the bit about magick on his Wikipedia page, though.'

I nodded. 'That was well over a thousand years ago, so I'm guessing that he didn't abolish staff kings.'

Saffron shook her head and drank some of her spritzer. 'He let the elections go ahead, then forced the new staff king to appoint himself, Alfred, as staff regent for life and accept Christian titles in lieu. Earl or bishop.'

I remembered Saturday morning, when the Mages in my kitchen had all had text alerts about the death of the Earl of Tintagel, who also got a mention in Drummond's briefing this afternoon. I made a mental note and asked Saffron to continue.

'William the Conqueror gave the seven English staff kingdoms charters, all slightly different, and he added a couple of the old British ones, too. He also created the staff lords.'

She started to colour up again. When she blushes, the red really stands out against her hair. She swirled her wine and said, 'Being a staff lord or lady is an honour for life. It's not hereditary. You get one for being a big cheese in the world of magick.' She paused. 'Like my mum.' She gulped her drink. 'Yes, I am the daughter of Staff Lady Hawkins, but she doesn't use the title. Much.'

It was an open goal. 'So we don't have to call you the Honourable Saffron or My Lady?'

'Only if you don't want children one day.'

It was Saffron's turn to get a slap from Mina. 'Hey. I'll be the one to decide that. You can find your own punishment if he steps out of line.'

I racked my brain. 'I've heard of Lady Kirsten. Is she one?' Saff nodded. 'And Rick said that someone called Milton was a big cheese.'

She frowned for a second, then slapped her head. 'Dummy. Me, that is. It must have been Rick's South London accent. He must have actually said *Melton*. That's his nickname – Melton Mowbray, as in the pork pie. Lord Mowbray of Pellacombe in Cornwall is as big a cheese as they get. The late Earl of Tintagel was his uncle. When the staff earl dies, there's an election.'

I thought for a moment. 'So, Her Majesty Queen Elizabeth is Regent Staff Queen as well as Sword Queen of England?'

'Close. The Duke of Albion is regent staff queen.'

The Duke of Albion is the member of the royal family who looks after magickal duties. The current Duke is female: Princess Anne, the Princess Royal. 'How many staff kingdoms are there?'

'Eleven. The English Heptarchy and four others in north west England, Scotland and Wales. It's bonkers, but the staff kingdom for Edinburgh is English, but the one for the Lake District is Scottish. Do you want to know where they all are?'

'Is there a list and map on the Merlyn's Tower server?'

'Yes.'

'Then we'll leave it there for now. Thanks very much, Saffron.'

Saffron stood up again, and this time I didn't object. 'See you both later.'

Mina got up, too, and stretched. 'You'll want another pint, won't you?'

'Please. Let's enjoy the peace, and the weather. No doubt you've got lots to tell me about the Bollywood party.'

'I am still not sure whether having Hannah is a good idea, but I've forgiven you for inviting her.' With that, she went to the bar.

When she got back, she grinned. 'It's not just the party. It's the cruise and the Cloister Court I need to worry about first. Would you mind if we went to London on Wednesday?'

'Not at all. So long as you remember that shopping is bad for my leg.'

'Hah. You'll be pleased to hear that I swallowed my pride and called Annelise van Kampen to ask about the dress code for the Cloister Court. She said that a dress and jacket would be fine.' She scratched her nose. 'She could be lying to wind me up.'

Annelise is both a Watch Officer and a lawyer. She assists Iain Drummond and is a bit of a flirt, I'm afraid. 'She wouldn't dare,' I said. 'It could be a sin of omission, though. Did she tell you to take trainers?'

'Trainers? Why? She said medium heels.'

'In court, yes, but it's a half-mile walk to get there through the Old Network. The tunnels.'

'Hmmph. Thank you.'

4 – All Rise

'I see what you mean,' said Mina as we emerged from the concrete, human staircase into the Dwarven tunnels of the Old Network under the City of London.

Not content with trainers, she'd brought a long coat to go over her new suit. The dress was black, with white panels down the sides and came from a designer with a franchise in Selfridge's. That's all I can tell you about it, I'm afraid. That she looked gorgeously professional you'll have to take for granted.

She looked up and down the tunnel as far as she could in the light from the LED lantern and torch. Real Mages use Lightsticks. 'If Dwarves are so short, why do they build such high tunnels?' she asked.

'It's only their bodies that are small. They need these tunnels to fit their egos and their greed. It's also good for business: remember, they can't stand daylight. Their customers have to come to them. Can I show you something?'

I led her south for fifty metres and stopped. I took her hand and opened my inner eye. With our hands joined, she could see what I could see – a blue plaque with this legend:

> *This Section of the Old Network*
> *was dug by the first*
> *Lord Mayor of Moles,*
> *who lived and died nearby, under Mansion House.*
> *Erected in his Memory by*
> *Watch Captain Clarke*

I gave Moley a moment.

'I wish I'd met him,' said Mina. 'It was kind of you to do that.'

'He deserved more. Come on.'

I kept hold of her hand and led us north, past the staircase down to Hledjolf's Hall. The Old Network is as old as Roman London, perhaps older, and was dug by Hledjolf the Dwarf. It all looks ancient, even the bit we were in now, which was only created when the tube network displaced the older system deeper underground. Some parts are very, very old, such as the junction we came to a few minutes later.

'Salomon's House is up there,' I said. 'And that totally blank piece of wall is where the Dragon's egg was found. This whole area was once on the surface. That's how the Dragon landed to lay the egg, two thousand years ago.'

Mina squeezed my hand. 'Someone's coming.' Her hearing is much better than mine. She turned to face one of the many tunnels, and I heard it, too:

running footsteps. A sweaty figure appeared: the Earth Master of Salomon's House. He runs a lot, does Chris Kelly, and almost didn't see us. When he did, he slowed, stopped, ran on the spot for a few seconds and finally came over with a big smile.

Chris is a Geomancer, an expert on Ley Lines and such like. He's not a colleague, but he's more than an ally. If he hadn't taken a risk on me and held out a helping hand, I'd have been roasted by that Dragon. We're not friends. Not yet. A point he soon made after we'd said hello.

'If you're serious about accepting our hospitality, we should make a date,' he said.

Chris has asked me – us – round to dinner on several occasions. Being a Watch Captain does not make it easy to plan in advance, but there was an edge to his voice that made it sound like he thought I was trying to avoid him. Anything but.

'I am serious, Chris. When are you around?'

He looked deflated. 'We're off to Germany for most of August.' He brightened up again. 'How about the August bank holiday? Saturday night?'

'Couldn't be better. There's no cricket until the Monday. We'll be there. Apocalypse permitting, of course.'

He nodded slowly, as if I'd just given him a Nobel prize. 'That's very good. I'll text you our address when we get back.' He looked at us properly, from my RAF uniform in a suit carrier to Mina's tights and trainers combo. 'I'm sorry. You must be on the way to the Old Temple. Everything okay?'

'It will be for him,' said Mina. 'He takes things like this in his very long strides. I look forward to seeing you and … Tamsin, isn't it?'

The funny look came back into Chris's face. 'Yes, it is. Good luck.'

When Chris had jogged off, I pointed to a tunnel leading due west. 'That way.'

'Is it far?'

'About ten minutes. Well, fifteen.'

'Fifteen with my little legs, yes, I get the message. Is there no entrance nearer?'

'Loads. Bank Station is the only one I have the key to. Come on, at least it's cool down here.'

Eventually the Network branched, and we turned south west up a rising tunnel. We stopped at a pair of doors. A proper pair of iron-bound bog-oak doors, with a grille for the gatekeeper to peer through and enough magick to deter anything except a Dragon. And Moley. He'd have got through.

'Do we knock?' said Mina.

I checked my watch. 'Any second now.' On the stroke of eight thirty, the sound of bolts being drawn back came through the door, and footsteps came from the tunnel behind us. The doors were heaved open and I did a double-take.

The gatekeeper was a young woman, dressed in the navy blue and royal red costume of a Yeoman Warder (or Beefeater). They are the crew who guard the Tower of London, and whom I pass every time I go to Merlyn's Tower. The Yeoman Warders are an excellent bunch, but they're all over forty and ex-service. The Cloister Court must have adopted their dress. Or vice-versa.

'Mina, this is Deputy Bailiff Stephanie Morgan. She's normally to be found avoiding her father in the Undercroft.'

Stephanie gave me the eye and shook hands with Mina.

Mina said, 'Your Wardroom Cake recipe is excellent. It's already being traded at the Clerkswell WI.'

'I should ask for royalties. Mind your backs.'

The footsteps behind turned into the Merlyn's Tower posse of the Boss, Iain Drummond and Annelise van Kampen. I saluted. Mina made namaste and checked out Annelise's footwear (trainers). A grim smile spread across her face. Annelise would pay for that sin against the sisterhood one day.

Through the doors, we found ourselves in a functional ante-room lit by LEDs and with wooden lockers on one side. The other side had coat hooks framing a full length mirror.

'We've been asking for a separate female robing room for some time,' said Annelise dryly. 'The rule is gentlemen first.' She saw my suit carrier. 'Do you need us to give you privacy?'

I took my civilian jacket off. 'Not unless you're more easily offended than I thought.'

'Another rule is no swords in court,' said Stephanie. She looked pointedly at my belt. 'It doesn't say No Guns, but we can assume that.'

The women turned away while I swapped my trousers and Iain Drummond put on his advocate's bands and gown. We left them to it and I followed Drummond into the lobby of the court.

This was more like it. The ceiling was much higher and Lightsticks glowed above the oak panelling. The doors to the Cloister Court itself were still firmly closed, the royal arms above reminding us that this might be a magickal court, but it was very much part of the state, something that many Mages refuse to accept.

The Court entrance wasn't the only opening. Stephanie Morgan had moved to lurk by a door marked Bailiff, and a corridor to the left had modern signs for washrooms next to it. Further doors were marked for Witnesses and Lay Counsel. The furniture was both functional and intimidating: green leather benches round the walls and two tables with hard chairs. Nowhere looked comfortable. I know, because Myfanwy had told me, that prisoners are brought directly into the courtroom from Blackfriars Undercroft.

Mina and Hannah emerged together. The Boss had put on her uniform jacket and was still fiddling with a new headscarf. This one was black silk, with the Peculier Constable's shield embroidered at the front. 'Is that new?' I asked.

'Birthday present from Tennille.' I raised my eyebrows. 'She and Ruth are the only ones allowed to know when my birthday is.'

Mina looked nonplussed. 'But Ruth is your twin. Doesn't that make your birthday rather obvious?'

Hannah dismissed such quibbles with a wave. 'It's boring to celebrate your birthday on the day you were born. Especially when there's two of you.'

'Okay,' said Mina.

Drummond returned from the washrooms as Annelise emerged from the Crown Robing Room (which is what it said on this side of the door). Annelise's heels were definitely *high* rather than *medium*. Another black mark for the girl from Gendt. That's in Holland, and not to be confused with Ghent or Genk in Belgium.

'We've had a change-round,' said Drummond. 'I'm going to speak in the Wessex business, so Annelise will lead in the Flint Hoard. Do you want to go through anything?' he asked, looking from Annelise to Mina.

'Ja, for certain,' said Annelise. She moved to one of the tables, taking a nervous Mina with her. Drummond drifted off to talk to Stephanie.

'Where's the new addition?' said Hannah with a grin. She paused long enough for me to get uncomfortable. 'The dog. Your Familiar Spirit.'

I gave her a look. 'Scout is at home, with my magickal half-sister. He can draw Lux from her, and he's big enough to be without me for a couple of days.' I pointed to the court doors. 'I checked the rules. Bonded Familiars are allowed. One day.'

'And Sofía?' She said it softly, like an old friend, giving me the chance to change the subject.

'Gardening. Thinking. Crying. Cora got in touch. Thanks very much for that; I'm seeing her later.'

'Here we go,' said Hannah, nodding towards Stephanie.

The Deputy Bailiff picked up her monstrous blue hat and donned it. If you haven't seen one, and can't be bothered to Google, it looks like the chopped off funnel of an American steam locomotive, with added brim. White gloves completed the outfit.

Stephanie opened a tall cupboard next to the Wardroom and took out a long-handled battle axe. As soon as it left the cupboard, it shimmered with magick until she ran her gloved hand over the face of the blade. We fell back as she approached the inner doors. She turned to face the room.

'The Court of the Queen's Cloister is now in private session,' she announced. 'Only officers of the court and interested parties may approach.'

I had no idea why, but I was an interested party: it said so on the list outside the doors. So was Hannah. We stepped forwards, leaving the others behind.

'Miss Desai, you are an officer of the court,' said Stephanie. 'You may approach.'

Mina did her frightened rabbit scuttle and joined me. 'What's this about?' she hissed.

'You'll see,' said Hannah.

Stephanie banged the axe three times on the floor, and the doors opened of their own accord. 'We sit on the left,' said Hannah.

We processed into the court and I took a good look round. With the name *Cloister*, I expected something monastic, but I was looking at the wrong name. The Court of the Queen's Cloister can sit anywhere, but this building is known as the Old Temple, and that's what it is: an old Roman temple, small but perfectly formed. A row of columns down each side demarcated the courtroom, and it was lit not with Lightsticks but a burst of natural light from above. I craned my neck, expecting a Skyway, but no, it was a long way up to a glass roof with wrought iron struts.

The side aisles beyond the columns had walkways and seating, and we headed left. The main body of the temple had been fitted out like a regular courtroom, with a few differences. For example, there were no tables or fittings for lawyers; they had to stand at lecterns.

The bench for the judge(s) was long, because up to five of them sit for a contested case. There is no jury in the Cloister Court, and the biggest difference of all was behind the bench: a ten foot high block of stone, roughly carved and bound with rusty iron. I pointed to it.

'The original London Stone,' whispered Hannah. 'Officially, it's known as the *London Palladium*, but no one calls it that any more because of the theatre of the same name. *Palladium* means protective Artefact. It's very powerful.'

A door banged in the darkness behind the London Stone.

'All rise … no, don't,' said Stephanie. What?

Heels clicked on the tiles, and the Honourable Mrs Justice Bracewell appeared, wearing a simple blouse and black trouser suit. Her hair was up, badly pinned; she was clearly undressed, with robes to follow. She passed by the steps to the bench and came to sit with us. In the background, I saw Stephanie place the axe in a holder.

'Good morning Constable, Watch Captain,' said the judge. 'Good to see you again, Ms Desai.'

'My Lady,' said Hannah.

Mina and I nodded, letting the Boss answer for us. We've met the judge before, in her chambers at the Royal Courts of Justice where she also sits in mundane cases. She is human, and happily married, but you have to look very hard to see it.

'All four of today's cases are a first for the Cloister Court,' she began. 'That's not something I'm entirely comfortable with, because as we lawyers say, *hard cases make bad law*.' She looked at some papers. 'Later, we have our first video link, we have the first appearance by the Peculier Auditor and we have the first sitting of a Staff Court since the Restoration in 1660.' She hadn't looked up as she rattled off the list, but she read the sudden tension in Mina's body when her title was announced. 'Don't worry, Ms Desai. I appointed you to be Peculier Auditor, and I'm not going to throw you to the wolves.'

Mina swallowed hard. 'Thank you, My Lady.'

The judge nodded. 'And our first first is another matter entirely. Never before has the Old Temple seen a family court. That's why I'm half-dressed and you didn't have to stand up.' She looked at Stephanie. 'I'm not sure the axe is appropriate for a family court, but as the girls aren't here, we won't quibble.'

Girls.

The girls. Wales. The Dragon.

There were a lot of casualties at the end of the Dragon Brotherhood affair, including one of the principal Druids responsible for hatching Welshfire – a woman called Surwen. I have many reasons to hate her, and she's the only person I've killed who I thought got off lightly. As well as releasing the Dragon, she also created the Lord Mayor of Moles, and did such a bad job that she condemned him to an early, unpleasant death.

Surwen's husband, Gwyddno, is locked up, and she left twin girls behind. Those twin girls are the reason for the family court and for the total privacy. Surwen did something terrible to one of the twins, so terrible that I don't want to go over it again here. Judge Bracewell had had to seek the advice of a colleague, and this was her judgement.

She cleared her throat and began. I'll spare you her reasoning and skip straight to the end.

'Finally, there is Guinevere's condition to consider. To have the best chance of developing into any form of healthy adult, she needs medical and magickal help. The Gathering of Caerleon, where the twins grew up, is not a fit community for them now. I have therefore decided to place them in the foster care of Watch Captain Helen Davies of the Swansea gathering, under the supervision of the Daughters of the Goddess.'

She looked up. 'How did I do?'

'Why Helen?' I asked.

'We consulted her. She's met the girls, and she volunteered. She fits all the criteria.' The judge took off her glasses. 'The Daughters of the Goddess will support and advise, but they're acting for the Court. The reason you're here, Mr Clarke, is that Helen Davies wants you to be her safety valve, in case she needs help or advice beyond that needed by all mothers of teenage girls.'

Was that the wry smile of experience? I think it was.

She replaced her glasses. 'They're keeping their names, and one day their father may be back in their lives. As regards Myfanwy Lewis, you're not to tell her anything until September, understand? The girls will be starting secondary school then, and word will get out anyway, I'm sure.'

'Yes, My Lady.'

'Good. Out you go. I need to get changed and my clerk has to set up the video link.'

We all stood up (without being asked) and nodded our respect to the royal arms over the bench. Stephanie retrieved the axe and led us to the doors in silence.

Poor kids. I hope they get a decent shot at life, and I can think of no one better than the Davies clan to give them that chance.

The doors parted and we returned to the lobby. Mina bumped into me when I stopped abruptly.

'Conrad! What are you doing?'

'That's Augusta Faulkner. Over there in the robes with gold edging. And she's coming this way.'

'It looks like all your ghosts are coming to haunt you,' said Mina.

'My daughter is not a ghost,' said Faulkner. By Odin's eye, she must have superb hearing. We've met once before, when she served me coffee at Lunar Hall.

Augusta Faulkner was a member of the congregation of the Lunar Sisters, and her mother was then the First Sister. Augusta's daughter, Keira, had been at the heart of my first magickal experience – saving the Thirteenth Witch.

'Could I have a word in private?' said Faulkner.

'Tell me later,' said Mina. 'I need the ladies room.'

We stepped aside, taking an empty corner. 'I thought you'd retired from the law,' I said.

'My retirement plans didn't work out quite the way I envisaged,' she responded, trying to maintain the dignity of the courtroom. Stuff that.

'Would those plans have changed because your daughter betrayed you and got you kicked out of Lunar Hall?'

Her lips pressed hard together as she bit back her first response. Augusta Faulkner had a reputation as the best defence lawyer on the magickal circuit. Iain Drummond had opened a very old bottle of single malt the day she hung up her wig.

She composed herself. 'I'm here to represent Irina Ispabudhan. It's a fascinating case, but that's not the reason I took it. I wanted to talk to you. On neutral ground.'

The Merlyn's Tower team were watching us closely. I made sure that Faulkner had seen me make eye contact with them. 'Go on.'

'Keira wants to come home.'

'You were her counsel. It was your job to explain the implications of lifetime exile. Especially the bit about "life".'

'Don't, Mr Clarke. Tormenting me won't make any difference. Yes, I've seen Deborah Sayer's sister, and Mother Julia's missing arm. You can't add to my pain by rubbing in my failings as a mother. And as a daughter. I can't hurt any more than I do already.'

She had a point. I could snipe all I wanted, but it wouldn't make anything better. There was one thing missing, though. 'Anna. Have you been to see her, by any chance?'

She looked away. 'Keira didn't kill Lika. I thought you accepted that.'

'I accepted that it couldn't be proved in court, which is a different matter. Even you won't deny that Lika would still be alive if you hadn't let Deborah Sayer and Keira into Lunar Hall. Will you?'

She shook her head. She was on the verge of tears.

I thought of my mother, and of what she'd do if Rachael or I were in trouble. I tried to soften my tone. 'I hate to say this to a top QC, Ms Faulkner, but it's not up to me, is it? It's up to the court.'

'If Keira does two years in France, she can petition the Cloister Court for return. The Court will listen to you. If you can find it in yourself to forgive her, she might have a chance.'

'I'm not a Christian. I don't do forgiveness.'

She tried – and failed – to hide a look of disdain. 'I had thought better of you, Mr Clarke. For some reason, the Goddess chose you, of all people, to carry my mother's body to its final rest. The Goddess does not do that without reason.'

'I didn't say I wouldn't help, I just said that there would have to be restitution first.'

'Tell me.'

'Start today. Go easy on Mina in the Flint Hoard hearing.'

'Irina is my client. She's entitled to the best service I can give.'

Her answer told me everything I needed to know: Irina had instructed her barrister to go for Mina's throat. 'Then convince her that you have a better strategy. Going for Mina won't endear you to the judge.'

She grimaced. 'Reluctantly, I agree with you. That's only the start, isn't it?'

'Yes. Visit Anna. Pay the blood price for Lika.'

She nodded, bracing herself for more.

'And if your daughter really wants to come home, she'll find and deliver Adaryn ap Owain. Tell her to start looking in Brittany.'

'That is a heavy, heavy price, Mr Clarke.'

'If Keira has reformed, she'll want to bring a fugitive to justice, won't she? Here's my card. Tell her to get in touch when the blood price has been settled.'

The doors banged open again. 'The Court of the Queen's Cloister is now in open session,' boomed Stephanie. 'All parties in the case of Irina Ispabudhan should enter.'

42

'What the hell was that all about?' hissed Hannah as we walked into court.

'Tell you later.'

The empty space in front of the bench was now filled with lecterns, and a TV screen had been mounted on a trolley.

We took our places on the Crown side of the court while Annelise and Augusta Faulkner took a lectern each. 'All rise,' said Stephanie, looking at us with a half grin.

The Honourable Mrs Justice Bracewell was almost unrecognisable in her scarlet robes and full length wig. Even the glasses were different.

'That shade suits her better,' said Mina.

'The robes?' I said.

'No,' said Hannah. 'The lipstick.'

Oh.

The judge took her place on the bench, and two new figures, both male and gowned, appeared. One sat in front of the judge; her clerk, presumably. The other fiddled with the TV. In a miracle of modern technology, it worked first time.

Irina Ispabudhan was at the centre of my most recent case, a gruelling hunt for a trio of magickal money-launderers and counterfeiters. Two of the three were now dead, and Irina was seriously injured. We could see her chained to a hospital bed with enchanted handcuffs. Her right knee was in a serious medical brace, hence the video link. This was only a remand hearing and not scheduled to take long.

'Are you Irina Ispabudhan?' asked the clerk.

'Irina Rybakova. I have taken my husband's name to honour his memory.'

'Noted.'

The clerk read out the full list of charges and sat down. There was a bit of discussion about the terms of her remand, and then the judge made the order. With a bang of the gavel, she dismissed the prisoner and the video screen was wheeled away from centre stage. It was left switched on because Irina had an interest in the next case.

'Moving on,' said the judge. 'Bring in the parties to ...' She hesitated. 'I know you're all calling it the Flint Hoard, and that's as good a name as any. Let's go with that.'

Mina took a deep breath. This was her big show, or it would be when I'd finished the warm-up act. But first, we needed an audience.

A small crowd of lawyers and their clients made an entrance. I recognised one of the clients – Saunders, Chief of Clan Flint. He is a repellent little Gnome who would be quite happy if I died. The feeling is mutual. They took their places, lawyers under the glass and clients behind the columns, and the clerk asked a nervous Annelise van Kampen to begin.

She cleared her throat. 'My Lady, the matter before the court is a considerable one: a large quantity of Alchemical gold. Our suit concerns the ownership of this gold, but first I would like to establish its existence.'

'A good place to start,' said the judge.

Annelise held her nerve. 'Thank you, My Lady. I would like to call Watch Captain Clarke.'

I emerged from the shadows and stood before the bench, turning my body so that Irina couldn't see my face on her monitor. 'I call upon Odin to witness that the evidence I shall give ...' No going back now. Unlike other witnesses, I literally couldn't lie on oath.

I could, but it would be the last thing I did.

Annelise took me through the discovery of the gold in the First Mine of Clan Flint, and the fact that I'd weighed it and counted it, all 440,000 Troy Ounces of enhanced Alchemical Gold.

'Does anyone have any questions for the Watch Captain?' said the judge.

A short barrister, clearly another Gnome, spoke up. 'Quintus Octavius, acting for Clan Flint, My Lady. My client does not dispute Mr Clarke's evidence – as far as it goes. We reserve the right to recall him if necessary.'

'Noted,' said the judge. 'Thank you, Watch Captain.'

I returned to my seat, and it was Hannah who patted my hand and said, 'Well done.' Mina was staring at the spot I'd vacated and saying something under her breath. A prayer in Sanskrit, I think.

The judge wrote something down and held up the paper. 'This court recognises the existence of the Hoard. We now move on to the question of ownership, to which there are many parties. Knowing this, the court appointed its own auditor, Ms Desai, and I would like to hear her evidence as to how the gold got to the First Mine. Ms Desai?'

Mina jumped up and straightened her jacket. She tossed back her hair and walked across the open space. Unlike me, she stared at the monitor. Mina is the reason that Irina is in a hospital bed. Irina looked away first.

Mina took the oath on a copy of the Mahabharata and looked at her papers. With great care, she said, 'My Lady, may I submit my report, Document One in the bundle?'

And that was it: she was up and running. My heart swelled as she started to give evidence. This was all her work, and she was as proud of her spreadsheet as I was of my Military Cross.

I sat there, grinning like a teenager watching his girlfriend on stage, even after she lost me, so about thirty seconds then. I have many skills, but double entry accounting is not one of them. After two refills from the water jug, she got to the end and bowed to the bench.

'Thank you, Ms Desai,' said the judge. 'I have a note that Mrs Rybakova wishes to object to this evidence.'

Augusta Faulkner shook her head. 'No longer, my lady.'

'Good. Mr Octavius?'

The Gnome was caught flatfooted by Augusta's capitulation and hummed for a moment before beginning. 'Clan Flint objects to the appointment of Ms Desai on the grounds of conflict of interest. Her association with the King's Watch is well known.'

Mina dropped her head and shifted her weight from one leg to the other. She knew this was coming, and putting up with it was a price she had to pay.

Annelise spoke up. 'My Lady, the Watch is not a party to this suit. I am acting for the Crown, not the Constable.'

'I agree,' said the judge. 'Ms Desai's evidence stands.'

'In that case,' said Annelise, 'as none of us has seen the document before, we would like an adjournment to prepare for a full hearing at a later date.'

'Does anyone object?'

Octavius spoke first. 'We agree with the adjournment, but this gold must be stored and guarded. We submit that Clan Flint should be paid a fee.'

'I concur. That seems reasonable. You'll also have to replace it if it gets stolen. Anyone else?'

No less than six barristers got up to agree, just to ensure that their clients had to pay them a court fee, a point that was not lost on the judge.

'I am not going to let the Flint Hoard turn into Jarndyce and Jarndyce,' she announced. 'There will be a full hearing beginning Monday the fifth of October. Now, I don't know about the Crown, but I'm ready for a break. We'll take forty-five minutes before the next case.'

'All rise.'

45

5 – Meet the Mowbrays

Mina's shoulders slumped when the judge had disappeared. I was limping across the court towards her before Annelise had even picked up her papers.

'You were brilliant, love,' I said, taking her in my arms. I earned a sniff from Annelise and scowl from Saunders for my pains.

'Come on, you two,' said Hannah. 'I've got another present. This way.'

The north side of the court had cleared, and I could see two doors, both closed. Hannah pointed to the right hand, more substantial door. 'That one goes down and along to the Undercroft, and only the Bailiffs can open it. Anyone who's drunk from Nimue's hand can open the other one. It's one of the few doors like that in the kingdom. Try it, Conrad.'

I did, and felt the tingle of magick. I pushed and had to push again. Behind the door, a steep staircase led up. 'After you,' said Hannah.

The top of the staircase had no door, and emerged into an exquisite courtyard garden. Most of the area was taken up with the glass roof of the Old Temple, but in the margins exotic plants flourished, sheltered by the high walls and obviously well cared for. This is where Myfanwy had been allowed for one hour a day to get relief from the Limbo Chambers in the Undercroft.

There were no doors in the garden walls. The only access was from below, though I did see another staircase to the east. A small shed nestled in the shady spot. 'There's a bench over there,' said Hannah, 'and you can smoke, Conrad. I'll be back shortly.'

Mina sank on to the bench, and I lit up. She leaned back and let the sun warm her face. 'I am dreading the fifth of October. That's when they get to cross-examine me. This was only the start.'

'You were brilliant. I think. I loved the bit where you said that polar bears are not native to East Anglia.'

'Did I say that? Really?'

'Yes. At least three of the barristers nodded in agreement.'

'I can't wait to read the transcript. I've no idea what I said at some points.'

Hannah reappeared, with Annelise and Drummond. Stephanie brought up the rear. Between them, they had flasks, cups and pastries. I was starving.

The Boss wanted to know what I'd said to Augusta Faulkner. When I'd told them, she blew out her cheeks. 'You know, technically it's none of my business. You weren't in the Watch during the Battle of Lunar Hall.'

'I know, ma'am, but I'd have said the same if it was a Watch matter.'

Hannah frowned. 'Not without checking with Iain, first. Understand? As it happens, I agree with what you said. If Keira can deliver Adaryn, I wouldn't object to a reduced sentence.'

'Time,' said Stephanie. 'Bring the tray, Conrad.'

I followed her down the second staircase and entered the Wardroom, a small but comfortable space. 'Leave it by the sink,' said Stephanie. 'You don't need magick to get out into the lobby, only to get in.' I waited for the others to catch up and opened the door.

The lobby was full, a sea of colour, of women and of talk. One man in a black suit stood out, like a rock protruding from the waves.

Mina pushed me aside and said, 'Now that is a crowd I wouldn't want to face. All those women. All that colour. Who are they?'

'The Daughters of the Goddess, in full fig,' said Hannah.

'Fig?' said Mina.

'Ja?' echoed Annelise.

'A Salomon's House term,' said Drummond. 'It suggests that the sacred robes of the Daughters are akin to fancy dress.' He looked pointedly at my uniform. 'We would never do that, would we? Or wear wigs.'

They both had a point. Underground, here, the flowing robes and hoods did look out of place, but they wore them naturally, comfortably and totally unselfconsciously.

Now I'd had time to adjust, I felt the air warming, not with heat but Lux, and the collective magick had made the crowd seem a lot bigger than it actually was. The bolder, brighter colours were mostly worn by the older women, the younger ones favouring lighter pastels. A couple even had their legs on show. All of these women were Mages, yes, but because they'd learnt their magick in the circle and not at Salomon's house, they are normally known as Witches.

'Axe coming through,' said Stephanie.

I jumped out of the way as she passed, and for the third time she opened the doors. As we streamed in to the court, one woman in a regular, high street stretch dress and leggings stayed seated, checking her phone with one hand and stroking her small baby bump with the other. Her head was down, so I couldn't be sure, but she looked strangely familiar.

We all took our places and Stephanie put the axe in its socket by the bench. She picked up a folded cloth. 'Conrad, can you give me a hand You're much taller than the clerks, and I've got no chance.'

'Of course. What do you want?'

'I need to get this over the royal arms, and I don't want to embarrass myself.'

I took one end of the black cloth. 'Why?'

'It's a sign of mourning and that this court is not the Cloister Court. It's the staff court of Wessex.'

'Oh. That makes no sense.'

We got the fabric in place, and I retreated as the clerks appeared, followed by the judge, in her third outfit of the day – her own, black, version of the Daughters' robes, with the hood pulled up over her now loose hair.

Instead of saying *All rise*, Stephanie read from a card. 'The Staff King of Wessex is dead. Let us pray for his soul.'

We joined in to make a circle, and the black-suited man called on all the gods not to stand in the way of Harold Mowbray on his journey to the next life.

'So mote it be,' we echoed.

'The king is dead,' said Judge Bracewell. 'Who would address the Staff Court of Wessex?'

The young man who'd led the prayers stepped into the circle. His black suit was impeccably tailored to show off his shoulders, and the only colour in his outfit was a blue tie that echoed his eyes. Even his curly hair was black.

'Is it me or is it hot in here?' said Mina.

'I don't know about you,' whispered Hannah, 'but he's definitely hot.'

'Ja, for certain,' added Annelise.

Three professional women, all achievers, and they couldn't take their eyes off the prime Cornish beef. I offer no observations at this point; I am simply stating a fact.

The whispered exchange had attracted the attention of a woman to the man's right. I'd missed her before, as she was slightly shorter than the Daughters and much, much shorter than the man. I knew she wasn't one of the Daughters because she was in black, modern dress and had her hair cut short and spiked. All the Witches wore their (long) hair plaited into the three-strand Goddess braid.

The woman stared at us, and it was obvious, even to me, that she was closely related to the man, and a couple of years older, about thirty. She wore a much cheaper suit, the jacket buttons straining over her thin white shirt and the trousers clinging to her hips but shapeless lower down. The only colour was a silk band at her throat that appeared to have been cut from the same cloth as the man's tie. A poor relation? She'd obviously spent longer on her eyeshadow than on buying her clothes.

'Go ahead,' said the judge.

Before speaking, the man looked over at us. Not at the Boss, but at Iain Drummond. Whatever he saw satisfied him and he began. 'Cador Mowbray,' he said. Cador? They do have some strange names in the world of magick. 'I act for Lord Mowbray of Pellacombe, Elector of Wessex.'

A woman with greying brown hair stepped forward. Her robes were so fine that they could have been silk, a shimmering white with a pale blue sleeves and a matching pale blue cloak. I noticed her belt, then the belts of the others. They were all made of rope, and red was the most common colour, mostly worn by the younger women. Otherwise, the cords were pale yellow, green, brown or white. The woman about to speak wore yellow.

'I am Brook, Seventh Daughter of Ash Coven in the Homewood at Glastonbury. I speak for all the Daughters. Our suit is simple: stay the election and let us petition the Sword King for a new charter. Women are explicitly forbidden from standing or even voting in the existing charter. In the twenty-first century, this is illegal and unsupportable.'

'Mr Mowbray?'

'What my learned friend calls the "Charter" is no such thing. A charter is granted by a king to a lesser body like a city or a guild. The document is a deed, a constitution if you prefer. Only a staff king in office can change it, and it is not subject to alteration by this court. There will be no staff king until an election is held.'

These two opening statements from the lawyers were the legal equivalent of boxers taking the ring and touching gloves. They now proceeded to slug it out with precedents and citations that only four people truly understood – the combatants, the judge and Iain Drummond.

'Who's winning?' I hissed when there was a pause.

'Cador,' replied Drummond. 'She can't land a glove on him.'

So I wasn't the only one with a boxing metaphor in their head. Either that or Drummond is telepathic, and true magickal telepaths are rarer than hydra's teeth. Or so I'm told. Lord Mowbray probably has a pet hydra.

Drummond continued, 'It'll change in a minute. Brook is going to take her ball home. Watch her sidekick.'

A glossy young Witch stood next to Brook. She had very short robes, above the knee, and the same light blue sleeves to her robe. She also had a holiday tan and wore very simple leather sandals. Her belt was red, and tucked into it was a rolled piece of parchment, secured with a rainbow ribbon. The Witch had her left hand on it.

The judge used her pen to point at Brook. 'No,' she said. I understood that bit.

Brook turned to her junior and accepted the parchment. She tapped it against her palm and waited until every eye was firmly on her. 'This is not directly relevant, My Lady, but I thought the court should know that the Chapter of Gloucester met yesterday.' She held up the scroll. 'They have put their seal to a proxy vote, with the Eldest as proxy.'

'Ooh,' said Hannah.

'Shit. Fucking shit,' said Cador's sister/cousin. The judge went ballistic.

She pointed to the woman and said, 'Who is that?' in an icy tone. She obviously knew, but it's a legal thing.

'My sister, Eseld Mowbray, My Lady. She …'

'Ms Mowbray, you are in contempt of court. You will apologise now or spend the night in the Undercroft.'

Everyone froze, all eyes now on Eseld. The young Mowbray paused for half a second, then slowly got on her knees. Her trousers cut into her thighs, and she had to hitch them twice before she got all the way down.

'Mercy, My Lady. I am truly sorry for my outburst.'

Her brother's accent was pure public school; his sister's vowels stretched in a very Cornish way. Interesting. Her chest was now in sunlight, and through the cheap shirt, I saw the outline of Artefacts on a chain. A Mage, then. Even more interesting.

Judge Bracewell allowed the silence to stretch out. 'One more word out of turn and it's a week. Understood?'

'My Lady.'

'Get up. Daughter Brook, you were saying?'

Cador helped his sister to her feet, and squeezed her shoulder supportively. Eseld was white with fury and embarrassment.

'Thank you, My Lady,' said Brook. 'We now have ten votes under proxy. Enough to block the election in perpetuity, and we will block it. The choice will then pass to the Sword King's deputy, Her Royal Highness the Duke of Albion.'

Iain Drummond was now the centre of attention. 'I speak for the Duke of Albion,' he said. 'Her Royal Highness is as keen to remain impartial in magickal politics as her mother is in mundane affairs. If the election of the staff king is unresolved, it will be passed to the Occult Council with a request for a commission to review the constitutions of all seven English staff kingdoms.' He paused. No one looked happy. 'The Crown urges the parties to compromise.' He finished with a bow and stepped back.

The Mowbrays started to confer, and an older Witch in green robes with a white belt whispered urgently in Brook's ear.

'Well?' said the judge.

'My Lady,' said Cador, 'Lord Mowbray would like to offer a conference of reconciliation, at Pellacombe, under the seal of hospitality.'

'That is generous, and a positive step,' said the judge. 'Daughters?'

Brook was caught. 'Could we have a short adjournment?'

'Ten minutes,' said the judge. 'And you can all stay in here. When the Bailiff lifts the axe, the blocking Ward will be released and you can get a mobile signal if you need to phone home. Bailiff, call me in ten minutes.'

The Daughters, the Mowbrays and the King's Watch retreated to their corners. 'You knew that was coming, didn't you?' said Hannah to Drummond. Her tone reminded me of an older sibling, surprised and respectful that the younger one has got one over on them. I used to use that tone a lot with Rachael.

'I knew it was in the pipeline,' he replied, 'and that's why I went to the Palace yesterday to check, just in case.'

'What is the Gloucester Chapter, and why have I never heard of it?' I asked. After all, Clerkswell is in Gloucestershire.

'One of the many hangovers from the Reformation. Basically, it means any Mage willing to go to the cathedral and pray.' He grinned. 'You could go, if you're willing to take the risk of being struck by lightning.'

'I'll pass, thanks.'

'What now?' said Hannah.

'I think the Eldest will go for it, if Brook can get her on the phone.'

'Aah, yes. How is she?'

'Recovering. She can still perform the Miracle.' He saw my face – and Mina's – and added, 'Their leader is called the Eldest Daughter. She keeps the job as long as she can perform the Miracle of Glastonbury, but don't ask me what it is. She had a small stroke recently.'

Mina had been watching the Daughters closely. 'What is it with the belts and the colours? I think the short green outfit over there, the one with the red belt, would really suit me. It would suit me better than her.'

Drummond deferred to the Boss.

'The belt says which Coven they belong to. There are loads of Covens up and down the country, all limited to thirteen Witches. They all have equal standing, except the top ones, and a red belt means that they don't come from one of the top Covens. The red ones here are all young Witches based in London, I imagine, come along to see and be seen by the top brass.'

'And the others?'

'White is Hawthorn Coven of Highgate. Do you see the one who spoke to Brook? That's Síona, First Daughter of Highgate. Top Witch outside Glastonbury. She sits on the Occult Council for the Daughters. She's a bit too ascetic for my tastes.'

'That leaves yellow, green and brown, doesn't it?'

'Yes, and they are the three Homewood Covens. Homewood is their sacred grove complex, south of Glastonbury. Did Conrad tell you about the Forest of Arden?'

'He did, and that it exists on a different plane of energy, invisible to mundane eyes.'

'Homewood is the same. You get access by going through one of three trees: an oak, an ash and a willow, and those are the Covens. Yellow for Ash, green for Willow and brown for Oak.'

Mina nodded to herself. 'Brook is Seventh Daughter of Ash. I see. If there are only thirty-nine members of the Homewood Covens, seven is a lot to come here.'

'This matters a lot to them. The last elections were held in 1974 when the last Duke of Albion died.'

'Let me guess,' I said. 'The Duke of Gloucester?'

'Got it in one. The Daughters tried to get things changed then, and they succeeded in Strathclyde and the Isles, but not in the Heptarchy. This is the first chance since, and Wessex is their home turf.'

'What's Lord Mowbray like?' I asked.

Drummond grimaced. 'Wait and see.'

Hannah pointed to me. 'He doesn't like the sound of that, and neither do I. What have you cooked up, Iain?'

'Gather round!' said Stephanie. Drummond grinned at Hannah and took his place in the circle.

Judge Bracewell glided back and lowered her hood. 'Well, counsel?'

Brook checked a piece of paper. 'The Daughters welcome this suggestion, so long as it is backed with genuine intent, and we accept the offer, subject to safe passage, guarantee and witness.'

Hannah shook her head at Drummond. 'Sneaky,' she whispered.

'Mr Mowbray?' said the judge.

'My father's intent is always genuine. The other conditions are acceptable, so long as they come from this court.'

Judge Bracewell gave Drummond a long, searching look. Our Deputy is clearly a gifted back stairs operator, and he went up in my estimation. Very neatly done.

The judge spoke. 'Now I know what the Watch Captain and the Peculier Auditor are doing here. And there was me thinking that it was an educational visit.'

'Me?' said Mina in a small squeak.

'Mmm,' said the judge. 'I appoint Watch Captain Clarke as guarantor of safe passage and Ms Desai as witness.'

Hannah nodded and said, 'My Lady, I request that Watch Officer Hawkins be named also, to advise Mr Clarke on the more advanced aspects of magick.'

There was a snort of derision from one of the older Witches. Clearly my reputation precedes me: they know how little magick I have.

'Fine,' said the judge. 'I name Officer Hawkins as co-guarantor. Mr Mowbray?'

Cador Mowbray bowed low. Eseld was trying to make herself look small. 'An excellent choice, My Lady.'

'Good. Agree the dates amongst yourselves.' She took a look round the circle. 'So mote it be.'

We all bowed, and she left us.

The Daughters couldn't wait to get out when Stephanie opened the doors. All of them looked at us – Mina and me – as they left. The older ones covered their curiosity with a respectful nod to the Constable, and I distinctly heard the word *Dragonslayer* passed around.

Eseld Mowbray looked very uncomfortable. She was trying to brush dirt off the knees of her trousers, to little avail, and she shook her head when her brother pointed to us.

'Well, well, well,' said Hannah. 'I did not see any of that coming. Except Eseld getting in trouble. I predicted that.'

'What does all this mean?' said Mina. 'What do I have to do?'

'You can find out over lunch,' said Cador Mowbray, coming over and shaking hands. When Mina made namaste, he followed suit smoothly.

At the mention of lunch, Mina panicked. She had shopping to do – we were going on a cruise in four days. 'No need to come, love,' I said. 'I'll take notes. You get off.'

'But I can't get out of the tunnels!' she said.

'Where did you come in this morning?' said Hannah. 'Surely he didn't make you walk from Bank Station?'

Mina looked at me. 'He did. He says he has only one key.'

'Oy vey! You shall come with me, and Annelise shall give you a key to the Middle Temple entrance. It's the nearest, and you'll be here again often enough.'

'Thank you, Hannah. See you later, Conrad.'

I kissed her goodbye and everyone left except Cador and me.

'There's someone I'd like you to meet,' he said. 'Or should I say *renew your acquaintance*. Oh, damn.' The last remark was uttered when his phone rang. 'Excuse me, won't be long.'

'I'll get changed,' I said.

'After you've helped me with the cloth,' interrupted Stephanie.

By the time I'd helped her remove and fold the black drape, Mina and company had left the Crown Robing Room, and I was able to get changed. Cador Mowbray was waiting outside the door when I returned to the lobby.

A stream of Daughters emerged from the Lay Counsel's room, now in their street clothes. No one had a suitcase, though.

'Where are their robes?' I said.

Cador gave me a strange look. 'They're wearing them. These are only Glamours. That's one of the things the Cord does.'

'Cord?'

'The Cord that Binds. Mostly used as a belt.'

A pair of Witches smiled and passed. Behind them, the pregnant woman saw us, stood up and saluted.

'Squadron Leader. Good to see you again, sir.'

I thought I recognised her. 'Flight Lieutenant Kershaw. It's been, what, three years? Is it Ms Kershaw now?'

'I'm still in the Reserves, sir, and it's been four years. I left after that tour in Syria.'

'That was a bad one, wasn't it. Congratulations, by the way. When are you due?'

'Beginning of December, but I won't be able to fly, soon. Didn't Mr Cador tell you?'

'All in good time,' said Mowbray. I noted the old fashioned use of *Mr Cador* to distinguish him from his father, *Lord Mowbray*. 'Let's get out of here,' he continued. 'Have you seen Eseld?'

'In the ladies. Here she is.'

Eseld was not wearing a Glamour. I could tell that because she was stuffing the cheap suit, thin shirt and plastic shoes into a carrier bag bearing the logo of a fast fashion chain. She was not wearing a Glamour, but what she was wearing was something else entirely, even if it did keep to the black and white theme.

Her blouse was frilly, but not in the least feminine. Think eighteenth century army officer. Or pirate. It was teamed with a short black and white plaid skirt, black leggings and aggressive leather boots. There was more leather for her jacket, belt and a pair of wristbands. Leather wrist bands? I know. There was one splash of colour: the piece of blue silk that matched her brother's tie had been fastened round her belt. Oh, and she now had purple lipstick.

She thrust the shopping bag on to Cador. 'Here. You can keep these for one of your conquests, in case they need something for the walk of shame.'

Her accent was pure Cornish, all right. How did the older sister, a Mage, end up with the local accent and sporting a look that most teenagers wouldn't touch with a barge pole?

Cador tucked the bag under his arm. 'I'll bet you're glad I made you go shopping now. You would have been in even more trouble otherwise. I have known the Honourable Mrs Justice Bracewell to order that offending items of clothing be removed.'

Leah Kershaw found this very amusing. She also hid behind Cador so that Eseld couldn't see her grinning.

Cador introduced me to his sister formally, and we shook hands. Her fingers were warm, and I could feel Lux trickling down them. Ah. *That's* what the wrist bands were for.

'Lunch,' said Cador. 'For some of us. You'll have to excuse Eseld and me. That phone call was something we've got to sort out. I'm sure that you and Leah will have plenty to talk about, Conrad.'

'And it gets me out of shopping,' I added.

'Good. Follow me.'

We left via the Lay Counsel's rooms, now deserted. A corridor ran through them leading to a heavily enchanted steel barrier at the end, and Stephanie was waiting to lock up behind us, having checked the other rooms first. Stairs beyond the barrier led up to a door that opened with a mundane key, and we emerged into a church that both Leah and I know very well – St Clement Danes, the RAF church.

I walked instinctively to the aisle where hundreds of slate badges have been set into the floor. Leah and I served with 7 Squadron. I still do.

Eseld was looking angrily at her brother. Still.

'We'll leave you here,' said Cador. 'I'll see you at Pellacombe, and say Hi to Rachael if you see her first.'

Before I could respond, the Mowbrays were gone. That was something I needed to follow up as a matter of urgency: if Cador Mowbray knew my sister, I needed to know how and why.

Leah and I found the badge for 7 Squadron and bowed our heads for a moment. 'Granddad was in 7,' she said. 'Made his day when I got in. Want to see any more? I get terrible morning sickness and now I'm starving.'

'Where are we going?'

'The Kernow room at the Waldorf. We can walk from here. I'll just light a candle.'

The Waldorf? Nice.

Leah's own Cornish accent had got stronger since she left the RAF, as had the bridge of freckles across her nose. Did I fancy her when we served together? You bet. Did I do anything about it? No. I had a strict rule – never hit on the junior ranks. I avoided a lot of trouble that way.

I sat down for a moment and sent three text messages while she lit her candle, then we left the church to the tourists and crossed to the Royal Courts of Justice, where Judge Bracewell was no doubt ensconced.

'You must know how I ended up in the Watch,' I said. 'Everyone seems to know my business. How did you end up with the Mowbrays?'

'My dad works on the estate and he met my mum there.' Leah held her finger and thumb a quarter of an inch apart. 'Mum has magickal talent that big. Just enough to get her a job in the big house. I'm completely mundane.'

'And what do you do?'

She grinned. 'Lord Mowbray's personal pilot. You're going to do part of my maternity leave.'

'Am I now?'

'Mr Cador saw it coming, and that's why you're here. I'm going to be your pilot trainer so that you can fetch the Daughters down for the conference.'

'What have you got? A Chinook?'

'As if Lord M would slum it in a Chinook. He has an H155.'

My my. The H155 Eurocopter is the Bentley of helicopters. 'Does it have the leather seats?'

She showed me her right hand. On the third finger was a ring with an enamel badge in the same blue as Cador and Eseld's neck wear. 'The upholstery is in Mowbray blue leather. I'll fly up to Cheltenham and we'll put in the hours over the next few weeks. If you're okay with that, of course.'

'I'll look forward to it.' I'd noticed a wedding band on her other hand and pointed to it. 'Who's the lucky fellow?'

She shook her head. 'One of the reasons I joined the RAF was to get away from the farm next door. Now I'm a part-time farmer's wife. At least being pregnant gets me out of milking.' We were walking along Aldwych, with the Waldorf coming into view. 'And how are you, Conrad? I've heard all the magickal gossip, of course, but I didn't serve with a Mage.'

I took a moment to stretch out my leg. 'I think I'm the same person underneath. Older. Wiser. Definitely more scars. Happier, too.'

'Sorry about the leg.' She paused, because we both knew I'd got off lightly compared to many former comrades. 'I saw Ms Desai with the Constable. She isn't your normal type … sir.' A smile drifted over her lips.

I started walking again. 'In what way is Mina unusual, lieutenant? Short? Indian? Ex-convict? Widow?'

She laughed. 'I was going to say *public*. You had rather a reputation for secrecy in your love life. It was discussed in the lipstick lounge. Occasionally. When we'd read the latest *Vogue* and run out of things to talk about.'

I should point out that this last comment was delivered with a thick layer of irony. Female officers in Afghanistan didn't have it easy.

'Misdirection,' I said. 'A lot of the time, I was up to something illegal and having people think I was in a secret relationship was good cover. I will admit to the German liaison officer, though. That was all true.'

'Hah! If I ever see Helen again, she owes me a tenner.'

It was time to change the subject. 'What's the story with the Mowbray siblings?'

'Bear with me,' she said. '*Eseld*, with two Es is the Cornish spelling of *Isolde*, as in Tristan and Isolde, right?'

'If you say so.'

'Their mother was Isolde. I-S-O-L-D-E. She still is their mother, of course, but she divorced Lord M when he was still plain Mr Mowbray. She took the kids with her to the Daughters in Glastonbury, for a bit.'

'What happened? Did he sue for custody?'

'Oh no. When Eseld developed magick, she cut off her Goddess braid and hitched a lift back to Pellacombe. She hates the Daughters. And when Cador turned out to have no more magick than I do, Isolde-with-an-I sent him packing. He got a first at Cambridge and became a barrister. He looks after the politics of Pellacombe.'

'And Eseld?'

'Powerful Mage. She's her dad's right hand.'

'So which one is the heir?'

'Neither. The son and heir is Kenver, from Lord Mowbray's second marriage to Aisling. It's very complicated.'

'Is she still around?'

Leah looked away. 'She died when I'd just joined up. Some sort of accident. They had a daughter who'd be in her twenties now. Morwenna. Hasn't been seen since Aisling died. Lord M was devoted to Aisling. No one talks about it.'

We passed through the revolving doors of the Waldorf and headed to the Kernow room. 'Remind me again what *Kernow* means. I know I've heard it before.'

'It's Cornish for Cornwall, if you see what I mean. You'll hear it a lot at Pellacombe. They've leased this room for years as their London base.'

Lunch was excellent, as you'd expect when you get the individual attention of your own chef. Leah told me a lot more about the Mowbrays (I had to take notes), and we fixed a provisional date for my first lesson in the H155. I was very much looking forward to it.

6 – Lovers of Secrets and Secret Lovers

During the lunch, two texts arrived which sorted out my afternoon nicely. I gave Leah a hug and she headed for her room and a lie down. The nice doorman got me a taxi, and I headed for Hyde Park and an assignation.

The cabbie dropped me at one of the south side entrances, and I made my way to the Diana statue. That's Diana the Huntress, and not to be confused with the Princess Diana memorial fountain further west. Cora Hardisty, Dean of the Invisible College, was waiting for me on a bench in the sun. Cora has a few things in common with Eseld Mowbray, starting with magick and being a woman, of course, and that leads straight to the most obvious: short hair. Cora wears hers in a feathered, shaped cut that wouldn't look out of place on a mundane university vice-chancellor, but stands out in the world of magick. Her outfit of loose trousers and linen blouse looked as expensive as her haircut

When she heard me limping along, she stood up and we embraced. She took off her dark glasses and, judging from the bags under her eyes, she was as ready for a holiday as I am.

'How's the wound?' I asked.

'Internally, all organs are healed. The muscles will take a lot longer. You're probably wondering why we're meeting in a park like Cold War spies.'

'Or secret lovers.'

She looked alarmed. Cora is happily married, as far as I'm aware. I tried to smile in a non-threatening way.

'Quite, Conrad. I thought Mina would be with you.'

'Shopping. We're going on a cruise next week.'

'Oh.'

She'd have sounded less surprised if I'd said we were going on a tour of French plague pits (there's one in Rouen. Don't ask how I know).

'Hannah told you about Sofía, I presume.' She nodded cautiously. 'She's keen to study at the Invisible College. I wouldn't normally bother you, but…'

'…But it's not every day you acquire a sister. So she really is a Mage?'

'Yes. Vicky and Saffron say she'd matriculate easily.'

She nodded again, more slowly. Vicky was once Cora's pupil, and she trusts her judgement. 'How is Victoria?'

'Like you: getting there.'

'I'm glad. There must be good reasons for Sofía to study here and not in Spain.' She paused, giving me a chance to fill in the gap if I wished. The implication was that I had to say something. Cora will take Vicky's word on trust, but not mine.

'There are good reasons, and they have to do with her mother, not Sofía. Mercedes wants her daughter to study in the land of her fathers, and that's that. My half-sister is just a normal, Spanish teenager as far as I can tell.'

Cora smiled. 'She'd be the first Spanish Aspirant since the Peninsular War. I checked. Is there a rush?'

'Not really.'

She looked at the fountain and at a couple sitting opposite us. She pointed. 'Those two are definitely married, and not to each other.' I agreed, and she continued. 'I can see her on Wednesday 2nd September. That's a couple of weeks before term starts.' She turned back to face me. 'I like to start the academic year with a big barbecue on Bank Holiday Sunday. Would you and Mina like an invitation?'

No one says *Would you like an invitation?* to a party they're throwing themselves. They say *Would you like to come?* The Dean was waving a red flag, and I had no idea what it meant. As I've said, she is the consummate politician, and far too devious for a simple man like me. I decided to shock her into the truth.

'Why wouldn't we, Dean? It's not a Swingers party, is it?'

She shook her head, more in sorrow than in anger I think. 'You'd be nailing your colours to the mast. My mast. It's a campaign barbecue this year: Vote Cora for Warden.'

'Aah. I see.'

The Dean got her wound when the last Warden of Salomon's House was blown up. She's standing to replace him, not just as Master of the Invisible College but as the leading Mage in England.

I smiled. 'We don't have a vote, but you'd have mine if I did. Has anyone else declared their candidacy?'

'Didn't Saffron tell you? Heidi Marston has thrown her welding mask into the ring.'

'Saffron joined the Watch to get away from her family. She only talks about them if I tie her to a chair and threaten her with violence.'

'That sounds like Saffron. How's she getting on?'

'Good, so far. She's not short of courage, that's for certain.'

Cora checked her watch. 'I really do have an appointment shortly, Conrad.'

I weighed it up. 'Would you be offended if I said that we'd love an invitation, but that I'd have to check with the Boss first?'

'Not at all. I'd expect nothing less from Hannah's … most high profile officer.' Whatever it was she was going to say, she'd changed her mind. 'Thank you, Conrad.'

I stood up. 'It's good timing, actually. We're already booked in for dinner at Chris Kelly's the night before.'

'Dinner? At his house?'

'Where else?'

'Oh. Right.' She desperately wanted to add something to that response and couldn't find a polite way of putting it. 'Enjoy the cruise, Conrad, and love to Mina and Victoria. We're off to Florida, would you believe. Kids, eh?'

After we'd kissed again, I lit a cigarette and watched her walk away. I toyed with the idea of following her, just to see if she were heading for a romantic assignation. There was definitely a touch of guilt going on during our conversation, and regret, too, but for what? The reason I didn't follow her is that she's a powerful Sorcerer. If she used her Sight, she'd spot me easily. I finished my fag and headed for Knightsbridge, very much not my usual stomping ground.

There is a group of people, mostly mundane, who have helped me out in the past and whom I call the Merlyn's Tower Irregulars. One of the founder members is Alain Dupont, a young Frenchman on a postgrad business course. Alain has done all sorts for me, and part of his payment was my getting him an interview with Rachael at the wealth management company where she is something of a superstar. He got the job, and when I messaged him from the church, he suggested meeting at the Café du Bordeaux, adding *If you're paying. If not, then Starbucks.*

Alain was hovering near an empty outside table, but hadn't sat down. When we did, and when I looked at the wine list, I discovered why: a bottle of Bordeaux from his home region cost £80. I ordered two. 'Mina is meeting us here.'

'At last! I get to meet 'er. Salut, Conrad.'

'Salut. How's life with my sister, Alain? Has she driven you mad yet?'

'She is abroad, so I 'aven't seen much of 'er I was going to thank you for this job, Conrad, but I am not so sure now.'

He looked genuinely troubled. 'What's up?'

'It is a great opportunity, mon ami, don't get me wrong. But … I am out of my depth. Financially. They pay the London living wage to interns yet they expect you to buy a round of drinks in places like this. The other guy, 'e 'as a title and a 'ouse in Belgravia. Already, I get looks.' He gestured at the café. 'That is why we meet 'ere. Already five people see me, which is five more than I can afford on my own.'

'Can you keep it up?'

He gave me a shrug that would score 9.9 in the body language olympics. 'Who can say? Sorry, Conrad, but you got me this job, and I don't want to lie to you.'

'You got this job yourself, Alain. Rachael does me no favours.'

'Perhaps. What did you want?'

'Do you remember I asked you to locate a guy called Milton in Cornwall?'

'I do. I could find no one.'

That was a while ago. One of the reasons I value Alain's help is that he is not in the world of magick, and has only his own interests to protect.

'I got the name wrong. It's actually *Mowbray*, and …'

Alain spat out his wine and coughed. '*Non, non, non.* No. Absolutely not.'

'Eh?'

He looked at me. 'Seriously?'

'What?'

'You are not lying. You do not know?'

'No I bloody don't. Get on with it, man.'

'The Mowbray Estate is our biggest client, your sister's biggest client. If she keeps them for another year, she will get a partnership. Please do not tell me you are investigating them. Please.'

I held up my hands, then gave him a cigarette to calm him down. 'Don't worry. My department is doing a job for him, to help him, actually, and I'm on the security detail. That's all.'

'*Mon Dieu.* You worry me.' He looked around. 'I cannot tell you anything, Conrad. Please do not ask me.'

'I only have two questions, Alain.'

'Go on.'

'In broad terms, just how big is the estate?'

He nodded thoughtfully and picked up his phone. A few clicks later, he showed me the screen. 'This is public knowledge. It is forty times too small. At least.'

It was the Wessex rich list, which valued the estate (under its mundane name of Truro-Fal) at thirty-seven million pounds. Wow. That made Mowbray a mundane billionaire. No wonder they had a suite at the Waldorf and their own personal helicopter.

'And your second question?'

'Has Rachael slept with Cador Mowbray?'

He laughed. 'You are more like your sister than you know, mon ami. You 'ave your values and you stick to them, and so does she. You know 'ow she came to this job two years ago, no?'

'I don't. I was in Afghanistan at the time, and we weren't speaking.'

'She 'ad the Mowbray account at the other place. Cador tried it on with 'er. She complained to 'er boss, and 'e told 'er to take one for the team.'

It was my turn to choke on my wine. 'You what?'

'*Oui.*'

'Why did she tell you and not me? Or our parents?'

'Your mother knows. Rachael told me the day I started, in this bar, over several bottles of wine. She wanted me to understand.'

'What did she do?'

'She walked out and came to the new firm. One month later, the Mowbray account followed 'er. She told me this because she 'as never and will never sleep with a client.'

'She was clipping your wings.'

He closed one eye. 'She said exactly the same thing. I 'ad to look it up.' His shoulders slumped in a sort of anti-shrug. 'I 'ave been on only two dates since I started this job. It is not good.' He looked over my shoulder and his face changed. 'I think you should talk to your sister about becoming our client.'

'What?'

He pointed. 'Look at those bags. You must 'ave a lot of money.'

Mina barely paused to kiss me before dumping a rainbow collection of designer shopping bags on the ground and downing half a glass of wine.

'Salut,' said Alain.

'Salut,' said Mina. She tilted her head to look at me. 'I have had a telephone call from your sister. She and Carole are going to be in the Inkwell tomorrow evening. You are to report for interrogation at 18:30. Alone.'

'I shall pray for you,' said Alain.

'Budge up,' said Myfanwy. 'There's room for three on this roller.' Ben and I moved apart and she squeezed between us. 'What's that mad dog doing now?'

Scout was running round the cricket pitch, a huge distance for such a small dog. 'I have no idea. Perhaps he's casting a spell.'

Ben is very, very new to the world of magick, and like my mother, he tries to ignore it. Living with Myfanwy makes that a difficult task. 'Really?' he said. 'I thought that wasn't allowed.'

'He's winding you up,' said Myfanwy. 'Familiar Spirits can't make Charms – that's casting spells – and if Scout could do anything, he'd make a Charm that made everyone forget about tea so that he could eat all the sandwiches. He's mostly dog and only partly a Spirit.'

'Still bonkers, though.'

'He is that. Anyway, Conrad, how did it go last night? Carole didn't call or text or nothing. I bet Ben hasn't even asked you, and she's his sister.'

'I had more important things to think about,' said Ben, aggrieved. 'Like who to choose as our fourth bowler.'

She shook her head in sadness. 'Men. Come on, Conrad, tell all.'

'That's because Ben's sister, unlike mine, is a good person. Carole accepted my story about Isaac/Ivan and is ready to move on with her life. Once I told her that Isaac's wife had claimed the body for burial, it finally seemed to sink in that he had never been hers. She cheered up a bit when I told her that Isaac had paid for the wedding in full, in advance, in joint names.'

'That's a bit horrible,' said Myfanwy. 'I didn't think Carole was that mercenary.'

'She's not,' said Ben. 'It means that Irina couldn't reclaim any of the money. It means that Isaac cared enough about her not to leave her with any debts.'

'He didn't plan to die,' I added. 'Whether or not he planned to go ahead with a bigamous wedding, he wanted Carole not to suffer financially.'

Myfanwy was having none of it. 'Only a man would say that. He was married! He was stringing her along. No amount of money can make up for that.'

'That's what Rachael said, pretty much. Carole just shook her head and finished her drink. She only stopped half an hour then went home to her parents.'

'Leaving you with Rachael.'

'Yes.'

'Do you want to talk about it? Was it bad?'

I grinned. 'Not after I went to the gents.'

'No! Don't tell me you did a runner,' said Myfanwy.

'I wouldn't blame him if he did,' said Ben. 'But does Conrad ever run away?'

'Yes, he does,' I said. 'Nothing wrong with a tactical retreat. Nor is there anything wrong with calling in reinforcements.'

'Who? Mina? She didn't say when she messaged me this morning.'

'I thought it was best to keep Mina out of it. I had Vicky and Sofía outside on standby. I sent a text from the gents and they came in.'

'Sneaky,' said Myfanwy. 'And also rather sad that we're talking about a drink with your sister as if it's a military manoeuvre.'

'You've only met her once,' said Ben.

Myfanwy banged him with her hip, nearly dislodging him from the roller. 'What happened next?'

'We chatted for ten minutes, then Vicky said that her ribs hurt and I asked if I could escort her back to Elvenham. Rachael waved us off and we left her and Sofía to bond.'

'Wow. How did it go?'

'They discovered their mutual love of tennis and dislike of cricket. They're going to play tennis later then go to the spa to get to know each other properly.'

'Talking of cricket,' said Ben. 'What do you reckon after that rain? Bat or field if we win the toss.'

Myfanwy shook her head. 'The men should definitely bat first. I don't think it will make much difference to the Coven. My first game as captain and we're doomed either way.'

Ben loyally tried to reassure her. I didn't bother, because all three of us knew that she was right.

Later that morning, Clerkswell Ladies, aka The Coven, were soundly thrashed, and only Mina and Myfanwy stopped to watch the men edge our game by a dozen runs and move into the promotion places.

Rachael and Sofía enjoyed their day together. I think that Sofía was as anxious about meeting Rachael as we were, and when it went okay Sofía decided to go back to San Vicente until her interview with the Dean. I collapsed into bed on Saturday night surrounded by open suitcases and outfits on hangers suspended from every hook and hold.

The traffic in central Birmingham on Monday morning was awful, and I was glad I'd insisted on leaving early. Saffron was dropping us at the station for the train to Liverpool before beginning her solo stint as Officer of the Mercian Watch. I sent Mina into the station to get coffees and arranged the luggage outside the car before having a last word with Saff.

'I want you to call on Lloyd Flint next week. He'll have a package for me.'

She made a face. Saffron does not like Gnomes. 'Do I have to?'

'Yes. Clan Flint are an important part of our Watch, so you should keep in touch anyway.'

'Fine. I'll stock up on latex gloves and wear trousers. What's in the package?'

'Nothing dangerous. It's personal.'

Understanding dawned in her eyes. 'It's not a ring! Are you going to…'

'…Just collect the package. And don't even think of opening it to take a peek.'

'Yes sir. Have a good time.'

When the train pulled out, Mina fiddled with her bangles and said, 'Do you think anything bad will happen on this cruise?'

'How bad are we talking? Socially awkward bad or tragically bad?'

She took my hands and ran her fingers round them. 'I don't know. Attack by Norwegian Trolls. Kidnap by Frost Giants. The Wild Hunt. Something like that.'

'None of them would dare spoil Mother's bridge tournament. We should be safe. My biggest worry is trying to hide a border collie on a ship for twelve nights.'

Scout was curled up at our feet. When I thought about him, he lifted his head and yawned.

'I trust Saffron, even if you don't,' said Mina. 'If she says that the collar will hide him, I'm sure it will. It was nice of Sofía to help her finish it.'

Saffron's speciality is making Artefacts and enchanting items. Over the weekend, she'd brought a present from her cousin, the even more talented

Artificer known by her family as the Great Geek of Oxford. Saff and Sofía had spent Sunday adapting it to Scout's individual Imprint.

You can't hide a dog for very long, but you can make every one without magick ignore him and think that he's an assistance dog who belongs to some other passenger round the corner. All we had to do was smuggle him on to the ship in the first place.

She changed the subject. 'Have you got your pilot's licence through? I'd hate to miss this trip to Pellacombe because you hadn't sorted your paperwork.'

'It came on Saturday, while you were being bowled for a duck. The postie left it with Rachael.'

'Good.' She digested the comment about her batting for a second. 'This Leah Kershaw. I think we should meet her.'

'Is that the royal "we"? I'm seeing her the day after we get back.'

She waved her hand as if such details were beneath her. 'For your last lesson, you should land in that field you own, behind the garden, and she can come in for afternoon tea.'

She was being serious. I have no idea why, but she was. 'Fine. I'll ask Leah about it.' I checked my watch. 'Time to turn our phones off.' I dug mine out and powered it down.

'Why should I do that?'

'Because in ten minutes, Alain will tell Rachael about my involvement with the Mowbrays and she will go through the ceiling like a moon rocket. If she can't get through to me, she'll call you.'

'What? Why didn't you tell her yourself?' Mina scrambled for her phone.

'Alain needs the money. I bribed him to do it. It'll save us a lot of hassle.'

She watched her screen go dark and breathed out. 'Your poor mother. She'll get it instead.'

I settled back and nudged Scout out of the way so that I could stretch out my legs. 'The holiday starts now.'

Mina's fingers hovered over her phone, itching to turn it back on. She looked up. 'In that case, I'd better prepare, hadn't I?'

She took out a copy of *Bid Better, Play Better* and didn't speak to me until we got to Warrington. That's one of the many things I love about Mina: you always know exactly where you are with her, and right now, I was in the doghouse. I leaned down to tickle Scout's ears. At least I had good company.

Part Two — Hospitality

7 – Intelligence Quota

Food can be made with love, with resentment or for a living. It can also be made out of duty, and that was what the plate of sandwiches under clingfilm represented. Mina pressed the film into place and rotated the plate before depositing it on the kitchen table next to some fruit and a box of flapjacks. She stood back and looked at me.

'You've done this deliberately, haven't you?' she said. 'Just to stop me meeting her.'

'You were the one who wanted to invite a pregnant woman with morning sickness to a tea party.'

'I thought she'd be okay in the afternoon.' She pointed a finger. 'You had lunch with her last month.'

'You didn't see what she ate: chicken soup and vanilla ice cream. I had to drink my coffee at the other end of the room because she couldn't stand the smell. The poor woman's in a state.'

'Hmmph.'

It was bizarre that a man should be defending the rights of pregnant women to one of the sisterhood, but there you go.

'I shall see you later. Say Hi to Rick.' She picked up her cricket bag and headed for the door.

It's been nearly three weeks since Mina and I smuggled Scout on to the Queen Anne for our Baltic bridge cruise. We had a lovely time, thanks, and Mina still polishes her trophy for Best Newcomer every morning.

We had returned to the news that Leah simply couldn't fly at the moment, and my training was carried out by the Mowbrays' relief pilot, a man of few words, no gossip and absolutely no entanglement in the world of magick. He's not even on their payroll and works for an agency. Instead of preparing a confection of dainties to soften up Leah Kershaw, Mina had prepared a snack for Rick James, the Senior Watch Captain, who was making a (metaphorical) flying visit.

Mina has never met anyone from my days in the RAF, still less a woman. Had Leah been feeling better, she'd have been grilled like the anchovies about my time in the service. I'll count that as a bullet dodged.

Rick was on time, despite the Friday traffic, and was escorted to the back door by Scout. He has his uses, that dog. Rick is the only non-white Watch Captain, and rose to be Senior by having a good nose for trouble and knowing when to nip things in the bud. He and I are technically equal in rank – I'm the Watch Captain at Large, but I work directly for the Boss, something that Rick had had to come to terms with. That he did, has made life a lot easier.

'Some animal, that,' said Rick. 'How's the training going?'

'Hard to tell. I might need to call on a specialist Mage before he gets too much older.'

Rick looked round the empty kitchen. 'Where is everyone?'

The simple, honest answer would be *avoiding you.* I opted for diplomacy instead. 'The Clerkswell Coven have got their first away game tomorrow, so it's extra nets for them. Vicky still needs to rest in the afternoons. They all said Hi.'

'Saffron doesn't play cricket.' Ah. Yes. That was my decision.

The others were avoiding him in solidarity with Vicky; Saffron was on a mission because I wanted to keep her away from him. 'Gone to see a Gnome about a gift,' I said.

He nodded acceptance and turned his attention to the table. 'Are these mine? I'm starving. Any chance of a beer?'

He ripped off the plastic film while I got a bottle of Inkwell Gold from the fridge. Rick's appreciation of Inkwell beers is one of the many things that make him hard to dislike, unless you've been dumped, cuckolded or two-timed by him. Thankfully, none of those has happened to me. Unlike Vicky.

He lifted a sandwich and eyed it with approval. 'What do you know about the Daughters?' he asked before biting into it.

I told him what I knew while he munched away, and then I went on to my scant gleanings about the Mowbrays. My lunch with Leah had been good for gossip, less useful on magick. Rick drained his beer and pushed his plate away.

'Tea?' I offered.

'Please.'

Rick's Watch covers most of the staff kingdom of Wessex. No one knows it better. He should be doing this job, not me. There's a good reason for that, something he didn't shy away from. 'You know Cordy's gonna be in the party, yeah?'

I nodded.

'Well, first thing you need to know is never call her that. It's *Cordelia* or you'll be in trouble.'

'Are you having the kids next week?'

He grinned. He and his ex-wife, Cordelia, have two children. Cordelia is also known as 11th Daughter of Ash.

'Yeah. I get them for the weekend, too. Weather looks good for next week, so we're going camping. If you can scupper the talks, or better still make them drag on for a few days, I'll get them for the bank holiday, too.'

We both knew he was joking. 'I'm afraid that the Boss is expecting me on Friday.' I poured the tea. 'What really happened between the two of you? It won't go any further. I promise.'

He looked at his mug of tea. 'On a good day, I tell myself it was because she got an invitation to join Ash Coven and had to dump me. On a bad day, it was because I got caught playing away once too often.'

I am not the guardian of Rick's morals and I let the silence speak for me. Rick nodded and reached into his bag. He passed me a brace of folders, one each on the Daughters and the Mowbrays. 'This is all my notes that aren't on the Merlyn's Tower servers. The Daughters are a funny bunch. I can't get my head round them. I'll tell you this for nothing: they rarely tell you what they're really after. A bit like Melton.'

'I'm not going to refer to him as *Melton*. I might slip up and use it to his face. I'll stick to *Lord Mowbray*. Does he even have a first name?'

'Arthur. He hates it as much as Cordy hates being called Cordy. Even his girlfriend calls him Mowbray.'

'According to Leah, she's his fiancée now.'

'Is that right? Leah would know.'

'She flew the Mowbrays all round Britain, Ireland and the Low Countries, but Lord Mowbray never talked business once. The files say he's a Geomancer, so…?'

Rick nodded. 'There's a few notes in there, but there's a problem with old Arthur: he's both very good and very deep. In the last thirty years, he's done more to restore the old Ways of Lux than anyone since the Romans. Ever heard of Thomas Brassey?' I shook my head.

'If you were a Victorian railway pioneer with a vault full of investors' cash and parliamentary approval for a new railway, you'd write to Thomas Brassey and he'd build it for you. When he died in 1870something, one mile in twenty of all the railways *in the world* had been built by him, and no one ever had a bad word to say about his work.'

'Impressive. I had no idea. You're saying that Mowbray is the modern day magickal Thomas Brassey?'

'Professionally, yes, but Brassey never stood for parliament, still less did he try to become king of anything, and that's why I've got no idea what Mowbray is up to with this business. Neither has the Boss, nor Cora. He used to be friends with Roly Quinn, not that Roly would have given any secrets away.'

Roly is the late Warden, the job Cora would like to have. 'Thanks, Rick. Did Hannah send any off the record briefings?'

'No. Not even a sarcastic one telling you not to crash the Mowbrays' helicopter. She's genuinely stumped.' He gave a micro-shrug to show that he was equally in the dark and moved on. He took a slim, leather bound volume out of his case. 'Special delivery from Francesca. She says it's her personal copy.' He looked at the title. 'What's this? *Ueber die Zauberei?*'

I accepted the book and said, 'It's a basic primer on magick written in German. Old textbook from before the First World War.'

He didn't ask any more questions about the book and finished his tea. He tapped the file labelled *Homewood*, and said, 'There's one story I haven't written down. Nor should you.'

Mages have few superstitions, for obvious reasons: if you know what goes bump in the night (and why), you're not inclined to avoid walking under ladders. Where Mages do have what looks like superstitions, they should be followed religiously. I know you're about to read what he told me, but I didn't write it down; this section, I dictated.

'You know that Cordelia is Page to Raven, 1st of Ash, yeah?'

'I saw that, yes.'

'You're in for a shock when you meet Raven.' He grinned. 'She has something in common with Chris Kelly.' He paused, the smile still on his face.

'What? They're both bald as a coot?'

He shook his head. 'I won't spoil the surprise. Raven is thirty-five years old, but looks a lot younger, as you'd expect given her life so far.' He hesitated and shifted his shoulders, reluctant to get on with it.

'One of the Daughters tends a sacred flame through the night, every night. Have done since … whenever. One night just as she was saying the prayer before dawn, a giant raven flew down from nowhere and landed with a bundle hanging from its beak, just like the stork in the baby cartoons.'

'There was a baby?'

'Too right. The bird lets out an ear-splitting cry. Literally. The poor Witch went deaf for a week. Every Daughter wakes up and comes running. At least six of them saw the bird for themselves, and saw it rise up and take off. The draught from its wings knocked them over. One of them swore that she saw two faces looking down on her from the sky.'

He drummed his fingers on the table, moving the rhythm from his right hand to his left and back again. 'One of the faces was male. It had one eye. The other was the Morrigan. All the Daughters know her.'

'You're saying that Raven, 1st of Ash, is the daughter of two gods, Odin and the Morrigan?'

'I ain't saying nothing, Conrad. I'm just telling you the story.'

I nodded and cleared the things off the table while Rick rummaged in his bag again. He pulled out a box made of shiny, pale, new oak, a cube about six inches on each side. The lid was formed on the diagonal rather than on the flat. It was held shut with a silver clasp. He put it on the table, along with a letter addressed to Mina using her official title – The Peculier Auditor.

'Mina will need this,' he said, 'to witness the agreement at Pellacombe, if there is one. It's magick, but anyone can bond with it, so she has to be the one to open the box first or it won't work for her.'

'Right.'

'Thanks for the food and good luck, Conrad.'

'Will I need it?'

He grinned again. 'In Cornwall? I hope not. In the cricket? Most definitely. According to the Internet, you're playing the league leaders tomorrow.'

'We are. Safe journey, Rick.'

'And you. Love to the girls.'

The gravel in front of Elvenham is both decorative and a good alarm. As soon as Rick's car had crunched away, Vicky appeared, wrapped in a pristine white dressing gown bearing the logo of a country house hotel in Lancashire. It was a sort-of present – she nicked it, and I had to pay for it.

'Is that tea still hot?' she said.

I poured and put it in front of her. She opened the Tupperware box of Myfanwy's flapjacks and started munching. 'Low blood sugar. Ooh! What's in the box?'

'Seal of the Cloister Court or something. Mina needs to bond with it, so don't touch.'

She peered closely. 'That's new, that is, and it's been sealed with a Jackson Spiral.' She remembered who she was talking to and explained. 'It doesn't hide the fact that there's magick inside, it just completely camouflages it.'

'Are you going to give the girls moral support at the game tomorrow?'

'Aye. They've even made me the scorer, would you believe. I hate the game, but with you and Ben otherwise engaged, they need all the help they can get.' She turned the mug around. 'I feel so old, Conrad. That's the real reason I couldn't face Rick.'

I made myself comfortable opposite her and said nothing. Vicky is twenty-four years old. Only two years older than Saffron. Younger than both Mina and Myfanwy. Her long face got even longer.

'It was only January that you caught me and Desi out clubbing and wearing Illusions. I haven't been on a date of any kind since I met you, d'you know that?' She raised her hand to stop me objecting. 'A booty call from Li Cheng does not count as a date.' She lowered her hand and pushed her mug aside. 'Any chance of a fresh pot?'

I put the kettle on and sat back down.

'It's not just the stab wound, though that's bad enough. I can't risk any vigorous exercise for at least a week, and that's really frustrating. Mind you, I never thought I'd miss doing exercise, but it's true. I just feel like I've missed out on something. Instead of having a weekend of romance and escape with Rick, I'm keeping score at a women's cricket match, and that's wrong.'

She subsided, and I took the chance to fill the pot, placing it in the middle of the table. Vicky picked up the stained, yellow, hand-knitted tea cosy with appliqué flowers. 'Mary's cosy,' she said, pointing to the frayed yellow wool. 'You bought it for your Mam, didn't you, and she left it behind?'

'I did. I was eight, and I spent some birthday money at the WI Sale of Work. It was a present to her.'

'Had you done something wrong?'

71

'I don't think so. With hindsight, I reckon that woman was a Witch who enchanted it and made me buy it.'

'You could be right. There's a lot of that about. What was it your Mam said when she left it behind?'

'She said, "I've treasured its misshapen ugliness for decades, but it really won't do in San Vicente. I'll leave it as a reminder of me." She chooses her words carefully, does Mother.'

'Aye, she does. That's about how I feel – a misshapen ugly old tea cosy who's kept around because they're useful.' She looked up, with a smile to show that she wasn't *too* serious. 'It's not just me. Desi hasn't been on a night out, either, and she used to be the real party animal. The shock of seeing you in Club Justine, and of you knowing what she was up to drove her back to the church big time. Poor lass.'

'If that's what she wants…'

Vicky shook her head. 'I'm afraid she'll be driven out of that church and end up doing something she'll regret. Something's come up.'

'Oh?'

'You remember Dr Nicola, me flatmate?'

'I do. She must miss you.'

Vicky grimaced. 'And half. It's me own fault for coming here to recuperate. She's moving out tomorrow. No warning, nothing. She's paid up till the end of the month, but after that I won't be able to afford the rent on me own, and besides, it's time I bought somewhere. I've given notice to the landlord.'

I sat back, stunned. 'You're not moving out of London, are you?'

'Why naah, man. You must be joking. I'm going back down with youse two next Friday, after your Cornish adventure. Desi and me are going house-hunting. She's already started messaging me property details.' She poured herself some tea and stood up. 'I'm gonna get dressed, then you and I are taking Scout for his walk. I need the exercise.'

Scout was waiting by the door before she'd tightened her dressing gown.

We stuck our heads into Mrs Clarke's Folly and left quickly when we saw Jules Bloxham laying into Erin like a sergeant major telling an officer cadet that she was a disgrace to the uniform (been there). Vicky had a different simile.

'Takes me back to school, and not in a good way. We had one like that.'

'A PE teacher?'

She shivered in the sunshine. 'No. Geography. Why do you think I'm allergic to maps?'

We headed east, away from the railway line to avoid any steep hills, passing Clerkswell Manor as we did. You can't see Elvenham from the road; my ancestor made sure of that. Clerkswell Manor (Grade II listed, Jacobean with later additions, if you're interested) was built to be on show. The family that owned it ran the village for generation after generation until there were no more generations left and they died out.

We could see Stephen Bloxham and his children sorting something in the garage and hurried past. We took a footpath south and Vicky visibly relaxed as she realised that her lung wasn't going to give her any pain, even with brisk walking. I risked a question.

'Have you heard the stories about Raven, 1st Daughter of Ash at Homewood?'

Her eyebrows shot up. They're well-shaped eyebrows because she's been bored. Mina informs me that Vicky's legs are also well waxed. I wouldn't know. 'Don't tell me that Raven's going to the conference,' said Vicky.

'I just found out from Rick.'

'That'll be fun for you.'

'I'll look forward to it. If you met her, could you tell if she really was a child of the gods? You knew who Sofía was straight away.'

She gave me that look, the one that says *You don't know nowt, man.* I've seen it a lot since we first met. 'Do you know how many natural Imprimatists there are like me?' I shook my head. 'About six in the UK and Ireland. There wasn't one at all in Salomon's House when I was an Aspirant. I had to go to Napier College in Edinburgh for a week every term for one-to-one tuition. That's how I met Lady Kirsten. They're all bonkers up there.'

'So I hear.'

'Aye. When I was staying with Rick, he introduced me to a few of the Daughters. Not Raven, obviously.' She hesitated. She stayed with Rick because they were lovers for a while, and I think that during her stay, Vicky was searching online for wedding dress ideas. She was very disappointed.

She picked up her own thread and carried on. 'One of the Daughters was a *Prima*, as we call ourselves, so we compared notes. She was really old, and she'd been there that night, when the raven delivered its little bundle. The Eldest Daughter asked her to look at the child, as you'd expect. Now, I've seen adults do this deliberately to hide things. Roly Quinn did it, and I bet that Lord Mowbray does, too, but I've never seen it in a child.'

I could see where this was heading. 'Do what?'

'Raven's Imprint is hollow. Like a doughnut. All the core stuff is not there. It is, of course, but this Witch couldn't see it. It was hollow then and it still is. Apparently Raven herself can't see it. They tried to force her to look when she was a teenager. She broke the Witch's nose who tried to make her do it.'

'I'll bear that in mind.'

She stopped to lean on a gate and we admired a golden crop, right on the cusp of harvesting. 'Is this one of Ben's?'

'I think so.' Ben is not a farmer; he's a cereal agronomist. 'I also think that Myfanwy and he have been here together.'

'Ooh! Frolicking in the wheat, eh?'

'It's barley, and she was trying to help him. I think. I hope she doesn't tell Hannah that during the inspection visit.'

'Hell, aye. That would be suicidal.'

'It would, but you know what she's like: no filter. Let's go.'

'Oh yeah, you're doing tea tonight. What are we having?'

'Salad.'

'Noooo. Not again.'

'We've all got a match tomorrow. Even you.'

'First and last time, Uncle Conrad. First and last time.'

8 – By Sea

Saffron was waiting for us at Lamorne Point, overlooking the River Fal in deepest south Cornwall. I wound down our window and she shouted, 'Where've you been?' She was leaning against her Land Rover in a short blue floral dress and soft trainers. I mention this because it's what Mina noticed first.

'She's not going to wear that to meet the Mowbrays, is she?'

'She's the daughter of Lady Hawkins. She can wear what she wants. She'll have to change before we get the chopper up.'

Mina gave me a sly grin. 'You're not going to make her wear uniform, are you?'

'Of course.' I saw the glee in her eye. 'Combat uniform, not dress.'

'Does she know?'

I shrugged and got out of the Volvo. Scout was bouncing around in the back, desperate to escape. 'Stay! Not long, but stay,' I told him.

I walked towards Saffron and pointed to the dog. 'He's why we're later than I planned. Had to keep stopping for walkies.'

Mina had joined me. 'Rubbish. You just wanted a smoke. How are you, Saffron?'

'Good, thanks. I hear that I missed a bit of a party.'

Mina and I grinned at each other. We'd both left the field of play with a victory on Saturday, and there had been a bit of a shindig afterwards. Clerkswell Men were now only one win from promotion and the Coven have met the league requirements for entry and will now be playing competitively next season. Juliet Bloxham had handed in the papers herself this morning.

'Oh yes,' said Mina. 'There was even dancing at one point. See?'

The girls huddled over Mina's iPad and I went to get Scout. We were actually twenty minutes early, so I went for a walk around the Point.

I'd been here last Thursday. Briefly. The Mowbrays' relief pilot had flown down with me to the Fal estuary to show me the Lamorne landing zone (or *LZ* in aviation jargon, which I'll try to keep to a minimum). He knows that Pellacombe exists, across the river, but he just doesn't think about it. Such is the power of a good Occulter, and Ethan Mowbray is supposed to be almost as good as Saffron's mother. We're meeting him later. When I'd touched down for practice, I'd taken in the overall layout of the area, but it's a different feeling when you walk around and look properly.

Lamorne Point sticks out into the River Fal, about ten miles upstream from Falmouth, and is only accessible from a private road with big electric gates. That still makes it more accessible than Pellacombe itself. Only estate employees are allowed to drive up to the house; all others have to arrive by boat (or helicopter, but more on that later).

Safely in the middle of the Lamorne mini-peninsula is a graded LZ (with lights. Posh), and the H155 was sitting waiting for me. I ignored it for now, and walked towards the bluff over the river, past the ancient cottage on the edge which is home to the Ferrymistress and her family.

The top of the Point is flat which makes it a good place for the helipad and the car park. From here, the drop to the river is quite steep. You can take the well-surfaced, gently sloping path that curves round or you can take the short, steep steps. Scout is a great believer in short-cuts and was half way down before I could call him to heel. He bounded back up, as fast as his little legs could negotiate the big steps.

At the bottom of the steps, the path met the jetty. A golf buggy and trailer were waiting to collect luggage and passengers, attended by a teenage boy and his little sister. They'd seen Scout appear, then me. The boy waved a welcome and pointed across the river. He lifted his hand to show five fingers – five minutes. I gave him a thumbs-up and lit a cigarette. I rubbed Scout's flank and said, 'Go on, boy. Go say hello.'

He picked his way down, tail wagging, ready to seduce the children. I looked across the water to get my first proper glimpse of Pellacombe; the visible parts, anyway.

The river is tidal here, more sea than river, really, and about two hundred metres wide. On the opposite bank there was a substantial farmhouse made from blocks of Cornish granite. It was well up the bank, away from flooding, and with its own boathouse on the water. It was surrounded on three sides by mixed woodland and looked like the sort of place the local MP would live. This part of the river is pretty inaccessible, and any stray visitors would see the house, admire it, and move on.

When I'd got it fixed in my head, I went back to the cars. The girls had moved on from videos of drunken dancing to unloading the cases (slowly). They were currently looking at the helicopter.

'It's rather gaudy, isn't it?' said Saffron.

The H155 didn't only have Mowbray blue upholstery: the outside was painted in the same colour. Here in the sun, I realised that it was the exact blue of the Cornish sky in summer. It also had the Mowbray boar's head in grinning gold on the doors.

Mina gave Saffron a puzzled look. 'Of course it's gaudy. It is the private helicopter of a billionaire staff lord. It's very essence is gaud, if that's a thing. If Conrad ever buys a helicopter, it will be painted sapphire blue. Possibly with red trimmings.'

Saff thought that this was hilarious. 'Yes, Rani.'

Rani. Princess. It's their nickname for Mina, and I've even heard it shouted across the cricket field – *Great catch, Rani*. She quite likes it, but she wasn't laughing about the colour of the chopper.

The whine of a buggy climbing the hill broke the moment and we turned to look. 'That dog is incorrigible,' said Mina.

Scout was in one of the front seats, having relegated the girl to the back. The boy, brown from living on the water and with sun-bleached hair was very polite, and asked if anyone wanted a lift. The girls shook their heads and picked up their hand luggage before setting off to walk down the slope.

'Never mind, lad,' I said. 'I'll give you a hand.' He could have managed, I'm sure, but if Mina's dress blew off the trailer into the river, someone would be in deep trouble. 'It's Michael, isn't it? Leah Kershaw told me about your family and what you do.'

He nodded in acknowledgement of his name, then went round the other side of the trailer. Leah had said that he used to follow her around like a puppy. She wasn't sure whether it was an adolescent crush or whether he really wanted to go in the helicopter. I told her it was both: teenage boys are quite capable of thinking about two things at the same time (so long as one of them involves attractive women).

We secured the cases and I gave Scout his marching orders. 'You are not riding down again.' Reluctantly, he disembarked and followed me down the steps.

Our ride across the river was on its way. A substantial, shallow-bottomed ferry boat was half way across. Overall, it was the length of three cars and yes, it was painted Mowbray blue. It was also much bigger than the boathouse on the other side, so where had it come from? The front half of the ferry was flat deck for cargo and had a ramp at the bow which could be lowered for a vehicle or pallet truck to get on board. The rear half was a passenger lounge with big glass windows.

In the centre was a wheelhouse, from where the Ferrymistress steered the boat carefully up to the jetty, cutting the engine at exactly the right moment to glide into the rubber fenders. An older girl, her firstborn, threw a rope to her brother on the jetty and he fastened it in seconds.

The girl on board must have been hot. Not a centimetre of skin was exposed to the sun, not even her hands. Leah Kershaw had told me that the girl had started her magickal education last year, and that the next Ferrymistress would be a Ferrymaster, her brother, Michael.

There was only one passenger in the lounge. Michael pulled down a plank and got ready to hand her off the boat. We were still on the dock, well away from the jetty and out of earshot.

'My god, will you look at the state of her,' said Saffron, gesturing at the newcomer.

'A most unusual choice of outfit,' said Mina.

Saffron shook her head. 'Outfit? You mean costume. If that counts as an outfit, she's a long way from home.'

Saffron was right, but only by accident. 'Shh,' I said, walking up to meet the passenger.

The woman was wearing a traditional Austrian dirndl: a royal blue dress and bodice teamed with a Mowbray blue apron. As she walked down the jetty, she moved as naturally in her outfit as Mina does in a kurta; this was her being her and wearing what she wanted to wear. She definitely hadn't got dressed this morning with a view to impressing the likes of Saffron Hawkins.

She was young, only twenty-four, and wore her long straw-blonde hair in a single plait with a blue ribbon at the end that matched her dress. Another ribbon round her neck held a heavy enamel badge with the Mowbray arms. This was Lena, fiancée to Ethan Mowbray and a Healer.

She had a strong face, big boned and with a jutting jaw so pronounced that it made smiling difficult. Very few would call her a beauty. Probably not even her mother. When she did smile, it went up her cheeks and creased her eyes, and then I knew why Ethan had asked her out.

She curtsied, just an inch, and said, 'Welcome. I am Lena, Steward of Pellacombe. I hope you are having good journeys.'

Mina frowned as she made namaste: Lena's voice was deep and her accent so strong that it almost smelt of edelweiss. I don't think Mina actually understood a word she said.

I bowed and went to shake hands. I'd been preparing for this bit, and said to her in German, 'Thank you, Fraulein Lena. It is an honour to be here and to accept Lord Mowbray's hospitality.'

Lena gave me that smile again. 'Do you really speak German?' she asked in her mother tongue. I responded in kind:

'Slowly. I'm afraid that neither of my companions do.'

'And neither does anyone in Pellacombe. Not a single person.'

Saffron was now frowning, and Mina was giving me the *Wait till I get you alone* look. I switched back to English and completed the introductions.

Lena took three metal badges out of the concealed pocket in her dirndl. Close up, I could make out fine white embroidery on her apron – plants and trees, all no doubt significant to a Tyrolean Mage; there was no sign of the Mowbray boar. Lena may be Steward of Pellacombe, but when she marries, she and Ethan will be living in Kellysporth on the north Cornish coast, near Tintagel. It's currently a house in mourning for Ethan's father, the Earl of Tintagel.

She held the badges in her open hand, one red, one white and one blue. 'You know of these?'

'We do.'

Leah Kershaw hadn't flown to Cheltenham, but she'd briefed me extensively by phone on the special arrangements for flying over and landing at Pellacombe. Not the helipad on Lamorne Point, but the one at the house itself, across the water. Before I could even see the place, I had to bond with it.

These badges were identical in all but colour, but they had very different implications for the three of us. Mina, having no magick, would have to wear hers all the time. She picked the blue one and started fastening it to her kurti.

Saffron chose white and gave it a good rub. For her, it was a simple exercise in using her Sight. 'Wow!' she exclaimed, staring over the water. Mina got her badge fixed and joined in Saffron's admiring gaze.

Saff dropped the depleted Artefact back into Lena's hand without looking, and Lena offered me the remaining, red, badge. 'Shall we go?' she said. 'The luggage is loaded.'

I took out my handkerchief and Lena dropped the badge into it. 'I'll wait until we're moving,' I explained.

Michael cast us off and the Ferrymistress backed away from the jetty. I left the passenger lounge and walked across the open deck to the bow. She swung the boat around and I closed my eyes. I took the badge in my left hand and opened my Sight.

Later this afternoon, I had to fly that H155 over the river and land it on the lawns of Pellacombe. Leah uses her Mowbray ring to do it, but that's not an option for me. Her ring is a symbol of her status, pledged to the Mowbrays. I have drunk from Nimue's hand and that relationship is monogamous, I'm afraid. And before you point out that I'm the Swordbearer to Clan Flint and that I wear Odin's ring, those relationships are different. The appointment to Clan Flint is just that – an appointment, not a pledge, and my association with the Allfather is just that – an association.

I was keeping my eyes closed because that's how I perceive magick best: by feeling it. The badge's flat surface became alive with swirling lines of Lux. They flowed out of the one inch disk and hovered in the air; I couldn't see them, of course, so I held out my hand, like holding it over an electric hob to feel the heat.

The badge was in my left hand, and it was drawing Lux from me to project the pattern. My head was already starting to throb. I lowered my fingers, resisting the reflex to pull away. The heat burned but didn't destroy. Not yet. I ran my fingers over the lines, seeking order in the chaotic swirl of energy. It was like putting your hand into a bag full of angry snakes and trying to count them as they slipped under and over each other.

But what if there were only one snake? There. I found an end and pinched it. I passed it to my left hand and held on, following the length of the line with my right. It crossed itself, retraced itself and tried to tie my fingers in knots, burning and searing them as it moved. I was gritting my teeth and suppressing a scream when I finally found the other end, and when I did, not only did the pattern make sense, it wrapped itself round my arm and dissolved into my skin. A tiny part of me was now in tune with the essence of Pellacombe.

If that sounds scary, it isn't. It's no different to knowing how to lift that awkward kitchen drawer that sticks – instinctive. All the badge had done is lay that instinct bare in symbolic magick. I opened my eyes and drank in the true glory of Pellacombe.

The farmhouse was still there, facing the river, but now it was only one storey high and formed a bank, with the Mowbray mansion above and behind it. The real Pellacombe was also built from grey granite and grey slate, but that seemed a technical detail of construction compared to the shape, the angles and the acres of glass that made it a thoroughly modern architect's dream house. The thinner windows had pointed tops that hinted at gothic, and a couple of the larger balconies resembled the verandas of a cruise ship. Even the many chimneys had been gathered together like those of a steamship. Surely they couldn't need them all? No new house is *that* reliant on fossil fuels.

And it was definitely new. Lord Mowbray had inherited only the original farmhouse and lands, his mother being the younger sibling and Kellysporth being the main family seat. When he became successful, Mowbray had sliced the top off the farmhouse and built himself a Mage's palace fit for the twenty-first century, complete with solar panels covering the steeply pitched roof slates.

Most of the forest had disappeared with the illusion, replaced by glimpses of gardens on the upper terraces. The boathouse had doubled or trebled in size and gained a concrete dock with twin piers. A selection of powered and sailing craft were moored low in the water, too low to use at this tide, hence the flat bottom of the ferry.

A warm presence approached me. Two. Scout tried unsuccessfully to jump on to the bow platform, and Mina stooped to lift him up. 'Don't fall in, OK?' she admonished.

'It's beautiful, isn't it?' I said.

'It's perfect,' she replied. 'Like your manners. Lena keeps looking out at you from the lounge. You've got another admirer.'

She made it a statement, not an accusation. The reason she doesn't get jealous – I think – is that she makes sure that any women I'm close to (Vicky, Hannah, Myfanwy etc.) are also close to her.

'What's Saff doing?' I asked.

'Ignoring Lena and sending messages on her phone. You're right – Saffron needs to learn a little humility before she comes a cropper.'

I turned to face the lounge and gave Lena a big smile and a thumbs-up. She smiled back and crossed to the wheelhouse. The Ferrymistress had been taking the longest, slowest route across the river to give me every chance to crack the pattern. She opened the throttle and headed for the empty south pier. Another reception committee emerged from the boathouse and came to wait. It looked like Mina would have her wish to meet Leah granted after all.

9 – By Land

Leah Kershaw perched on a bollard and a woman who could only be her mother put a protective arm around her shoulders.

'You made it!' said Leah. 'Thank goodness for that.'

I made the introductions (it was her mother), and Mina tried to hide her disappointment when Leah said that she wasn't going to be around much, and not at all once I'd managed to land the chopper at Pellacombe.

'Do you want me with you for preflight?' asked Leah.

'Thanks, but if I can't do it on my own, I'm in trouble,' I replied.

She nodded. 'Then I'll be waiting at the LZ for you coming in. Good luck, sir. Not that you'll need it.'

'You taught him well, did you?' said Saffron, giving me that *I'm a better Mage than you* look.

Leah blinked at her. 'Conrad is the best pilot I've ever flown with. Bar none. You'll see.'

Saffron had the grace to look embarrassed and said nothing.

A minibus was being loaded with our luggage, and Lena offered us a lift. I looked at the girls. 'I'd rather walk,' I said. 'If you don't mind. I've been sitting down too long already today.'

'A walk, please,' said Mina. 'Only slowly. Scout has very short legs.'

Lena took a moment to process that, and nodded dubiously. 'I shall escort you and practise the talk I must give tomorrow.'

The afternoon sun was on our right as we ambled up the path. Its rays picked out the tightly bonded granite blocks in the mansion and brought the gardens to life. The more Saffron saw of the house, the grounds and the Wards (Lena was giving a magickal talk, too, but that went over my head), the more that Saffron was impressed by how much Lord Mowbray had achieved and by how many staff wore his ring. We saw several men tending the gardens, and Lena said that they'd been drafted in from the farms and woods to make sure that everything was just so for the Daughters' arrival tomorrow.

'And the pub will close,' said Lena. We looked at each other. 'The Mowbray Arms,' she explained. 'In the village. All the staff will be here. Tourists will pass by and not notice. It often happens.'

'That's so smart!' said Saffron. There was definitely jealousy now, and Lady Hawkins will be on the receiving end of some suggestions about running Cherwell Roost fairly soon, I'm sure.

We got to the level of the mansion and could see that its most impressive side faced a manicured lawn. At the end of the lawn was an elegant summerhouse with views over the river.

Lena pointed to the grass. 'Do not land the helicopter on this. I will never forgive you if you do. We shall see your ...' she waved her hand. 'Your *Hubschrauberlandeplatz*. Ach. What is the word?'

I knew that one. 'Helipad.'

'Helipad. Good. This way. I am glad that no one has heels.'

Below the knee-length dirndl, Lena wore a sturdy pair of fell shoes that matched her sturdy calf muscles. She led us across the lawn, up yet another path and on to the plateau above the house. A separate set of steps and an accessible path led down from the plateau to a formal entrance on the eastern side of the house. The minibus was there at the moment, for a few seconds, until a young surfer drove it away.

The grass on the top plateau hadn't been cared for nearly as much as the south lawn, and it was browning from lack of water, which made the bands of artificial turf stand out even more. They formed a huge circle and bullseye that would make landing a lot easier. The centre even had a radio transmitter buried underneath it.

'All is good?' said Lena. I nodded. 'Then come.' We descended the steps to the main entrance and our third welcome.

Despite the publicity, the sun does not *always* shine in Cornwall. A lot of the time it rains, and visitors to Pellacombe can shelter under a canopy that straddles the road, as can the hosts while they wait. The more I saw of Pellacombe, the less I could work out whether it reminded me more of Downton Abbey or of a really top class, five star country house hotel.

Cador and Eseld Mowbray flanked their cousin Ethan in the doorway. All were dressed casually, and all had at least one item of Mowbray blue clothing. For the men it was a polo shirt with boar's head crest and jeans; for Eseld it was a long-sleeved blue athletic top (also with crest) over black jodhpurs and long socks. Her face was flushed from exercise – Leah had told me that Eseld loves to ride and has several horses. The spikes in her hair had collapsed from sweat and wearing a helmet.

As we descended the steps, Saffron whispered, 'It's like a bloody cult round here. Who wears a shirt with their own crest on it?'

Mina nodded her Indian nod, and I let her reply. 'Some of the world's most successful businesses do it. Even the chief executive.'

Saffron's face said what she thought of that idea. She quickly switched to a smile when we got to the bottom of the steps.

Lena presented us, and I got a good look at her fiancé. Ethan Mowbray was much shorter than Cador, and squarer in shape. He had the Mowbray colouring of black hair and blue eyes, but none of the others' poise or expensive skin-care routines. He was in his late thirties, and wrinkles had already spread around eyes that never wavered from mine during the introductions.

Lena stepped aside and Ethan spoke. 'On behalf of Lord Mowbray, welcome to Pellacombe. Please accept our hospitality and enter in peace and fellowship.'

I accepted on behalf of the group and everyone shook hands or made namaste. We were now guests, under Ethan's protection, but he looked to Cador to continue the conversation. The smooth young lawyer stepped forward and said, 'I'm sure you're tired after your journey, and Conrad has a job to do later, so we'll leave you alone until supper. Lena will show you to the King's Watch suite.' He grinned. 'We've named it in your honour, as you'll be the first to stay there. We only finished re-modelling it yesterday.'

'This way, please,' said Lena.

I'll save my account of Pellacombe for later. Cador was right: we needed some down time. The King's Watch suite was on the top floor at the north end of the house and had a lounge with views over the river, three bedrooms and one big bathroom. The luggage was waiting for us, as was a selection of cakes and sandwiches. Behind the aroma of freshly brewed coffee, the lingering scent of fresh paint haunted the air. All the windows were open.

'This, I like,' said Mina. She slipped off her sandals and curled up on the couch. 'You can serve, Conrad.'

'In a minute. I'll get changed first.'

When I emerged, Saffron was standing by the picture window, admiring the view. When she turned round and saw me, her mouth opened in shock. 'Do I have to wear combat uniform, too?'

'Yes. Of course.'

She looked at the back of Mina's head and wisely clamped her mouth shut. I hadn't heard the last of this.

'There's something up with Lena and Eseld,' said Mina from the couch.

Saffron and I joined her and Saff made an effort to get back to the present. 'Not half.'

'In what way?' I asked, totally nonplussed.

'You were too busy having a staring match with Ethan to notice,' said Mina. 'When Lena had introduced us, she was on your right, the same side as Eseld. The natural thing would have been to go and stand next to Eseld, but she didn't. She went all round the back and stood next to Cador.'

'And none too close to him,' added Saffron.

'Where's Scout?' said Mina. 'I am about to open the sandwiches and he's not here. That must be a first.'

'He's in our room,' I said, 'which is beautiful, by the way. Housekeeping have provided a dog basket and a bone for him. He's getting acquainted with it.'

'Ugh. Does he have to sleep with us?'

'I'll move it out here later. I think I'll pass on the cakes, thanks. That tour of the grounds took longer than I thought, and I want to get the landing over with. I'll see you at the *Hubschrauberlandeplatz* in about an hour, Saff.'

'And me,' said Mina simply. 'I will be there also. And don't ever call it by that word again. You're just showing off.'

That put me in my place. I gave her a kiss and left them to their afternoon tea.

10 – By Air

We'd been shown to the King's Watch suite via the main staircase. As Lena had taken us down the short landing, she'd pointed to a fire door and said, 'This goes to the family wing and also to the place of staff.' Guessing that this was the shortest route to the dock, I wound down two flights of stairs and bumped into Jane Kershaw (aka Leah's mum).

She took one look at my uniform and said, 'Looking for the short cut?'

'Please. I know the dock's that way, but…'

'This place is pretty counter-intuitive, I'm afraid. Follow me.'

She led me in the opposite direction, to a windowless corridor dimly lit from above and sporting several ancient portraits. I stopped to look at both the light source and the unblinking eyes of the watchers. This was a seriously creepy place, a fact written all over Jane's face when she asked, 'If you want to know about them, I'm not an expert.'

She was already waiting at the first door, her hand on the knob.

'Perhaps later.'

She pushed open the door and led me down below the level of the mansion's basement.

'Isn't there a less … gloomy route?' I asked.

She made a wry smile. 'Was it that obvious? No one likes using this staircase except the Mowbrays, but it saves a ten minute walk. That top corridor leads to the Lab.' She opened another door at the bottom of the stairwell. 'Welcome to my domain.'

Jane's domain was a busy, open-plan office with views down to the dock. I'd descended a long way from the King's Watch suite and we were standing in the gutted shell of the original farmhouse. 'Leah never said what you did here, Jane.'

'I'm the Assistant Steward in charge of HR and recruitment. It's all hands to the deck right now, so I've even been making beds.'

'Thanks for the shortcut. I'll no doubt see you around.'

She smiled and turned away. Two of her colleagues were already making a beeline to intercept her. I left through the open door and took the short path to the dock.

The tide was on the turn, slowly filling the river and floating the boats. The dock was deserted, except for the busy head of Michael bobbing around in a sharp looking sailboat. Not that I'm an expert, but this looked like something rigged for racing, not messing around on the water. I gave him a shout.

'Just you to cross, sir?' he said.

'Just me, and I'll be coming back in the chopper.'

He hopped on to the dock with ease and looked at me properly. 'Are you really in the Army, sir?'

'RAF, like Leah. That's how I know her. I did nearly twenty years before I joined the King's Watch.'

He jumped down some concrete steps to a rigid skiff and then watched me descend with a limp. At the last moment, he held out a hand to help me on to the boat. A wise head on young shoulders.

While he fiddled with the engine, he said, 'I'd love to join the Navy.'

'Why don't you? Pellacombe will still be here if you want to come back to it.'

'It's Mum. She says she wants to retire at fifty. That's only eight years away – and if I don't take over from her, someone else gets the job. And the house.'

'How old are you?'

'Fourteen.' He powered up the engine and we shot across the river. When he'd pulled in and fastened the boat, he said, 'Shall I run you up in the buggy?'

'Please.' He helped me out and we wandered along to the waiting buggy. On the other side of the jetty, the big ferry rocked gently, probably sleeping for the night. 'Has your mother been happy here?' I asked.

Stupid question, really. Michael is a teenage boy: he had no idea of his mother's happiness. To be fair, I'd have shrugged helplessly if someone had asked me the same question at his age. I know better now.

I rephrased myself. 'You know what I'd do, Michael? I'd tell her you're too young to make that decision at eighteen. Ask her to give you five years in the Navy. If that's really what you want. If you approach her in the right way, you know, focus on your little sister's welfare, and how much you'll learn by going away, I reckon she'll come round.'

He nodded thoughtfully and drove the buggy up the hill, dropping me right next to the helicopter. 'I saw Dad out earlier, checking it over. Do you want me to call him?'

'No need. If Leah trusted him, then so do I. Thanks for the lift, Michael.'

He strained his brow, trying to think of something to offer me in return for my advice. 'If you give me your number, I'll text you. Then you can call me for a ride any time. Or a trip on one of the boats.' I passed him my card and waved him off.

Unlike some Mages, the Mowbrays don't stint when it comes to mundane technology. The girls reported super-fast Wi-Fi in the suite, and I'd been given an iPad with 4G reception. The tablet was loaded with a whole suite of helicopter-related apps, including a program that recorded preflight checks and service notes. I checked, and Michael's father had passed it 100% A1 ready.

Even so, for this first flight I was going to do the full thing myself. I opened the app and performed the first check – *#1 - Door. Does it open?* It did, and I put the tablet on the seat.

At half past five, I started the twin engines and got ready to lift off. The Mowbrays had put a lot of trust in me. It was entirely possible that I would crash into the mansion and wipe them out. Let's hope not.

I flew in a lazy circle around the Fal estuary, avoiding Falmouth town and taking the blue bus well out to sea. The H155 is not the most responsive helicopter, but it beats a Chinook. Did I indulge myself and burn Lord Mowbray's fuel on a jolly? Of course not: this was important familiarisation flying, and I defy you to prove otherwise. Besides, if my last sight on earth wasn't going to be Mina, that view of the Cornish coast is as good as any memory to take to Valhalla. Or wherever.

I made my first pass over Pellacombe at a good height, just to see if I could see it. I could, even if it looked like it was in shadow when the rest of the earth was bathed in sunshine. I looped round to the east and got ready to descend properly.

There was a nice clear run to the helipad with no hills or trees to complicate things. I double-checked the map and started losing height. The granite chimneys of Pellacombe came into view ahead of schedule, and I dropped a little faster, on a line with the Ferrymistress's cottage.

A cold sweat prickled my neck. I was half a kilometre early, according to my internal map and compass, but right on track according to the visuals – that is, what I could see in front of me. I closed my eyes in desperation and tried to feel the muscles in my arm where the magickal key had entered. A throb of heat. The key was stuck there, pulsing gently, inside my arm but not bound with my Imprint. I used every ounce of willpower and focus to pull the end of the twisted rope up my arm.

Slowly, very slowly, it snaked up my arm. I twitched the collective a fraction to get a bit of height back, and the magick rushed up my arm, into my chest and hit my heart with a burst of Lux. I opened my eyes and I was heading into a hillside.

I don't know what I did next, because I wasn't thinking, I was doing what thousands of hours of practice told me to do to get the chopper over the hill and skim the roof of the summerhouse. In its shadow, three women stood unflinching as I nearly wiped them out. That was bloody close.

I could have taken the long way round to let my heart slow down. No chance. I needed to try that landing again, and I needed to do it as quickly as possible. I banked hard to the south and made a big loop back to Pellacombe.

This time I took the descent at borderline idiot speeds. If I was going to hit the hill, or trees, or the summerhouse, I didn't want to know about it. Do or die. It was the sort of speed you only do when you're desperate or under enemy attack.

The chimneys lined up with Lamorne Point as they should have done, and I brought the blue bus to land right in the centre of the artificial grass. I closed my eyes, took a deep breath and started to shut down the engines.

Mina ran across to grab me, scarf trailing and blowing in the dying wash of the rotors. I lifted her and span her round before burying my face in her hair. 'Sorry, love. That was too close.'

'I knew you'd do it,' she said. She gave me a quick kiss and we walked over to meet Leah and Saffron.

Leah saluted. 'That was well done, sir. So close I thought you'd practised it.'

'The implication being that if I *hadn't* practised it, then I was clueless.'

'Your words, not mine,' grinned Leah.

Saffron looked less happy: in half an hour she had to get in the chopper with me. No wonder she said, 'What happened, Conrad, if you don't mind me asking?'

'I'd be more worried if you hadn't asked. You've every right to know, and the answer is that I have no clue. I think the Glamours around Pellacombe must be dynamic and shift depending on how you approach them. Either that or the house is alive. Or both. The illusion changed at exactly the right moment to put me into that hillside I managed to re-bond in time. It won't happen again.'

Mina had been watching Saffron's face and asked the question that Saff was too afraid to ask. 'How do you know?'

I tapped my chest. 'I felt it, and there was no shadow on the land the second time.'

'Come on,' said Mina. 'There's tea in the summerhouse and I brought out the cake. I thought you might need it.'

Leah joined us, and in ten seconds conversation had moved on from helicopters to babies. Scout appeared, too, and curled up on my feet. According to Mina, he'd been with them until I nearly crashed, at which point he'd howled like a wolf and run off round the estate trying to catch up with the chopper.

'Do you mind if I go and say goodbye?' said Leah, rising and reaching for a hug. She'd just had a text.

'To whom?' said Mina.

'Smurf.'

The girls looked at each other blankly.

'What else would you call a bright blue helicopter?' I supplied.

Leah grinned. 'I know you'll take good care of him, Conrad. It's the others who come after you that I worry about.'

We watched her stride across the grass and pat the side of the helicopter. Then she leaned down and kissed the grinning wild boar on the pilot's door. Saff looked to the right, as did Scout. Their hearing's much better than mine.

A battered pickup bounced into view and did a circle round the chopper to face the way it had come. It stopped near Leah, and she gave us a last wave before climbing in and kissing her husband. She was turning a page in her life. The next time we met, she would be on maternity leave. I silently wished her luck and gave belated Thanks to Odin for still being alive.

'I too must go,' said Mina. 'I got a call from Cador – or Mr Cador as everyone insists on calling him. He wants to go through something.'

'I wondered why you'd got changed,' I said. 'I thought you were saving that outfit for tomorrow.'

'I am,' she said, repositioning the emerald green scarf. 'Tomorrow has started early, that's all. Come on, Scout, you're not flying today.'

They left us, and I went to stand under the veranda for a smoke. Saffron joined me (upwind) and asked something about our imminent trip. She's a good person, really. She'd decided that my near-death experience was not the best preparation for an argument about uniform.

'Mmm. What have you got against your outfit, Saffron? Or costume if you prefer.'

She went red. 'I don't mind the ceremonial occasions, Conrad, even if the dress uniform is grossly unflattering for women. I can cope with that. Just. It's this.' She passed her hand down the desert camouflage. 'You don't wear it any other time, do you? So why now? I think it demeans your status as a Watch Captain.'

'And yours?'

'Yes, but I thought we were partners. What demeans you demeans me. And vice versa.'

'What did I tell you about Irina when we finally arrested her?'

She frowned. 'A lot. Which bit?'

'That motives can be mixed. There is rarely a single reason for human behaviour. We are not Dwarves.'

She nodded, keen to avoid a serious argument.

I continued. 'When we meet the Daughters tomorrow, how do you think they'll react?'

She opened her mouth, closed it and tried to put herself in the Witches' shoes. Her mouth twisted in a bitter smile. 'I know what they'll think of me. They'll think, "Oh, that's Lady Hawkins' daughter. Heidi Marston's cousin. You know the one." It's happened often enough.'

'And me?'

She looked away. 'Hard to say.'

'Don't worry, Saff. You won't upset me.'

She looked back and blinked. 'I know what my mother said to my auntie. I overheard them when they found out I'd been teamed with you.' She lapsed into silence.

'Let me guess. It involved *jumped up mundane thug*. Or similar.'

'Close. *Ignorant magickal tourist* were the exact words. *Tourist* is the Hawkins family code for non-Mages hitching a ride.'

'I'm proud of the uniform. Maybe you will be one day. Until then, focus on that badge.' I pointed to the two pips on the tab around her chest button. 'It's the Queen's commission. It reminds Mages who we are and who we have at our backs.'

She grinned and nodded her head. 'The Daughters can look down on you and me, but they diss the Watch at their peril.'

'Too right, Lieutenant Hawkins.'

'In that case, can I say something else?'

'The day I tell you to keep your opinions to yourself is the day you ring the Boss and ask for a new partner. Go on.'

'Who's going to handle their luggage tomorrow?'

I let that sink in for a second and did myself what I'd made her do: put myself in the Daughters' shoes. 'That's an excellent point. After all, we're Guarantors, not footmen.'

'Not that manual labour is beneath us,' she added, a little unnecessarily.

'Of course. Hang on.' I got out my phone and dialled. 'Hello, Michael … No, I don't need a boat, thanks, what I need is a loadie, as we call them in the RAF. How do you fancy a chopper ride tomorrow, to help with logistics? … Of course you'll have to ask your mum and dad. I'll have to ask the Mowbrays, too. Text me and I'll get back to you.'

'Who?'

'Michael. The Ferrymistress's lad. The one who drove the buggy.'

'Why him?'

'Instinct. And he's non-threatening to Witches.'

'Other than being a man. You do know that some of them are complete androphobes and we're taking two men to meet them.'

'Three. Don't forget Scout.'

She laughed. 'As if I could. What do you want me to do in the helicopter, exactly? I promise on my life not to touch any buttons if you let me sit in the front.'

'Of course you're in the front. Your controls will all be switched off. Don't worry, you can't make us crash. Let's go.'

I passed her the iPad and showed her the apps. 'If you call out the preflight checks and tick them off, it'll save loads of time. In the air, I'd like you to learn how to use the radio.'

She nodded, full of serious purpose. 'Right. Don't worry. I've got it.'

11 – Happy Families

Saffron was a model assistant throughout the flight, and cast a wistful look over her shoulder when we left the Smurf on the ground at Lamorne Point. She'd caught the chopper bug. A serious affliction.

'I don't mind the walk,' she said, 'but why did you land on this side and not at Pellacombe?' She carefully didn't suggest that it might be because I was scared of crashing.

'True love.'

'Eh?'

I pointed to the neat cottage with killer views over the river to Pellacombe. No wonder Michael didn't want it to go out of the family. 'The Ferrymistress was born to the job. She fell in love with the apprentice mechanic who's now the senior Estate engineer. That concrete bunker at the back of the landing zone? He'll be there tomorrow morning to service the Smurf.'

She laughed. '*Service the Smurf.* That sounds sooo wrong. How do we get across? I'm not good with boats.'

'You grew up in the country, yet you don't shoot, sail, ride or ramble. What did you do?'

'Cherwell Roost isn't a country house; it's a house in the country. If you must know, before I went to boarding school, I used to do a lot of sewing with my Nana. Dad's mother. Why do you think my uniform fits better than Vicky's or Desi's?'

'Erm...'

'You tried not to notice, didn't you?'

'Well...'

'Just don't you dare tell Mina or Myfanwy that I can sew, okay?'

'Right. Your personal dress-maker isn't your grandmother is it?'

She looked alarmed. 'How did you know about that?'

'Because you talked to her in the car after the Battle of the First Mine. My hearing's not that bad.'

'Oh. No. It's a girl from school who's getting into fashion the hard way, from the bottom up.' She waved her hand, as if having a personal dressmaker with your exact size was an act of charity rather than a manifestation of privilege. I left it there

'To answer your original question, the Ferrymistress has to provide a crossing between dawn and dusk. After that, we're on our own. As the sun won't set for another hour, we're good.'

Michael's older sister, now in fewer layers, was sitting on the jetty reading an old book that looked distinctly magickal. She jumped up when we approached and packed the book carefully into a canvas bag.

She took us across in the same skiff that Michael had used earlier, and although we were never in danger, it was clear to me that the water genes in the family had all gone to her brother.

Back in the King's Watch suite, Saffron headed for the bathroom and a well-earned shower. I poured myself an equally well-earned single malt from the generous bar and gave Mina a kiss. 'What did Cador want?' I asked her.

'To check me out. In a non-sexual way. Lord Mowbray had clearly told him to ask me some questions and he wanted to get them out of the way before dinner. It doesn't get any easier.'

'What doesn't?'

'Being asked delicate questions about my time in prison and my Indian heritage. It might have been less unpleasant if he'd hit on me. Part of me would have found that flattering, so long as he kept his hands to himself.'

'I'm sorry.'

She stood up. 'It's not your burden, it's mine. I can't change the past or re-make the world, and most of the time I'm very lucky. I'm going to get changed. You definitely need a shower, Conrad, so don't leave it too long.'

The girls had discussed their outfits for tonight while I was busy nearly dying in the helicopter. They'd even roped Leah into it on the basis that she must have eaten with the Mowbrays while on road trips. Saffron (and Leah) had persuaded Mina to wear western dress and go short in the skirt. Blue is her favourite colour, but red sometimes works better, and it meant she'd co-ordinate with Saffron's yellow number. And me? Who the hell cares what I wore, so long as it didn't smell of jet fuel.

Lena knocked on the door at five to eight. She'd changed, too, and wore a floral Seasalt dress (or so I'm told).

'Tomorrow, I am showing you all of the house,' she said. 'Tonight it is best if I take you. The family room is hard to find.'

She led us down that second staircase, but not as far as the entrance to the Lab (whatever that was), and took us into a snug dining room on the middle floor. When I say *snug*, I mean that relative to Pellacombe, not your average semi-detached. It seated ten people and had patio doors on to a terrace.

The first to greet us was Eseld, who was also the most formally dressed, if your calendar for formality was dated 1819. Another beautiful silk pull-over shirt was held by a leather belt over silk knee breeches.

Yes, you read that right. Knee breeches, complete with buckles at the bottom to stop them riding above her knees. She also had white stockings and flat black leather shoes with a bar across. The overall effect was definitely striking, and the breeches emphasised her hips in a way that enhanced her femininity.

Eseld said hello and bent down to greet Scout, squatting to get down to his level. He eyed her nervously, his tail wagging slowly. Unlike every other human he'd met, Eseld didn't try to stroke him. 'You're a funny one,' she said to Scout. He backed off a pace and she straightened up, turning her attention to me. 'Leah says you ride. D'you fancy a gallop tomorrow morning?'

'I'd love to, but I'm not sure I'll have time. Lena needs to prep us for the conference.'

The slight curl to her lip said what Eseld thought of Lena. 'That's at nine. Breakfast's at eight, and I'll see you in the stables at six thirty.'

It was a challenge. A gauntlet thrown down. In this instance, I had nothing to lose and everything to gain by finding out more about one of our hosts. The thought of riding around the estate was also very attractive. 'I'll look forward to it. Where are the stables?'

'Tell your Familiar to go find the horseys. It'll do him good.' She pivoted with a dancer's grace and intercepted Saffron, whisking her off to the drinks tray.

Ethan and Cador came over to say hello and I noticed that they were undressed in one unusual way. Eseld was sporting a Mowbray blue silk scarf around her neck to complete the Regency gentleman look. As for the men, it was shirts and chinos, and no Mowbray blue at all. Not a stitch. Interesting. Perhaps Cador had deliberately given his sister the wrong dress code for tonight. It's the sort of thing I'd have done to Rachael if she'd upset me, and I whispered as much to Mina a short while later.

'Oh no,' said Mina. 'If anyone has misled Eseld, it would be Lena, but I think Eseld likes being different. I wonder why.'

'Does she need a reason?' I asked.

'We all have reasons for conforming or making ourselves stand out. I wonder what on earth she's going to wear for the conference.'

The sun was lighting up the Fal with golden flickers as Lena invited us in from the terrace. The meal was a little nervous, but not in the least strained, mostly thanks to Cador. He has a knack of getting the best out of people when he wants to, and he could afford to be relaxed and take risks because he has nothing to prove or to lose tomorrow. He will never be staff king. He will not have to play hostess. He does not have to use a magickal seal, or fly helicopters or guarantee anyone's safety.

Scout was pretty relaxed, too. He curled up on the sundeck and went to sleep.

By half past ten, it was dark and everyone was ready for bed, but duty called for me. Or rather, Scout called, standing by the door and letting us know it was time for his last outing. Mina swapped her sandals for trainers, grabbed her coat and joined me for a walk down to the dock, taking the long route now that the offices were closed. It was one way of getting some time on our own, and we held hands going down the track, loving the quiet and being together.

It was magical by the dock. Lights flickered across the estuary, cosy beacons from the cottages. Rigging snapped against the masts of the sailboats and a few night birds called out to each other. It was full tide now, and down by the water you could smell the sea. Mina slipped her hand under my coat and snuggled up. 'It's cold,' she said. 'Is it me or is autumn around the corner? It shouldn't be. This is August.'

'Welcome to the countryside. The days might be warm, but summer's definitely over.'

'Hmmph. Remind me not to wear a short skirt next time we come here at night. If my legs weren't brown, they'd be going blue.'

I bent down for a kiss, and we were enjoying ourselves when Scout trotted up and barked. Time to go.

'Did you notice,' said Mina, 'who never exchanged a single word during dinner.'

'I did. Lena and Eseld. Not so much as a *pass the coleslaw*. No one seemed to mind, though.'

'I wonder what it's like when they don't have guests,' she mused.

'Eseld has her own place down Penzance way. She's never normally here unless Lord Mowbray is also in residence.'

'Hmm. I wonder why that is, and I wonder why she's so desperate to get you on horseback tomorrow.'

'Rachael used to do that sometimes: make guests play tennis at unsocial hours, just to prove a point.'

'Possibly. The longer I'm here, the more I get the feeling that we've been given parts in a different film to the one our agent promised.'

'Was that a Bollywood metaphor?'

'Of course. When not acting as Peculier Auditor, I am 100% focused on the party next month. We will start selling tickets on Monday.'

'Right. That puts me in my place.'

We'd reached the lights under the canopy by the front door. Mina lifted her cold hand and stroked my face. 'Your place is at the back, looking moody and as far from the dance floor as possible. And that is why I love you. Let's hope these granite walls are soundproof.'

Part Three — Meet Me in the Middle

12 – Game

'Go on then. You heard her last night. *Find the horseys.*'
Scout scanned the white wool that had descended on Pellacombe, then turned round to face me and tilted his head on one side. The message was clear: *in this????*

After such a clear night, it wasn't surprising that mist had taken over the estuary, even up to the heights of the Mowbray mansion. The sun was just peeking over the horizon (or would be if I could see the horizon). This wasn't proper fog and it would burn off soon enough. I looked down at my reluctant hound and said, 'You're supposed to be a dog. You don't need to see the stables, just follow the scent.'

He shook himself, and a few water droplets from the dew flew free. Without further ado, he bounded off to the north, disappearing into the mist.

'Bloody dog,' I said to myself. 'How am I supposed to follow you now?' From within the mist, a bark showed he'd taken pity on me.

Away from the public face of Pellacombe, a paved path led through the small woods that clustered nearby and which had formed the magickal basis for the illusion of a forest. On the other side of the wood was the start of a village where most of the estate workers lived. There was no wall around Pellacombe. Not one you could see, anyway. One of the nearest features was a collection of functional buildings that included the stables. There was a tiny puddle at the bottom of the sign warning of private property. I wish he wouldn't do that, but he is a dog, I suppose.

Eseld was busy saddling a powerful stallion whose chestnut flanks glistened under the artificial light. The name outside the stall said that he was Uther. In case you can't remember, Uther Pendragon was the father of King Arthur. Fitting for a beast like that.

'You found us,' said Eseld. 'Your Familiar stuck his head in and ran a mile.'

'Morning. That is some beast. Does he live here or in Predannack?'

'Mostly in Predannack. I brought him up here when Dad decided he wanted to be King of Wessex.'

Dad. That brought me up short. Cador has only ever referred to his father as *Lord Mowbray*. At dinner last night, we all avoided business so his name never came up. I certainly couldn't imagine Ethan referring to him as *Uncle Arthur*.

I looked around the immaculate stables and could see three other stalls in use. 'Which one should I take?'

She didn't answer until she'd finished checking the saddle. She had eschewed all fancy dress today and was looked like any other woman about to go for a ride. Apart from the purple lipstick. And the leather wrist bands.

'Why do you think I invited you here this morning?' she said, then answered her own question. 'To get you alone.'

I tried not to react. Honestly.

She gave me a feral grin. 'Don't worry. You're not my type. Have you noticed that Mages, even the nicest ones, rarely do each other favours?'

'Not free of charge. There's usually a price.'

'There is, but not today because it's not for you. Call your Familiar.'

I whistled loudly and two of the horses whinnied at the noise. Scout came nervously into the stables and made a dash for the sanctuary of my legs.

'I had a Familiar once,' said Eseld. 'When I was a kid.' She lifted a finger and pointed it at me. 'And don't laugh when I say that it was a bat.'

'I'm not laughing, I'm just puzzled. Aren't they rather short-lived?'

She shook her head. 'It should still be alive. They can live for forty years. Twenty is normal.' She paused for a moment, screwing up her purple lips as if trying to keep something penned in that was trying to escape. She shook her head and blinked. 'You've bonded with Scout, but not properly. It's not your fault, I can see that you've been trying. Who taught you?'

'I got most of it from a book. I'm afraid that a lot of it didn't apply to me for obvious reasons. I simply don't have the magick.'

She squatted down, like she had last night, and put her hands out wide on either side of Scout's head. I felt the warmth of Lux and Scout whimpered. 'A Familiar needs to be a true union of Spirit and animal, neither one nor the other and greater than the sum of its parts. The Spirit part is getting edged out as he grows up. That's normal, but not to this extent. You need to intervene. To enhance his Imprint and open a channel for Lux that doesn't rely on physical contact.' She rested her hands on her knees.

'How do I do that? I thought only serious Mages could project Lux without a physical link, and I have no idea how to enhance his Imprint.'

She held up a hand and I hauled her to her feet. 'Do you trust me, Conrad?'

That was a leading question. 'In this, yes.'

'Good enough. Strip off all your magick and leave it here, then follow me.'

I wear some of my magickal Artefacts all the time now. Yes, *all* the time. I felt naked without them, and when I'd followed Eseld into an empty stall with a wall heater glowing brightly, things got worse. She asked me to take my top off.

She peered at my arm. 'Did you have some ink there? They didn't do a very good job removing it.'

'I have no tattoos. That's a scar from a shrapnel wound. You should see my leg.'

She brushed her fingers against the scar tissue. 'Dead. It's a blank spot on your Imprint.' She shook herself like Scout does and frowned. The emotional temperature dropped several degrees, much to my relief.

'How does your Sight work?' she asked.

'Heat. I close my eyes and feel lines of heat.'

She chewed her lip. 'Shit. That's so not helpful. We'll have to improvise. Right. Call him in, squat down and put your hands on his shoulders. I'm going to stand behind you and put my hands on yours. I have to avoid touching him at all costs. You should be able to feel his Imprint within his body, and you need to enlarge it somehow. I can't tell you more than that. When you feel my fingers start to really dig into your shoulders, that's the signal for you to let go. I'll help you form the air-bond, but I can't help with the Imprint. Okay?'

'I'll do my best, except I can't squat for long. You really do need to see my leg to understand why.'

She got a feed bucket and turned it over. I lowered myself down and she moved behind me. Warm hands touched my shoulders and I called for Scout. He came and sat in front of me and his blue eye turned green, the way it does when he's using magick.

'This might hurt, lad,' I said. 'Sorry.'

I moved my hands above his doggy shoulders and closed my eyes. I pressed down through his fur and instead of heat, I got cold. A metal shell under the skin. That's what it felt like anyway. Eseld flexed her fingers and I felt heat radiate across my chest.

I tried to press without pressing, to move my awareness inside his body without crushing him. He gave a little whine to show I wasn't succeeding. I squeezed my eyes so tightly closed that spots appeared and tried again.

Whoah! My hands stayed on his shoulders, but I grew another pair of hands that sank into the flesh. I nearly jerked away because my brain isn't equipped to receive data from four hands. The physical hands stayed and my head throbbed like I'd been hit by a bouncer. Tentacles. I was feeling inside Scout's body as if I had tentacles, not extra hands, and deep inside his canine form, I felt something glowing red hot. It was my turn to swear.

It was knobbly, it had bits sticking out and it was vaguely dog shaped. It also felt like a piece of lava. Somehow I had to make that thing, his Imprint, much much bigger. Images slid round my brain, of volcanoes, hot springs and furnaces. What comes out of a furnace? Metal, yes, but also glass. I had an idea.

Somewhere at the front of that lump of fire was a mouth, and I was going to blow it like a bulb of glass. If I could only turn that tentacle into a tube...

OWWWWWWWWWWWWWW! OWWW!

That's the noise I made. Apparently. I also managed to get an invisible tube into the Imprint and blow Lux down it. The pain was worse than when my leg was blown up.

Slowly, the Imprint expanded, growing more dog-shaped as it did. My shoulders burned almost as much as my hands as Eseld gave me Lux. I heard her hiss with pain, and I redoubled my efforts. I got as far as three-quarters of dog size when her fingers dug into my shoulders like twin vices.

I didn't just let go. I withdrew my Sight from his body as slowly as I could bear until it was back with my hands, and the ice-cold metal of his shoulders was now much warmer and softer. I tried to visualise a streamer of glass connecting us as I moved my hands away. There. Still attached. We were now more bonded than ever. With a thump, I fell off the stool and fainted.

'Here, drink this,' said Eseld.

She was lifting my naked torso off the floor and supporting my head. My side felt wet. Had I cut myself? I opened my eyes. No. I was being licked back to health by Scout. I took a sniff and was soooo tempted.

'Sorry. Thanks, but the alcohol limit for RAF pilots is zero.'

'Oh. Right. Never thought of that. Can you sit up?'

I levered myself into a sitting position. 'Any chance of an aspirin?'

'Coming up.' She passed me my top and disappeared.

I looked at Scout. His right eye was now permanently green. Very disconcerting. I reached out and stroked him. He flinched, squeezing his eyes closed. I think the poor thing just got a taste of my headache.

Eseld returned with water, aspirin and a chair. I managed all three with some difficulty.

'That was interesting,' she said. 'You've made a huge difference to Scout. It'll work out over the next six months or so. I didn't know you were a Geomancer.'

'Neither did I. I can do bits of dowsing and follow Ley lines, but my only genuine talent is Navigation.'

She disagreed. 'You made that Work like a proper Geomancer. Sort of. I've seen my dad work, and you have similar styles in a way. Don't take offence, but Dad's like a surgeon and you're more of a digger driver.'

'Being in the same sentence as your father is a big compliment.'

'Do you still fancy a gallop?'

'I think I need it. After I've had a cigarette, if you don't mind.'

'I'll join you, and we can give Scout a job.'

'He'll try most things, but using a brush is a bit beyond him.'

She held out a hand and pulled me up. 'Tell him to choose a horse for you.'

Outside the stables, the mist had nearly gone. I asked Eseld to tell me where we were going, and she described a route round the Pellacombe estate that should blow the cobwebs away. When we went back inside, Scout was sitting looking at one of the stalls. He heard us coming, barked, and trotted outside.

'Good choice,' said Eseld. 'I'll get a saddle while you say hello to Evenstar.'

What a beast. Scout had chosen a two year old filly just reaching maturity. She had a beautiful grey coat (which means white in ordinary language), and I went into the stall to get acquainted.

Evenstar isn't a thoroughbred, and didn't have a thoroughbred's temperament. What she did have was a lot of strength in her legs, something I discovered when we gave Uther and Evenstar their heads on a gallop to Mowbray's Hill. Eseld is a better rider than me, and Uther faster on the flat, but up the hill Evenstar dug in and won by a head.

'Do you come here a lot?' I said, drinking in the view down the valley. I could see both Pellacombe and Lamorne Point coming to life. The Ferrymistress was making her first crossing, smoke was coming from the mansion chimneys and even the Smurf looked wide awake.

'I try to come every day. Predannack is beautiful, but it doesn't have anything like this.'

'Thank you for sharing it with me. And for what you did to Scout. I am in your debt, Eseld.'

She shook her head violently. 'No. No you're not. Freely offered, freely given.'

That was not done lightly. She had gone out on a limb for Scout and me, and to insist on no favour owed was very generous. 'Then accept our thanks, from Scout if not from me.'

His little legs had left him well behind the horses, about half way up the hill. He struggled to the top and barked plaintively.

'From him, yes,' she said. 'From you, reluctantly, but yes. Let's go. We've got a conference to prepare for.'

We turned the horses and walked down the hill. Eseld was trying to keep a barrier between us for reasons of her own, but it's hard to do that when you've shared magick. Even harder when there's been physical contact. I decided to risk something personal but not intimate. 'What have you got planned for today's outfit?'

She laughed. 'You're brave.'

'Cador made you go to Primark before the Cloister Court.'

'And I haven't forgiven him yet. Do you like 80s pop, Conrad?'

'Not as much as my father. He used to sing power ballads to get me to sleep when I was a baby. Apparently. I think it turned me to classical music at an early age. If you'd heard my dad on karaoke, you'd never look at Bonnie Tyler in the same way again.'

She laughed again and picked up the speed to a trot. 'Then you're in for a real treat.'

13 – Set

'That had better be all she touched,' said Mina. She was holding a mascara wand in one hand and peering carefully at the bruises on my shoulder.

'I thought it was Lena that I had to steer clear of.'

'Hmmph. You smell of horse today. Go away and let me finish.'

Saffron emerged into the lounge as I went to the bathroom. Her hair was in an MOD approved bun and her uniform looked ironed. She bent down to say hello to Scout and stood straight up. 'Woah! What's happened here?'

'Eseld took him in hand. I'll tell you later.'

My curiosity about Eseld's outfit also had to wait. She was still in her riding gear at breakfast and already tucking in when the King's Watch party descended. At least she gave me a proper smile today. Fleetingly. When no one was looking.

She also said something to Mina. Something that involved touching her on the back. I couldn't hear them, but I saw Mina's nose go up. I'm sure Eseld was trying to be nice, but she'll need to watch out: Mina's like a cobra when her nose goes up. It means she's ready to strike.

'Excellent breakfast,' I said to Lena when I'd put down my knife and fork.

'Danke. I am telling the butcher about proper sausage. Maybe in winter he makes *rohwurst*.'

'You'll have to send us some.'

'And now for the tour,' she said to the group. The Mowbrays drifted away and Lena led us out of the dining room.

I'll give you my impressions of the public rooms in a minute. When Lena showed us the staircase to the old farmhouse, I asked about the Lab.

'*Ist verboten*,' she said with a shrug. 'Only the Mowbray Mages go in there. Lord Mowbray's *Zauberwerkstatt*, I think.'

Magickal workshop. Made sense. We went back upstairs and started from the front.

Inside the formal entrance doors is an equally formal reception hall with the main staircase rising at the back. Portraits faced each other across the slate flagged floor. One could only be the Earl of Tintagel, Ethan's father, a fact confirmed by Lena. The other portrait was a woman in early middle age, slightly hunched in the shoulders and with long black hair loose around the shoulders. Her face didn't look strong, but her gaze was deep and directed straight at the artist. 'Lord Mowbray's mother,' said Lena, crossing herself. 'This room will not be used properly for the conference. Tonight we eat in the dining room. As Cador is saying, the action will all be in the Aisling Rooms.'

Aisling. The name of Lord Mowbray's second wife, who died in mysterious circumstances. I wonder what the next Mrs Mowbray thought of having a suite of rooms named after her sainted predecessor. Then again, how would Aisling's child, Kenver, feel if his father erased the Aisling suite and called it the Kerenza Room?

'This way,' said Lena. A grand door led to a room that was intimate without being small. There was no bare slate here. A huge carpet in blue and yellow covered the floor, and light wallpaper brightened the room further.

There were pieces of furniture around the wall, all exquisite. My father would be salivating if he were here, and my mother would be saying, 'They look naked.' They did. All ornaments and photographs had been taken away and there was even a pair of shadows on the wall where pictures had been removed.

The purpose of the room was obvious from the circular table in the middle surrounded by five chairs, three on the south side and two on the north. Set back from the table, each side also had a small desk and chair. Lena frowned in concentration and spoke slowly.

'The Mowbrays and the Daughters have one observer who cannot speak. They are Eseld and Síona. In the talking, Cador and Brook will lead. They are the lawyers, ja?'

'Yes.'

Saffron had read the brief as thoroughly as you'd expect. 'Why isn't Lord Mowbray coming? Or the Eldest Daughter?'

Lena shrugged. Today's dirndl was a light green with white flowers. The apron was the same. I supplied the answer.

'In case things go badly. The principals only turn up at the end for tea and a photo opportunity after they've done the signing ceremony. Or sealing in this case. Ethan and Alys will be in constant contact with Mowbray and Hedda. If it all goes to plan, we'll be off to fetch them tomorrow.'

Lena nodded. 'Ja. That is right. Today, Ethan is in charge.'

Mina raised her eyebrows. She'd got the message: this is not Cador or Eseld's show.

Saffron went to check the windows. Most were sealed units with just one door into a garden. This room didn't have the river views.

Lena went right, to a door on the Daughters' side of the room and opened it. 'When they come, I give them the keys to this room. See?'

It was a pleasant, if cramped, sitting room with only a high window. I suspected the bathroom off it would get more use than the room itself. Lena led us to the corresponding door on the opposite side of the main room and threw it open. She didn't invite us to enter, and I could see why.

'Lord Mowbray's study,' she said.

I peered over her shoulder and glimpsed a lot of pale oak. Pleasant. He could easily have made it a gloomy man-cave, but this room was perfect for conducting Estate business. Even the desk was pushed into a corner rather than dominating the space. The only one of our party who crossed the threshold was Scout, who stuck his nose in, sneezed and backed out just as I was trying to focus on one of the paintings. Lena shut the door behind him.

When he sneezed, I got a ripple, like water lapping over your nose in a swimming pool. I'd never had that before, and I had no idea what it meant. What I did know was that the room was guarded by a Ward of some description, and I don't know how I knew that, either. This morning's pain was paying off already.

There was more to the tour, and it finished back in the main hall. When Lena had said that it wasn't going to be used *properly*, I think she meant that it wasn't going to be filled with liveried footmen and trays of champagne. What it did have was a cosy corner by a fireplace with a settee, three armchairs and a coffee table. They were tucked away at an angle but they had a good view of the whole hall, including the entrance to the Aisling rooms. This was our spot.

Lena opened a decorative wooden cabinet on the wall and showed us a telephone handset. There was a list of extension numbers on the back of the door. She used the phone to call someone and said, '*Ja. Bitte.*' She replaced the handset and said, 'Coffee is on its way. Do you have any questions?'

'Will the dinner go ahead tonight regardless?' said Mina. 'Even if they're at each other's throats?'

'Oh yes. Everyone will make nice. I have told Ethan that I will kick them out at six thirty to get changed. Dinner will be at eight o'clock.'

The coffee arrived and Lena stayed with us until she got a text and disappeared in a flurry.

'Someone's in trouble,' said Saffron.

'Possibly. See you at the dock in twenty,' I said. I poured myself a second coffee and took it outside for a smoke. Part of the tour had included the little hut with ashtray. There was even a water bowl for Scout next to one of the cloakrooms. Lena had thought of everything. Or someone had. Being the Steward of Pellacombe was not a job she'd expected to do when she was growing up, and this was her biggest test so far. I wondered how much of what was happening had come from her and how much from the collective memory of the Pellacombe estate.

I finished my coffee and went to get my case from the King's Watch suite.

14 – Match

Saffron had one job to do on the flight to Glastonbury, and she executed it perfectly, advising Air Traffic Control that we were entering a specified area and repeating their permission word for word with a clarity that her drama teacher would be proud of. I put the Smurf into a slow circle and we all admired the view. Except Scout. He was curled up in a dog basket with his paws over his ears to fidget with the bonnet we'd given him. It's too loud for a dog in a helicopter.

'I've never seen it before,' said Michael. 'It really stands out, don't it?'

They don't call them the Somerset Levels for nothing. All around us, flat fields soaked up the sun with only the odd tree breaking cover. And then there's the Tor.

The hill on which the tower stands rises like a film set from the flatness, a perfect tear-drop mound of green with the tower standing proud. In the summer sun, it looked like Merlyn himself was about to saunter up and engage in a spot of Necromancy. No wonder the largest coven of Witches in England is based nearby.

'I'm taking her down now,' I said. There was only the lightest of breezes this morning, and I'd had a good look at the landing zone already so I let the Smurf do most of the work for once.

The Daughters of the Goddess have their base south-south-west of the Tor, near a river. The Homewood itself exists on another plane and is invisible even to Mages like Saffron. Vicky's seen it, but she's a Sorcerer. To the west of the Homewood is an old country house that advertises itself as a women-only spiritual and holistic retreat. It's quite popular in the local community because it employs people, it sponsors things and a lot of the staff live there.

It's also the Daughters' main point of interaction with the rest of the magickal world. It's a centre of learning, the biggest outside the Invisible College. It's a hotel for visiting Witches, and it's a farm. Thirty nine Daughters live in the Homewood. Most spend most of their time on the higher plane, but they have to eat and they have to have somewhere in the normal world to live, and it's here at Home House that they register their address on the electoral roll.

The Daughters had made a temporary LZ out of their all-weather sports pitch and the Smurf settled down right on the centre spot. I shut down the engines and took off my headset.

'Where are they?' said Saffron.

I pointed to the main building. 'See that minibus? They'll wait until we get out, then they'll drive up.'

'Oh. A power play.'

'You could say that.'

Scout was the first out, and he headed straight for some trees. He came trotting back as the minibus bumped over the grass and drew up in front of us.

The first to get out of the bus was their Guardian for this trip, Isolde, first wife of Lord Mowbray. Her picture still hangs in the family area of Pellacombe, so she was easy to recognise. Twenty years older now, but still the angular, awkward woman who had bequeathed her genes to Eseld and Cador. Like all the Daughters on this trip, she was wearing street clothes for the journey, in her case a pair of jeans and a red jacket. In fact, all but one of them were in their favourite pair of jeans and trainers.

Behind her came Alys, the Little Mother. It's an odd title for such an important position: the Little Mother of Homewood is the second most powerful Daughter. Alys was looking behind her as she got out, talking to the two women behind her. Alys could best be described as powerful, and what she lacked in height she made up for in square-shouldered determination.

The next two were the ones I'd seen before at the Cloister Court, Brook and Síona. Brook was their counsel, who'd gone toe-to-toe with Cador and earned a draw, and Síona was the Witch from London, presumably representing the many, many Daughters who don't live in Glastonbury. They were still talking as the fifth member of the party unfolded herself and straightened up to survey the scene.

'Will you look at that!' said Saffron.

'Will she fit in the chopper?' said Michael.

Scout whimpered and jumped behind me.

I just stared, trying to let my sunglasses hide my shock and incipient naked terror, because I now knew what Rick had meant about Raven and Chris Kelly having something in common. They are both taller than me, and I'm six foot four.

The best way to describe the First Daughter of Ash is *statuesque*, and that's because she was like a regular sized female athlete who'd been made into an oversized statue. Everything was in proportion, but so much *bigger*. The shoulders, the chest and the powerful thighs were all emphasised by the singlet and the leggings. Odin only knows where she gets athletic shoes in her size.

A long black braid snaked its way down her chest until she flipped it over her shoulder and looked at us. Raven, 1st of Ash, had deep set eyes and strong, high cheekbones. As well as being unmissably striking, she would have been beautiful, too, if it wasn't for a slightly heavy jaw. She grinned and flashed a huge set of brilliant white teeth.

I stepped forward and met Isolde half way between the bus and the chopper. I took off my glasses and introduced myself. Isolde did the honours for them, and there was a big round of handshakes (excluding Michael, who

106

had vanished without trace). When it came to Raven, I felt my hand enveloped by power, both physical and magickal, and she was the only one who made a comment.

'Can we go the scenic route? I've always wanted to see the land from a helicopter.'

Alys stiffened visibly, but it was Brook who spoke. 'I'm sure the Watch Captain has to follow a flight plan or something.'

I don't like being talked about in the third person. Who does? At least she didn't call me *the pilot*. There's been a few high-ranking passengers who've regretted doing that. I turned and focused on Raven. 'If I get the chance, I'll ask Lord Mowbray. I'd be happy to oblige.'

Raven gave me a short nod and stepped aside so that I could meet Cordy. Noooo! Banish that thought.

So that I could meet *CORDELIA*. There.

Rick's ex had a knowing smile on her face for some reason. Rick's taste in women is best described as *omnivorous*, yet Cordelia was the one he'd asked to marry him. She was the shortest of the group, barely above Mina in height. I wondered if that was why Raven had chosen Cordelia to be her Page: they did look very odd together. I barely had time to take in more than Cordelia's impish grin when Alys started walking towards the Smurf. I stretched out my legs to get there before her and help her on board.

That wasn't an act of chivalry (misplaced or otherwise), it was because I had a problem to solve.

'Could you please sit at the sides and leave this seat for Michael?' I said, pointing to the single by the door.

Alys paused with her hand on the grab rail. 'Is there a reason for that?'

'Weight distribution.'

She took her hand off the rail and confirmed what I thought: the Little Mother is a very, very nervous flyer. 'Don't you need to check everyone's actual weight?'

I shook my head and bent to whisper. 'Would you be more comfortable with a view or without?'

'With.'

'Then take that one, over there. The closer to the middle, the less movement.'

A smile flickered and died. 'Thank you.'

Michael had reappeared. I think he'd run around the field in a huge loop to get to the back of the bus without having to meet the Witches, and he was now piling their luggage next to the hold. I left Saff to finish loading the passengers and went to help Michael. Balancing the cargo really is an issue, and I hefted every case before telling him where to place it.

'I can feel her,' he whispered. 'She's awesome.'

'Raven?'

'Yeah.' The poor lad was smitten. I just hope for his sake that Raven doesn't notice.

'Listen, Michael, you need to watch out on the way back.'

'Sir?'

'Alys is a bit nervous, which is quite normal, but she has the power to kill us all if she panics.'

'Oh.'

'Yes. Keep an eye on her. Without staring, of course. If you're worried, use the intercom.'

Saff, Michael and I were the only ones with headsets.

'They might hear me. Some Witches have superb hearing,' said Michael.

'True. If you're worried, bend down, feel his pulse and say that Scout's feeling ill.'

'What if Scout really is ill?'

'He's my Familiar. I'll know if he's ill. Put that last case there and start strapping them down. I'm going to check the engines. Airborne in five.'

Raven had chosen the seat closest to Michael, presumably because it had the most legroom. Saffron had channelled her inner cabin crew and was busy checking seat belts and pointing out the limited range of controls available to passengers.

'These windows don't open, do they?' said Alys with alarm.

'Oh no,' said Saff. 'And the doors lock centrally.'

That did nothing to calm her down, and I was starting to get nervous myself. Scout trotted up and whined. I lifted him into the cabin and he nearly jumped out of my arms to get away from Raven, at which point a thought struck me. 'Alys?' I said. 'My Familiar is very young. Would you mind if we put his basket next to you? If you could give him a stroke now and then, I'd be grateful.'

It worked a charm, and the flight back to Pellacombe was as smooth as I could have wished for.

I didn't get out, because I was moving the Smurf over the water as soon as it was empty. Saffron was responsible for escorting the Daughters to the formal reception, and other hands would help Michael unload. As a special treat, I was taking him up front on the short hop to his home.

By the time Michael had personally taken me back across the river, the Daughters had disappeared to their rooms and I found Mina showing Saffron something that Mina found hilarious and Saffron found mortifying.

'What?' I said, pouring myself a coffee.

'I'm telling you, she's used a filter,' said Saffron.

'She didn't need to,' said Mina.

'Oy,' I said. 'What's going on?'

Saffron folded her arms and sat back, like a teenager in a strop. 'It'll be all over Salomon's House,' she muttered.

With the serene grace of a princess, Mina passed me her iPad.

At the exact moment that Raven had turned her gaze on the helicopter at Home House, Cordelia had taken a picture and sent it to Rick, who had sent it to Vicky, who had sent it to Mina and Saffron.

The picture showed the four of us on parade in front of the Smurf. I was immobile with my hands behind my back and Scout was peering through my legs like a rabbit in the headlights. Michael looked like a saint who's having an epiphany and Saff had taken off her dark glasses to stare. Her mouth was round and open, and you could almost hear her saying *OMG* like Janice from Friends.

Everyone who'd forwarded the picture included the previous comments:

Cordy -> Rick: *So this is the King's Watch's newest recruits????? One cardboard cutout, one child and one flapper. Even the dog looks scared.*

Rick -> Vicky: *You need to tell Conrad that Top Gun have been on the phone. He failed the audition. LOL. I'm guessing they've just seen Raven for the first time.*

Vicky -> Mina & Saff: *I am going to treasure this. I laughed so much my lung hurt. BTW, is that a new uniform Saff????? Desi & Myvvy are gonna love it too.*

'Let me guess,' said Mina. 'You're going outside. I shall join you.'

15 – Daughters. Mothers, too.

'And it worked?' said Mina when I'd finished my story. 'Alys really calmed down when she stroked Scout?'

'Gave her something to worry about. Scout just absorbed the Lux like a free snack, I think.'

'What was your plan B?

'I gave my mundane SIG to Saffron and told her to be ready to shoot Alys if she kicked off.'

Mina shifted her scarf. The shiny material kept sliding off her matching green tunic. 'I weep sometimes, Conrad. Not for you, but for me. If I had not seen what I have seen and been through what I have been through, I would have been appalled by what you just said. The saddest thing is that I think it was a good idea. Are you sure Saffron would have done it?'

'Saff has a very highly developed survival instinct, and she's a Mage. If she'd seen a senior Witch about to combust in flight and kill everyone, she'd have had no hesitation. Her only question was whether the cabin was pressurised. Actually, that was plan D. Plan B was an emergency landing and Plan C was the other Daughters dealing with Alys.'

'I'm glad I wasn't with you.'

'Why?'

'Then I would have been in Cordelia's picture. I would have freaked out, too. Raven is something else, isn't she?'

'And half.'

Saffron had wandered out to join us, having given us some privacy first. She heard the tail-end of Mina's remarks about Raven and asked, 'Conrad, did your Troth ring show any reaction when Raven shook hands?'

'No, but that doesn't mean anything. It's only sensitive to me or the Allfather himself. What did you get from her?'

Saffron squinted at the cloudless sky. 'Dunno, really. I'll tell you one thing, as soon as she strapped on her seatbelt, she dialled the magick right down like a volume control. She didn't dial it up again until she was walking down the steps to Pellacombe.'

'And how did that go?'

Saff looked at Mina and gestured for her to tell the story. 'I was too busy trying to remember everyone's names,' she added.

'It was mortifying,' said Mina, shaking her head. 'Humiliating for everyone involved. I had no idea that Eseld hasn't seen her mother for fifteen years.'

'What!'

'Tell me about it,' muttered Saffron.

'Isolde had the grace to stand well back,' said Mina. 'Saffron introduced the other five Daughters, and that was all very cordial. Then Ethan formally offered hospitality, and Alys accepted. When Lena went to lead the others upstairs, Isolde came forward. Cador went and gave her a hug. As you'd expect. They've been in contact since he went to Cambridge. She even stood next to Lord Mowbray at Cador's graduation. I know, because I saw the picture, and talking of pictures, Eseld made me take one to show you.'

Mina was almost trembling with fury as she got out her phone. She found the picture and shoved the phone in my face. 'Why did she ask me to do that, Conrad?'

'A joke. When we were out riding, I asked her what she was wearing, and she said I had to wait and see.'

Eseld was posing on the staircase, one foot on a higher step and her body turned to face the camera. She'd promised me a connection to 80s pop, but I hadn't expected Adam and the Ants. With a big grin, Eseld was in full pirate mode: black and white wide striped leggings, over the knee leather boots, a black shirt and a short, black frock coat with silver facings.

'Mmm,' said Saffron. 'Eseld has issues, I think.'

'You think?' said Mina, stowing her phone. 'While Cador was welcoming their mother into the house, Eseld started talking to Ethan about the secure Wi-Fi router. Ethan wasn't listening, of course. Even a block of wood like him knows something is wrong. When Isolde finished hugging her son, she turned to her daughter, and do you know what her daughter did? She said, "Your room is at the top of the stairs. Lena will show you which one." And then she turned and walked into the Aisling suite.'

'Ouch. That was harsh.'

'You have no idea.' Mina turned to look at Saffron and decided that she was enough part of the Elvenham family to continue. 'It makes me so mad. Eseld has a perfectly good mother and treats her like that. I think I shall apply to be Isolde's daughter when this is over. To make it worse, Eseld clearly has history with Raven, too, but I can't work out what.'

I did some sums. 'Raven would have been about eighteen when Eseld fled Glastonbury.'

Lena stuck her head out of the main doors. She couldn't see the other two, just me, and spoke in German because it was quicker. 'The opening ceremony will be in ten minutes, okay?' She disappeared without waiting for a reply.

I translated and lit another cigarette. 'How did they treat you, love?' I asked Mina.

'Like a funfair curiosity. I don't know whether that's because I'm a mundane accountant doing a Mage's job or because, yet again, I'm the only non-white person in the room.'

Sometimes Mina apologises after venting. Not today.

Saffron tried to smooth things over. 'It's not your skin, Mina, it's definitely the mundane thing. In Homewood, all the mundane sisters are there to serve in one way or another. They're not used to having non-Mages at the top table.'

'Are you?' said Mina.

Saffron was taken aback. 'Yeah. Of course. My brother, for one. He's still a Hawkins. Like Cador here. After all, you can't say that the Mowbrays haven't made you welcome, can you?'

'Hmm. Perhaps you're right. Shall we go?'

Ethan passed round small glasses of apple brandy, distilled from apples gathered on the estate and infused with herbs by Lena. My flying was done for the day, so I accepted one gratefully and took my place standing around the table in the Aisling suite. The Daughters were now all in their robes, unbleached white wool and worn long. Except for Raven. Hers were above the knee and the colour you'd expect: deep black with the yellow cord a bright line. It made her look a bit like a wasp.

Eseld's pirate outfit looked even odder in the flesh than on the picture. In backstage clips you sometimes see actors in the most bizarre costumes talking like actors, their voices completely at odds with their appearance. Eseld's Cornish accent made her sound like she was in role, to my ears. At one point, I'd swear her hand went to where a sword would be. Ethan cleared his throat and lifted his glass.

Mina described Ethan as a *block of wood*. It's true, he's not the most communicative host, and he didn't waste his breath on a big speech. He meant every word, though.

'What we do here, we do in peace and in the shadow of the Earl of Tintagel,' he said. 'The earl loved this land and its people. Let us do his memory justice in our commitment to its future. To the Earl of Tintagel!'

Alys was not happy. Ethan had forced her to drink to his father's memory. It didn't seem to bother Raven or Brook, though. Even Isolde spoke out clearly, and Lena seemed sad that he would never be her father-in-law.

We were in a circle, and Eseld had waited until the last moment and forced herself between Raven and Alys. That way, she could hide behind Raven and avoid her mother.

'Shall we begin?' said Cador. 'We'll break for lunch at one thirty.'

Everyone shuffled round or headed for the exit. I noticed Eseld use Raven as a shield again. We left the principals to their talks and Lena shut the doors behind her, using her Steward's badge to activate a Silence over the doors and turning to face the exiles.

Isolde, Cordelia, Saffron, Mina, Lena and I were all now at a loose end for two hours. There were refreshments aplenty inside the suite, and both side rooms had exits. It wasn't as if they were locked in like the election of a Pope. Even so, one of us had to be outside at all times, just in case.

Mina had already set up her laptop in our little corner and volunteered to take first watch. She has a lot of reading to do now that the transcript of the first session of the Flint Hoard hearing has been released. The various lawyers have started submitting their papers, too.

When Isolde walked out on Mowbray, twenty-five years ago, the new mansion at Pellacombe was only a dream. Now that her children were locked away, she asked for the tour. Cordelia nodded happily and we drifted outside as a party, with Lena in the lead. I fell into step with Cordelia and got a better look at her.

Her face was as impish as her smile. Pointy and mischievous. Alive, too. 'I may never forgive you for that picture,' I said. 'I'm surprised Rick could get a signal to receive it if he's off camping.'

She laughed. 'I think your idea of camping and Rick's are very different. His is more *glamping*, but yes, he is in the great outdoors, helping the kids to get back to nature. I'm hoping to Facetime them later.'

'And you should watch your step with Saffron. She may get her revenge when this is over.'

Cordelia grinned. 'And not before?'

'She's on duty.'

She nodded. 'Rick said you could be a humourless bastard at times. He also said you were a good laugh. I'm still waiting for proof of the second part. I like what you did with Alys, though. That was thoughtful.'

'She's not the first nervous flyer I've had to transport. I'm surprised she agreed to come.'

She slowed down, allowing the others to get ahead. With Lena's voice booming, Isolde couldn't hear us.

'Are you really neutral, Conrad, or has the Mowbray charm seduced you? You loved flying that helicopter, I could tell. Saffron loves being treated like royalty and I'm sure Mina's been flattered, too.'

'Don't forget Scout. He's anyone's for a bone and a game of catch. If he was a few months older, they'd probably lay on a few bitches for him.'

'What!!! You can't say that.'

'It's what they are. Don't you have dogs at Homewood?'

'Actually, no. Apart from a sheepdog on the farm, they're banned as pets. You haven't answered my question, have you?'

'I was trying to be funny.'

'Don't give up the day job. Still not answered me, though.'

'I am the Guarantor. I gave an oath. A Clarke's word is binding. I'm surprised Rick didn't tell you.'

'He did. I wanted to hear it for myself. So nothing we say will get back to the Mowbrays?'

'And vice versa.'

I was beginning to think that Cordelia's presence in the party was not as simple as being Page to the First. I have no idea what that purpose might be, but it was something to chew over later.

We had arrived at the summerhouse. Lena got a call on her phone and when it was over, she swore in German (*Rot in Hell with the Devil*, to be precise). 'I cannot show you the dock,' she said to us. 'I must go back.'

'And me,' said Isolde. 'It's best if one of us is in the house.'

'Good idea,' said Saffron. That left me and Cordelia, as Saffron no doubt intended. She's learning.

'I'll show you the tradesman's entrance,' I said. 'It's lovely by the water.'

'Great.'

Half way down the path, she returned to her original point. Cordy … damn. No. *Cordelia* isn't stupid, and whatever she said next was to someone's agenda. Raven's? The Daughters'? Even her own, perhaps?

'Mowbray did it deliberately,' she said. 'He invited us down by helicopter because he knows it's a bloody pain to get from Glastonbury to Pellacombe any other way. People think that Glastonbury's in the west country. It is, but it's not in Cornwall. Three bloody hours by car. At least. Raven jumped at the offer, like Mowbray knew she would. And Brook. Alys had no choice but to fly or be humiliated. He's sneaky like that.'

We arrived at the water and I did my own impression of a tour guide. Cordelia seemed genuinely enchanted by it all, and we fell silent for a bit, just soaking up the beauty of the place, enjoying the breeze and admiring the skill of a yachtsman, probably Michael. I think he had his little sister as crew.

'What's she like to work for?' I asked.

Cordelia turned to face me and gave me the pixie grin. 'You mean, "Is she really a child of the gods?" don't you? Everyone asks me sooner or later. Rick asks me every time he picks up the kids, though I reckon it's more of a joke than anything.'

'It's your turn not to answer the question,' I responded. 'I'm fully aware that you don't know her nature. I just wanted to know what she's like as a leader.'

She held her hands up. 'You got me there. Fair enough. I'd only been elevated to Ash Coven a month when Raven became First Daughter of Ash. She upset a lot of people when she asked me to be her Page. Everyone said she'd chosen me because I was no threat to her and didn't know any better. They're wrong.'

She said the last words with some passion and turned to look at the water again before continuing. 'Raven chose me because I had two small children and because she wanted someone who'd had a life outside the Coven. Working for Raven is easy.'

'We'd better get back. I know a shortcut through the house, though I may get in trouble for using it.'

The office fell into complete silence when I walked through the door with Cordelia, and every eye followed us to the staircase. When the fire door had closed behind us, Cordelia said, 'It must be you. I never have that effect on people.'

'That's because you've never been to the Mowbray estate before. Enjoy it while it lasts.'

'You what? That was scary … but not as scary as this place.'

We'd emerged into the portrait corridor, and her eyes flicked between the pictures and the Lab. I pointed to the next staircase and she almost ran up it. Interesting.

Lena was standing guard outside the doors to the Aisling rooms when we got back to the main hall.

'They have decided to eat separately,' she announced. 'I am sending food to the King's Watch suite for you. Someone will be there to serve and get you anything else. Back here in one hour.'

The doors behind her opened. Ethan smiled at her and said, 'All is good.' It was a tiny glimpse into their intimate lives when, for once, he didn't care who noticed. She stepped into the room with him, and the two Witches followed.

Isolde scanned the room for her daughter in vain; Eseld had already disappeared into the Mowbray's side room. Isolde tried to talk to Cador but Síona intercepted her. I don't think Síona even realised what she'd done.

'Food,' said Saffron. 'Definitely a good idea.'

Over the excellent lunch, I repeated what Cordelia had said once the Mowbray staffer had left us.

'So?' said Saffron. 'What does that mean?'

'It means the Daughters have clear factions,' said Mina, 'and Raven is in a different faction to Alys. For some reason, Cordelia wanted us to know that. I wonder if the three Covens are really three factions. Don't forget, Brook, Raven and Cordelia are all in Ash Coven. The other two are in Willow, and the Eldest Daughter is in Oak. No one from Oak is here.'

'Do we really care?' said Saffron.

'Yes,' chorused Mina and I.

Mina pointed her fork at Saffron. 'And so should you.'

Saffron frowned. Previously, she's gone into a huff when picked up like that. This time she thought about it first. 'We're here to protect the Daughters from the Mowbrays not from each other, right?'

'True,' I said.

'I'm sure the Boss has an opinion about the politics inside Homewood, and I know my mother does, but do we? Yes it's interesting and all that, but isn't this a distraction?'

'That's a good question. You didn't really talk to Cordelia, so it's hard to explain. She mentioned Rick a lot when she was talking to me. It's as if she wanted what she said to get back to him for some reason.'

Saffron nodded. 'Fair enough, but you didn't see Eseld and her mother either. If there's a situation to keep an eye on, I reckon it's that one. Isolde's not going to hurt her own child, but if she forces the issue, I can see Eseld lashing out.'

'She's right,' said Mina. 'That would not be good.'

We'd all finished eating. Saffron leaned out and picked up the internal phone to summon coffee. 'What's the plans for this afternoon?' she asked when she'd put the phone down.

'If no one objects, when they've locked the doors I'm going to sleep for a couple of hours.'

'Really?' blurted Saffron.

'Yes, really,' said Mina. 'He will use the excuse that he was up before dawn to go riding and that he's been flying, but yes, he will go to sleep for a couple of hours and actually be awake when he gets up. I cannot do that.'

'Me neither,' said Saffron. 'Do I get a break later?'

'Of course. The afternoon session is 14:30 to 18:30. We'll take two hours each.'

The coffee arrived. I reluctantly said no to more caffeine, took some water and went to the smoking shelter. When I got back to the main hall, the parties were all ready to go again. Isolde and Cordelia were already outside the space, and the distress on Isolde's face was starting to be really noticeable. Lena closed the doors and put the Silence in place.

I made my excuses and left them to it. Mina had a very interesting story to tell when I relieved Saffron a couple of hours later, and I'll let her tell it herself.

16 – What Mina Saw (and heard)

The swastika at the top of this page is a Hindu symbol of good luck and prosperity, and I hope you don't mind me including it. It's up there to show you who is in charge while Conrad is asleep, and if you don't like looking at it, remember that I have one tattooed on my chest; I have no choice but to look at it.

I don't know what we would have at the top of the page if Saffron were telling the story. I would choose a silver spoon for her, or maybe a halo. If we asked her, she'd probably pick a hawk. For Hawkins. Very boring.

Conrad limped off up the stairs after saying something about the weather. He keeps talking about the Jet Stream as if it means something to me, and he even started talking about a hurricane in the Caribbean. I nodded and told him to go.

Lena wiped her hand over her face and muttered something in German, then said, 'For me, a rest. You are all good, yes?'

I could watch Lena's jaw all day. It really is that big. I only watch it because it is so painful for me to look at it. Every time the muscles work in her face, my head aches. When you have had your own jaw smashed to a pulp and then rebuilt, you become very sensitive to these things. I was very glad to see the back of her.

Cordelia took out her phone and said, 'Gonna FaceTime the kids, yeah?' Isolde nodded to her, and Cordelia wandered outside. That left Saffron, Isolde and me. Saffron is getting better at taking a hint. 'If Conrad is asleep,' I said, 'can you call the Constable? I think her meeting is over now.'

'Good idea,' she said. 'I'll go to the summerhouse.'

And that left Isolde and me. She was no longer wearing the red jacket and she badly needed some colour about her, because Isolde is not the most striking person you will meet, especially given the competition from the other women around here.

No one can compete with Raven, of course. She is just immense in every sense, and that carries its own burden. Raven has to live up to that effect every day. When she walks into a room, everyone looks at her, which is fine, but it's what you do when you have their attention that matters.

Look at Chris Kelly, who is just as far off the ground. As soon as you've noticed him, he tries to deflect attention away from himself. Raven, I have not worked out yet.

Isolde is the thinnest of the Daughters. None of them are what most people would call overweight and most of them glow with health, but not Isolde. She looks like her mother needs to take her in hand and feed her up.

I have no idea whether her mother is still alive. She probably is, somewhere, in a little Cornish cottage, wondering what happened to her daughter. If her mother were a Mage, I'd know all about it, but these magick people have a habit of forgetting mundane parents and siblings. Saffron was right, I should give Lord Mowbray credit for having Cador at the heart of his empire.

'How are the negotiations going?' I said. 'Do I need to practise using my magickal seal yet?'

Isolde squeezed her eyes closed like she was trying to squeeze away a headache. She blinked and tried to focus on me as if I was a real person and not a decorative ornament.

'Would you like me to get you some tea?' I asked. 'It's been a long day already and it's only just after lunch. Longer for you than most, I think.'

'That would be very kind. Thank you.'

I rang the kitchens and moved to a different chair so that I was a bit closer to her and my laptop wouldn't be in the way. The servants must be on stand-by for refreshments because a young boy appeared with a tray before I'd finished asking a question about Isolde's Goddess braid. Hers was tightly pulled in and I wouldn't be surprised if it was making her headache worse.

I poured the tea and said, 'Will they go back to the table after dinner if there's been no progress?'

'I doubt it,' said Isolde. 'Brook and Cador might burn the midnight oil on the legal language, but not the others.'

'So it's going well?'

She summoned a smile. 'You're persistent, aren't you, Mina?'

'Oh yes. Conrad calls me the little itch he has to scratch.' He has never called me anything like that, believe me. I would hit him if he did.

She drank half a cup of tea and relaxed slightly. 'Thank you. That's good. Alys won't have proper tea in the little sitting room. It's herbal tea or that rocket fuel coffee. Raven's on the coffee, so Cordy and I missed out.'

'You call her Cordy and you still live? Rick told us to avoid it at all costs.'

'I wish those two would grow up. She prefers Cordy but won't let Rick use it, so he warns everyone off.' She shrugged it off and finished her tea. I poured some more.

She stood up for a second to rearrange her robes and do something with that rope belt. When she re-tied the knot, the scar on my arm throbbed. She'd just used magick for some reason. I wonder why. When she sat down, she leaned back and relaxed a bit more. 'Mowbray wouldn't have suggested the conference if he wasn't ready to concede the main point. When they started this morning, Cador tabled a simple statement: If the Daughters voted for Mowbray, he would commit to issuing a completely new gender-neutral Deed. According to Brook, Cador actually said, "You can be home for tea if you want." If only.'

'I take it your party wanted something else.'

'Have you done any formal negotiating?'

I had a choice. I could talk about negotiating with the Inland Revenue, but I am well aware that other people's opinions of accountants does not reflect the years of sacrifice we put in to achieve our skills. I studied as long as a doctor to qualify, but what credit do I get? If I was going to win Isolde over, I had to trade weaknesses.

'I watched my lawyer negotiating with the CPS for a plea bargain. Does that count?'

'You don't mind talking about it?'

I don't shrug much. I had no idea about that until Conrad pointed it out to me. Shrugging is one of his many little obsessions, like the weather forecast. He is a man and has time for such things, of course. Instead of shrugging, he says I nod or shake my head. I would say that instead of nodding, he shrugs. Having thought about it, I gave Isolde a shrug.

'It's part of who I am, Isolde. Have you met the Constable?'

'No. She famously never leaves London.'

An interesting comment. I filed it away for later. 'Hannah doesn't hide the damage to her head, really. She could wear a proper wig if she wanted to, but she doesn't. She wears a headscarf or that red monstrosity that scares me more than her magickal power does.'

'Is it really that bad?'

'Oh yes. Her wounds are there, but she doesn't talk about them. It's the same with me and prison. The only difference is that I had a choice about going into money-laundering. Not much of one, but it was a choice.'

She nodded, digesting what I'd said. 'In that case, you'll know that it's how you play your hand that counts. I can tell you what Brook said, but I can't tell you what was important to us.'

'I know about bluffing and expectations. I play bridge, Isolde.'

'Really? So does Hedda – the Eldest Daughter. You must tell her. Anyway, this is what happened. Cador's proposal would have left everything in the Deed untouched, including the Restoration language. Brook said that it was an ideal opportunity to clear up some other areas. The distribution of votes, for example, and don't ask me to explain *why* there are twenty-seven electors or who decides where they're from, okay?'

'That sounds complicated.'

'It is. Perhaps too complicated for this conference. Brook also asked for an end to spousal titles.'

'You've lost me.'

'In the mundane nobility, the wife of a man with a title gets a spousal title – Duchess of Cambridge, for example. The next time Sir Mick Jagger gets married, his wife will be Lady Jagger. Doesn't work for men, though. Sir Elton John's husband doesn't get one, nor did Prince Philip. When his wife became Queen, they had to pass an act of parliament to make him Prince Consort.'

'I see. I can't say I've given it much thought. When I was little, I always wanted to be a princess in my own right, not because I'd married a prince.'

'Right.' She looked a little alarmed at that. I smiled and said nothing. 'Well, in the world of magick, there are no spousal titles.' She gave me a very sad smile. 'Even if I hadn't divorced him, I wouldn't be Lady Mowbray. There's an anomaly, though. If Mowbray becomes staff king of Wessex and marries Kerenza, she will be the staff queen.'

'You're right, Isolde, that shouldn't happen. It seems perfectly reasonable to me.'

'It is perfectly reasonable. You know it, I know it, and so does Cador. Unfortunately he has his own perfectly reasonable suggestions, too.'

'Aah. What are they?'

'He wants the right to move the staff king's place of power from Old Sarum.'

I am not a walking atlas, unlike some people. 'Where is that?'

'Near Salisbury, in Wiltshire. It's where the election has to be held, if there is one. Mowbray has a place in Wiltshire called Ethandun and we think he'd like to move it there. He's one of the few people in the world who could actually do that.'

'I take it he needs to do more than call in the removal men and redecorate.'

She looked at me as if I were stupid, then she remembered I'm not a Mage. 'The place of power – Locus Lucis if you prefer – is at the centre of a web of Ley lines. It's like, I don't know, moving Heathrow airport to Essex.'

'I see. I think.'

Isolde wasn't finished. 'There were a few other things. Brook wants to limit the staff king's power, for one. We all know that Mowbray won't appoint the Duke of Albion as Regent, so that could cause real problems.'

She tilted her head. 'I'm surprised that the Constable hasn't had something to say about this. Or Judge Bracewell.'

'I'm sure they have, but not to me. Or Conrad. They may have spoken to your bosses.'

'The Sisters of the Eldest – that's our council – are not our bosses. They are our elders.'

120

She'd just given me an easy catch. I grabbed it and said, 'And you are a good Daughter.'

She looked away. 'Unlike my actual daughter, you mean. I'm sorry you had to see that.'

'How very English of you, Isolde. We can all see the hurt on your face, we can all feel your pain. It's you that should be upset, but instead you apologise. Surely Eseld's father doesn't encourage her to behave like this or wear fancy dress outfits?'

'To be fair, he doesn't encourage her. He pushed Cador to keep in touch, but Eseld ...'

'Is that the only reason you came? To see her?'

'Yes.'

'Is there anything we can do to help? It's not fair. It's wrong, Isolde.'

'You don't know what happened.'

'It was fifteen years ago! She needs to move on for her own sake. I should know.'

Isolde shook her head. It could have meant a number of things. She might have been about to ask me about my mother or she might not. She decided to drop another hint instead.

'As for the outfits she wears, it started when she met Raven and ...' She heard a noise and turned round. Someone was coming downstairs – Cordelia.

Cordy came over and said, 'Do you want to take a rest, Isolde?'

'I think I will,' said Isolde, standing up. I did the same. 'Mina, will you do me a favour?'

'Of course.'

'Ask Lena not to put me near my daughter at dinner tonight.' She looked at the staircase and then the door. 'I won't rest, I'll go for a walk. The pre-conference letter said that we were free to wander anywhere on the grounds.'

She left through the main doors and Cordelia took her place. 'Is that tea fresh?'

'I'll get some more.'

The tea arrived with Saffron, and we sat down. I'm afraid that the conversation moved on to men at that point, specifically Rick and his shortcomings as a husband. You don't need to know about those.

It went very quiet when Conrad emerged from his slumber, and I left him to it. It had been a long day for me, too.

I was coming out of the bathroom when Saffron appeared. 'Are you going to sleep?' she asked.

'No. Just a lie-down and a break from being on duty. I may give Vicky a call.'

'Good idea.' She hesitated with her hand on the bathroom door. 'Did you learn anything? I know you haven't had a chance to tell Conrad yet...'

'We are a team, Saffron, and I won't tell him anything until you're there, too. That's simply because I don't want to repeat myself.'

She smiled and opened the bathroom door. I did ring Vicky, but only after I'd spoken to Myvvy about the Bollywood party. I don't want Saffron to think that I'm completely shallow.

17 – Eavesdropping

Mina whispered that she'd tell me later about her encounter with Isolde, then she wandered upstairs. Saffron followed me outside and stood away from the smoking shelter.

'I've updated the Boss,' she said.

'Thanks. Did she have anything to say?'

She frowned. 'Not really. It was almost as if she already knew what was happening.'

'Don't look at me, Saff. I haven't spoken to her since the last conference call, and you were in on that. If she's got a spy in camp, it's not me, or Mina.'

'Right. I'll see you later.'

That was interesting. I mulled it over and went back to keep watch. Scout had been asleep with me upstairs and nipped out for a leak. I found him making friends with Cordelia and Lena.

'You take him for a walk,' said Cordelia. 'I'll mind the shop.'

'I'm tempted. I could do with a stretch myself, but something would happen the minute I got to the dock.'

'Can I take him?'

'Be my guest. Scout? Be nice to Cordelia, okay?'

He barked and bounced up and down, backing towards the doors until Cordelia followed him and they left.

Lena switched to German and asked me how I was.

'All good. Is Ethan learning your language?'

'He's trying. He was doing really well until his father got sick at the end. Don't worry, I'll make sure he keeps up.'

'So there *is* someone at Pellacombe who speaks German.'

She shook her head. 'No. Ethan is not of Pellacombe. He is Kellysporth. It matters. He may be here now, and he may be wearing the blue, but he is Ethan Mowbray of Kellysporth.'

'Why did you take the Steward's job, if you don't mind me asking?'

'I made him let me. They desperately needed someone they could trust after the last one retired. He said it was beneath me. You know he is a big Mage, yes? Much bigger than me.'

'So I hear. I can't tell.'

She nodded. 'I grew up in a …'

'Sorry, I don't understand.'

'Nunnery orphanage,' she said in English, before switching back to German. 'My parents gave me up when I was little. They didn't know for certain that I'd be a Mage, but they knew there was a good chance.'

'Were you still in the convent when…?'

She shook her head violently. Her jaw flexed and her braid flew around. 'It was not like *Sound of Music*. I was not a nun. I refused to take the vows. I was working as a nurse in their infirmary. Paid. Professional. Mowbray and Ethan came to the valley to do work on the Ley lines and that's how we met. They were there for two weeks. When Ethan asked me to visit him, I came here on my own.'

I got the message. She didn't need rescuing. She wasn't the magickal equivalent of a Thai bride.

She breathed out and smiled. 'Kellysporth is not as big as Pellacombe, but it is still big. The estate is larger, even. I took this job to learn about what I need to do. Thank you for listening, and listening in German.'

That smile. It would brighten up a whole valley. The room was a lot dimmer when she headed off to the kitchens, and nothing of any significance happened between then and 18:30 when we all gathered for the Opening of the Doors (which was a bit of a non-event).

The last to arrive were Lena and Mina. They'd clearly been talking about something, and I found out what when we adjourned to the King's Watch suite. Mina said that she'd been asking Lena about the seating arrangements, and then she went on to tell us about her chat with Isolde. Saff and I looked at each other.

'There's definitely a spy in the camp,' I said.

'And my money is on Síona,' said Saffron.

'Why?' said Mina.

'She lives within walking distance of the Boss, that's why.'

'And she has to think about the whole country, not just the South West,' I added. 'Interesting. Does that make a difference?'

'To history, yes,' said Mina. 'To us, probably not. Hedda, the Eldest Daughter, will have to agree, and we have no idea what her agenda might be.'

'Good. What did Lena say when you asked her to keep Isolde and Eseld apart?' I asked Mina.

'She'd already had the same request from Eseld. Except Eseld expressed it via text and as an order. Did you get anything out of Lena?'

'Not really. I scraped away a layer or two, but that's all. Her loyalty is definitely to Ethan rather than Lord Mowbray, though. I think we guessed that already. I wonder what Eseld will wear for dinner tonight?'

'We'll find out in half an hour. Do you need a shower, Saffron?'

'If you don't mind. I'm getting used to combat uniform, but it's still a sweat box.'

It was a beautiful evening and we were shown to the best place to enjoy it: the main terrace outside the ballroom / dining room, next to the gardens and with the best views of the river. The Mowbrays (except Eseld) were there first, and when Lena detached herself from Ethan to talk to Mina, I dived in for my first conversation with the enigmatic lord of Kellysporth.

'How did it go this afternoon?'

Lena had carefully listed tonight's meal as an *informal dinner*, so Ethan was wearing a shirt and chinos. Unlike last night, he'd made the effort to sport some Mowbray blue in a silk handkerchief sticking out of the shirt pocket.

'Not bad. Have you heard about the queen issue?'

'It was mentioned.'

He grunted. 'They see it as part of gender neutrality. We don't. It's a good job that Hannah Rothman is quite young. If it was any other Constable, there might be some issues about who's responsible for criminal justice. I think they'll have a huge row about it tonight. Hopefully they'll be willing to negotiate tomorrow.'

Lena brought me a glass of sparkling wine from the Mowbray vineyard in Dorset. 'It's getting better,' she said. 'In a few years it might be worth taking to market. Right now, we keep it in the family.'

I took my glass and soaked up the view. On a night like this, any wine would taste good. I turned round when Scout barked at the new arrivals. Eseld appeared from one direction as the Daughters came from another, and Eseld headed straight for me. That way, she wouldn't have to greet her guests.

I think someone had read the riot act to her about the dress code. Tonight's outfit was a simple blood-red blouse and black jeans. The Daughters were all in their robes.

'By the gods, I wish I was out riding,' she said. 'Are you as bored as I am?'

'I'm used to it. I'd rather be bored here than bored in Camp Bastion.'

'Eh?'

'Afghanistan. Have you forgotten about it already?'

'How can I forget something I never knew. Were you there a lot?'

'Years. I survived, give or take the odd rebuilt leg. Thanks for the ride this morning. It set me up nicely.'

'And me. Same again tomorrow?'

'Do any of the Daughters want to join us?'

'You must be joking. That's too much like fun for them.'

I sipped my drink. Lena was right, once the chill was off, it wasn't wonderful. 'Was it really so tedious in there?' I asked.

'It's so slooooow! Every time they wanted to discuss something, they insist on going into conclave. I had to download a new game to stop me going mad. Ethan's told me not to say anything at all about the talks, so don't ask. How's Scout?'

'He detected a Ward on Lord Mowbray's study, and I felt it.'

The petulant overgrown teenager was gone in a blink. 'That's excellent. That's about what I'd expect for his age. Try to go to more places with magick and explore together before he matures completely. You haven't got long.' She tipped her wine over the balustrade on to the path below. 'Get us a beer, would you?'

I swapped our glasses for two bottles of Mowbray's Kernow Blonde. Their beer is a lot better than their wine. I gave Eseld her beer and a cigarette. Once we'd lit up, I knew that no one would approach us.

I stared at Isolde's back. She was talking to Cador and had deliberately turned away from Eseld. It was time to stir the pot. 'What did she do that was so bad?'

The pot refused to be stirred. 'Why? Does it upset you that a daughter won't speak to her mother?'

'I was in the chopper while you humiliated her this morning. It's upset Mina and Saffron. I can't speak for anyone else.'

'They'll get over it and no one else cares. Are you riding tomorrow or not?'

'It'll wake me up.'

'See you at six-thirty, then. Thanks for the smoke.'

She picked the right moment to detach Saffron from Síona and took my partner away from the crowd. I took her place and asked Síona whether she wanted another drink.

'You've switched to beer. Wise man. I'll take anything except that gnat's piss they call wine.'

And Hannah said she found Síona a bit ascetic????

I fetched her a Pimm's and took a grateful swallow of my beer. Close up, I could see that Síona was both older and younger than I'd thought. Older in that she had done absolutely nothing to hide the ageing process: no makeup, no hair colour, no nail polish. Younger in that she really was younger than I'd thought. No more than sixty, I reckon. When she turned to the side, I got a glint in her eye. Aah. Contact lenses.

I remembered Michael's comment about Witches' hearing and lowered my voice. 'Saffron spoke to the Constable this afternoon. She seemed happy enough with your progress.'

She blinked. 'I have no idea what you mean.'

I said nothing.

She sighed. 'Is it that obvious?'

'To us, yes, but not to the Mowbrays. They have no idea. Neither do Isolde or Cordelia.'

'Good. Let's change the subject.'

'Do you know what happened to Eseld and her mother?'

'No, and no one's talking about it, either. I know it was something to do with Raven, because Hedda was thinking about chucking her out.'

'Really?'

'Yes. One of my roles is to listen to the Eldest. I have no stake in Glastonbury politics, so it's good for her to have a sounding board outside the Homewood. I hadn't been in the role long when she said that Raven had been involved in something. She wouldn't tell me the details and she decided to take no action. Would you mind if I asked you a personal question?'

'You can ask…'

'About that Dragon.'

So, not personal at all. Having given a seminar on Dragonslaying, I couldn't refuse now, could I? She did seem genuinely interested and it wasn't just to change the subject.

Síona was standing quite close to the sliding doors that led to the dining room, and while I was telling my tale, I could see movement inside. Ethan and Lena appeared to be having a domestic of some sort, standing either side of the dining table. No one else could see it and no one could hear them. It ended when Lena gave a monumental shrug, lifting her arms in surrender. She swapped two place cards and came out to announce that dinner was ready.

I'd made a mental note of the places she'd exchanged, and the net result of her work was that Eseld ended up next to Cordelia instead of Saffron. What was that all about?

If you've wondered what Witches eat, particularly the Daughters, the answer is anything sustainable. Very few Mages are vegetarians, for some reason. Way below the mundane population. When it comes to Witches and Warlocks, they often insist on sustainable, organic produce, and tonight's feast was almost all from the Mowbray farms or locally caught fish. There was a distinct Austrian flavour to the meal and it was all placed on the table for us to help ourselves.

I've told you that because you might be interested, and it puts off me having to tell you who Lena had placed me next to.

It was Raven.

And she was charming. Every time I asked her something about herself, or the Daughters, she neatly deflected me and asked something about helicopters, or Scout, or the RAF or anything. The only topic she opened up about was Spain. Yes, really. She'd done an exchange with a coven in Catalonia when she was younger and waxed lyrical about Spanish food, the climate and lifestyle.

No one lingered over coffee and I soon found myself down on the dock with Scout and Mina. At the last minute, Saffron had attached herself to us. I waited until we were leaning on the rail and said, 'What's up, Saff?'

'Eseld hit on me before dinner.'

'Nooo!' said Mina. 'I got that one wrong.'

'Did you say anything?' I said.

'Course not! Why?'

'Because Ethan made Lena swap the places. You were originally supposed to be next to her.'

'Are you sure?' said Mina. She said it to Saff, not me.

'I know when I'm being hit on, thank you very much. No one's run their hand down my waist like that in a long time, and she wasn't checking out my magickal potential.'

'What did you do?'

'I squeezed one of the pressure points on her wrist. She got the message.'

We swapped notes on the evening. They were both intrigued by the thought that Raven was involved in Eseld's sudden departure from Glastonbury. Mina was furious about what Eseld had said about her mother, and there wasn't a lot else. I think the principals in the negotiations were too tired to gossip much, but Saffron did have a couple of tidbits.

'I heard Alys talking to Isolde at one point. They were discussing who would go to the Election in Old Sarum and who would go to the celebration banquet afterwards. They had no idea I was listening.'

'So they expect to strike a deal. I'm glad I only had one beer. Let's go to bed. Some of us have to be up very early.'

Saffron stiffened. 'You're not going riding again, are you?'

'Yes. I enjoy it.'

'Will you say anything to Eseld?'

'No. You can look after yourself. I would like to know if she tries again, though.'

She nodded and I whistled softly to summon Scout.

Mina heard me return to the King's Watch suite the next morning and appeared from our room. Saffron was already lounging on the sofa, looking hungry.

'Is your virtue intact?' said Mina. 'No attempts to seduce you in the loose box?'

There hadn't been, as it happened, so I didn't have to lie or look embarrassed. 'No. She was the model Mage this morning, and arranged some exercises to test Scout's ability to spot Wards and Glamours, and for me to sense that he'd spotted them.' I started moving equipment around. 'It was quite sad at the end. She said how much she was looking forward to us meeting her father, like we were her new best friends.'

Mina shook her head. 'I wonder how many men *or* women she's met who treat her like a normal human being. I have to keep reminding myself that she's four years older than me and not Saffron's age.'

'Oy!' said Saffron. 'I am here you know. Why is breakfast in the dining room today?'

I finished putting my stuff together and answered her question. 'Lena thought, quite rightly, that it would be very bad form for the Watch to eat with the family, so we're all in it together. It's good to mingle.'

And mingle we did. Up to a point. I noticed that Brook and Cador were eating together and that they'd chosen a distant corner of the vast space to do it in.

'Looks promising,' I said to Cordelia.

'Mmm. Don't go for a long walk this morning. I think you could be in business.'

She was right. At half past ten, (metaphorical) white smoke appeared and the doors were opened. The Daughters and the Mowbrays had reached an agreement. It was time to collect the VIPs, starting with our absent host.

18 – Lord of All he Surveys

Most people who visit the Isles of Scilly begin their journey at Land's End Airport. I've never been before, and when I looked it up I was quite impressed. Two runways. Don't often get that. But we weren't heading for the runways.

I took the Smurf along the coast so that Saffron (and I) could see Land's End from the air. 'Is that it?' she said when I told her to look for the car park. For such a famous landmark, it's otherwise very hard to spot.

'What did you expect?'

'I dunno. Something bigger and pointier.'

'Tough crowd. I'm going to make a tight turn. When we're heading south west, you can contact ATC for landing.'

Saffron is very keen to learn. She has the radio off pat now, and she's also asking questions about what some of the instruments mean. She even has a sixth sense about when not to speak. She got us clearance to land at one of the off-runway zones, and I took the Smurf down to a spot close to an access road and well away from the terminal building.

A black Range Rover bumped through a gate and pulled up as we got out of the chopper. 'It's not blue,' said Saffron. 'This is a first.'

'Check out the rear bumper. It has a boar's head sticker, along with a black and white Kernow badge.'

She peered. 'Can you really see that from here?'

'Yes.'

We walked over and a woman with a runner's physique got out of the driver's side, somewhere between me and my mother in age. She was wearing black trousers, black trainers and a blue blouse with the boar's head on her left breast. Her hair was black with grey streaks, worn short and styled. She's been driving the Mowbrays around for many years, going ahead of them to various jobs while they take the chopper.

She gave us a big smile. 'You must be Mr Clarke and Miss Hawkins.'

I shook hands. 'Either that or we've just stolen Lord Mowbray's helicopter. How d'you do.'

She looked alarmed and peered at the Smurf in case it cried for help after being kidnapped. 'Sorry. I'm Maggie Pearce. I'm afraid there's a bit of a flap on. Kenver has gone missing.' She saw the alarm in my eyes. 'Oh no, he's alright, but he's not where he should be. If you see what I mean. No, you don't. Could you get in the car and I'll take you to Lord Mowbray?'

It was the biggest model of Range Rover, with seven seats. Saff and I strapped ourselves in and Maggie drove off the airfield. Behind us, an automatic barrier rose back in place. 'Lord Mowbray had to pay for that himself,' she said.

She drove with meticulous precision around the perimeter of the airfield, always at 95% of the speed limit or less, and pulled up next to the offices of a very small airline. 'Lord Mowbray's in the conference room. Could you come with me, Miss Hawkins? We need to collect the others. I'm afraid that things are all at sixes and sevens this morning.'

Saff and I looked at each other. Clearly Mowbray wanted a word with me on my own. She nodded to show she'd got the same message, and I jumped out.

There was no one on duty outside the conference room, so I knocked and entered.

My first thought was *so that's where she gets it from*. Arthur, Lord Mowbray of Pellacombe, was wearing a black frock coat over a black and white waistcoat. It didn't have the eighteenth century flair of Eseld's outfits, but it was definitely the mark of someone who wants to be noticed. He stood up and came to shake hands.

Underneath the outfit, he was wiry, strong and had the piercing blue eyes he'd passed to his children. His hair was all grey and cut so short that he'd get in the US Army with no problem. Years of outdoor living had lined his face and if they were casting for a film about the Peninsular War, he'd be a shoo-in for a battle-hardened British officer who'd fought his way through Spain.

'Clarke. Good to meet you,' he said. His words were clipped, the Cornish *r* in *Clarke* was unmissable. Eseld had it, too, but not Cador. He probably left it in his rooms at Cambridge. 'Sorry about the mess this morning. Coffee?'

'Please. What's happened?'

He poured coffee from a flask and we sat down. When he spoke, he looked at the window. 'My boy Kenver went out last night and never came back. Didn't know until this morning. Cue panic. Then he texts to say he'll get to Pellacombe under his own steam if there's a deal done.' He turned his coffee cup round and looked at me properly.

'Are you worried?'

'No. It was his text all right. We have a code that only he and I know, and he's not in danger. Kerenza insisted on staying at Nanquidno in case he turned up. It's not far, so they won't be long. If she's finished packing.'

He sat back. 'Wanted to thank you properly for all this, Clarke. What you've done means a lot down here.'

'It's been fascinating, sir. We've enjoyed it.'

'No need for the *sir*. Eseld tells me you're a Geomancer like me.'

'In that same way that I also play cricket but I wouldn't say that to the England captain. I know my limits. I also know Chris Kelly.'

'Good man, Chris. Kenver's going to study with him in the autumn.'

131

I made sure he was looking at me before I said, 'And did you know Isaac Fisher, aka Ivan Rybakov?'

'Yes. By reputation, of course, but we didn't move in the same circles. I've heard you've got a problem with the Fae.'

We have. One of the reasons I've enjoyed this jaunt is that it has no connection with our search for the *Codex Defanatus*, a book full of powerful, old magick. It's on the loose, and some of it had come into Isaac Fisher's possession, with fatal consequences for several people, including him. At the source of this poisonous well is a Fae Prince.

'How did you hear that?' I said.

'My uncle was approached, many years ago, by an intermediary trying to sell some of the things that have turned up recently. Helen of Troy. The Lions of Carthage. They must have come from the same place. I was still on the way up in those days. They didn't approach me, and my uncle said no to them.'

'That's the late Earl of Tintagel?'

'He's the only Mage uncle I've got. Or had.' We were leaning closer to each other. Just a fraction. 'I ain't a Clarke. My word isn't binding unto death, like yours is, but I promise you on the stones of Pellacombe that I had nothing to do with it and that the Earl never told me who it was who approached him.'

I nodded to show that I accepted his word. 'Do you know of anyone else who was approached?'

'No. This is bad, isn't it?'

'Yes. We think it will get worse.'

He rubbed his face. 'I'm telling you this now because I wanted to see you in action first. What I reckon is that the Fae didn't approach the really big players at the time, just the ones who were willing to take risks to get ahead. I know a few people he might have gone to. Now that I know for certain there's a problem, I'll ask a few questions.'

'Thank you. That would be useful. It could also be dangerous.'

'Not as dangerous as a Dragon. It's the least that I can do.'

'Then thank you again.'

'I also hear you're a smoker. Shall we take a refill into the sunshine and wait?'

'Suits me.'

When we got outside, he said, 'I know you won't tell me anything about the Daughters, but how did Team Pellacombe get on?'

'Like a well-oiled machine. I'm sure you knew they would.'

'Even Eseld?'

'What do you want me to say? We've only just met.'

He nodded. 'You're right. It's not fair to drag you into my family's problems. I tried to tell Isolde not to come, but she's still as stubborn as she always was. That's where Eseld gets it from. I could have told my ex that there wouldn't be a happy reunion.'

I'm guessing that Eseld gets her stubbornness from her father more than her mother, but it's not for me to say. And having refused to get drawn in, I couldn't very well ask what had happened all those years ago. Mina would have handled this conversation a lot better than I did. Sorry, but there you go.

'Thank you for the loan of Evenstar. She's a superb mare.'

'Pleasure. I don't get to ride as much as I'd like. More's the pity. I'm looking forward to meeting the Peculier Auditor. She's made quite an impression.'

'Is that because she's young? Short? Indian? Mundane?'

He laughed. 'All of the above. Plus she said that Cornwall is too hilly for cricket. Anyone who can say that and get away with it must have something.'

'She certainly has something.'

'She also has the new Seal of Wessex. Cost me a fortune that, and I may not get my money back.'

'I thought it was the seal of the Cloister Court.'

He shook his head. 'It is at the moment. The new staff king will then have to pay to get the head changed. The magick is all in the body.' He looked around. 'Where are they? Even Maggie couldn't take this long.'

'Shall I call Saffron?'

'No. Here they come.'

The Range Rover drew up. Behind it was a smaller 4x4. 'Who's that?' I said.

'It's not a *who*, it's a *what*. That's the luggage. Kerenza doesn't travel light.'

Saffron got out of the car, followed by an eight year old girl and the girl's mother, Kerenza. If you do your research online, Kerenza will get you a lot more hits than Lord Mowbray. She is a Mage, in a small way, but she earned her money and her reputation as a model and actress. She's fifteen years younger than Mowbray and she'll stand out in the family photographs for being taller than all of them and blonde. She put on a radiant smile and came to wow me.

Kerenza doesn't just have a model figure, she has even, symmetrical features, wide blue eyes and poise. She must have tact and charm, too, because Leah said that she's quite popular in Pellacombe.

'I'm so sorry for all this,' she said. 'Cador text me to say that Eseld has gone to get changed and won't say what she's wearing for the ceremony. I had to pack some extra things in case.'

'Did that include your pirate outfit?' I said.

Mowbray swore under his breath so that his soon-to-be stepdaughter didn't hear. 'Eseld won't be wearing that again,' he muttered. 'Let's get going.'

Rather than force the women to rearrange themselves in the Range Rover, Mowbray got into the Suzuki and I joined him. 'Does Maggie always drive like that?' I asked as we made a stately procession around the lanes.

'Safe and Steady Maggie we call her. There's a reason her daughter gave birth in a layby.'

There was a lot of milling about at the airfield. Saffron whispered, 'Did Mowbray offer you refreshment?'

'Yes. Coffee. Why?'

'Kerenza made us try some of Maggie's flapjack.' She shuddered. 'I've brought some in case we need to create an emergency landing zone.'

I went to supervise the loading and I was joined by Kerenza's little girl, Grace. She's eight years old and looks set to take after her mother in looks, if not in temperament. She seemed painfully quiet at first until I asked if she liked flying in the Smurf.

She giggled and put her hand to her mouth. 'You're not allowed to call it that. Leah said it was a secret name. Mowbray doesn't like it.'

At great risk of pain, I squatted down to her level and said, 'We'll call him Smurf if we want to. We can call Mowbray *Arthur* if you want.'

She thought that was really naughty. 'And you can call me *Izzi*.'

'And why would I do that?'

'Because it's my name. Isolde. Mummy said I had to use my middle name when she met ARTHUR. She said there were too many Isoldes already, but Granny still calls me that, and so does my friend from my old school.'

Poor kid. Her home was London until she was whisked away to Cornwall, and as well as Granny, her school, her friends and her father, she'd even had to give up her name. Not that her father had been around much.

'What do you like best about Pellacombe?' I said.

'The horses. I'm getting a pony after today.'

'I love horses, too. I was riding Evenstar this morning.'

'She's soooo beautiful. I wish I was big enough to ride her. Mowbray says she might have a foal, and if she does, it's going to be mine as well.'

I'd made sure to squat down near the rear wheels so that I had something to hold on to when I got up.

'What's wrong with your leg?' said Grace/Izzi. She's too young for the truth, so I said that I'd had an accident. I peered into the hold and moved a hat box. A hat box? Really? Whatever. At that moment my phone rang and I took the call that was going to change everything for everyone.

'Hello Michael.'

'Can you talk, sir?' He was breathing heavily and I could hear outdoor noises in the background.

'Yes. We haven't set off yet. What's up?'

'I'm up top at Lamorne, and Kenver's just turned up. He's got Morwenna with him.'

'What! Are you sure?'

'He introduced her. I'm on my way down to get the buggy. I don't have anyone's number except yours. Could you tell Lord Mowbray?'

'Of course.'

He disconnected. Grace was still there, staring at me with a frown. 'Go and get Arthur,' I said. 'Tell him it's very, very important.'

She ran round and stuck her head in the cabin. Mowbray jumped down and came round to the back.

'Is there a problem with the Falcon?'

Falcon? Is that what he calls the chopper? Give me *Smurf* any day.

'No. I've just had a call from Michael. He says that Kenver has turned up with his sister.'

He looked at me with utter incredulity. 'Morwenna? Here?'

'So he says. Michael's organising the ferry for them right now. I thought you'd want to know before we got in the air.'

'Too bloody right I do.'

He took out his phone and stared at the screen then made his mind up. He jabbed a Contact and put the phone to his ear. Meanwhile, we'd forgotten Grace, who'd heard Mowbray say Morwenna's name and had run to tell her mother.

Kerenza marched up and said, 'Is it true?'

Mowbray held up his hand to silence her as his call connected. 'Ethan, I've just heard that Morwenna's crossing the river with Kenver. Get down to the dock and head them off … Yes, really. Morwenna. If it's not her, deal with it. If it is her, get them into the boathouse until I get back … I don't care, just do it … We're ready to leave now.'

He terminated the call and started to move. Kerenza grabbed his arm. 'Not now,' he said. He didn't move or try to unhook her hand, he just waited.

She took one look at his face and stepped back. 'Come on Grace,' said Kerenza. 'Time to fly.'

It was. Saff had followed to see what the fuss was about and heard everything. I made a zip-it sign over my lips and waggled my phone at her.

We flew back to Pellacombe with only helicopter related conversation in the front. In the back, they were completely silent because if they put the headsets on, we could hear them. What they couldn't do was see what Saff was doing with her hands. She was busy texting.

If you're wondering where Scout is in all this, he didn't come. When we'd started preflight checks, he'd whined and I got a sharp pain in my ears. We'd proved he *could* fly if necessary, so I sent him back to the ferry with Mina, and she can take over again.

19 – Homing Instinct

When Saffron messaged me, I was playing a game outside with Scout. Not that trying to stop him digging holes in Lord Mowbray's meticulous borders is much of a game.

It did have the advantage of distracting me, because I was very nervous. These nerves were not because Conrad was flying a helicopter, though that did not help. These nerves were because of the magickal seal sitting like a bomb in the ballroom. While Conrad was off riding this morning, Saffron had helped me open the box and take out the seal. My arm throbbed when I picked it up and it became very warm in my hands. Other than that, nothing.

Saffron had said that she was pleased. It was now bonded to me. It's all very well for her. She does not have to stick it on a crucial document and hope it works.

My phone pinged, and I had to read the message twice.

Saffron: *Morwenna Mowbray crossing the river with Kenver. CC says get down to the dock with Ethan.*

Morwenna? Who? Aah. The missing daughter. I replied *On it* and shouted, 'Scout! Find Ethan.' And then I ran down to the dock as fast as my sandals would let me. I made it just in time.

Ethan was already at the start of the pier, hands on his hips and breathing hard. Scout skidded to a halt on the dock and barked loudly to let me know that he had, indeed, found Ethan. The ferry was just coming up to the pier, and I could make out two young figures at the front. They turned away before I could get a proper look at them.

Ethan had been ignoring Scout and he only turned round when he heard me arrive. 'What are you doing here?' he said.

With any other Mowbray, that would be rude; with Ethan, that's what you get. Before I could answer, he said, 'This is family business.'

I nodded. 'And if she comes ashore, it is also King's Watch business. The agreement clearly lists members of the family present, and I'm afraid that Miss Morwenna is not on the list.' I nodded again, just to make the point.

Ethan blinked. 'Mowbray told me to keep her in the boathouse until he gets back. He won't be long.'

'And if she stays in the boathouse, that's not a problem. No matter what happens when her father gets here, she can't go up to the house without the Daughters' approval.'

Ethan was clearly not used to being told that what happened on the Mowbrays' property was anyone's business but theirs. I had told him, and if he had a problem, it was his problem, not mine. I turned to face the young couple coming down the pier.

I have got so used to seeing the Mowbrays – Lord M, Ethan, Cador, Eseld and the portraits in the hall – that I couldn't believe that these children were from the same stock. Perhaps if there were a picture of Aisling on display, it would make more sense.

The only way that I can describe Kenver Mowbray is *weedy*. He was gangly, thin and looked like he spent way too much time indoors. He was the whitest person on the whole estate, the Ferrymistress's older daughter notwithstanding. He also looked very nervous. As well he might.

His sister was just as pale of skin, but you didn't notice that because of her mane of barely tamed wild red hair. Together with the killer cheekbones, you had a very striking young woman in her mid twenties. She was wearing a red maxi dress and a denim jacket. A heavy looking canvas bag was slung over her shoulder.

They walked towards us uncertainly, Morwenna a step ahead of Kenver. She stopped about ten feet away and spoke. 'Been a long time, Uncle Ethan.' She turned to me and frowned. 'Sorry, are you Lena?'

I was so busy getting over the shock of her Irish accent that I didn't register at first what she'd done. She sees a strange Indian woman and assumes that I must be the only foreigner – Lena. All I could do was laugh.

Kenver touched her arm. 'No! Lena's ...' He was going to say *Austrian* until he realised that I could be just as Austrian as Lena. He made a quick recovery and said, 'You must be Miss Desai, the Peculier Auditor.' At least he spoke to me like I was a real person. I forgive him.

'Namaste, Mr Kenver, Miss Morwenna,' I said. When I straightened up, I realised that Ethan had run out of words *completely*. Totally dry. It was up to me to move things along, so I said, 'I'm afraid that the Watch Captain is not here yet. Perhaps you'd like to wait in the boathouse?'

'And why would I want to do that?' said Morwenna. She tossed her hair away and her eyes flickered. This was bravado. She was scared.

Ethan woke up. 'Because she asked nicely. You know your dad's not here, don't you? They were delayed, waiting for you to turn up. They're in the air now, and Mina's right – for the moment, Pellacombe is neutral ground. It would be very awkward for everyone if I let you go up to the house. The chopper will be here soon.'

That was the longest speech I've heard Ethan make in two days.

Morwenna's voice was enchanting. I've always loved an Irish accent, and she had that *seize the day* intonation that makes telling you the time sound like an invitation to dance the night away. I was falling in love with her already.

'C'mon, Kenver,' she said. 'I expected to cause a stir, but this is creeping me out, so it is.'

She gestured behind me, and I turned to see what she meant. Every member of staff in the old farmhouse had come out to look, as had many of the ones in the mansion. About forty people were staring at us. At Morwenna.

Ethan turned and marched to the boathouse door. I stood out of the way to let them pass, blocking the route away from the pier in case they changed their minds. They didn't, and followed Ethan indoors.

The boathouse is basically a huge shed, big enough to house the ferry at night and for refuelling and maintenance. There's also a boat lift to get smaller vessels out of the water and enough space to work on them.

We gathered a little way from the door, which Ethan was locking, and Morwenna found time to notice the hyperactive hound bouncing in front of her. 'Who are you, gorgeous?' she said.

I answered on his behalf. 'This is Scout, the Watch Captain's Familiar Spirit. Do you have food in your bag by any chance?'

Morwenna bent to say hello and I got the tingle in my arm that tells me magick is being used. So she really was a Mage. She'd disappeared from Pellacombe before her talents had shown. She also kept her bag well away from Scout.

I took a closer look at Kenver. The file said that he had been nominated heir to Pellacombe because he was a Geomancer like his father and because Eseld wasn't interested in becoming the big cheese in the Mowbray Creamery. I wonder how much of that is true, and if it changes now that Morwenna is both here and a Mage herself. Did Eseld really say *No thanks, I don't want to inherit a mansion and thousands of acres*? Kenver may be a first class Mage for all I know. That is not my department. I can tell you that he is a long way from being a natural leader. Even Ethan has more presence than Kenver.

Ethan had finished with the door (and finished sneaking a text on his phone). He came over slowly, and we all turned to face him. He was still breathing hard, and that wasn't from exercise. He was displaying actual emotions for once. Real ones.

'I should say something,' said Morwenna. 'If I don't answer to my name, it's because I'm not used to it. They couldn't cope with Morwenna in Galway, so I got Maeve.'

Ethan showed no signs of responding, so I filled the silence. 'Does that have one of those Irish spellings?'

'Sure it does. M-E-D-B-H.'

'You really are Morwenna, are you?' I said it with a smile, but it was the sort of question I had to ask because I'm not a Mage. Kenver looked like I'd slapped him in the face, but his sister (if she is his sister), thought it was hilarious.

She was still laughing when Ethan showed why he doesn't need to ask embarrassing questions. 'See for yourself,' he said. He raised his hands and my tattoo started crawling with magick. Morwenna changed in front of my eyes. First, her denim jacket disappeared, then her maxi dress changed from red to a green floral and the cut changed from low-waisted to high. She grew half an inch and her hair dropped and straightened. Finally, her face aged and changed from pointed to heart-shaped. I found I was holding my breath.

The woman underneath the spell smiled and lifted her skirts to do a twirl, then slashed with her hands and the magick disappeared. It was Morwenna again.

Kenver was furious. 'How dare you bring our mother in like that! You sick bastard, I'm going to...' His hand was raised and magick was on the way. I jumped between them, facing the boy and raising my finger.

'No, Kenver.' I swung round. 'Why did you do that, Ethan?' He lifted his hands in a lifeless shrug and had no words. 'You loved her, didn't you? You loved Aisling.'

'No!' said Kenver. 'How could you?'

Ethan shook his head. 'Grow up, Kenver. I was a teenager when she died. Yes, I loved her. As a mother. I didn't have one of my own. If anyone's going to get angry, it's me.'

Scout barked and ran towards the door. 'Shh, everyone,' I said. They did. 'There! Incoming Smurf alert.'

We all stared at the roof, tracking the noise of the helicopter as it came lower. The sound echoed round the boathouse and Kenver flinched as it passed overhead. In a second, it fell in pitch and started to die. They were down and safe.

'Do we just wait?' said Morwenna.

Before Ethan could answer, my phone rang. It was Saffron. I answered and couldn't hear her at first for the noise of the rotors. They quickly faded and I heard her running. 'I'm following Mowbray. Where are you?'

'In the boathouse. Where's Conrad?'

'Dealing with the Smurf. And Kerenza. He's also going to tackle the Daughters before they go apeshit ... By the Goddess, Mowbray can run ... He's on the dock now.'

I disconnected the call and said, 'Lord Mowbray is here.' We all moved towards the entrance, and Ethan made a gesture of magick. The door banged open and a man came through, black silhouette against the sunshine. He slammed the door closed behind him and he came into focus.

My first thought was a stupid one. It often is. It's a good job I know to keep my mouth closed because all I could think was *How did he run in that coat?*

His face was displaying more emotions simultaneously than Ethan or Cador have shown in two days, but it was Ethan who spoke first.

'You knew,' he said. 'You knew where she was all the blasted time, didn't you?'

'No,' said Mowbray. 'Not for years. I knew she was alive, but not where.'

'Why didn't you tell me?'

Mowbray ignored his cousin and turned to his daughter. 'Why now, Medbh? Why today?'

She was scared. The emotional temperature had gone through the roof and it didn't get any lower when Saffron banged on the door and rattled the handle. Ethan and/or Mowbray had locked her out.

'Mina! Are you okay?' she shouted.

I do not like to draw attention to myself unless it's in a good cause. I retreated into the shadows, dialling Saffron as I moved. She must have had her phone in her hand, because she answered immediately.

'We're fine. At the moment,' I said. 'What have they done with the door?'

'Activated a built-in Ward. It's way out of my league. Given enough time…'

'Fine. Stay on the line.'

The family group had quickly forgotten me and resumed their drama.

'You called her *Medbh*,' said Ethan. 'All those trips to Ireland. You've been to see her, haven't you? Is *any* of it true? What happened that night, is any of what you told me true?'

'Not now, Ethan,' said Mowbray.

'Then when would be a good time, because I can't think of a better one.'

Kenver had gone white. Even whiter, if that were possible. 'What do you mean? Of course it's true.'

Ethan held his ground, well into Mowbray's personal space. He'd also run out of words again. Mowbray took half a step towards his daughter and Ethan lifted his hand.

'Not looking good,' I whispered to Saffron.

Morwenna/Medbh reached out and touched Ethan's sleeve. 'Please. Uncle Ethan. Please. I shouldn't have come. I'll go.' Ethan lowered his hand, but he wasn't moving. She shivered and looked down. 'Tell him. They both have a right to know.'

'Are you sure?' said Mowbray.

She nodded.

Mowbray sighed heavily. 'It was mostly true, but it didn't happen in the Lab. Aisling drowned. Her own creatures did it.'

Ethan's nostrils flared. 'How?'

Morwenna made a grab for his hand and held it tight. 'He's not lying. She died saving me. I'd gone too close to the pens and fallen in. When it happened, I ran and ran. I thought it was my fault, you see? I just kept running. All night. When the sun came up, I hid. Then I ran again. A policeman found me.'

Ethan seemed to find that the most unbelievable fact of all. 'A policeman? A mundane one?'

She smiled. 'Well, it wasn't the King's Watch, was it? I said I'd run away from home and hidden on a train down from London. I gave the police Granny's number and they didn't know any better. Granny was in Britain at the time and she took a leaf out of Dad's book. She hired a helicopter and came to fetch me. The police patted themselves on the back and didn't notice that by the time I'd left, they'd forgotten all about me.'

Lord Mowbray chipped in. 'Don't forget, Ethan, we thought Medbh had been eaten alive. Aisling's mother rang me two days later, when they'd already left the country.'

'What happened to you?' said Ethan, finally talking to … Damnit. I'll call her Medbh. It suits her better.

'That really is a story for another time,' she said. 'And not here. We have an audience, Ethan, or had you forgotten?'

He turned and glanced at me. 'I hadn't forgotten. As soon as I heard that it was Saffron outside, not Conrad, I decided that now was the best time to talk.' He saw the phone in my hand and made magick towards the door. 'Tell her to come in.'

The door burst open and Saffron burst in. She ran forward and saw that I was safe, then slowed down.

'What are the Army doing here?' said Medbh.

'It's the new designer look for the King's Watch,' said Ethan. Was that a joke?

Mowbray pulled himself together. 'Where do we go from here, Hawkins?'

'I, erm, I'll call Conrad. Sir.' She fumbled with her phone for a second, then stopped when she heard a whistle from outside. Scout bounded out, suddenly happy again.

Medbh looked at her father. 'Can this guy really send me packing?'

'No. But he can pull the plug on the conference.'

'And he's not the only one,' said Ethan. 'So can Mina.'

'How come?'

Ethan smiled.

I supplied the answer. 'Because Conrad always does what I tell him, that's how come. Here he is.'

It was a big door, so for once he didn't have to duck when he came in. I stood that little bit taller. Not much, just a few millimetres. He looked at Saffron first, who nodded to show she was okay, then he looked at me. 'Everything under control?'

'I'm fine. I think they have a lot to talk about. Medbh has given them all a shock,' I said.

'Medbh?'

'A lot has changed since my daughter was last here,' said Mowbray. 'Including her name.' I was watching Kenver, and he didn't seem happy that his sister was no longer *Morwenna*. Mowbray continued, 'Have you spoken to the Daughters, Clarke?'

'I have. To say that they are surprised would be an understatement. As things stand, they are content for … your daughter and your younger son to join the party eventually. If you still want me to collect the Eldest and her colleagues, Medbh and Kenver will have to wait over the water, with the Peculier Auditor to keep an eye on them.'

Mowbray rubbed his chin. 'Let me guess. That's a take-it-or-leave-it offer.' Conrad nodded. 'Typical. Just to prove a point. Fine. I'll take it.' He turned to his children. 'If you're happy, of course.'

'As if that leaves us a choice,' said Medbh with a sigh. 'I suppose it was a bit dramatic, coming over like this. Perhaps I've got more in common with Eseld than I thought. How's she taken it, Mr Clarke, if you don't mind me asking?'

Conrad glanced at me. I know when he's laughing inside because his nostrils contract a tiny fraction. He thought all this was very funny, given what happened with Sofía last month. He put on his driest voice and said, 'Eseld doesn't know yet. She's grooming the horses. Or something. Cador took charge of keeping her out of the loop for the moment.'

'She's not that bad,' said Mowbray.

'Yes she is,' said Kenver with more sibling bitterness than I expected.

'Right,' said Mowbray. 'You two get back on the ferry and I'll go see Eseld. And Cador.'

He started moving and then Ethan spoke. 'I'm going with Kenver and Morwenna. It's not just Eseld and Cador who need to hear the whole story. As far as I'm concerned, the Agreement can go fuck itself.'

Mowbray stopped in his tracks. He opened his mouth, then closed it. He shoved his hands in the pockets of his frock coat and bounced on his feet. 'You're right. It's up to you. They may not want to talk, but I can't stop you going with them. And do you really want a complete stranger to hear what's being said?'

'If you'd been here, Mowbray, you'd know that Mina isn't a stranger.'

I wouldn't have gone that far. Nice of him to say it though.

Mowbray shrugged, and moved towards the door. Conrad came over and held out his hand to me. In the centre was an egg. A small blue egg. Don't ask me what species, because I don't care. He glanced right, then bent down and kissed me quickly on the lips. He straightened up and said, 'Raven gave me this. It's like a magickal attack alarm. If they give you any trouble, crush it and run.'

'An egg? What if I break it accidentally?'

'It's stronger than it looks. Let me.' He took my scarf, placed the egg near one end and tied a quick knot. 'There you go. And you'll have Scout.'

'Be careful in that helicopter.'

'I will.' He spent a few seconds talking to Scout, then left with Saffron.

I turned to the Mowbrays. 'Shall we go?' We walked to the pier, and everyone glanced at the buildings. The audience had all gone inside. 'It's a shame the ferry doesn't have a café,' I said. 'I don't know about you, but I could do with a cup of tea.'

'Sorted,' said Medbh. 'Not the tea, we can get that at the cottage, but I do have cake. I think we need a moment, don't you, Uncle Ethan?'

He grunted. Back to normal, then.

And while we enjoy some tea, Conrad can take over again.

20 – Yet More Sisters

The first thing I did when Saffron and I left the boathouse was to get a full report. I only asked one question. 'What did you do when you found that the door was locked?'

'I checked the walls. They're only metal. I found a place with minimal Warding and I was getting ready to blast it open when Mina called. Once I knew she was safe, I stood ready.'

'Excellent. Well done.'

She grinned. 'Thanks, sir. It means a lot that you trusted me to look after Mina.'

'As it should be, Saff. Guess whose idea it was to send them over the river with Mina.'

'Alys. Got to be.'

'Correct. And there's more. They wanted you to do the job.'

She stopped. 'Why aren't I? Doesn't this put Mina at more risk?'

'Mina can cope. She'll come over all *Rani* on them.' Saffron's eyes bulged. Wisely, she said nothing. 'Besides, I need you with me in the Smurf.'

'Is that for my skills with the radio?'

'That's a bonus. You know full well that I'd feel naked turning up to collect the country's senior Witch on my own.'

'So long as you're not actually naked, that's good.'

'Not likely to happen today. We need to get back in the air as soon as possible and get everyone together before something serious happens. Come on.'

We got up the hill as fast as I could manage. Michael's father was casting his eye over the Smurf's vital signs. He pointed to a pickup at the far edge of the lawn. Behind it was an aviation fuel bowser. 'I'll fill her up when you get back from Glastonbury,' he said. 'Saves going over to Lamorne.'

'Thank you.' His son was finishing the windows with a polishing rag. 'Michael's doing a good job there.'

'Do you think he's really cut out for the Navy, then? Big difference to life in Pellacombe.'

'Not really. He'll fit right in. Let's get going.'

While we waited for the engines to warm up, I asked Saff to check the manifest again.

'Oh. There's been an addition. Zoe is joining us. Isn't she …?'

'Alys's twin sister. Yes. She must have used Morwenna's arrival as an excuse to add one to their number. I wonder if she's as a bad a flier as her twin.'

'They're fraternal twins, so probably not. We've now got six adults, like last time, but minimal luggage. Why aren't we flying them back tonight?'

'My flying hours will be up by this evening. Mowbray offered to let them stay another night, but they preferred other arrangements. Some are going back by coach, some are visiting covens nearby.' The readout showed that everything was ready. 'Here we go.'

I landed in the same spot at Home House and the same minibus bumped over the grass. We got out and Saff muttered something about banning mobile phones to avoid embarrassing pictures. When the Daughters came to meet us, she kept her shades resolutely in place.

First was the Eldest, Hedda, accompanied by her daughter, Signe (pronounced sort of like *Seenyer*). Hedda was everything you'd expect a powerful Swedish Witch to be, but much much older. She wasn't going to bother getting changed and wore her pale yellow robes with great dignity. She carried a staff of oak and managed not to look as if she were leaning on it. Her daughter walked exactly one step behind and looked as if she'd been doing it all her life. The only surprising thing was that Signe had brown hair and brown eyes. She was about my age.

I bowed low, as did my comrades. Hedda held out a hand to be shaken, and I felt nothing of her power. That says a lot about how great it must be. I was about to say something suitable when she got in first.

'Good morning, Watch Captain. Is everything well? Good.'

She walked past me, and I motioned for Michael to help her. He'd already lowered the step and handed her on board like the young professional he is. Signe followed behind.

The other four Daughters were an assorted bunch, but none of them stood out like Raven did. For one thing, they were jostling for position. Subtly. The two with the brown cords of Oak Coven won out.

'Good morning,' said the one who got to me first. 'Where do we sit?' She hadn't offered to shake hands. Her problem.

'Good morning, ma'am. Could you identify yourselves for the manifest?'

From her reaction, you'd think I'd insulted the Goddess. She actually flinched back, and that allowed the other woman with the brown cord to take over. She offered a smile and a handshake, both of which I took.

'I'm Kiwa, 4th of Oak,' she said, and went on to introduce the others.

Kiwa, 4th of Oak (the same Coven as Hedda) is the Traveller, and her role sits awkwardly with Síona's. The Traveller visits the covens which are affiliated to Glastonbury and makes sure they're behaving themselves, whereas Síona's job is to represent their interests in Homewood. According to Rick, Kiwa gets on well with everyone. That surprised me, because if she's supposed to be an inspector of some sort, you'd have thought she'd be rather unpopular.

In person, she was in her forties or fifties and would double the non-white contingent at Pellacombe. Rick said she was born in Jamaica but grew up here. Any trace of a Caribbean accent had long gone. Her hair was in a Goddess braid, but only just.

The Witch who'd refused to shake hands with me was Georgia, 2nd of Oak and Keeper of Homewood. She was the one who'd been on duty when Raven descended from the skies and would be about sixty now. She had a round face and light brown hair. I'm sure I could detect a hint of Geordie in her voice. Her robes were immaculate and cut lower than the others at the front. I could see a heavy chain of Artefacts round her neck.

The two Daughters from Willow Coven were happy enough to shake my hand, but neither said more than hello. Zoe, 5th of Willow and the Daughters' Treasurer was very obviously Alys's sister. Her taller, thinner sister. She stood as far away from Georgia as she could.

That left one of the few Witches I've met who wears glasses. Morning, 6th of Willow, is the Dame of Homewood. That rather bizarre title means she's in charge of magickal education. I'd put her as the youngest of the four, early forties, and she matched her name – pale and intense.

When the introductions were finished, I turned and looked Georgia in the eye. 'To answer your question, ma'am, you can sit anywhere on the sides except the seat by the door.'

Saffron was making faces at me. I think she was trying to tell me that Georgia was one of the Witches who were less happy dealing with men. Georgia ignored what I'd said and ignored Michael when he offered to help her up. There was only one seat left, jammed in the corner, facing backwards and opposite Michael. It was where Raven had sat, and she'd chosen it for the legroom and filled it as if she were on a throne. Georgia huddled against the pillar and snapped at Saffron when she pointed to the seat belts.

Saff closed the doors and took out her phone. She went away from the Smurf to make a couple of calls while I got the engines going. She waited until we were in the air and protected by the roar of flight to report back.

'No answer from Mina. Probably not surprising. Lena says that it's all gone quiet now, and that Eseld didn't seem too bothered when she got back from the stables with Mowbray. I can't wait to find out what the story is with Medbh.'

When we got back to Pellacombe, Lord Mowbray was on hand to welcome the Eldest Daughter, as you'd expect, and Saff led them across the lawn to the reception committee. There were now eleven of the thirty-nine

Homewood Coven members in Pellacombe. Only one of the most senior Witches had stayed behind – Verity, First of Willow and Daughter of Memory. She is the chief priestess and leads the religious ceremonies.

I finished handing the Smurf over to Michael's father and headed straight for the dock. The return of the Smurf was the signal for Mina's party to cross back over the river. I couldn't wait to see her and hear Morwenna's story.

Sorry. I mean *Medbh's* story.

21 – Out of this World

The Ferrymistress delegated her older daughter to drive us up the hill in the buggy and to make the tea. I was dying to have a look in the gorgeous little cottage, but she showed us to the garden instead and rejected my offer of help in the kitchen.

Ethan, Medbh and Kenver had already sat down at an outdoor table under a parasol, and Medbh was looking for something in her bag. 'Go away, you hungry hound,' she said.

There was no way that I was going to miss this story. On the other hand, they did need a little family time. I called Scout and walked round the beautiful garden for a few minutes, admiring the way it had been terraced to maximise views of the river and of Pellacombe opposite. Scout left his mark in a few places and I had to warn him off drinking from the bird bath. Ugh. When I went to get him a proper bowl of water, the tea had arrived and Medbh was handing out slices of cake.

'It's barm brack,' she said. 'Irish tea bread. I made it myself two days ago. It's at its best now.'

It was good. Not as good as Myvvy's cakes, but very nice. 'Did you make it in Ireland.'

'I did indeed. Just before I got the plane over from Shannon to London.' She looked at Ethan. 'I caught the Night Riviera sleeper train to Penzance and Kenver picked me up yesterday morning.'

It is brave of a woman with red hair to wear a red dress. I don't think it would have worked without the denim jacket, even if she did look rather hot. She lifted her hair away from her neck and shook it looser, then turned back to me.

'He's a tall one, your fella the Watch Captain.'

'Height is just one of his many qualities,' I replied. 'But don't let him hear that.'

'How did youse two meet?'

'Now that would be a long story, Medbh. A lot longer than yours, I imagine.'

Ethan looked from me to Kenver and then to Medbh. 'Which name would you honestly prefer?'

She took it in her stride. 'You mean the one I was born with or the one that got thrust on me? Ach, sure I don't mind. Honestly. I think Dad's set on *Medbh*, though.' She turned to her brother. 'Sorry, kiddo. I know you want me to be a Mowbray through and through, but I'm not.'

Kenver looked down. 'You're here. That's what matters.'

She squeezed his arm. 'And I'm here to stay. I'm done with Ireland now. Except for holidays, of course.' She gave a forced smile. 'Only Dad knows the whole story, and you know nothing, do you Mina?'

I nodded. 'Forget I'm here.'

'It's hard to ignore someone with a permanent Ancile. A bit like wearing body armour to dinner. Do you not feel a thing?'

Now that was interesting. Only Sorcerers can sense my Ancile without looking hard, and Vicky says she tunes it out. Either Medbh is very sensitive or she's not fully in control of her powers. I gave her the standard answer. 'Only when someone shoots at me. Please don't do that.'

She laughed. 'I'll do me best. You do know that my Ma was a Zoogenist?'

'I did.'

Conrad has a low opinion of Zoogenists. They are the Mages who can use magick to change and adapt animals. One of them created the Lord Mayor of Moles, whose memorial plaque Conrad erected. He shot her in the end, and after she died he discovered worse crimes. When it comes to magick – like my Ancile – I am like a blind person in a picture gallery. I have to rely on what people tell me. I did not like the sound of this.

Medbh carried on speaking to me as if this was something that needed reporting beyond the family. Ethan was being tight-lipped, and Kenver was troubled. 'She had a thing for octopus, you know. Thought they were the bees' knees, she did. Wanted to create a species that could survive in tidal waters. It was more of a hobby than anything.'

She was being very flippant. I don't like that. 'My hobby is cricket. Breeding mutant octopuses is not a hobby.'

'She got a bit carried away with one of the brood. Some of them turned out huge. A dead end. She'd separated the males and females to stop them breeding, but she was too attached to them. A lot of Mages would have killed them out of hand.'

Kenver couldn't take any more. 'Why did Dad say that it all happened in the Lab?'

Medbh's eyes narrowed. 'To keep the King's Watch out of it, you eejit. Those pens should have been licensed and they weren't.'

Ethan looked troubled. For now, he kept his counsel.

Medbh rubbed her eyes and took a deep breath. 'Long story short, I was fascinated by the great creepy things, and I was trying to make friends with one of the females. I was only nine and they looked cute.' She paused again. 'I didn't fall in, I got dragged in. Ma had to dive in to save me. Look.' She lifted

149

the skirt of her dress, all the way to the waist. I am used to Conrad's scars, and I have my own. These were different. From her knee, up her thigh and disappearing round her back were white disks. Ethan gasped. I shuddered. Kenver looked like he was going to be sick.

She held the dress up a while longer and said, 'There's no Healing can get rid of these bad boys. At least the red hair gives me an excuse to cover up in the summer.' She dropped the skirt and we all breathed out. 'Ma had to jump into the pen to get me. She chucked me out and tried to shock them all. Dad thinks she panicked and some of the Charm blew back onto herself. He says she drowned.'

Ethan recovered first. 'So where have you been, and why the secrecy?'

'Do you remember Granny, Kenver?' It seemed an odd question, and it was.

'Why are you asking me? I never knew her. Dad said she blamed him for what happened to Mum and wouldn't have anything to do with us.'

'That's all true, but it's not the whole story. He wouldn't let her come near you because she was hiding me.'

Ethan and Kenver could see where this was going and looked both angry and upset.

'Hiding you?' I said.

'I was sick,' said Medbh. 'Octopus poisoning, if you'll believe it. The police fella who found me got the station nurse to check me over and she saw nothing. It was all going on under the surface. The marks had just started to appear when Granny took me away. I fainted on the plane, and when I woke up, I was underground.'

I twigged. 'The Fae!'

'I was in the sídhe of the Princess of Corrib herself. It was my life for nine years.' She lifted her hands as if to say *this is who I am. Take it or leave it.*

Kenver knew. Ethan had guessed. The pain on Ethan's face came out in sweat on his brow. He wiped it with his hand and looked away.

'Forgive me, Medbh,' I said. 'What does that mean?'

'It means they treated me like Cinderella for four years. A complete slave. When I got magick, they taught me as best they could. They don't really understand human magick. I still had to work, as well. On my eighteenth birthday, they threw me a party. I walked out the next day.'

I nodded. 'That is half your whole life that you have dismissed in a few sentences, Medbh.'

'Aren't you the nosey one?' She said it with some asperity, and she was looking at my nose when she said it. I held her stare. Only Conrad, Myvvy and Vicky are allowed to make jokes about my nose. She blinked first and looked down. I don't think the men had even noticed. Typical.

'I took a taxi to Galway city,' she said, staring at her dress. 'I spent the next three years in therapy and learning copper magick.'

150

'Copper?'

Ethan answered. 'The Fae don't like copper much. It's in their biology, same as ours, but they're vulnerable to it in some way. They call human magick *copper magick*. Where were you? In Galway?'

She shook her head. 'Away up the coast with the ...' She said something in Irish that went over my head. 'That's a coven of Irish Witches in Donegal. After I'd finished with them, I did go to Galway. For one thing I had to re-learn English. The Fae don't use it in the sídhe, and neither did the Witches.'

'So why are you here now?' I said. 'And why have you left Ireland behind?'

'Dad came. It was him who had the taxi waiting outside the sídhe. I know this hurts, Uncle Ethan, but Dad wanted me to make my own choices, and I'm afraid that I chose not to see you until today. I first came over a couple of years ago. I met Kenver then.'

Ethan was hurt. He stood up and went into the cottage.

Medbh wasn't finished unburdening herself. 'Before you ask, Mina, I know I haven't said why I've shaken the dust of Galway off me shoes. It took me a while to figure it out, and several visits, but in Wessex, I'm a Mowbray. In Ireland, I'm just an ex-Fae bitch. I'll even give it a go learning Cornish, but it's very different to Gaelic, hence the Princess of Corrib naming me *Medbh* instead of *Morwenna*.'

'Why now?'

'Dad. He wanted to bring me back at the Election. I jumped the gun because I wanted the spotlight in Old Sarum to be on him, not me. I didn't reckon on things being quite so edgy here, but it's done now.'

Ethan returned from the cottage, rubbing water off his hands. 'Have you met Kerenza?' he said with an edge to his voice.

Medbh shook her head. 'I wouldn't dare see Dad's woman before I saw you. It was different with me little brother.'

I really was beginning to feel like an intruder now. Medbh had allowed me to hear her story for the very good reason that it would go straight from me to Conrad and then to the Constable in London. It goes without saying that she must be hiding *something*, but what? I believed a lot of what she said. Everything, probably. And the hurt and pain I'd seen in Ethan, Mowbray and Kenver was also real. Medbh would use that pain to exclude me from now on. Family business. I am very used to that.

I stood up. 'Where's the bathroom, Ethan?'

'Left inside the door.'

'I'll get more tea, too.'

When I went into the cottage, my plan to inspect the kitchen was foiled by the utility room. The small bathroom was off a room full of muddy boots and waterproofs. I would have gone further after paying a visit, but Scout was doing his early warning bark when I pulled the chain. By the time I got outside, we could see the Smurf coming down in a graceful arc. It disappeared behind the chimneys of Pellacombe and we started moving towards the buggy for the trip back to the ferry.

I fell into step beside Medbh when she paused to admire the view. 'It's beautiful,' she said. 'It was still being finished the last time I was here.' She gave me a grin. 'I hope they're not in a rush over there. I need to get changed.'

'You and me both. And they can't do it without me, so they'll have to wait.'

'Sounds like a plan. Are you wearing another sari, Mina?'

'This isn't a sari, It's a kurti, and I shall be wearing a suit.' I realised something. 'Are there more scars on your arms? Is that why you're wearing a jacket?'

'No flies on you, are there, Mina? It's not scars, it's a rather unfortunate tattoo on me shoulder. Cap sleeves cover enough of it. Talking of outfits, is it really true about Eseld and the pirate get-up?'

When we got in the buggy, I showed her my phone.

'Would you look at the state of that,' she said.

I couldn't possibly comment. That, I'll leave to Conrad.

Part Four — Agreement

Chapter 22 – Putting a seal on the Day

There were already two people waiting at the pier when I got down – Eseld and Cador. Eseld fished a tin out of her jodhpurs and offered me a hand-rolled cigarette. It seemed churlish to refuse. I thanked her and said nothing. After all, I was waiting for Mina. It would have been rude to intrude.

'What's she like?' said Eseld.

'I only saw her for a minute. Less.'

'Dad showed us a picture. She's the spit of her mother if the portrait is anything to go by, but you haven't seen it, have you? I told Dad to take it down when he started dating Kerenza.'

Another contradiction from Eseld. I'd expected her to resent her stepmother-to-be, not be solicitous of her feelings. 'Don't you remember Medbh or Aisling?'

'I was still at Glastonbury when Aisling died. I remember her having a little ginger kid that I met once.'

'Well, she's still ginger. Does that help?' Eseld thought that was much funnier than it deserved. 'She's got an Irish accent. A strong one.'

Cador had moved as far away from the smokers as he could while remaining in earshot. 'That'll be the Fae,' he said.

'What?'

Eseld looked across the river. 'Here they come.'

The Ferrymistress had the tide with her and I'm sure she opened the throttle further than normal. The ferry hit the fenders with a big bump that nearly threw her daughter overboard. Ethan led the party off the boat and down the pier. Except Scout, who was already letting me know how glad he was to be back.

I stepped away from the pier to give them some room, and Mina dodged round the back.

'Careful,' she said when I hugged her. 'You don't want to detonate that egg.' We hugged some more.

She looked at the Mowbrays, who were moving slowly across the dock towards the old cottage. 'You first,' she said. 'I'm saving my story until Saffron is with us … What are you doing?'

154

I had my phone out. 'Ordering coffee to be served in the summerhouse.'

'You are not! You can order it to be served in the King's Watch suite. Some of us need to get changed.'

Lena brought the coffee herself. She was now on to her fifth dirndl, a plum number, and she amazed us all by collapsing on to the sofa. She closed her eyes for a second, then realised that she was in Mina's place. She held out her hand to Saffron and said, 'Pull me up. I may not stand on my own again.'

Saffron jumped to it, and Lena reverted to hostess mode long enough to pour four coffees. She took one and sat on a spare chair. 'How is Ethan?' she said.

'How long have you got?' said Mina.

'All is good. Nothing is happening for an hour. For now, they need to be alone.'

Mina looked at me. I shrugged and picked up a sausage roll. Coming up here was either the wisest or most stupid thing Lena had done since we arrived. With a deep breath, Mina started her story.

When she'd brought us up to date, Lena was very quiet for a minute while we discussed what some of it all meant. Then she shook herself and said, 'Forgive me. I must go. Also, I have a message.' She stood up and looked at her watch. 'You are invited to meet the Eldest Daughter at one o'clock in the morning room. That is the new name for the Aisling suite, apparently. Lunch is at one thirty. The Agreement will be sealed straight after.'

Mina rearranged her hair and frowned. 'Tell the Eldest Daughter we'll be there at one fifteen.'

'A pleasure,' said Lena.

When she'd gone, Mina said, 'Are you really going to wear your combat uniform for the ceremony? Both of you?'

I was already getting ready to head outside for a smoke. 'Yes.'

'And me,' said Saffron. 'The alternative is too horrible to contemplate.'

'Wise choice,' said Mina. 'Be in the hall at one fifteen, Conrad.'

Rather than head to the summerhouse, I wandered through the woods to take a break. It was shady in there, and there were more interesting smells per square metre than in the formal gardens, so Scout was happy, too. Plus, there was no problem about him digging holes.

I went as far as the stables and checked on Evenstar, then turned round to go back. At the edge of the wood, close to Pellacombe, I heard a familiar *caw caw* from the tallest tree. Scout heard it as well. He was hiding behind my legs and whimpering as fast as he could run. What interest does Odin have in these proceedings, I wondered? I dug in my pockets and found half a sausage I'd purloined from breakfast. Being a dog owner makes you do things like that. As we left the trees, I placed it on the ground and made a bow to the raven.

I wasn't the only one in the hall at 13:15.

Hedda had sent the rest of her sisters packing, and they were milling around making conversation. It was painfully obvious that they'd formed two groups around Raven and Alys with Síona and Isolde in the middle. Literally.

Raven was with Cordelia, Brook and Georgia; Alys with Zoe and Morning. These were obviously their core supporters, and I'm guessing that Síona and Isolde didn't want to pick sides. Yet.

If you're keeping track, there were three missing, all of them inside the morning room. Hedda was sitting by the round table where the negotiations had taken place, resting one hand on the wood and holding her staff in the other. Signe was seated behind her and Kiwa had been at her side. Kiwa stood up when we entered and moved away. What did Kiwa have that the others outside didn't?

Saffron closed the doors behind us, and Hedda gestured to three empty seats that would leave us facing her when she turned to face the table. She didn't get up; we nodded and sat down.

'Please excuse my behaviour this morning,' said Hedda. 'I know that I rushed away when we met. I didn't want to linger while the children introduced themselves, or worse still waited for me to introduce them.'

'Ma'am,' I said. It was a way of avoiding reference to her obvious physical frailty. 'It's Conrad, please. You've already met Saffron, and this is the Peculier Auditor, Mina Desai.'

'A pleasure to meet you, Mina.'

'Namaste, Eldest.'

'May the blessings of the Goddess be with you, Mina. Are you ready for your part, my dear?'

'I would have preferred to practise, ma'am, but suitable treaties are hard to come by.'

'Well, you look the part, and that's half the battle inside, isn't it?' She turned to me. 'I saw that Georgia endeared herself to you, Conrad. I make no excuses for that. Or apologies.'

'Neither are needed, ma'am. The 3rd of Oak does not have to like me, she only has to let me guarantee her safety.'

'Nicely put. I'd ask you to call me Hedda, but no one else does. Except Signe, of course. She calls me *Hedda* because everyone else calls me *Mother*.' She turned and smiled at her daughter, who smiled back as if this was the first time she'd heard her mother say that. They must be devoted to each other.

'I have a question for you, Conrad. Have my children behaved themselves?'

She said it with a smile and almost a twinkle. I replied in the same vein. 'No one had to be put on the naughty step.'

'Good. I ordered two of them not to mention certain events. They all know about you and the Dragon, of course, and they all saw Gwen and Elowen, but of the first group you brought here, only Raven and Síona know about the Lunar Sisters, and that's why Kiwa is here.'

Kiwa bowed fractionally. 'Thank you, Mother. The daughter covens are my responsibility, and without your help in Lancashire, I dread to think what would have happened. I know that you didn't go up there to save the coven, but you did, and I am very grateful. Please also pass my gratitude to your colleague, Victoria Robson.'

'I will, but it's Vicky, not Victoria. How's Abbi Sayer getting along?'

'She's getting there.'

Mina cleared her throat. 'Please excuse me for interrupting. What Conrad is trying to find out is whether Abbi blames him for what happened to her mother. He likes to keep track of potential enemies.'

Hedda tried to stifle a smile. 'A sad situation to be in. I also ordered them not to use the word *Witchfinder*. Now that the others are here, I can't guarantee that.'

'It goes with the territory,' I said.

'As for Abbi, she blames Keira Faulkner, not you. She also forgives her. Is that what you wanted to hear? Good. You chose a difficult path, Conrad. You too, Saffron.'

'Mine wasn't an informed choice,' I said. 'The Allfather was light on the downsides of the King's Watch.'

Hedda looked up. 'Thank you, Kiwa. No need to stand there anymore.'

The Traveller left us, and Hedda relaxed ever so slightly. 'You were also in the presence of the Goddess, weren't you, Conrad?'

'I was. Mina has felt her, too.'

'How was that, my dear?'

Mina moved her hair round from the back to hang over her shoulder. 'In Lakeland. A Witch made a Goddess braid for me, and I felt the Goddess move in the wind over the water.'

Hedda nodded slowly. 'We live in very strange times. Have you ever wondered why you have Odin's number in your phone, Conrad, yet we only ever talk about *being in the presence* when it comes to the Goddess?'

'I find that thinking too much about the gods causes unnecessary headaches.'

'How do you think I feel, then? It's because the Goddess does not need to manifest herself. Many of us have dedicated our whole Spirit to her, and through us she speaks. In Homewood, it is through Verity. Mostly. The Goddess is not at all similar to the Allfather. You should remember that. And you don't need to pretend that his raven isn't here. I felt Odin's interest as soon as the bird arrived.'

'Ma'am.'

157

'Does flying give you an appetite, Conrad? It does me. Let's go and get this circus started.' She smiled at her own metaphor. 'Lord Mowbray makes a good ringmaster, does he not?' She put her hand on the table, and Signe moved to help her stand. 'And you are a proven lion tamer, Conrad. I will let you decide who fills the other roles. Juggler. Acrobat. Contortionist. Sword swallower.' She moved towards the doors. 'And of course, there are plenty of clowns.'

We hung back to let her go through the doors and collect the rest of the Daughters. Lena was standing outside the dining room and welcomed us. One of the Daughters waited inside and intercepted Mina. It was Zoe, the Treasurer.

Hedda may have warned them off certain subjects, but she'd said nothing about not discussing the Flint Hoard. The Daughters have a big interest in that. Before Zoe could kidnap my love (who was too polite to resist), Lena stepped in with a rescue.

It turned out to be a bit of frying pan into fire moment when Lena said, 'Mina, you are on the top table. With Lord Mowbray and Hedda.'

'Errrr....'

'This way.'

The dining room had been rearranged from the informal buffets we'd enjoyed. A small rectangular table with settings for three had been put near the window with four round tables of five in front. Lord Mowbray had chosen to honour his guest by putting Hedda in the centre, with him to her right and Mina to her left. Mina did not look happy, not that anyone except Saff could tell. She'd let her hair come forward and no one could see her face.

The place settings for the lesser tables had been designed to keep some people apart – Eseld and her mother, for example. In fact, I think that Lena had worked out my table and then thrown the others in the air. I found my place on the table with Eseld, Alys, Brook and Kiwa and leaned on the back of the chair. We all stood until everyone was sorted, then we turned to look at the top table.

Lord Mowbray cleared his throat and said, 'Today is a special day. Each one of you honours me by sharing my bread and my board, and it would be a special honour if the Eldest Daughter of Glastonbury called for a blessing on our food.' He bowed to Hedda and stood back.

The Eldest, without thinking, gave her staff to Mina and lifted her arms. Mina looked at me and her eyes bulged with shock.

Hedda took a deep breath and spoke the words,

Lord and Lady,
Sun and Moon,

EIGHT KINGS

Accept our thanks for the sacrifice of Mother Earth,
And help us return it threefold with grace.
So Mote it Be.'

We echoed the last line and sat down. From the sides, blue-shirted staff started to circulate with food and, from a young lad, drink. He was very young and very flustered. Instead of bottled beer and cider, we got two lots of cider. I must admit that I hate the stuff, and asked Kiwa to pass the water jug.

Eseld was on her best behaviour, and had followed her father's instructions regarding a tone-down of her dress. Up to a point.

I'd admired Lord Mowbray's blue frock coat when he got up to speak. Very flamboyant. Eseld had exactly the same coat. You couldn't miss her.

Over lunch, Eseld was the model hostess, asking everyone questions and trying to get as many neutral topics of conversation going as possible. I did my bit, especially when it came to the Arden Foresters. They are a coven in Warwickshire that I was involved with when Vicky and I were called in to sort out the incident of the Phantom Stag. I didn't say too much about the deadly incident and its traumatic aftermath, but as soon as I mentioned them, Kiwa wanted to know as much as possible, much to Alys's discomfort.

It took me a minute to work out why: the Arden Foresters is a mixed coven. Kiwa clearly knew the theory of their organisation and wanted to know much more about how it worked in practice. Alys started squirming at this point, and suddenly said, 'But do the men really *add* anything to the coven?'

I shrugged. 'I'm not a Witch. Or a Warlock. I didn't grow up in a coven or attend the Invisible College. I can really only comment on the King's Watch.'

Eseld's black eyebrows flicked up and she said, 'All the Druid gatherings are mixed, aren't they? Tell us about Caerleon…'

'Oh yes, the Dragon,' said Kiwa.

We were lingering over Mowbray estate cheese when Lena nudged Ethan and he got up to say that coffee would be served at the other end of the room, and could we leave our seats to allow the staff to clear the tables ready for the ceremony.

Before we could stand up, Raven bounced to her feet. When Raven speaks, everyone listens.

'I would like to propose a special toast at the end of our stay at Pellacombe. You can join in if you agree with me. This toast is to all the staff here who have looked after us, and especially to our hostess, Lena. You have done a magnificent job. To Lena!'

Not a single person held back. Lena went redder than Medbh's hair and when Ethan went to start a round of applause, she grabbed his hands to stop him, so he kissed her instead. I caught something out of the corner of my eye, and a lot of what had happened since Monday made a lot more sense.

'I'll grab the coffees,' said Eseld to me. 'And I'll see you outside.'

'Thanks, but I need to see Mina first.'

Eseld reached up to pat my shoulder. 'No you don't. I've been watching, and she's not sending you distress signals. Go and take some of that cheese to your Familiar or he may never forgive you for shutting him out.'

I wasn't going to take her word for it. I went on my toes and peered over the crowd. Mina had her back to me and was being introduced to Kerenza. I put some of the brie and a couple of oatmeal crackers in a napkin and headed for the terrace.

I half expected someone to join us in the sun, but we had the place to ourselves. I turned and leaned on the balcony and thanked Eseld for the coffee when she appeared. When we'd lit up, I risked all sorts of hell by saying what I'd seen when Ethan kissed Lena.

'You love him, don't you?'

She turned and kicked the stonework. Hard. So hard it scratched her patent leather lace-ups. 'Bastard. Fucking bastard hell.' Her anger wasn't directed at me; it all went inwards. When you lash out at masonry, the pain takes a few seconds to register. When it did, she started hopping. 'Oww. Oww fuck.' She turned to me. 'I knew you were trouble, Mr Conrad Bloody Clarke. How did you guess?'

'There had to be a good reason why you don't speak to Lena.'

'She's a freak.'

'It takes one to know one. When Ethan kissed her just now, I was the only one who could see your face.'

'Like I said, you're trouble. Dad said I had to smarm you. I didn't think you'd actually take any notice of me.'

I let that pass; I'm not her therapist. She put her foot on the balustrade and tried to rub the scratch out of her shoe. 'Go on then. Say something.'

'Like what? You're entitled to your obsessions, so long as they don't hurt anyone but yourself.'

'You're a brutal sod, aren't you? Never mind.' She sighed and gave up polishing. 'It was never really reciprocated, and we never did anything that cousins shouldn't do. Dad found out and warned him off. And me. He brought the Imprimatist down from Glastonbury and she showed us why we were too closely related to ever be a happy couple.'

'Now *that's* brutal,' I said.

'If you're born to the staff, it comes with the territory. Are you going to tell anyone other than Mina?'

'Like Saffron? No. Not unless it's relevant. It wouldn't hurt you to talk to Lena, though.'

'Too late for that. Can I cadge another fag?' After she'd lit up, she continued. 'I thought I was over him. I really did. Then Lena turns up. Maybe it'll be different when they're married.'

She was near to tears. It wouldn't take much to tip her over the edge. While she was vulnerable, Mina would have switched the conversation to Isolde or Medbh and reduced her to a complete nervous wreck. And people call me brutal?

'Any chance of a last ride tomorrow morning?' I said.

She tried to smile. 'Of course. When do you have to leave?'

I didn't answer, because Saffron appeared and waved us in.

In our absence, the tables had been cleared and cleaned. Every place had a sealed envelope by it with the words *Text of Agreement* printed on the front. In smaller letters it said *To be opened after the Ceremony.* Glasses had been set out and jugs of iced water were busy gathering condensation. I poured for everyone (long arms) and looked at the top table. They didn't have a jug, just glasses, to avoid the danger of spillage on the elaborate piece of parchment which took centre stage. Next to it was a brass dish containing sticks of red sealing wax. In front of each chair was the occupant's seal.

Lord Mowbray's was gold, as you'd expect, as was Hedda's. Unless my eyes deceived me, both bore the trademark of Dwarven handiwork. Mina's little number in sterling silver looked very much the poor relation.

When the last jug had been thumped on the table, Mowbray rose to his feet. In his left hand was a bunch of index cards. He glanced at the top one and then flicked through the rest before looking round the room. His eyes stopped at the fourth table, the one with Raven, Kenver and Medbh on it. Something changed in his eyes and he dropped the cards on the table. He smiled at the room and began to speak.

'I did not expect my third child to return to Pellacombe today. That alone would have made it special for me. This Agreement is a bonus. I don't need to tell you how hard you've worked to achieve it, or what it means for the future, because you all know that, too.'

He paused and took the bottom card off the pile on the table. 'What I will say is this: the Agreement we're about to sign is the future of the Heptarchy. Of that I have no doubt. It will be many years before those who helped create that future will know for certain that we can be proud of our work. Until then we should be proud that we've tried our best to shape it for the good of our land and of those who will come after us.'

He smiled at us. 'Don't worry. You'll be on your way soon.' And then he sat down.

Hedda turned to her right and nodded graciously. She folded her hands on the table and said, 'Raven has already saved me the trouble of thanking our hosts, and Lord Mowbray has put into words my hopes for the future.' She lifted her seal, using both hands to pick up the gold weight, and said, 'On behalf of the Daughters of the Goddess, I make this mark of Agreement.'

Mowbray snapped off an inch of sealing wax and placed it, whole, on the document. Hedda brought down the seal and molten wax flowed from under it as magick flowed out to illuminate the writing. Literally – the ink glowed for a second. A suitable Mage could now see that the text and the seal were linked: tamper with either and it would leave a trace.

Hedda thumped her seal down and winced at the sound. Mowbray broke more wax and repeated the sealing. For the next step, he had to do things differently. He began by sliding the Agreement well to his left.

Mina stood up and the parchment was now in front of her. Mowbray came round and placed some whole wax on it. On top of that, he placed a tiny wafer of Alchemical Gold – Mina can't use her own Lux to work the seal. He stood back and nodded.

Mina looked up. 'By the power vested in me through the Cloister Court, I certify that this Agreement is duly concluded.' She pressed down her own seal and the text lit up for the third time. When she bent down to blow on the wet wax, Hedda put her hand to her head and collapsed forward onto the table, knocking her glass over. Without thinking, Mina snatched the parchment out of the way of the water.

'Mother!' screamed Signe. She stood up and ran to the front of the table.

Lena moved even faster, hurtling round the back and shoving Mowbray out of the way. Signe had tried to cradle her mother's head, but Lena dragged Hedda backwards, out of her chair, and laid her on the floor. She pressed her hands to Hedda's head and set her jaw in rigid concentration. By now, almost everyone was crowded around the table.

'Back!' shouted Mowbray. 'Give her some room!'

He and Mina moved the chairs and most people took a step back. Signe lifted herself onto the table and swung over to the other side. She was about to take her mother's hand when Mowbray hauled her away. 'Let Lena heal,' he said.

I'd seen enough and backed right out of the crowd, searching for the white halo of Saffron's hair. There. 'Saff!' I called, and beckoned her away. She walked back, trying to crane her head over the crowd.

I took her arm and yanked it enough to get her full attention. 'Can you remember the basic engine start?'

'Yes. Power on, wait for the OK then grab and twist the collective stick without moving it. Press the button and hold it for twenty seconds.'

'Spot on. Run. Do it now. Go!'

There is a lot, lot more to starting a helicopter than that. Most of it is dedicated to making sure that all the controls are in the right position, and I knew that they were because I'd left them there.

Saff legged it out of the dining room, and I spoke up. 'We're starting the helicopter if she needs transport.'

There was a tense silence for a few seconds. I looked at Mina, who had a ringside position. She was biting her lip and rubbing her left arm where the scar would be itching with all the magick. Then Lena looked up and scanned around. When she'd found me, she said. 'Ja. It is eine brain hemmage. She must be moved, but I cannot let go. A stretcher we need.'

'Quickly!' said Signe. 'We must get her to the Homewood.' She whipped her head round to Mowbray. 'Do you have a stretcher?'

'Sod that,' said Raven. 'Let me through.'

She didn't wait, and shoved Eseld almost into the window. Mina jumped back and stumbled into the curtains. 'Take hold,' said Raven, then she bent down and scooped up Hedda in one flowing movement of muscle and power. Lena kept one hand on Hedda's head and moved to Raven's side. I turned and started my slow jog towards the front door.

The whine of the starter began as I climbed the steps to the landing zone. I crossed my fingers as it built, and headed for the pilot's door. Saffron released the starter at the right moment, and the turbos carried on winding up to ground idle speed. So far so good. She jumped out and took another step into adulthood by not grinning at what she'd done. Instead, her face showed nothing but concern for Hedda.

'Doors!' I said. I climbed into the pilot's seat and started to get ready. The Smurf is a clever creature. If anything was seriously wrong, he'd be telling me. The only red light showing was for oil pressure, which is what I expected. I turned to my right and saw the massive frame of Raven cradling a limp Hedda across the lawns. Lena was attached to Hedda's head like a human IV drip.

Saff got inside the cabin, and between her and Raven, they eased Hedda inside. They had to lay her on the floor and bend her legs. Saff fastened Lena's belt, and I saw Lena pointing. Saff got a headset from the hook and popped it over Lena's head before getting out of the other door and closing it behind her.

They'd been followed by a crowd. Everyone had come, and then stopped behind Mowbray at the edge of the safety circle, fifteen metres from the chopper. All except two. Alys and Signe kept going. Saff ran round the front and got ready to close the cabin door. Raven had got in the rear section of the cabin and held out a hand to pull Signe inside.

Alys stood there, paralysed by fear. She wanted to go. She desperately wanted it. With time and help, she would have done. Saff counted to three and slammed the door closed. She pushed Alys gently away from the chopper, but the woman froze. Eseld sprinted across the lawn and grabbed the Witch as gently as she could. Saff left them to it and ran round again. By the time she'd got her belt on, we were at ground idle.

She switched the ICS to intercom and said, 'Lena, is everything okay back there?'

'*Ja. All good. Conrad, nicht Heimwald. Bring sie ins Trauro Krankenhaus.*'

What? The hospital? 'Are you sure, Lena?'

'*Ja. Oder sie wird sterben.*'

163

Or she will die. That was clear enough. I opened the throttle and leaned over to flick the ICS to crew only. When the engines were loud enough to drown out anything, I told Saff what Lena had said. She nodded.

'When we're in the air, I need you to put out a Mayday. Tell them we're coming in to Truro and describe the situation. Use my rank and squadron. Anything.'

'Sir.'

It took longer to turn in the right direction than it did to fly to Truro. Saff didn't just use my rank, she promoted herself to captain in Military Intelligence and used her Head Girl voice over the radio. It worked a charm. Or should that be Charm. As far as I know, you can't project magick over a digital radio, but you never know.

The problems started when it became obvious that I was on a fast descent. The ICS was switched back to intercom, and Lena's mike picked up screams from Signe. Saff swivelled round to see what was happening, and I gritted my teeth. I couldn't afford to join in this one.

'She'll lose her magick,' said Signe.

'She will die!' said Lena.

'Turn round. Go to Homewood. Or…'

'Oh shit,' said Saffron.

Raven's voice boomed through the cabin and over the sound of the engines. Now that was definitely magick. 'Hurry the fuck up.'

I could do no such thing. What I could do was waggle the tail a fraction and make everyone think I was hurrying. 'Status?' I said.

'Raven has Signe in a restraint,' said Saffron, deadpan. Right.

The Royal Cornwall Hospital in Truro has a very small helipad. Right next to A&E. As we dropped out of the sky, I could see men and women struggling into Hi-Viz vests to implement the emergency protocol and make sure I didn't land on an ambulance. They already had a stretcher at the edge of the LZ. This was going to be a hot off-load.

'No one move,' I said. 'Wait for my command.' Lena passed the message on to Raven.

We touched down and I slowed the engines. 'Ready, Saff?'

'Yes sir.'

'And go.'

She dived out and scuttled round, waving the paramedics over. They were good. Professional. Right up to the moment that Raven grabbed the one who tried to disengage Lena from her mission. They rolled with it and adapted their procedure. The rotors hadn't reached ground idle speed before Hedda disappeared through the doors.

'What now?' said Saffron when she'd climbed back in.

'We do a quick check and take off again. They don't need us here.'

She waited until we were in the air before speaking again. 'Are we going to pick anyone up and come back?'

'No. This helipad is for emergencies, not taxis. We're heading for Lamorne Point. You'd better text Mina and tell them what we've done.'

'I already did. On the way over. You were busy flying, so I used my initiative.'

'Good. Give them an update, and well done, Saffron.'

23 – Goodbye for Now

There was a welcome party of one as we touched down at Lamorne Point. A tiny black and white welcoming party.

'How did he get here?' said Saffron. 'Did he swim?'

'He's not stupid, and he's not wet. I bet he ran up the steps though.'

The buggy appeared over the crest of the hill and Mina hopped out. Michael must have brought them over in the fast skiff; it was him at the wheel.

'I so want to take a picture of that,' said Saff.

I was focusing on the instruments. 'Of what?'

'Mina's shoes.'

I looked up. 'On your own head be it if you do. I'm certainly not that brave.'

'Me neither.'

Mina's jacket had gone and her bare arm showed off the slash of the scar for anyone to see. That was strange enough, but not as strange as her feet. Her black tights were pushed into woolly socks and they were poking out of blue walking shoes.

We looked at each other and said as one, 'Lena's spare pair.'

When I slipped off the harness, Saff said, 'I'll get the doors.' It was her way of leaving me to get a free hug and a kiss.

'How is she?' asked Mina.

'In good hands. I hope.'

'Mowbray tells me that Truro has a specialist stroke centre. She couldn't in a better place. What happened up there?' She looked at her phone. 'Saffron says you made it despite Signe. What does that mean?'

Saff had joined us. 'It means that Raven used brute strength and magick to stop Signe attacking us. That was a close call, Conrad. I was on the verge of grabbing your gun.'

'What's happening at Pellacombe? What are the Daughters doing?'

'I don't know. I told Mowbray what was going on in the air and I guessed that you'd be coming here. I told Scout to find Michael and left them to it.'

When we got back across, in the regular ferry, the dock was deserted. We went through the office and Mina collected her heels from the cupboard where she'd purloined Lena's shoes. Every desk was empty. Not a single person around.

That was because they'd been summoned to help with the packing. As we got to the main hall, the Mowbray minibus doors were being slammed shut on the Daughters' luggage. The Witches themselves had already left in their own vehicle, which they'd rented locally.

In Lena's absence, Kerenza was supervising. Being an ex-model, she must have a higher pain threshold for heels and still looked as poised as she had this morning, and with equal poise, she swept us into the family rooms where everyone clustered round to ask questions, especially Ethan. When he'd got the gist, he said, 'I'm off to pick up Lena.'

Ten minutes later, Saffron came up to me on the little terrace. 'What now, Conrad?'

'Home. Unless you're too tired to drive.'

'Home? Is that it?'

'Our mission's over. We were only going to stay tonight because some of the Daughters were staying as well. Now they've all gone, we're redundant. There's a bed if we want it, but I don't want to intrude on the Mowbrays' family time.'

She sighed. 'You're right. You get all involved in this, and then suddenly it's over and we're not welcome any more.'

'We'll be back for the election, don't forget. We're not hired gunslingers in the King's Watch, despite what some people say. I'm still dealing with the fallout from all of my cases. Except the one in Lakeland. Heard nothing from them at all.'

She smiled. 'And for Mina it's a job. I looked at one of those Flint Hoard printouts this morning. My eyes started swimming before the end of the first paragraph.' She yawned. 'I think I will stay here tonight. I'm not sure I could manage a four hour drive on my own.'

'Sensible.'

'You're off to London on Friday, aren't you? With Vicky.'

'We are. I've told the Mages of Mercia to take the weekend off, so you should get a chance to put your feet up.'

'Fat chance. You're really going back to Clerkswell on Sunday night, just for one cricket match?'

'We could get promoted. I've been guaranteed a game. You have to prioritise, Saffron.'

'Very funny.' She took one more look at the river. 'I think I'll base myself at Elvenham, if that's okay. I'll come up on Monday, if Myfanwy doesn't mind me being there.'

'She's getting the weekend with Ben. After that, she really does prefer to have company.'

Mina appeared with a cup of tea in one hand and a cardboard tube in the other. She swapped places with Saffron and said, 'What would have happened if Hedda had been taken ill before the ceremony?' she said. 'Lord Mowbray was very insistent that I look after the Agreement.'

'That's a question we'll never answer,' I replied. 'Technically, Alys is her deputy, but I don't know if she can use the seal. Or if she'd want to.'

Mina frowned. 'I thought that this was all Alys's idea.'

'Eseld let something slip over lunch. Alys may have taken control, but it was Hedda who first realised that Mowbray was buying up electors and started to do the same. We'd better start packing.'

24 – A Perfect Fit

On the way north to Clerkswell, I took a call from Lena, who said that Hedda was having surgery for a haemorrhagic stroke, but the prognosis was good.

'What did you do to help her?' Mina asked.

'I do not have the English for that, and Conrad does not have the German. I stop the blood, yes?'

There was a lot more, about who was going where and who was keeping vigil with Signe. Lena would not be paying a visit: it seems that Signe was furious with the decision to go to Truro rather than Glastonbury.

The lights were on in Elvenham House when we arrived. They were comforting, even if we knew that no one was at home. Vicky had offered to get takeout from Bishop's Cleeve and we'd succumbed. She was going to pick up Myfanwy on the way back. I decided that there would never be a perfect time, so now was as good as any.

'Let's go up to the well first,' I said. 'It's a mild night, and Myfanwy said that the electrician's finished installing those lights.'

Mina looked at the empty house and said, 'Why not. I'll nip to the loo and see you up there.'

We got out, saluted the dragon, and made our way round the back. Autumn is definitely on the way, because even a couple of weeks ago there would have been residual light at this hour. Tonight, the sky was black, stars fighting with the heat haze to be seen.

I was glad to arrive at the well on my own. There was already a power supply here, for the pump that sends water to the Inkwell brewery, and Myfanwy had decided that such a crucial part of the property should have its own lights. My magickal journey began here when the Allfather enhanced me. Effectively he turned me from mundane into Mage, and hundreds of years ago it was the gateway to a (now abandoned) Fae realm.

In keeping with all this, Myfanwy had made the lights semi-magickal. There is a switch, hidden in the junction box and there's a motion sensor, also hidden in a box. If we left the sensor exposed, it would be triggered all the time by foxes/cats/badgers and goodness knows what roaming through the garden. The trick is to set the sensor off without opening the box.

The sensor is totally mundane, as supplied. It's the box that's magickal. Saffron made it for Myvvy, with a little help from Erin. Inside the box is a Glyph, a painted picture of a firework. If you project a little Lux on to the box, the Glyph lights up and emits infra-red energy. A bit like clicking on an internet GIF. I stared at the box and spent a fruitless minute trying to project Lux from my fingers. All I achieved was nearly setting my jacket on fire.

I scratched my head and thought about how other Mages do this, and as I scratched, I remembered Eseld's hands on my shoulders. Of course. 'Scout! Here boy!'

He trotted up and tilted his head in query. I was now, consciously or not, projecting small amounts of Lux to Scout. If I could figure out how it worked for him, I might stand a chance.

Of course, he and I are bonded, which is a special case. I closed my eyes and found where the trickle of Lux was leaving my body. It was flowing out of my hands, like water running downhill. Downhill. Feeling like a complete numpty, I lay down in front of him. In strictly gravitational terms, the Lux was now flowing *uphill*, but it didn't feel like that. My brain was trying to turn a non-spatial event into a spatial one, because that's all it had to go on.

Power can flow in other ways. Oxygen flows into the blood through the lungs. Electricity flows from negative to positive. In both cases, there is a difference of power that tries to even itself out. I had more Lux than Scout. It was the same principle.

It was all a matter of Sight. Saffron and Erin had done the hard work by enchanting the box. All I had to do was use my Sight to find it. 'Scout, go find Mina,' I said to get him out of the way.

With his little beacon of Lux gone, and with my eyes closed, I reached out to sense the magickal terrain. There's the well. Can't mistake that. And there's the box. I pointed my finger at where I thought it was (eyes closed, remember), and tried to let Lux build in my fingers. When there was a big enough difference, it made the jump and I felt the Glyph activate itself. Bingo.

I smiled to myself and got ready to stand up. And then I heard an electronic *kercheek* noise. An iPhone taking a picture. What the...?

I snapped my eyes open and blinked. The lights had come on (good), and in the soft glow stood Scout and Mina (not so good). Mina was staring at her phone. 'What are you doing?' I said, scrambling to my feet.

'Conrad, you were lying on the grass, in the dark and pointing at the well. When the lights came on, I took a picture. What did you expect me to do? Ignore it?'

'You could have said *well done*. It took a lot of effort to do that.'

She ignored me and said, 'I sent it out and Saffron has already replied. She says *Where's his horse?*' Mina looked around. 'Nice. It is a special place.' She drifted over and sat on the edge of the well. Time for action, hopefully with better results than when I tried it with Amelia Jennings.

I dug out the box and got on one knee. Her eyes bulged.

'Mina, I don't know how I could live without you. You mean everything to me. Will you marry me?'

'Yes.' She paused. 'You need a hand up, don't you?'

'It's been a hell of a day.'

She braced herself and gave me a hand. 'What a way to start our engagement,' she said when I'd staggered around and sat down next to her.

'It's who we are. Sad but true.'

'Not sad. Never sad for what we have.' With that, she took my head and dragged it down for a kiss. A series of kisses. We only stopped when I heard barking from the house. The girls were here.

'We have a moment,' said Mina. 'I can see why *here*, but why *now*?'

'Because I love you. Because I want the world to know that we're heading for marriage.'

She tilted her head. 'That's a very odd thing to say. Now hurry up and show me the ring.'

I opened the box and held it out. She stared at it and said, 'Is this the diamond from the Dwarf?'

'Yes. It was 3.7 carats, and...'

'And you can't afford to waste a $25,000 diamond. It's beautiful, Conrad. Are those real rubies?'

'Of course.'

She lifted it out. The story of that diamond began in Niði's Hall, and it's entwined with our search for the *Codex Defanatus*. I had it emerald cut, which means flattish and oblong. On either side were two matching (smaller) rubies.

'Who made it?'

'A Gnomish friend of Lloyd Flint. Or a cousin. I've paid for the rubies, but if you say yes, then the ring is an early wedding gift from Lloyd.'

She weighed the ring in her palm. 'Does it have magick powers?'

'Yes it does. We talked it over for a long time, and he said that the only thing that made sense was to use your Lux to mask the Ancile. You should be a little less obvious to Mages now. Any other Work would be dangerous.'

We heard the sounds of approaching dog (and women). Mina held out the ring. 'Put it on me.'

I slid it over her finger (I'd done a lot of checking in her jewellery box, so it fitted), and said again, 'Will you marry me?'

'Yes.'

A burst of applause echoed around the garden. Mina stood up, and both Vicky and Myfanwy gave her a big hug. I'd had my back to the house. Had Mina seen them coming, and timed the last bit to perfection? Only a real diva would do that. Or a Rani. A princess would definitely want an audience.

We walked back in a line, Mina and I holding hands in the centre. Myfanwy (who has little filter at the best of times) was the one who brought up the elephant in the room.

'What about Pramiti?'

To get out of a difficult, possibly deadly situation in prison, Mina had prayed to Ganesh. The gods do not always hear our prayers and rarely answer them. What's more, a prayer is not encrypted. Any Spirit can listen, and one did.

Pramiti is a Nāgin, a snake-woman. You could call her a shapeshifter if you want. I wouldn't do it to her face though. Pramiti was owed a favour by Ganesh, and Ganesh transferred that debt to Mina. There is nothing to stop us going to Cheltenham registry office and getting married, but if Mina wants to get married with Ganesh's blessing, and she does, then we have to pay that debt. I looked down at Mina.

'When I am ready to start planning the wedding, we will go to temple and make an offering to Ganesh,' she said. 'It's up to him to tell Pramiti what is going on, not us.'

The rest of the evening was a delirious celebration. I'll spare you the details. The weirdest part, for me, was the intense concentration and moving of lights necessary to produce the perfect picture of Mina's hand with the ring on it. The circulation of that image was how our friends and family found out.

Later, in bed, I said, 'I heard what you said on the phone to Erin. About the wedding. You've already started making plans, haven't you?'

'Mmmm. Yes. We'll go to temple on Saturday. Might as well get it over with.'

Part Five — Returning Officer

25 – Skin Deep

'It really isn't a problem, Chris. Honestly.'

We were on our way to the Hindu temple in South London, and Chris Kelly had just rung to cancel tonight's dinner. His youngest child was ill, apparently.

'It's a bloody problem for us,' he said. 'Tamsin went to a lot of trouble for this, and she's furious.'

'It's no one's fault. Or is it?'

'Of course not. That's what makes it worse. She's bloody furious and has nowhere to direct her fury. Why do you think I volunteered to sit in the clinic waiting room for three hours? It's not safe at home.'

'I'm sure we'll find a way to amuse ourselves.'

'I'm sure you will. Is there any chance you're going to be in London next Friday?'

'Yes.'

'Good. See you then. Better go,' he said, and disconnected immediately.

'Genuine?' said Mina.

'He's no actor. It was genuine.'

'Then I have an idea. I shall need to research it a little. This is our stop.'

You may wonder why we were trekking all the way to a battered temple in a disused warehouse in South London when the magnificent Neasden Mandir is only five miles from my – our – flat in Notting Hill. The answer is Mr Joshi.

I'm going to ask for your indulgence at this point. Please. The story of our visit to Mr Joshi's temple, of our dinner with Chris, and of what Pramiti wanted all deserve to be told in full and told by Mina. You can read what happened in *Ring of Troth*.

One of the reasons she has to tell the story is that after our visit to the temple we had a huge row. A humdinger. One of those where you have to back down or risk everything, and then risk everything by backing down. You deserve to hear her side of the story, not mine.

We were back south of the river on Sunday, in the very different surroundings of Wimbledon, and with domestic harmony restored after our row last night. It's a cliché, I know, but it really does help if you make a point of not going to bed angry.

'Now that's a house I could aspire to,' said Mina.

I won't name the road itself, but I will tell you this: there were paparazzi clustered around two of the houses further along. A certain TV personality had been caught coming out of the wrong gate on Friday night, and the

Sunday papers were already talking about a divorce settlement of eight figures. How do I know this? Because the taxi driver told us. I don't think he believed that we were going to a barbecue for one minute.

Dean Cora Hardisty's house not only has three storeys, two wings either side of the grand entrance and a fountain at the front, it also has views over the park. 'It's a shame we won't get to see inside.'

'Why not!' said Mina, with genuine outrage.

'We're still in the outer circle. If she gets to be Warden, we'll be invited to one of the inside parties. According to Vicky, her Halloween bash is legendary.'

'Then I shall devote myself to her cause completely. How do we get through the gates?'

There was an intercom panel in one of the gate pillars. I took out the stiff invitation card and held it to the microphone. A small Work in the card discharged itself and the gates slid back. I'm telling you this because it is one of the few instances of digital-magickal integration that has made it out of the Salomon's House laboratories.

We headed round the side and I pointed to a small wall with a concrete finial on top. 'There, and nowhere else,' I said. Scout looked unhappy. 'I'm not joking. You can pee here or in the bushes, but nowhere else.'

'You do realise how ridiculous this is,' said Mina. 'You are having a battle of wills with a puppy and losing.'

I folded my arms and stared at him until he cocked his leg. It's good practice for when we have children...

'Conrad? What's the matter? Have you seen a ghost?'

'What? Sorry, love. Just a premonition. We'd better leave the scene of the crime.'

Smells of griddled meat assaulted us as we rounded the corner and found the party. Because this is England, and summertime, there was a small marquee on the terrace. Having a good shelter is the only way to guarantee that it doesn't rain. Without that marquee, it would have tipped it down.

The sun was shining, everyone looked relaxed, and the tent had been set up to contain two bars: salad and drinks. Cora detached herself from the crowd and came to meet us. Was it my paranoia, or did more eyes meet ours than usual on a social occasion? I'm not that famous. For the record, Mina was not the only non-white guest. A couple were of Afro-Caribbean descent, and a couple more from China. Mina was the only south Asian.

'Congratulations!' said Cora. 'Hannah told me your news.' She frowned. 'You look different, Mina.'

'Thank you. This is a new sari.'

Cora shook her head. 'I was coming to that. I meant your aura. I can't see your Ancile anymore, and I know you've still got it, so ... Aah. The ring. Nice work, Conrad. I do admire you, Mina. I could never carry that much fabric around.'

I wasn't wrong. There were way too many people watching our arrival. Yes, Mina looked gorgeous, and yes, her new sari was spectacular, but not *that* spectacular. I was beginning to suspect that my presence was more significant than I'd anticipated.

'… can be hot on a day like this.'

I tuned back in to the conversation as Cora ushered us to meet her husband, the only mundane adult present. He was where you'd expect a man to be on such an occasion – running the barbecue. He was tall, younger than Cora and had a blue cockerel tattoo on his bicep. If you didn't know, that marks him as a Tottenham Hotspur fan. At his side and assisting was a lad of about nine in a replica No 9 shirt.

Mina started wafting succulent smoke away from her sari, and I excused us.

'No problem,' said the chef. 'Catch you later for a beer, yeah?'

I made straight for the friendliest face – Dr Francesca Somerton, Keeper of the Queen's Esoteric Library. She gave Mina a kiss and told me off for not getting drinks. I went to the tent, and the conversation had moved on from weddings by the time I got back.

'I thought I'd know more people,' I said. 'I recognise Selena, over there.' Selena Bannister is the Mistress of Masques and Revels at Salomon's House. She and Cora are close friends and allies. Hannah had told me that Selena was Cora's unofficial campaign manager.

'There are only three guests from the Inner Council,' said Francesca. 'Selena, of course, myself and Oighrig Ahearn. She's gone to the ladies.'

'Who are the rest, then?'

'It's a bit like a reunion,' said Francesca with a smile. 'All but two or three are former pupils of Cora's. They'll all vote for her, of course, but she's brought them here to sound them out and sign them up to campaign on her behalf.'

'There aren't going to be speeches are there?' said Mina.

'Not today. I wouldn't have come if there were. The time for speeches is after the candidates have all declared themselves.'

'Has anyone other than Heidi Marston come forward?'

'Not yet. I hear rumours that the North is rising.'

There is no North in magick, so what was she on about? I asked.

'You may not have noticed, being from Wessex, that all the power in English magick is south of Birmingham. There are enough Mages from further north to be upset about that. Roly told me that someone was always pestering him to found a northern Salomon's House. He never said who it was.'

'Do I smell?' said Mina suddenly.

'Yes you do, dear,' said Francesca. 'Of jasmine. What do you mean?'

'There is a five metre gap around our table that wasn't here when we arrived.'

'Perhaps they don't want to interrupt us,' said Francesca with her usual tact and diplomacy.

'It's me,' I said. 'No one loves the King's Watch. I'll take myself off for a smoke and Francesca can introduce you to a few of them.'

'No!' said Mina. 'You are not going to leave me with a garden full of Mages who are all taller than me and with whom I have nothing in common!'

'You're the Peculier Auditor,' I said.

'I am proud of who I am,' she declared. 'I am also well aware that not everyone is interested in asset depreciation. Even your eyes glaze over when I try to talk about the Flint Hoard case.'

I'd already stood up at this point and got out my cigarettes. 'That's why you're the hero. Anyone can take on a bunch of homicidal Gnomes, but it takes a special person to deal with their accounts.' I started backpedalling towards the shrubbery before she could respond. By the time I'd reached the shade of an oak tree, the cordon sanitaire had already shrunk to two metres, and Francesca was calling over the only other woman standing on her own. Scout appeared from nowhere and I got a real smell of cooking sausage. 'Was that you boy? Did you just project hunger on to me?'

He sat in front of me and whined. 'You'll have to wait. Like the rest of us. You can't rush a barbie.'

I lit my cigarette, and the back of my neck suddenly felt warm. Mage alert. 'Do you smoke?' I said.

'Not any more I don't,' said an Irish voice from behind me.

It took all my willpower not to turn around. 'And do you always lurk in the bushes?'

I heard a rustling, and she appeared round the front. 'Only when I'm trying to figure out how a great lump like you has a Familiar and I don't. Oighrig Ahearn. We've not met properly.'

We shook hands, and she corrected my pronunciation of her name. As close as I can get it, Oighrig is pronounced *Oichrigh*.

'It means *Little Speckled One*,' she told me. 'I was a medical miracle, you know. Born with freckles.'

Almost all the women were wearing loose maxi dresses, as was Oighrig. Hers had thin straps, and every square centimetre of skin from her forehead to her fingertips was freckled. She wasn't like that when we'd last met, so either she was *very* sensitive to sun or she'd used a Glamour to hide it. I'd seen her briefly, once, in Salomon's House.

'I haven't seen you since the Inner Council meeting about my use of firearms. You gave me the benefit of the doubt on the crucial vote. Thank you.'

'God, that seems like *years* ago. Sorry I missed the Dragon seminar. I was out of town.'

'I'm going to start charging for that story.'

She stood back, further under the tree, and tucked some vibrant red hair back under her straw hat. Oighrig is the youngest member of the Inner Council of Salomon's House and is known as the Oracle because she's responsible for teaching and research in Sorcery and Divination. *Oracle* isn't a nickname, either. She got the job when Cora was appointed Dean.

'I'm still grateful,' I said. 'About that vote. So grateful that I won't object to you calling me a *great lump*.'

She laughed. 'It's what you are. My Great Aunt always told me never to say things behind people's backs that you wouldn't say to their face.'

'You know, that makes it worse. Speaking of family wisdom, my mother always told me never to leave an important question unasked. What were you really doing in the bushes?'

'I told you: looking at your Familiar. You've a good bond there, so you have. I was gonna try to call you, but all he was interested in was smelling me feet and whether I had any sausage. I think you're well suited, to each other.'

'You were going to *call* me? Via Scout?'

'Aye. I wanted to get you on your own.'

'I'd say I was flattered, but I've clearly no cause to be. What have you got against Mina?'

'Nothing! I meant without any of the other guests, though now you mention it, it's always easier to get information out of a man without his girl to fend you off.'

Now that was alarming. Frank, but alarming. I took a swig of beer.

She moved one foot in front of the other and glanced at the party. Not a single person was looking in our direction, which meant that everyone was secretly watching us. Paranoid? Me?

Oighrig turned her head back to me. 'I hear that you're either a real hero or the Devil incarnate. Depending on who you talk to.'

I took another swig. 'That was a bit Delphic for a great lump like me.'

The blood spread out under her skin. 'I shouldn't have called you that. Sorry. I was talking 'bout your trip to Cornwall. You either saved the life of the Eldest Daughter of the Goddess or you denied her the chance of magick forever.'

'I played my part. If you're after information, I can tell you that Hedda is still in a medical coma and that the surgeon was very pleased with the operation. I honestly don't know any more than that. My source in Cornwall doesn't have insider access.'

'That's good to hear. That she's doing okay, I mean. You were there, though, weren't you? All through the conference.' She saw me lift my eyebrows. 'Selena was right: you really can be tight-lipped when you want to.'

'I can tell you what was in the Agreement. Mina's got the text on her phone if you want a copy.'

'Is it all legal stuff?'

'Pretty much.'

'Then I'll pass.'

She'd come to the line she didn't want to cross. Should I help her over? Well, she had apologised for calling me a great lump. 'Are you related, or just nosey?' I said.

'Is it that obvious?'

I pointed the neck of my beer bottle at her freckles. 'The world of magick is even smaller than the RAF. You are a Mage from Galway. You have … shall we say *distinctive* good looks? If you're not related to Aisling Mowbray, I'll bet you know everyone who is.'

'That Great Aunt I was telling you about? She was Aisling's mother. Her sister was my Granny. We knew that Morwenna was alive, but not where she was. I couldn't believe it when I heard she'd turned up out of the blue. I was Facetiming everyone in the West who has a phone all day yesterday and I got nothing. Then you turn up today. Do you blame me for trying to charm you?'

'Medbh. She's called Medbh now. Unless she's changed back in the last forty-eight hours.'

Something didn't sit right here. Either Oighrig's family were a bunch of vacant eejits (as they say), or Medbh had been lying, or something else. It was time to play her at her own game.

'Would you describe your family as a bunch of vacant eejits, Oighrig?'

She spluttered. 'That's fighting talk, that is. What makes you say that?'

'Because Medbh told Mina that she'd been three years with a coven in Donegal and three years in Galway city. I've never been, but I imagine that flame haired Mages aren't *that* common.'

She looked troubled. 'Are you sure?'

'Of what? I'm sure of what she said to Mina. I'm sure that Lord Mowbray – all the Mowbrays – examined her Imprint closely, and that today's Medbh is yesterday's Morwenna. Beyond that, I'm sure of nothing.'

'Who's lying then?' she said. She spoke as if I were a lot closer to her than a ten minute acquaintance would warrant. She shook herself and put on the Irish smile (it is a thing, I assure you). 'Or perhaps the ones I left behind really are a bunch of bog-hopping culchies.'

'Why did you leave them behind?'

'You know that there's no Invisible College in Ireland, right?'

'Didn't you go to St Raphael's?'

'Hell, no. Only jackeens go there.'

I knew what a *culchie* was, but … 'Jackeens?'

'Dubliners. Outside the city, there's a whole network of circles for learning, and a nifty college in Galway city, but it's like Irish Dance.'

'Now you've lost me completely.'

I was suddenly conscious of being watched. Not from myself, but from Scout. On the edge of the party, Cora was taking a great interest in my conversation with Oighrig. If Scout's response was anything to go by, I'll bet she was eavesdropping.

Oighrig was oblivious of the attention. 'Irish dancing is all very well, if you like that sort of thing, but if you want to dance ballet, you have to go abroad. That's how come I ended up in Salomon's House.' She paused. 'Is there nothing else you can tell me?'

'I only saw her once. You could try Mina.'

She laughed. 'Because I'm sure that an officer of the Cloister Court is bound to be fountain of gossip. I'm getting a thirst, Conrad.'

'And me. I'm not driving today, either.'

We sauntered back and I got a severely raised eyebrow from Mina when I took her a large Pimms. 'Tell you later,' I said. 'How's it going?'

'Very well. No thanks to you. When is the food ready, and has Cora's husband kept the beef away from the rest of the meat?'

Cora herself was twenty feet away when Mina said that. She called across the gap, 'There is absolutely no beef on today's menu.' She'd definitely been listening.

'You must meet …' said Cora.

I've left that person's name out of this story because you've met enough new people already. The campaign for Warden is going to run and run, and if that person becomes important, I'll let you know who she was. There was one substantive development, and it came out of a hushed conversation with the aristocratic Selena.

We were talking about the Fae, and she managed to drift over to a quiet part of the garden. I'm sure she used magick, too, to keep things away from the others.

'You know that Cora sees your … recent caseload as a troubling development, don't you?'

'Recent caseload? That's one way of describing several near death experiences.' I paused to let her get the point. 'What I like most about Cora is that she's willing to change her mind and not let personal prejudice get in the way.'

'Quite. She sounded out the Constable about you. Informally. If Cora were to create the post of Director of Security at Salomon's House – part time, of course – would you be interested? And would you allow your name to be floated during the election campaign?'

It was a brave move of Cora's. A lot of Mages don't like the Watch on principle. On the other hand, they like being killed even less. 'On one condition,' I replied. 'I don't like the word *director*. Make it Security Attaché.'

'How quaint. I'm sure that won't be a problem.'

I also spent some quality time with Cora's husband and son when the cooking was over. 'How do you put up with them?' he asked.

'What? Mages?'

'No. Women. The whole world of magick is full of 'em. Does my 'ead in sometimes.'

'You and me both. There's even a women's cricket team in the village now.'

He shook his head sadly and turned to his son. 'What's the best thing about Saturdays?'

'Boys day out,' he replied. The poor lad put on a mournful face and added, 'But me little sister wants to play as well. Mum says she'll have to come too, next year.'

'I'll tell you, mate, the world's going to rack and ruin.'

We turned to look at the assembled gathering. I counted three men out there. 'Too late,' I said. 'Another beer?'

'Please. And a diet Pepsi for the boy.'

Just after we got in the taxi to go home, Mina got a text. From Pramiti.

'She can wait until Tuesday,' said Mina. 'You really think that Cora could hear you across the garden, with all that noise?'

'I feel Lux as heat. Vicky sees it as an extra colour. Sort of. Maybe Cora feels Lux as sound, and maybe that gives her an edge.'

'Maybe. Now tell me what you and that poor girl were talking about.'

'Poor girl? You mean Cora's daughter?'

'Don't be dense. The Irish one. The one with serious pigmentation issues.'

'Pigmentation issues?'

'Yes. And red hair. Poor girl.'

'Didn't she come to talk to you?'

Mina shook her head. 'No. After you parted, she got on her phone. She was the only one at the party who did that. Until the end. After that, she avoided both of us.'

When I'd told Mina what we'd been talking about, we were both puzzled and worried, but we weren't sure why. 'I'll tell Hannah and Rick,' I said. 'Perhaps they know someone who knows someone.'

Mina gave that a considered nod, then we sat back and held hands.

26 – Bank Holiday Pursuit

Monday was the must-win cricket match, the one that would see the Clerkswell men's team promoted to Division One.

We won.

And then we partied.

27 – Assorted Hats

One of my favourite coffee shops is opposite the Tower of London, up some stairs behind a souvenir tat shop and possessed of a covered smoking area at the back which doubles as a dog shelter. It's very handy for Merlyn's Tower, home of the King's Watch, and only fifteen minutes' walk from Salomon's House. I took the tray of coffees over to the table and distributed them. Two of them went in front of empty seats. Trouble with taxis.

'How's the house-hunting going?' I asked Vicky.

'Flat-hunting. We're a long way from being able to afford a house within an hour of the City. Thanks for the coffee.' She sipped her latte and looked at the pastries on the counter. 'Better not. The flat-hunting's going champion, if you enjoy sticking your neb into other people's lives. I must say I've got a taste for it since I met you.'

'Do you blame me for all your bad habits?'

She gave that some serious consideration. 'Yes.'

There was a blast of damp air and the other two members of our party blew in, trying to shake their umbrellas outside without getting wet. Mina spotted us and dragged a slightly dazed looking Sofía over to the table.

'Where did this rain come from?' said Mina.

'I told you last week. There was a change in the Jet Stream and a hurricane in the Caribbean.'

'So?' said Mina. 'That means nothing to anyone.'

'She's got a point,' added Vicky. 'I have no idea what it means either.'

'It meant rain in a week's time, which is why I told you a week ago, and you're ganging up on me again. Sofía, you have to stick up for me.'

'Why should I do that? You are big enough to look after yourself.' She sniffed her espresso and started adding sugar. 'Although, I have been talking to Papa.'

She gave me a strange look, as if I were responsible for all of my father's peculiarities instead of being their recipient.

She finished stirring and downed her coffee in one. 'He says that I must learn all about the weather and how to drink tea, and that this is all I need to fit in over here.'

'Sounds about right,' said Vicky with a sage nod.

'Totally,' added Mina. 'And get used to London prices. That helps.'

'Never!' said Sofía. 'Is it too late to go to Napier College in Scotland?'

'Yes!'

Her face fell. 'Tell me again about the Dean. I don't have to call her *My Lady*?'

'No, and you'll meet her yourself soon enough,' said Mina. She does like to use a little tough love on my little sister.

'Nice coat,' I said. 'Is it new?'

'Very new and very expensive,' said Sofía with a sidelong glance at Mina.

'Enough about the weather and shopping,' said Vicky. 'I want to hear all about Pramiti if you're gonna drag us off on a mission.'

That was our cue (Sofía and me) to head out for a smoke and for me to ask about how Mum was getting on. Fine, is the answer. Dad and Sofía have been meeting during bridge nights, so Mum could pretend it wasn't happening. When we got back inside, Vicky and Mina both had their phones out and were arguing.

'We're trying to get an Uber,' said Mina. 'My rating is higher than Vicky's.'

'No it isn't.'

I got out my own phone and checked for the twice-daily update from Lena. 'Good news,' I said. 'Hedda is awake and talking. Things are looking good for her.'

'That is good news,' said Mina.

'Ooh! I've got one,' said Vicky. 'Uber on its way.'

Mina and Vicky were off on a Pramiti-related quest that needed a Sorcerer and clashed with our upcoming appointment in Salomon's House.

'And we're walking,' I said to Sofía.

'In this rain?'

'Quicker and much more dog friendly,' I said, and zipped up my coat.

She hesitated a second, then joined me. 'It is not so bad, this rain,' she said. 'I do not like Ubers and I prefer to walk.'

We left the warmth of the coffee shop and waited patiently to cross Byward Street.

'If you spend any time with Vicky, you'll have to get used to Ubers. How are you feeling?'

She gave an epic shrug, so big the umbrella tilted away from her. 'About the college, I don't know. If it is good, it is good. I am more worried about dinner tonight. I can cope with Papa not knowing the world of magick, but Rachael… What will we talk about?'

'We'll talk about whatever Rachael wants to talk about. Haven't you spotted that yet?'

She laughed. 'Si. Also, I have been thinking about what to do if I get into the Invisible College.'

'You'll get in. The Dean owes me, so that's not a problem. It has to be your choice. If you think it's right for you.'

She was quiet for a second. I think she was nodding and had forgotten that I couldn't see her very well under the umbrella. 'Yes. I understand. I was thinking about my name. You know that I am not really called *Torres*. Mama picked it at random when I was born.'

'You've had it all your life, Sofía.'

'Yes, and Victoria says that they only use first names at the College. Everyone will know that I am your sister, so I want to take our father's name. If I don't like it, I can change back when I graduate. Sofía Clarke.'

She rolled the *r* when she said it. It sounded strange but good.

We entered Frederick's Place and I slipped Scout's lead off. A short way down, she stopped and lowered her umbrella. The portico of Salomon's House had just become visible. To both of us. To me through the token they gave me, and to Sofía via natural talent.

'Ready?'

'No. Let's go anyway.'

'Spoken like a true Clarke. Don't worry, you'll be fine.'

'That's what Mama said when she sent me to Clerkswell. And look what happened there.'

'Why have you invited Victoria?' hissed Rachael when Sofía and I arrived at St Cecilia's Dining Rooms. My older sister's flat in Mayfair could just about accommodate us, but that would mean her cooking or hiring a chef. Not going to happen.

'Very nice,' I said. We had a panelled room all to ourselves. 'Mina and Vicky have been on an engagement related mission, and you get on all right with Vicky, don't you? Besides, you invited Alain.'

'That's because I felt sorry for him. He's been dumped again.'

'You are not trying to set him up with Sofía, are you?'

She grinned. 'They have to meet sooner or later. Better to do it where I can keep an eye on him. Will they be long?'

'They're in a taxi right now. No more than five minutes.'

This was a joint celebration of our engagement and Sofía's admission to Salomon's House. Or as we're calling it, "Ironmonger's College." This was an old Mage's in-joke, because Salomon's House backs on to Ironmonger's Lane. More recently, the Occulters set up an online presence exactly for this purpose.

The real reason that Vicky was here was that I'd had a text from Alain: *Rachael wants to talk to you on your own. She has told me to make sure it happens.*

It would be a lot easier if Vicky was here to lower the temperature, and Vic wasn't going to say no to a free dinner in an exclusive Mayfair dining room, was she? Mina looked particularly gorgeous tonight, even if her dress did look familiar. 'Didn't Vicky wear that to the garden party?'

'She did. I thought it would look better on me, but don't tell her that.'

'I wouldn't dare. How did you get on with Pramiti?'

She gave me an equivocal, very Indian nod. 'We have made a start. We are back on the hunt tomorrow, but I will definitely be back for dinner with Chris Kelly. Don't worry.'

During a smoke break on the roof, Alain appeared and gave me a thumbs-up sign over Sofía's head. I didn't mess around with subterfuge. 'Could you give us a minute, Sofía?' I said. 'Alain is under orders to get me alone so Rachael can talk to me.'

'Why?'

'I have no idea.'

Sofía shrugged and left us to it. Rachael appeared seconds after they'd gone downstairs. She must have been waiting behind the door.

I had a terrible fear that Rachael was going to re-open old wounds about Elvenham House now that I was getting married. I was wrong.

'What happened in Cornwall?' she said when we were alone.

I shook my head. 'I can tell you about the food and the view from Lamorne Point, Raitch, but that's it. Everything else is classified.'

Rachael really is our mother's daughter, even if she tries to deny it sometimes. She put her left hand on her hip and tapped her right forefinger against her refreshed lipstick. In a flashback, I was six years old and about to be interrogated regarding a broken window at primary school. I tried to repress a shudder.

'Don't be dense, Conrad. I'm not talking about the secret negotiations, I'm talking about the fact that my biggest client has acquired an adult daughter. Bit close to home, that.'

'To be fair, Raitch, he's always known about his daughter. She's only just reappeared, that's all.'

'Then why am I having to spend the weekend in Salisbury? Do you know how many times I've met Mowbray? Once. He came in to sign the papers when he moved to our company. That's it.'

'Lord Mowbray is a busy man.'

'*Lord???* Since when does he have a title?'

Oops. That was a slip. 'Erm, it's like Mum's CBE. Secret. For services rendered.'

She gave me another of Mother's looks, the one that said *I don't believe you, but that's not the important thing.*

'Whatever. Why does he suddenly want see me now? I could put this Morwenna person into the trust without a face-to-face meeting.'

'Medbh. Her name's Medbh. The Mowbrays as a clan are pretty formidable. They'll expect you and me to talk but not say anything to each other, if that makes sense. If you get her name right, it'll give him something to think about.'

'I like that. Any other hints?'

'Sorry. I have no idea what he's planning.'

'Fair enough. How did Sofía really get on this afternoon? And are you sure that this Ironmonger's place is the right one?'

'It's the right place. She's got a scholarship there and they have a very good pupil-teacher ratio. She did very well at the interview, too.' I pulled my lip and thought for a moment. Rachael was about to go when I said, 'She's enrolling as *Sofía Clarke*. Her idea, not mine or Dad's.'

'Oh.' It was her turn to think. 'I spoke to Mum about their will. She says that they're not changing it. She thinks Dad will want to give Sofía something when she's finished her studies. She's going to cross that bridge when it comes.'

'She's a good kid, Raitch. Getting to know her father's been all the inheritance she wants.'

'Yeah. She is a good kid. Shit taste in music, though.'

'Tell me about it. Are you coming to the Bollywood party?'

'If there's room.' She straightened up. 'Anyway, what are you up to this weekend?'

'Mina needs to see a man about a missing ruby.' She rolled her eyes. 'Rachael, if I tell you something, will you just accept it?'

'That sounds serious. Yes, if it's important.'

'The case is tied up with Mina's ... heritage. She won't be allowed to marry if we don't sort it out.'

'Really? I thought she was completely cut off from her family.'

'No. This is about a very old debt being called in, and you'll meet her cousin at the Bollywood party. There'll be plenty of room at Elvenham because we're turning the old servants' rooms into proper bedrooms.'

She shivered and started to walk towards the stairs. 'We?'

I followed her. 'Team Elvenham. Myfanwy is already planning Christmas. Mum and Dad have booked flights.'

'Then it's my duty to come. Keep up standards.'

When we got downstairs, Mina was deep in conversation with Sofía about something, and Vicky shocked me by announcing that Alain was being co-opted into their flat-hunt. 'He needs to leave that place,' she said. I couldn't agree more.

'I wonder what tomorrow night will be like?' said Mina when we got back to Notting Hill.

'Interesting. So many people have dropped hints about Chris Kelly's domestic arrangements that I can't wait to find out.'

It was *very* interesting, and because it forms part of the search for Pramiti's missing ruby, I've let Mina tell it in *Ring of Troth*.

Our dinner at St Cecilia's had been on Thursday, and we didn't get back to Elvenham until Tuesday night, after a detour to Heathrow and Richmond. When we finally rocked up, Mina announced that the wedding would be early next summer, 'Now that our little difficulty has been dealt with.'

She didn't give anything away about the wedding details, not even to me in private, and there were no announcements about bridesmaids. Yet. I don't think she knows herself what she wants.

One thing that did change straight away was the corner of the library in Elvenham. For many years, James Clarke's desk had stood there, until I restored it to pride of place. On the Wednesday morning, Mina moved one of the reproduction console tables into the space and installed an altar to Ganesh on top.

She led me to the altar and took off her engagement ring. She placed it on top of a twenty pound note and recited a prayer in Sanskrit. She finished the prayer with a deep bow and took my hand.

'Ganesh, hear me. I release Conrad from his promise never to lie to me now that we are betrothed.'

She looked up at me and smiled. 'Now it is finished. You can lie as much as you want, which I hope is very little.'

Without waiting for a response, she picked up her ring and slid it back on her finger. 'I'm hungry. Let's go.'

She left the money behind as an offering. It would go into a pot underneath the altar. Mina had told the whole house that anyone was welcome to make offerings, and Scout was advised that there would be drastic consequences if he so much as *dreamt* of stealing them. Ganesh does have a sweet tooth…

28 – A Straw in the Wind

On Wednesday evening, the day before our departure to Cornwall, I got an unexpected phone call. I was alone in the utility room doing a spot of ironing. Honestly. Mina trusts no one else with her saris. Just before the phone rang, Scout came looking for me.

'What's up boy?'

He turned his head towards the staircase and whined. 'Are they not playing nicely up there?'

'Arff.'

Mina, Myfanwy and Erin were in the attic, arguing about a colour scheme for the new rooms. 'We're well out of it.' Scout eyed the laundry basket. Covetously. 'You are not making a bed there, old son. It'll be time for a walk soon.'

At that point my phone rang. It was Eseld's number, but not Eseld on the other end. It was her father.

'Lord Mowbray! How can I help?'

'My Enscriber's injured herself. Fell over on a boat and sprained her bloody wrist. I don't know another one I can get here in time. Eseld says you've got one on retainer.'

'Erin works here, yes, and she's here now. I'll just get her.' I muted the call. 'Scout. Fetch Erin. Now boy!' He scampered off and I returned to the call. 'She's on her way, and as far as I know, she hasn't got any plans for the next few days.'

'Good.'

'Apart from that, how are things going?'

'Fine. Everything's lined up and ready. Oh, and Lena asked me to pass on a message. Hedda wants to see you at visiting tomorrow night.'

'How is she?'

'Tough. Early exposure to Swedish winters, I suppose. Lena went to see her this afternoon and says she should make a full mundane recovery.'

'That's good to hear.'

'It is. The next two and a half weeks in Glastonbury are going to be interesting.'

'How come?'

'They choose the new Eldest Daughter at the next full moon.'

Because Scout couldn't explain why he wanted Erin in particular, all three women trailed downstairs after him with shouts of, 'Conrad! What's happening?'

I held out the phone to Erin. 'Lord Mowbray has a job for you.'

Once Erin had gone to the sitting room for some privacy, Mina looked at Myfanwy and said, 'Blue?'

'Blue.'

'Good. Shall we let her have a Japanese room?'

'So long as she sleeps in it.'

'Settled,' said Mina with some finality.

'Good. I'll start organising the builder while you're in Cornwall,' said Myfanwy.

'Are you going to tell me what you're talking about?' I said.

'No,' said Mina. 'You'll find out when it's finished. Here she comes.'

Erin held out my phone to me at the same time as she called Saffron on her own mobile. 'I'm going to scrounge a lift from Saff,' she said. 'There's no room in the Volvo with that dog.'

'I would go home tomorrow, if I could,' said Hedda, 'but there will be no one at home to take me. And I don't think the hospital believe that I'm recovered.'

'Brain surgery is a serious business,' I replied.

Hedda was out of bed and sitting in a family room. The only sign of her trauma was a walking frame and a woolly hat to cover the dressing. She looked pale and her left eye seemed dimmer.

'Thank you for the plums, and thank Lena, too,' she said. She held the box of Pellacombe plums in her right hand and felt some of them with her left. She caught me looking at her. 'I can use my hands and my speech. In most ways I am very lucky. The doctors do not know what I have really lost.'

'Totally?'

'It is like being blind or paralysed. I remember the feeling of magick, but it simply doesn't work any more. Even when Raven comes to see me, she is just a very tall woman.'

I smiled. 'What did she feel like before?'

Hedda looked away. 'I cannot describe it to you. Could you get me some paper towels? There is a bathroom just there.'

She ate two of the plums, slowly and deliberately, while I told her about the plans for the Election tomorrow. When she'd finished eating, she sighed. The effort had been immense, for some reason. 'Now you can tell Signe that I will be all right. She does not need to visit me. She must stay for the election and the banquet.'

'Why's that?' I said. I tried to make it sound like a joke.

'Because she must start to lead her own life now. I do not need a nurse, I need a daughter. A daughter with her own life.'

That was a very heroic declaration. You had to admire it, even if it sounded a bit premature.

She hadn't finished. 'Do not weep for me, Conrad. The Goddess has finished with me, and that is a burden I did not know was so heavy. It is only now that I have laid it down that I realise how bent my back was.'

I weighed up what I'd been thinking about since last week. 'I don't think the Goddess is finished with you yet, Mother.'

She pointed a crooked finger. 'Don't start with that. From the day of my stroke, I am Mother only to Signe. You will call me Hedda and you will tell me how you know the Will of the Goddess all of a sudden. It sounds most unlikely to me.'

'How much of the sealing ceremony do you remember?'

She frowned. 'I remember lunch. I remember the pain. I remember Lena's hand inside my soul and I remember the helicopter. That is why I wanted to see you. To say thank you. And don't say you were just doing your job.'

'I was doing what anyone else would do: trying to help. I did what I could.'

She nodded. 'As did Raven and Lena. Thank you.'

'I had help though. You had wine with your meal.'

'Did I?'

'Yes. We were supposed to have a choice of beer or cider, and the beer is very good and rather strong. One of the waitresses agreed to go on a date with our waiter, just before service. He was so delirious, he only brought cider. I hate the stuff.'

'I don't follow.'

'If he'd brought beer, I wouldn't have been fit to fly. I was off duty. I think the Goddess tipped the scales in your favour. Just a little.'

She sighed and said something in Swedish. It sounded like a prayer. 'You have made an old woman very happy, Conrad. Will you come and see me again before you go? I would like to meet your wonderful fiancée again. You know, my memory tells me she said that she plays bridge. Is that right, or is it playing tricks on me?'

'No tricks. She loves bridge. She describes herself as an enthusiastic beginner.'

'Promise?'

I got up and moved the side table closer to her. I topped up her water and bent down to kiss her cheek. 'No promises, Hedda, but I will make it my business to come.'

'Then the blessings of the Goddess be upon you.'

29 – Truth or Dare

The Jet Stream had blessed us with a subtle shift, bringing high pressure, clear skies and a drop in temperature. The perfect morning for a ride and for flying a chopper.

I picked up my clothes from the chair and slipped out of our bedroom to get dressed.

'Oh. Have you been up all night?'

Erin was collapsed on the sofa in the suite's sitting room. She had barely crossed the river yesterday before Lord Mowbray had grabbed her and dragged her into his study. I hadn't seen her since.

She made a monumental effort to turn her head and look at me. Her eyes were red and her hair had exploded. The blonde was now streaked black with ink where she'd pulled her hands through it. There was more ink on her face and her right hand was almost completely covered. I couldn't see her left hand because it was buried in Scout's fur. The cheeky rascal had seen a woman in a vulnerable state and jumped on the couch.

'Are you my friend?' said Erin. If I hadn't known she'd been performing magick all night, I'd have said she was on drugs.

I dumped my clothes and gave her shoulder a squeeze. 'When you need one.'

'Then don't tell me I look a sight, okay?'

'Did it go all right? All done?'

She nodded and winced. 'Yeah. That Enscriber with the dodgy wrist left me with the worst job ever.' Her Bristol accent had got stronger overnight.

'What's up?'

She moaned out a breath. 'You'll see, right enough.'

In that moment, when she had no energy left, I suddenly knew that I could trust Erin far more than I'd thought. Despite her very close friendship with Myfanwy (and Mina and Saff), she'd kept her client's secrets. Good to know.

'Can I get you anything?'

'Give us a hand up or I'll go to sleep here. I'm sorry I'll miss the election, but I have to rest.'

She turfed Scout off the couch and held out a hand. I hauled her up and shoved her gently towards her room. As she disappeared through the door, she raised her inky fingers in a wave. 'Night, Conrad.'

I gathered my clothes and got ready to head to the stables.

When I got there, a few minutes late, Eseld had nearly finished setting up.

'Did you manage to amuse yourselves last night?' she said. I'd only seen her for two minutes, long enough to make this appointment.

'I was shattered. It was a relief not to socialise.' We finished saddling and led the horses out into the crisp morning air. 'Your Dad certainly got his money's worth out of Erin.'

'The Enscriber? It was so manic last night, I didn't even see her, let alone get to talk. Race you to the lookout point?'

'Absolutely.'

'Do you want a bet on it?' she said with a twinkle.

I try to avoid gambling. It's addictive. 'A bet has to mean something, and any amount of money that would mean something to you would bankrupt me.'

She laughed, full of excitement. 'A forfeit then. Winner gets to choose the loser's outfit for the banquet tonight.'

'That would be no fun for you and dangerous for me. How about truth or dare.'

We locked eyes. She knew what might happen if she lost. She ran her tongue round her purple lips and sucked the end back in to her mouth. 'You're on. We'll trot to the long meadow gate and start from there.'

This time, she paced herself, holding Uther back for a flying finish. Now that I knew the route, I reckoned I could get one over on her, and pushed Evenstar to overtake just before the start of a track through some woods, a track that was only one horse wide. I slowed right down, and she got frustrated trying to pass me. Uther baulked at a patch of brambles and she had to pull up. I dug my heels into Evenstar and hollered her into a gallop. This time, I won by a length.

'You bastard,' she said. 'If it wasn't so beautiful up here, I'd be really angry.'

I dismounted and gave Evenstar's nose a rub. At the edge of my consciousness, I felt a twinge. Scout was coming back into range, and he wasn't happy at being left behind. I got out a carrot and a bag of treats for the animals and a smoke for the humans. Eseld joined me and we took a moment to be at peace with the morning.

'Well then,' she said when she'd finished her rollup. 'Truth or dare. If I'd dared you to sleep with me, what would you have done?'

I thought she might say that. Whether she'd actually have dared me to do it is another matter. As we were in the realm of the hypothetical, I replied, 'My promise to Mina goes above everything, but as a gambling debt is a debt of honour, I'd have done the next best thing.'

'What? Sent *Mina* to sleep with me?'

'Oh no. I'd have sent Alain Dupont. He's a very able deputy. Highly rated on Tinder.'

When she'd finished laughing, she picked up her helmet, ready to remount. 'And what about you, Conrad? How do you think I'll react if you make me tell the truth about my mother?'

'I wouldn't do that, Eseld. It would spoil a lovely morning. Tell me the truth about Medbh instead.'

'What truth?'

'Oighrig Ahearn,' I said, leaving the name dangling in the air.

'Shit. How did she get hold of you?'

'Walked up to me at Cora Hardisty's barbecue. A week last Sunday.'

'That explains a lot.' She put her helmet down again. 'Medbh disappeared a couple of days after that. Dad said that she was staying at Ethandun. Hiding more like. Then Ethan and me started hearing whispers that the Irish diaspora was abuzz with it all. We went to talk to Dad.'

'From the look on your face, that didn't go well.'

'He was furious with Medbh and he wouldn't say why. He muttered something about a tangled web and said that she hasn't been to the West of Ireland since she left the sídhe. She's going straight to Old Sarum this morning. He was hoping to keep a lid on it until after the banquet.'

'It's your business, not mine, Eseld. I won't say anything unless I have to.'

She put her helmet on. 'I can't imagine why you'd have to. The Daughters won't be interested, that's for sure.'

I mounted Evenstar and said, 'Why's that?'

'You'll see.'

I did see, but not as well as Mina did. I'll let her tell the story of the election. After all, she did have a starring role.

30 – The Boar of Kellysporth

Conrad likes to test me. He likes to see if I can forgive him, and so far, he's been lucky. His luck nearly ran out over breakfast.

I still couldn't believe that the dress code for electing a staff king was *outdoor casual with coats*. What? For Saffron, that meant combat uniform, and she was all ready when she arrived. I was playing it safe until I knew for certain.

She waved a sausage in the air. 'Old Sarum is in the middle of an old ruin. It belongs to English Heritage, and they're letting us have exclusive access to a cordoned off area until one o'clock. We're there because it's a Locus Lucis, and this Locus Lucis is on top of a hill in the open air, so we have no choice. It's going to be tight to organise.'

It was. Here we were in Cornwall, and in a short while we were travelling 150 miles to Wiltshire in the Smurf. It was going to be my first ever trip in a helicopter, and there was so much else to be nervous about that I'd barely considered it. After all, I do know the pilot very well.

Conrad tells me that there is a small airfield next to Old Sarum where we will land, and where another helicopter will be waiting. The Daughters of the Goddess are being taken from Glastonbury to Old Sarum by coach, and after the election both helicopters will leave together for different destinations. The Daughters will go to Perranporth airfield while we come here. Conrad will then use the Smurf to fetch them in two trips.

I was running that round in my head when he appeared from his ride. He got himself a huge plate of protein and joined us. 'News on Medbh,' he said. 'She lied about Donegal and Galway.'

Before we could absorb the implications of this, Lord Mowbray came in. 'Get us a bacon sandwich, will you, love?' he said to Kerenza. She jumped up from her seat and left her breakfast to go cold while she served him.

In one hand he carried a large cardboard envelope, the sort that Amazon use to deliver calendars (not that I've ever ordered a calendar from Amazon). In the other was the box that contains the Wessex seal. I shuddered when I saw it, and immediately had a flashback to Hedda's head hitting the table when she had her stroke.

He gave both items to Cador and pointed at us. At me! He poured himself some tea, took the plate with his bacon sandwich and disappeared. When the father left, the son wiped his hands and came over.

'Good morning,' he said. 'Nice ride?'

'Yes thanks,' said Conrad.

'Here you are, Mina,' said Cador. 'One ballot paper and one seal. All yours.'

'And why do I want these?'

He frowned. 'To conduct the election.'

I confess. I squeaked. 'Me! Why? Who says?'

Cador looked at Conrad. Conrad frowned and looked at the door where Mowbray had disappeared. When Conrad didn't answer, Cador said, 'Didn't you get the renewed warrant from Judge Bracewell?'

Conrad went red. Seriously red. He doesn't blush very often. He muttered something.

'What!'

'I got a message to pick up some post from Merlyn's Tower. I was distracted by the Pramiti business and forgot.'

I banged the table. 'You cannot use our engagement as an excuse!' Cador was trying to walk away. 'Stay!' I told him. 'And explain.'

He floundered a little until his legal training reasserted itself. 'Don't worry. Ethan is the Marshal. He'll be leading things. All you have to do is take the poll, record the results and seal them.'

'All? That is *all* I have to do? In front of your family, the Daughters and goodness knows how many other Mages?'

This time he did retreat. 'Yes. That's it. Just read the text and take the poll.'

'I'd start saving if I were you,' said Saffron to Conrad. 'We're talking at *least* a ruby necklace to make up for that.'

Somehow, he kept on eating through all this. He looked at the last rasher of bacon and put his fork down. 'I'm sorry. What can I say? I'm really sorry. And we've got to go, Saff. The Smurf is waiting.'

He purloined two sausages on the way out and left me to seethe. In another minute, I was on my own. Even Eseld had avoided me and eaten on the other side of the room. I picked up the toxic delivery from Cador and headed to the King's Watch suite to get changed. I would have cursed a lot more if Erin hadn't been asleep.

The moment I forgave him was the moment the helicopter made a lazy arc over Torbay. He'd told us we were going over the water rather than land, for some reason. The view was immense. Total. At that moment I relaxed and thought *what's the worst that can happen?*

After we landed, there was a one mile trip by minibus, and I reconsidered my decision to forgive him when I saw just how many people were waiting to be let in to Old Sarum fort. The Daughters were gathered together on one side, forming several groups and with a new presence at the centre.

You couldn't miss the Witch with the rainbow robes. This would be Verity, 1st of Willow and the chief priest. With Hedda incapacitated, Verity had taken it upon herself to come. She wouldn't be travelling to Pellacombe afterwards.

On the other side of the path was a mixed bunch of Mages. For once, the gender balance was about equal, probably because the age profile was skewed towards the older end. A couple had their best suits on and stood out a mile in the sea of nature toned outdoor fabrics. And me? Lena had forsaken her dirndls for leggings and a waxed jacket, and I did the same. Except for the bright red kurti. Without any height or magick, I need a way to stand out.

Our group was let through by the throng. As we approached the front, a burst of red hair announced Medbh Mowbray. She emerged from the crowd and joined her family, as far from me as she could get.

Ethan Mowbray had a short discussion with a man from English Heritage and then we streamed across the bridge to the gates. I was sticking to Saffron at this point because Conrad was going to miss the election completely. Helicopter business.

Inside the fort, we had to pick our way round several muddy patches and into an area at the top surrounded by ruined walls. Saffron sniffed the air and lifted her head. 'What can you smell?' I said.

'What? Oh. Lux. We're right over the join of three Ley lines.'

'I shall take your word for it.'

A small section of scaffolding had been put up by one of the walls, about eight feet high, as if it were being used to repair the stones. Ethan climbed up the ladder and I groaned. Out loud. I was going to have to do the same at some point. I put down my backpack and took out the form of election and the seal.

Ethan and Lena actually have his-n-hers waxed jackets. It's not a look I'm going to copy with Conrad, especially as his waxed jacket is old and smells of horse. From an inside pocket, Ethan took a piece of wood.

'What's he doing with that stick?' I whispered.

Saffron rolled her eyes. Now I know how Conrad feels. 'It's a staff. Magick. It's the staff of the Marshal of Wessex.'

Ethan took off his jacket and laid it on the top of the wall. He turned his back on us and my arm itched furiously. From around the space, I could hear murmuring.

Ethan laid the staff to one side, straightened his back and turned round to face us. There was an intake of breath as we saw what he was now holding. A golden crown.

'Behold the crown of the staff king!' His big chest carried his voice across the ruins. 'It was laid down by my father when he appointed the Duke of Albion Regent of the kingdoms of Wessex.'

Kingdoms? Plural? Was that in the Agreement? I made a mental note to check, and Ethan moved on.

'That Regency has lapsed. Mages of Wessex, I call upon you to elect a new staff king. Are you ready?'

There was a rumble of agreement, I half expected Ethan to shout *I can't hear you!* like a warm-up man. Instead, he laid the crown on the wall and picked up his staff. 'The court of Wessex has appointed a judge of the election. Let it proceed.'

Saffron nudged me in the back. 'That's you!'

I slipped off my coat and picked up my burden. The crowd parted and I found myself at the bottom of a ladder, with both hands full. Before I could breathe, a familiar voice said, 'Allow me.'

Raven took the packet and box and placed them on the platform; I was both annoyed and relieved in equal measure and would have said something if there was time. Instead, I hitched up my kurti and climbed to the top. Ethan had already picked up my goods and even produced a clipboard. Some of their organisation was spot on.

Ethan waited until I was composed, then turned back to the crowd. 'The election will be judged by Mina Desai of Elvenham in Clerkswell, Gloucestershire.'

I felt a surge of pride in my new life when he said that. To stop a silly grin appearing on my face, I made namaste to the crowd. A good few of them, including all the Mowbrays, bowed back. I almost felt giddy.

The Mowbrays had gathered at the front, slightly to my right. Little Grace, Kerenza's daughter, was with them, too. She had a look of awe on her face, as well she might: she'd been given a day off school for this. The Daughters were to my left, and the miscellaneous Mages made a semi-circle behind them.

'When you're ready,' whispered Ethan. Talk about being brought down to earth.

I'd studied the form, and Cador was right. I didn't have a lot to say. 'In the name of the court of Wessex I shall take a poll of Mages. Your right to vote will be validated by the Marshal. Step forward the Guardians of Sarum.'

Two men came from the crowd and identified themselves. Ethan nodded his approval and the older man said, 'We choose Lord Mowbray of Pellacombe.'

This was a completely open ballot. They could say who they liked, which meant that I had to write it down in full every time. The cardboard folder had included a silver Cross pen, especially Enscribed with the date, place and purpose. I wrote down their vote in my bestest writing, adding "2" to show that both Sarum votes had gone to the same person.

Mowbray got six more votes in similar vein and then I called for *Aquae Sulis*. That's the Roman name for Bath. Verity, 1st of Willow and Daughter of Memory came forward. 'I claim right of proxy,' she said.

Ethan challenged the crowd for the real electors of Aquae Sulis to step forward. When they didn't, he granted Verity the proxy and she also voted for Mowbray. I wouldn't say that I breathed a sigh of relief, exactly, but my shoulders definitely relaxed.

It came as a great shock when Tintagel voted. Mowbray had already picked up twenty votes and was home and dry. A well-built young Witch had the Tintagel votes and announced in a defiant voice, 'We choose the true Boar of Mowbray, Ethan of Kellysporth.' What???

Ethan stiffened. He clearly knew these people very well and said, 'Morgan! Do you want to repeat that? I don't think the judge heard you.'

'She heard me. Tintagel votes for you, Ethan. You should be the Boar of Mowbray and head of the clan.'

Ethan went quiet. I focused on the woman and said, 'How do you spell Kellysporth?'

For some reason, the crowd thought that was funny, especially Lord Mowbray. In five more minutes, I was placing my seal at the bottom and passing the parchment to Ethan. I descended the ladder to a prolonged round of applause.

'Well done,' said Saffron. 'You're a natural.'

'A natural clown, you mean?'

She looked offended. 'No. Why would I say that? You have natural authority, Mina.'

'Yeah, right, I…'

'Mages of Wessex!' I shut up and Ethan announced the result of the election, then called on Mowbray to accept the crown.

To further, greater, applause, he mounted the scaffold and accepted the crown. Just like that – Ethan handed it over with no speeches or ceremony.

Mowbray lifted the crown and showed it around. More applause. He lowered it and let it rest by his side in one hand, like a hat.

'Thank you all,' he said. 'This is the greatest honour. Unlike the sword king, there is no coronation, no oath and no ceremony. To get this crown, I made promises, and now that I have it, I renew them. To mark that, I would like to ask the Daughter of Memory of Glastonbury to lead us in honouring the gods we serve, the ancestors who made us, and the Spirits who guide us through this life.'

He placed the crown on the wall, and bowed his head. Verity stepped to the foot of the scaffolding and turned to face us. Half way through the prayers, my arm crackled and my neck got clammy. I barely remembered to echo the refrain at the end. Verity returned to the throng, and Mowbray picked up his crown. He also picked up Ethan's staff.

'My first act as staff king is to appoint Ethan Mowbray, or the boar if you prefer, as Marshal. Ethan, will you serve?'

Ethan bent the knee and accepted the staff.

Why wasn't Mowbray putting on the crown? I was itching for him to do it. Perhaps he knew it was too small. It didn't look very big. He had one more thing to say.

'There will be a new Deed for the kingdoms of Wessex, and it will be proclaimed from a new place of power. I hope that you will join me there. Until that time, thank you. If you don't want to be pestered by tourists, I suggest you leave now.' With an athletic flourish, Mowbray jumped down from the scaffold and re-joined his family. Ethan followed more slowly, gathering his bits and using the ladder.

The crowd parted again and the new staff king walked out through his people. I found myself next to the Daughters, and one of them looked very much alone. Instead of being at the heart of the group, Signe was now confined to the edge. She looked wretched, clearly regretting that she'd come.

'Have you heard from the hospital this morning?' I said while we waited to get through a gap in the walls.

'What? Sorry. Yes. Mother sent me a text to say that she was fine.'

'That's good. Conrad was thrilled to see her last night.'

'What's left of her.'

I didn't respond to that. We shuffled through the gap and I heard Kiwa, the Traveller, talking to Verity. I heard her because she wanted everyone to hear her.

'You see, there is life outside Homewood. And it definitely includes men.'

Verity took that in her stride. 'So it does. It also featured a mundane *woman* taking a position of responsibility.' She realised that the mundane woman could hear her and gave a slight nod of her head. 'The women of the mundane world have more to offer, if we let them.'

The group was moving slowly towards the main entrance. I dropped back a little, but not so far that I couldn't hear. Raven spoke next. 'There is already a queue of Mages to join Homewood. Why would we deny them a place?'

Síona jumped in. 'Which is precisely why we need a fourth coven.'

I wasn't the only person eavesdropping. Several Mages were now at the fringes of the group. Verity had had enough. 'Have you forgotten that the Mother is still in hospital? Signe does not want to listen to this. Not now.'

I'd been so absorbed by the gossip that the Mowbrays had moved well ahead, nearly at the car park. I put on a spurt and caught up with them as they were getting in to the minibus back to the airfield. Medbh was already at the back, out of the way.

'What's up?' said Saffron.

'Medbh is avoiding us.'

Conrad had a great smile on his face when we got out. I slipped over to him and he gave me a great big hug. 'You were brilliant,' he said.

'I was, but how do you know?'

'Saff sent me a text. You'll need these.'

He passed me a linen napkin with sausages in it. Ugh.

Medbh also took the furthest seat in the helicopter, so I forgot about her and enjoyed the return view. I expected the trip to calm me, as the one out had done, but something was niggling. This morning should have been a triumph for the Mowbrays, and on the surface, it had been. Underneath, there was a lot going on that sounded a dissonant note, like an out of tune bell in temple.

Medbh was one thing. The attitude of the Daughters another. Hedda's situation. The sudden burst of enthusiasm for the Boar of Kellysporth. It all added up.

At Lamorne Point, Conrad left the engines running and Saffron reminded us to secure all loose items before leaving the cabin. I was out second and had to go straight to comfort a distressed Scout, whom we'd left with the Ferrymistress's older daughter.

I gave him a hug and half a sausage, then held him while we waited for the Smurf to get airborne again. Just before giving himself completely to the machine, Conrad looked over and blew me a kiss. When the noise of the rotors had died away in the distance, they were replaced by the throb of diesel. I stood up and ran to the edge of the hill. The ferry and the Mowbrays were already half way across the river. I couldn't blame their urgency. They had a lot to do and no time to wait for lovesick auditors to wave off their fiancés. Convenient, though.

A third noise, the electric whine of the buggy, came up the path. Eseld, with cigarette clamped in her mouth.

'They were going to make you walk,' she said, 'and I fancied a smoke, so I volunteered. Besides, someone has to be on duty to welcome the Daughters.' She slipped out of the driver's seat. 'Well done, Mina. I could see you were nervous.'

If Eseld walked into a village shop today, even in her blue fleece, she would still turn heads. She is a striking woman.

I come from a big family. Two big families. Nothing is left of them except ghosts and echoes.

And memories. I remembered trying to copy my mother when she was dealing with someone she didn't want to get close to. That was how Eseld had treated me: polite, friendly, and never being together long enough to let the mask slip. She had done her best to spend as much time as possible alone with Conrad, so why was she here now?'

'I don't like it either,' she said.

'And what would that be?'

'Medbh. Dad won't tell us the truth, and told us not to push it for now. I saw you trying to catch up with her.'

'And Kenver kept getting in the way. He's very protective. For a younger brother.'

'That's brothers for you. You've got one, haven't you?'

'I had two. When I sent a message to the one I have left, telling him about the engagement, he replied *Are you sure?* I'm not going to give up, though.'

'Congratulations, by the way. That's one hell of a ring, Mina.'

'Thank you.' We weren't going anywhere, and Eseld clearly wanted to talk, so I said, 'I feel like I am carrying around a great weight.'

'You have strong shoulders. You must do to wear that Ancile. It's taken me days to figure it out, and I had to call someone to make sure. Is it really tattooed on to your skin?'

We were in the middle of nowhere, high on a point. I slipped off my bangles and held them out to her. With a start, she accepted them, and I peeled off my kurti. I kept my back to her while I did so, and when I turned round she swore. Then she put her knuckle in her mouth and bit it.

'You ... I want to say, *you poor thing.*'

'Don't.' I put the kurti back on and took my bangles from her. 'Satisfied?'

I do like to put people on the back foot. I also swore to myself that this was the last time I was going to get undressed to show my wounds. Doing it for Tamsin Kelly had been bad enough.

'I'm so sorry,' said Eseld. 'I had no idea.'

'Why are you here, Eseld?'

She lit another cigarette. 'I had no idea it was going to be like this.'

I nodded in encouragement. 'Like what?'

'When Dad said that he wanted to be staff king and *rule* as staff king, I thought it was a laugh. When the Daughters got involved, I thought it would be good to put one over on them. Then he came up with the idea of the conference.'

'I was there, remember? In the Old Temple. I saw the look on your face when Cador suggested the conference. You didn't know, did you?'

'No.' She laughed with no humour in it. 'Not my finest hour, that, being torn off a strip by the judge.' She looked at me again. 'She's your boss, isn't she. No, you're right: I didn't like the idea of the conference, and when they sent the list with Isolde's name on it, yeah, I suppose I lost the plot a bit.'

'Is it a wonder that your mother wanted to see you?'

She was shaking her head before I'd got the question out. 'Not the point. Hedda sent her to upset me. To destabilise me. Us. Put us off balance. She's like a great spider in the web of Homewood. Was. Ex-spider, now.' She tried to smile, to get some comfort out of Hedda's tragedy. I warmed to her a lot when the smile died on her face. She couldn't do it.

'And then there's you,' she said. 'You and Conrad. And Saffron.' She bent down to stroke Scout, who'd gone to sleep on the grass. 'And you, you mad mutt.' She stood up. 'You're the first family to break bread with us in the private quarters since Pellacombe was built. Did you know that?'

She was upset, clearly. She was opening up to me in her own way. She obviously thought that what she'd said made sense and constituted a confession. It didn't. It described a situation and said nothing about what had led her here, to this hilltop, to talk to someone she barely knows.

I have been to therapy. I went after my face was smashed in. A bit stupid, really, sending me to therapy when you can't talk. I could push Eseld further or I could bank what we'd got and invest it. I chose investment and turned the conversation.

'I won't tell Saffron you counted her in my family. She can be very prickly about the Hawkins clan.'

'Nouveau riche,' she said. 'Only been around since the 1700s.'

'And the Mowbrays? It's not a Cornish name.'

'We came down from Scotland during the Reformation.'

'William the Clerk, the first recorded ancestor of Conrad's family was alive in the 1350s, by which time the Desais had been in Gujarat so long that they were naming parts of the countryside after us.'

'Wow. That is old.'

'And yet here I am in Cornwall, Eseld, a footnote. A qualification on the accounts.' She frowned. 'I lost you with the accountancy metaphor, didn't I?'

She chuckled. 'Yeah. Just a bit. You haven't spoken to Conrad properly since the ride this morning, have you?'

'No.'

'We had a race. The forfeit was truth or dare. I lost. I told him what I'd have dared him if I won.'

I wasn't amused. 'It was something involving sexual relations, no doubt.'

'No need to be sniffy, Mina. It was just a bit of fun. I wouldn't have *really* dared him to sleep with me. Do you know what he said? He said he'd have sent someone called Alain Dupont in his place.'

'Aah. You wouldn't have been disappointed. From what I've heard, he's very good.' I took a step closer to her. 'My engagement to Conrad is many things, Eseld. Unlikely. Dangerous. Perhaps even doomed. But it is not *a bit of fun*. Are we clear on that?'

She looked down at her feet. 'Yeah. Sorry.'

I stepped even closer and put my arms up to give her a hug. She squeezed with all the strength of a woman who can control thoroughbreds, and I felt her chest heave.

'Arff! Arff!'

We pulled back and she blinked at the tears forming in her eyes.

'Incoming Smurf,' I said. 'You have about a minute to dry your eyes and stop behaving like the teenage daughter I won't have for a long time.'

'May the gods help you if she turns out like me. And don't let Dad hear you calling his pride and joy *The Smurf*.' She took in a deep breath and held it. When she released the air, she blinked again and the tears had gone. 'Now that we're here, how shall we sort it?'

'I can't drive the buggy. I shall go with the first party across the river and up to Pellacombe. You can wait and bring the rest.'

We could both hear the rotors now. 'Sorted,' said Eseld. 'And thanks.'

I paused for half a second to let her know that I'd heard her. 'Who do you think will be in the first party?'

'Raven and her acolytes. Alys may be deputy to Hedda, but Raven is 1st of Ash.'

It got too loud to talk as the Smurf dropped out of the sky, and for the fifth time today, I wished that I'd asked Saffron to put my hair in a plait. Eseld was half right about the passengers, but for the wrong reasons. To explain why, Conrad needs to take over the story back in Perranporth.

31 – Landed Gentry

Electing a new staff king was not today's most memorable event. Not by a long chalk.

The best thing was seeing the video on Saff's phone: Mina conducting the election. Second best was beating Eseld to the top of the mound; third best was Michael skiving a day off school to be our loadie, and the cherry on top was the news that he'd joined the local sea cadets.

'Are you ready, Michael?'

'Sir.'

Perranporth airfield is very near the cliffs. Less than 200m, which is nothing in an aircraft. My crew kept quiet about that when we passed over them and scooted in to land in a spare corner of the runway.

'Off you go.'

All the passengers today had been told that it was strictly hand luggage only. It was Michael's job to take their bags and escort them under the rotors. I was busy planning our return when Saff said, 'He's got a problem.'

I peered round and saw the Daughters trying to have an argument at the tops of their voices. 'Go and sort it, Saff.'

The Smurf has so many luxuries. One of them is the wireless headsets. Saffron jumped out and ran over. She keyed me out for a moment while she talked to the Witches, then turned her back on them to speak to me. 'It's Alys and Raven. Alys didn't do very well on the first flight and Raven wants her to get it over with by coming first. Alys is having none of it.'

'Tell her that it's get in now or wait for Maggie Pearce to come and get her. That's at least an hour for a forty minute drive. Oh, and tell Raven that she has to come, too.'

'Why?'

'I haven't brought my SIG. I'm not risking Alys losing it in mid-air with no one to stop her.'

'Right. Hang on.'

The engines had reached ground idle. They're quite happy like that, on a cold day in the Arctic. On a hot day in Cornwall, not so much. They'd already worked hard and my patience was limited by the thermometer.

Saffron had bad news. 'That idea's not going to fly. As it were.'

'In that case, tell them I'm going to make one trip with as many as can fit in. The rest will be sent for. Wheels up in two minutes.'

Raven handed her case to Michael as soon as she heard the offer, and Cordelia followed in her wake. With some touching of hands and shakes of heads, Brook, Kiwa, Morning and Síona joined them in the cabin. The last one to take her seat was Isolde, leaving four to wait behind. Saffron was busy on her phone before the engines had reached take-off speed.

Part Six — Dawn's Blessing

32 – Witnesses

I couldn't quite believe what I saw at Lamorne Point: Mina and Eseld standing by the buggy *almost shoulder to shoulder*. What?

My crew ushered the passengers out, and I watched Eseld give a smooth welcome and point to the buggy. None of this flight wanted a lift, so Michael drove the luggage down, and Eseld led them all to the steps. Mina tagged on to the end and waved to me. I waved back and carried on shutting down the helicopter. Scout was waiting patiently at the edge of the safety circle.

Something started pressing on my chest, in a not-good-heart-attack way. I gasped for breath, and it stopped as suddenly as it started, to be replaced by fear. Not my fear…

I looked up and saw a black shadow. A very tall black shadow. It morphed into Raven, and she was holding Scout in her arms. Even at this distance, I could see him trembling. She jogged across the LZ as I was opening the door. When she got close, she almost threw him into the cockpit.

He tried to climb up me, paws scrabbling for purchase on my jacket. I clasped him and lifted him until he could start licking my face. And neck. Even my bald patch did not go unwashed.

'Easy boy. It's all right. We're good. It's all good.'

Either he calmed down or he ran out of saliva. I eased myself on to the ground and put him down.

'Sorry about that,' said Raven. 'I didn't realise that he was so fragile.'

The 1st of Ash looked guilty and awkward. For the first time, she was uncomfortable in her huge frame.

'What were you doing with my Familiar? And why?'

She shook her head. 'You wouldn't understand. I'm so sorry, and it won't happen again. I'll make it up to him, if I can.'

When she said, *You wouldn't understand*, I don't think it was just magick she was talking about. I left that for later and tried to move on. 'It'll cost you at least a steak and a marrowbone. Perhaps even a grooming session.'

She squatted down like a collapsing jenga tower and looked Scout in the eye. 'Friends? Steak later?' He looked like he'd take some convincing. She stood up. 'I wondered if you fancied taking me for a spin? Might not get another chance.'

'Sorry, Raven. It's not my decision, and in half an hour I'll be timed out.'

She reached over and stroked the Mowbray blue door. 'I never realised it could be so liberating.' She shook herself. 'Sorry. I'll shut up. Have you got more to do?'

'A bit. We'll be about half an hour.'

'We?'

'Michael's dad will be here in a minute.'

'Then I shall leave you to it and see you at the banquet.'

I watched her straight back cross the Point and disappear down the steps. When even Cora's hearing couldn't eavesdrop, I bent down to Scout and said, 'What was that all about then, eh boy?'

'Arff.'

Fair enough.

Back in the King's Watch suite, Erin had emerged, wrapped in the complimentary fluffy robe with blue belt. Her hair was even worse – still ink-stained, and now flattened on one side. At least her eyes looked human again. She was snug in the middle of the sofa with Mina and Saffron on either side, and they were watching Mina's iPad. They'd already made inroads into the afternoon tea spread over the table.

I kissed the top of Mina's head and leaned over to see.

'Who filmed that?' I said.

On the screen, Mina was conducting the poll again, only this time in HD.

'One of the Mages from darkest Cornwall. St Michael's Mount, I think. Not that it makes any difference. Mowbray got him to film it for posterity and sent it to me,' said Mina.

'Sent it with thanks for a job well done,' added Saffron.

'I keep brushing the hair off my face,' said Mina. 'All the time.'

'Yes?' said Erin. 'It wouldn't be you if you didn't. Ow! That hurt.'

'I do not do that,' said Mina, retrieving her elbow from Erin's ribs.

'Yes you do,' I said.

'Totally,' agreed Saffron.

'I can't watch this!' said Mina. She made no move to reclaim the iPad or leave the couch.

'What's this party tonight?' said Erin in a pause where on-screen Mina was writing down a particularly long name.

'Election Banquet,' said Saffron. 'It would normally be private, but the new staff king has to deliver on his promises to the Daughters. The big one is the Proclamation feast. That won't be for a few weeks, and we're not invited.'

'What time?'

'Drinks from seven o'clock, then dinner at half past. Conrad and Mina have an appointment with King Mowbray to seal the new Deed first, so they get dibs on the bathroom. Rewind that bit.'

I desperately wanted to watch the election and see Mina in action. I also wanted to get my chance in the bathroom and left them to it after pouring a cup of tea and stuffing a sandwich in my face.

'How are we going to handle this?' said Mina. We were early for our appointment, and Lena, flying past at a run, had asked us to wait on the terrace.

'We're in an awkward position,' I replied. 'You have a job to do on behalf of the court, and asking questions isn't part of your remit. I'm here as a personal guest, now that my helicopter duties are over.'

'I thought you were the guarantor of safety.'

'Only up to Lamorne Point. That's why Saffron kissed me when I got the orders from Hannah: no uniform required tonight. Hence the new suit.'

Mina had made the decision to show off one of her scars – the bright blue slash of boiling tattoo ink on her left arm. That had meant a new dress, western and bright red satin. The swastika was going to remain under cover.

She nodded. 'It is a bit awkward to ask your host questions about his daughter. That's why I'm glad it's you that has to ask them.' She grinned. 'I'll back you up.'

While Mina was getting ready, we'd shared notes on the day, especially about Eseld; I've been mulling it over ever since. 'I've got a theory,' I said. 'About Eseld and Raven. I don't know where Isolde fits in yet.'

'Yes?'

'Eseld told me she had a Familiar when she was very young, only just coming into magick. Raven would have been about eighteen at the time. I think Raven killed it.'

'What! She murdered Eseld's Familiar?'

'Not murder. If it had been deliberate, either Raven or Eseld would be dead by now. Whatever happened, Eseld has forgiven Raven but not her mother.'

Mina drew a deep breath through her nose. It's her sign that she's come across something distasteful. 'I know what happened,' she said, 'and I know it because my mother did the same. I think that Isolde persuaded, or bullied, or ordered, or tricked Raven into trying to break the bond. I don't think Isolde wanted her daughter to have a bat Familiar. Or that particular Spirit in that particular bat.'

I mulled it over. 'It fits. You missed an option out of your list: blackmailed. Isolde could have had a hold over Raven.'

'Good point.'

I smiled. 'I didn't know you had a pet bat, love. What did your mother really do?'

'Got me to break up with my best friend. That's a story for another time. How are we going to test your theory?'

I felt a presence behind us. 'Not now, I don't think.'

Cador and Eseld came out of the house deep in conversation. I couldn't believe the transformation in Eseld. No comedy outfits or sub-Goth black.

She was wearing a stunning, loose, Mowbray blue jumpsuit. Mina lost no time in telling her how much it suited her.

'Thanks,' said Eseld. 'Dad's ready for you now.'

The clothes might be mainstream, but all of the mutinous anger was still there. She pivoted and turned it on Cador.

'What?' he said.

Eseld folded her arms. Cador pressed his lips together and straightened the cuffs of his jacket. He and I were both wearing hand-tailored suits, from very different parts of London and for very different reasons. And very different prices. When Eseld kept her mouth zipped, he sighed.

'We don't know what's going on,' he said. 'Dad's up to something, but none of us know what it is. All nine of us were at tea, and he wouldn't say a thing. Closest I've seen to a family meltdown in years. Eseld said you should know.'

'Damn right,' said Eseld.

'What about Medbh?' said Mina.

Eseld grinned. 'I called her the golden girl, and she swore at me in Gaelic. She is a good actress, but I don't think she's that good; she's as much in the dark as we are.'

'Enough,' said Cador. 'Let's not keep him waiting.'

Eseld led us round the front of the house, towards the morning room. The first of the Daughters had appeared in the dining room, and I saw a face of longing against the glass. Isolde.

The door to Mowbray's study was open and the new staff king was seated at his desk. He looked inordinately pleased with himself, a look Dad used to sport when he'd pulled off a particularly outrageous sale to gullible Americans.

'Come in, come in,' he said, rising from the desk and coming round. He looked at his children, standing in the doorway and said, 'Thanks.' Then he shut the door in their faces and locked it with key and magick. 'Take a seat.'

The small conference table had a tray with three glasses and a familiar bottle on it. No. Surely not.

'My lord king, would that be a bottle of Dawn's Blessing?'

'No need for titles,' he said. 'Unless it's a state occasion. That's definitely something that's got to go. And yes, it is Dawn's Blessing.'

'Is that what Hannah has?' said Mina.

'Oh, yes.'

Dawn's Blessing is a magickal spirit from Scotland. It's a sort of whisky, in the same way that the Tower of London is a sort of museum. Hannah's bottle is a personal gift from the Peculier Constable of Scotland; I presume Mowbray got his because he's incredibly rich

'For after,' said Mowbray. 'Business first.'

We sat down, and he moved the tray on to his desk and opened a cupboard. From the depths, he fetched two tubes, two large oak boxes and the smaller one that contained the seal of Wessex. From a desk drawer he got a heavy manila envelope and two strips of paper, about the size of a cheque. He began with these.

'You gave me your bank accounts so that I could pay your expenses,' he said. 'I've done that, and added a fee for personal services. Here's the advice notes.'

He put them in front of us, and we stared at the figures. 'You get a lot of service for £10,000 each,' I said.

'Worth it. Especially as you're going to leave my younger daughter alone tonight.'

Mina got in first. 'You can't bribe us not to ask questions about Medbh.'

'I know I can't. I can ask you, as a father, to leave her alone until I get on my hind legs to present the new Deeds. I'll say something then. The money is completely non-conditional. If you won't agree to leave her alone, I'll just put you on a table by the door and it'll be very awkward for everyone.'

We looked at each other. Mina moved her head in a circle: *it's up to you.*

'We're a team,' I said, 'and that includes Saffron.'

'I thought you might say that. She's got the same, and her advice slip is in the house mail.'

'Good,' said Mina. 'Now what's this about *two* Deeds?'

'Your Enscriber, Erin. She hates me because of this.' He slipped the cap off a tube and took out a long roll of parchment with a ribbon stitched into the bottom. 'Have a look at her work.'

We rolled out the parchment. A good Enscriber is both artist and Mage. From the elaborate coat of arms at the top to the final hatching at the bottom, it was beautiful. It was also written in Gaelic script and the Cornish language. No wonder she'd gone bonkers.

'It goes with this,' said Mowbray. He opened one of the large boxes and from a bed of velvet, he took a thin golden circlet, larger and less ornate than the crown I'd seen in the video.

'Kingdoms. Plural,' said Mina.

'Correct,' said Mowbray. 'I'll explain it all later. All you have to do is put your seal after mine.'

She lifted her hair away from the tops of her arms. I think it was tickling her. 'Do you think this will end up in the Cloister Court?'

'No. I think certain lawyers will be all over it, then they'll advise their clients that it isn't worth the risk of going to court.'

'And the first lawyer to examine it will be Cador, won't it?'

His face froze for a moment and his eyes unfocused. He tapped the table with his hand and turned away. 'Sometimes you have to act alone. I'll get the royal seal and some wax.'

The royal seal of Wessex was ancient and ornate. It was also huge and must be worth a fortune in scrap gold alone, never mind the artistic and magickal value. In two minutes, it was all done and Mowbray's good humour had been restored. He cleared all the boxes and tubes away and restored the drinks tray. The only other item on the table was the manila envelope.

He poured three small measures and sat back. 'I don't know what the Constable does when she serves Dawn's Blessing, but I'm a traditionalist.'

'Hannah drinks it. What else would she do?'

He laughed. 'The toast. Have a smell first.'

We inhaled the aroma of fresh peat bogs and misty mornings.

'I am not a whisky lover,' said Mina. 'For this, I make an exception.'

Mowbray lifted his glass, 'May the gods grant us many new days and bless our beginnings. To the dawn.'

'To the dawn.'

There was a shared moment of peace as the golden glow of dawn spread across the room. In one smooth motion, we all placed our empty glasses on the table. There was a sigh of pleasure from under the table and Mowbray laughed.

'I had no idea Dawn's Blessing could spread down the Familiar channel.' He reached down and gave Scout a scratch. 'Don't develop a taste for it,' he said affectionately. 'Bad for you.'

'Everything he wants is bad for him,' said Mina. 'He's going through a teenage phase.'

'Tell me about it,' said Mowbray. 'There's one more thing.' He opened the envelope and pulled out a mundane document of printed sheets on archive paper. The sheets were held together with a gold ring in the top corner. He turned to the last page and placed it in front of himself. From his suit pocket, he took a fountain pen.

'This is my mundane will. A new one, in anticipation of my marriage. I'd like you to witness my signature.'

'Of course.'

'It would be an honour.'

'Thank you.' He uncapped the pen and wrote today's date, the 10th of September. Then he signed it with a flourish and passed the document and the pen to Mina.

She studied the document and smiled. 'You've already put our names and addresses.'

'There's another identical copy in the drawer with Saffron and Erin's names on it. I can't use the Estate staff because most of them are beneficiaries, and beneficiaries can't be witnesses.'

Mina signed. 'I like being Mina Desai of Elvenham House. It has a ring to it.'

I also signed and returned the pen and papers. Mowbray pocketed the pen and slid his will into the envelope. He sealed the flap and slid it across to Mina. 'Will you keep that? The king's will should be lodged with the court.'

Mina passed it to me. It was too big for her small purse, and only just fitted in my pocket.

'Thank you both,' said Mowbray. 'I hope you enjoy the party.'

33 – Hustings

Saffron and Erin were waiting in the morning room when Mowbray released us. There was no sign of his family.

'You've scrubbed up nicely,' I said to Erin.

'Ha ha, Conrad. It was a close run thing. I nearly rang Lena and asked to borrow some evening gloves.'

'How did you get on?' said Saffron, 'and why have I got a note saying I'm rich?'

'You only need a mirror to know you're rich,' said Mina.

'Eh?' Saffron wasn't sure whether she'd been complimented or insulted.

'Nice work on the Cornish Deed, Erin. It was worth the extra soap and water.'

She showed her hands. They were bright red. 'You need a solvent to get that stuff off. I won't be able to use Merlyn's Ink until the rash has cleared up. Not that I get many commissions like that.'

'What's going on?' said Saffron.

Mina explained the double Deed situation, and Saffron agreed to leave Medbh alone.

'You three can carry on plotting if you like,' said Erin. 'I need a drink.'

We took a short cut through the Pellacombe maze to the dining room and found that (apart from the king himself), we were the last to arrive.

'Yes!' said Saffron when we got to the bar. 'Real Champagne.'

Lena overheard her. 'Ja. The house wine did not go down well. Please take two glasses each. You have some catching up to do.'

'That is a gorgeous dress,' said Mina.

I grabbed two glasses and headed outside. My opinion of Lena's dress was neither wanted nor useful (I didn't think it suited her, but what do I know?). Eseld was waiting for me, where she knew I'd be going. She'd even arranged a pillar ashtray.

'Is one of those for me?' she asked.

'No. Get your own.

'Michael! Over here!'

She swapped her empty glass for a full one and said, 'What shall we drink to?'

'I'm done here. So is Mina. Why not drink to endings and beginnings?'

We clinked glasses and made the toast. There was a whine from down below. 'What's up with him?' said Eseld.

'Your father shared Dawn's Blessing. Scout's disappointed that Champagne doesn't have the same magickal properties.'

'Lucky you! We're having a family get-together after the formal meal and speeches. If he doesn't crack it open then, I'll want to know why.' She took a long look at me. 'You're not going to talk, are you?'

'No.'

'Then give me a fag instead. I've got some gossip for you.' She smoked for a second and continued. 'I ran into Lena before. Literally ran into her – round a corner and boom! We were both in a hurry. I don't know what came over me after that.'

'Let me guess: you were nice to her.'

'Shocking, isn't it? I'll be losing my reputation. I said, "Are you okay? Is there anything I can do to help?" She nearly fell over again.'

'I'll bet. What did she say?'

'Dunno. It was in German. Then she said, "If you mean it seriously, go to the guest wing and sort them out. I give up." I nearly told her to jump off the Point, then I thought *You've got to earn this, Eseld*. I said, "I'm on it," and she jogged off.'

'Hang on,' I said. 'You agreed to go and talk to the Daughters? You must really want to get on Lena's good side.'

'No good deed goes unpunished, does it? There's been so much going on, I just didn't have the energy to hate her any more, and Lena saved Hedda's life.' She shrugged. 'Anyway, I ran up the stairs, through the fire doors and into the frying pan.' She gave a thoroughly malicious grin. 'The temperature dropped twenty degrees when they saw me.'

'What was going on?'

'Do you remember that floor?'

'Yes. There were four bedrooms, two bathrooms, two extra toilets and a store room.'

She gave me a look. 'Really? You remember shit like that?'

I wondered how much she'd already had to drink. I shrugged and smiled as if it were an affliction.

'Yeah, well, there are ten of them and Lena had arranged the beds as 4/3/2/1. She'd got in a state because they wanted her to start moving the beds around.'

'Are they really so entitled?'

She paused and put down her champagne. 'Not normally. If they'd been able to agree, it wouldn't have been a problem. It was war by proxy, though. Raven and Alys were keeping to the back while Georgia and Zoe slugged it out. When they couldn't agree who got the single room and the triple room, they'd called Lena.'

'Georgia and Zoe? Why them?'

'Georgia's signed up for Team Raven. Zoe does what her twin tells her.'

'They're completely divided, are they?'

'Totally. Raven has Cordelia, of course, and Brook. She bought Brook by getting her into Homewood. Brook is a good lawyer but not much of a Mage. Ironic really.'

'Why?'

'Because Raven's pitch is to make Homewood the premier centre of Circle magick in the world. No non-Mages allowed.'

'Interesting. Why is Georgia on board with this?'

'Because today, Raven announced that it should continue as women only.'

'And Alys? What's her pitch?'

'Business as usual, basically.'

'Do many people agree with Kiwa? That men should be admitted?'

'In Homewood, no. Outside, in the affiliated covens, a small but vocal minority.'

I took that all in for a while. 'I have to ask, how do you know all this?'

She looked around to make sure no one was listening. A bit late for that. They weren't, as it happens, because the Daughters were preoccupied with their own issues.

Hedda's stroke had been a supernova in Glastonbury, and the Homewood galaxy was reforming. Raven and Alys were the proto-stars, the ones with all the gravity, and the others were being drawn into their orbits.

Since my last visit, Isolde had joined Team Alys, which left only Kiwa, Signe and Síona floating freely. My brain ran with the astronomical metaphor – were Raven and Alys proto-stars or black holes? Would they give light and life, or would they suck the Daughters into a dark future?

Eseld leaned in to me. 'It's Morning. She was my tutor here when I left Glastonbury. She only got promoted to Homewood after she'd finished with me. We've kept in touch. Don't tell anyone.'

'So what did you do about the beds?'

'I said that in Hedda's absence, Signe should have the single room. Then I said that if they weren't happy with the other arrangements, Raven could move the beds on her own because all our staff were busy.'

'How did that go down?'

'They agreed. It would have been a loss of face if one faction had argued. Do you know what the best thing was? Lena said thank you.'

'And here she comes.'

Lena looked slightly dazed, as if she'd reached overload. It was easy to forget how young she was when you saw her being so competent and organised. Eseld's left hand twitched, as if she were going to put her arm round Lena. Then she thought better of it. Too soon.

'Five minutes,' said Lena. She looked at both of us when she said it. 'I thought you would like a warning.'

Eseld immediately snatched my cigarettes and lit up. 'Thanks for that.' Lena nodded and left.

I took my cigarettes back and said, 'I'll see you later.'

In my absence, the rest of my team had taken different approaches to the party. Erin had barely moved from the bar and appeared to be chatting up one of the staff. Saffron had managed to penetrate the event horizon around Raven and appeared to doing something with magick for some reason.

Saffron had a small hairclip in her hand and Raven was peering down at it. Cordelia was expressing a polite interest and Brook had wandered off to talk to Síona. And Mina? She had ended up with Grace, Kerenza's eight year old daughter.

'There you are,' said Mina. 'Grace was telling me about her new pony and I said that you knew more about horses than I do.'

'So does your Auntie Eseld,' I said.

Grace giggled. 'Mummy says I'm not to call her that but she likes being called *Auntie*. She's coming with me to choose one.'

'You'd better go and find your place,' I said. 'Dinner's nearly ready.'

She skipped off, already looking a little overtired. It had been a long day for her. 'How did you end up with the small child?' I said.

'Kerenza is very worried about something. After two minutes of small talk, she excused herself and left her daughter with me.'

'What's bothering her?'

'I have no idea.'

Ethan boomed across the room. 'Ladies and gentlemen, please take your places.'

Lena had opted for three tables of eight and managed the difficult feat of neutralising any potential hostilities. It also made the conversation rather bland, and I spent most of the meal talking to Kenver about Geomancy. On Mowbray's table, I think Mina was talking weddings with Lena, and that was one consolation: being separated from Mina meant that I could eat the mouth-wateringly pink Beef Wellington. Bliss.

The fun and games began as the last of the Wellington was cleared away; dessert and cheese was going to be a buffet after the formal part of the evening. I scraped the mushrooms and flaky pastry off two slices of beef and took them outside for Scout while a small dais was being set up.

I slipped back into the room, and instead of disappearing, I noticed that the staff had grown in number. A lot of chef's whites were now visible, along with office staff and the girl from the stables. I sat down, and at that moment, Mowbray moved to the dais, flanked by Lena and Kerenza. What?

'I've been asked to keep this very brief,' said Mowbray from the floor. 'In fact, I've been ordered to do so.' He looked around the room. 'That doesn't apply to you. You can applaud as loud and long as you like. Please join me in showing our thanks to Lena for organising this banquet, and to the Pellacombe staff for delivering it.'

When the applause had died down, he continued. 'Today marks many new beginnings and a few endings. I will never stop mourning the loss of my uncle, Ethan's father. Kellysporth will not be the same without him. It will be different, and that difference starts on Monday, when Ethan and Lena will become the new heads of the Kellysporth community. A new beginning for them, and a new start at Pellacombe. Lena? Would you like to hand over?'

Lena swallowed hard. I could see *You can do this* running across her forehead like a ticker-tape (in German, of course). She stepped forward and looked over the seated guests to the staff lining the walls. 'I would like to thank you all for what you have done. I will miss you. If any of you want a job at Kellysporth, you have my number.'

There was gentle laughter, which Lena acknowledged with a curt nod, then she reached into her dress and lifted out the heavy badge of the Steward of Pellacombe. She turned and handed it to Mowbray, and the staff began a raucous cheering and stamping of feet. With a crimson tide washing over her skin, Lena bowed to them and walked back to her seat.

Mowbray let her have it all. He didn't move to calm things down and let the cheering run its course. Only when the last whoop had faded did he speak. 'A house needs a Steward. I give you the new Steward of Pellacombe.' He placed the ribbon over Kerenza's head and stepped back.

It was bound to be an anti-climax. Kerenza was applauded warmly, but not cheered. There was no hollering or ironic cries of *All is good*. For one second I forgot that Mina wasn't next to me and murmured, 'I wonder whose idea that was.'

'Ethan's,' said Kenver. Oops. Interesting, though. Kenver is still very young, and didn't think it odd that I should be asking him awkward questions.

Kerenza resumed her seat on our table and practised her smile while she watched Mowbray fetch the props for the next part of the performance. The staff king of Wessex took one of the two tubes containing the Deeds with him on to the dais. I shifted my chair so that I could get a better view of the room. I knew what was coming and wanted to see the reactions.

He took out the new Wessex Deed and unfurled it so that the two seals dangled off the bottom on their ribbon. With a little Lux, Mowbray made them light up. 'Here is the new Deed for the staff kingdoms of Wessex, duly sealed by Mina and myself. I will leave it here for your inspection, and to save you the bother of decoding it, I've just messaged the full text to a few people. As it was agreed, so has it been delivered.'

He stepped off the dais to lay the unrolled parchment on a table, then took the other tube and a velvet pouch. He pointed down at the Wessex Deed. 'That document has one section you won't have been expecting. The old

Deed was light on geography. It didn't specify which of the ancient kingdoms had been brought together. This one does.'

He picked up the second tube and slowly extracted the other parchment while he spoke. 'We've all got used to England being a magickal Heptarchy. Seven kings. No more. From tonight there are eight kingdoms and eight kings. An Octarchy, if you're classically inclined. The new kingdom is also an old kingdom, and this is the new Deed of the staff kingdom of Kernow.'

There was a stunned silence. Not a single person had seen this coming. Shock, fury and sheer delight in the devilment of it passed across the faces, and soon each table had descended into murmurs and gesticulation. I felt a sharp pain in my shoulder as Kerenza leaned over and dug her nails into my flesh.

'Did you know about this?' she hissed. 'Or you, Kenver?'

'No, nothing,' said Kenver.

'No, ma'am. Not until six forty-five tonight,' I said, rubbing my shoulder and checking for tears in my shirt.

'What's he doing?' said Kenver.

'Ladies and gentlemen!' said Mowbray. The discussions stopped and we turned back to the stage. 'This Deed also follows the terms of the Agreement, as you'd expect. It makes it very clear that Kernow is its own kingdom, and I am proud to be its staff king. The new Deed also provides for separate Marshals, and I hope that Ethan won't think it a slur that I am relieving him of Kernow.'

He looked at Ethan. Ethan's face looked back. What the man behind the face was thinking, I have no idea. After a pause, Ethan nodded.

Mowbray took a short staff from the table and said, 'She doesn't know I'm about to do this, and I hope she accepts. I would like to appoint my daughter, Eseld, as Marshal of Kernow.'

For a fraction of a second, Kerenza had thought that she was going to get the job, and for a fraction of a second her anger showed before the smile came back. Eseld was on her way to the dais. She bent the knee to her father and accepted the staff of office. She didn't make a speech, but she did stand up and kiss him.

'Your first job,' he said, 'is to present the new crown. It's there.'

With nervous glances at the room, Eseld took out the crown. This time Mowbray bent his head and allowed his daughter to place the crown on it. A perfect fit. She backed away and sat down as quickly as she could. If Mowbray was expecting applause from his family or the Mages, he was disappointed. What he did get was three cheers that started with the loyal staff. They roared it out, and we joined in more politely

'To also be king of Wessex would be too much for one man,' said Mowbray, 'and so with immediate effect I am abdicating from the other kingdoms. I'm sorry, Ethan and Mina, but there's going to be another election.' Before more murmuring could break out, he took off the crown and said, 'The time for speeches will be at the Proclamation banquet.' He looked around, as if there were something he wanted to say. He shook his head and looked up again. 'Tonight's public business is done. Thank you.' He looked over at our table. 'Kerenza is now in charge.'

Kerenza's smile didn't falter as she stood up and thanked the staff. She then invited us to help ourselves to desserts and coffee. The second she sat down, chaos broke out. Polite chaos, but chaos nonetheless.

I leaned over. 'Don't forget Grace. I had to send Scout to escort her to her room.'

'She's quite capable, but thank you for taking the trouble. I'll send one of the girls to check on her.' I watched her snag one of the waitresses and whisper something, then I got up and turned to face the room.

Mowbray was still at his table, messing with the Deeds. Eseld had rushed to his side, holding the Marshal's staff like a sword. No one had approached them yet. Zoe was heading for our table to re-join Alys, and Cordelia had already found Raven. Ethan and Lena were at the centre of a crowd of staff, shaking their hands and taking selfies. I caught a glimpse of Mina, and her nose was up. She was on the hunt, and Medbh was her target. Mowbray had promised a statement. It had been the thing he'd bottled out of, right at the end.

I started to move in a loop, spotting the red hair and intending to get to the door before Medbh could escape.

'Excuse me, Conrad.' It was Signe. I hesitated and our quarry made it to the door before Mina could catch her.

'Sorry, Signe. How's your mother?'

'I don't know. My phone hasn't been getting a signal. I wondered if you had some government device on a secret channel. I know you've got her number.'

'Don't you have mobile signal jammers in Homewood?'

'What?'

'Mowbray turned off the Wi-Fi and used magick to jam the regular signal before dinner. He'll turn it back on in a minute, I'm sure.'

'How do you know?'

'Kenver told me. The magick is Kenver's first contribution to Mowbray enterprises and he's quite proud of it. I'm afraid the King's Watch doesn't have access to GCHQ's boys' toys. Yet.'

'Oh.' She took out her phone and smiled. 'You're right! Thank you. I'll nip outside and call her. She should still be up.'

That had taken all of a minute. When I looked up, the only Mowbray left in the room was Kerenza, and she was retreating backwards towards the doors. 'Ladies, Conrad, I'm sure you'll excuse us. Jane Kershaw is on duty tonight and will handle any of your needs. I shall see you all in the morning.'

'Bugger,' said Síona. 'What do we do now?'

'I don't know about you lot, but I'm having dessert,' said a rather loud and rather drunk Erin. 'Feel free to compliment my work on the Kernow Deed.'

'And *that* is why men are a bad idea,' said Georgia to Brook. Eh? Erin likes to let her hair down and it's the fault of the men in her coven?

I don't have much of a sweet tooth. I grabbed a coffee and made it on to the terrace before Mina and Saffron could stop me going outside, forcing them to follow me.

'What do you make of that?' said Saffron.

'Which bit?'

She gestured to the dining room. 'The whole thing. The abdication. The new kingdom of Cornwall. Sorry, of *Kernow*.'

'I think it's a good job that Cornwall is in Rick's Watch, not mine.'

Saffron looked disappointed. 'So that's it? We eat cake and go to bed?'

'Cheese, in my case,' I said. 'And I saw them putting out bottles of apple brandy.'

'I think Conrad is being flippant,' said Mina.

'You reckon?'

'What I was trying to say is that this really is none of our business. Not directly. We'll go back in and try to pick up some more gossip about the Daughters.'

We were on our way in when we heard Alys and Raven arguing. We stopped by the doors and listened.

'The time for debate is tomorrow,' said Alys. 'Now is the time for prayer and sacrifice, and you as First of Ash should be leading by example.'

Raven ignored her. 'We knew Mowbray was up to something. You heard that woman from Kellysporth this morning, voting for Ethan. I bet he's stitched it up for Ethan to get the other crown.'

'No he hasn't,' said Brook. 'Complete opposite. The only votes outside Cornwall that Mowbray can rely on are the three from Ethandun. All his other deals were for one election only, and he's changed the electors anyway. It's open season now.'

Alys's voice was loud and firm. 'Prayer and sacrifice. The sun has already set. Are you forgetting your obligation, Raven? Would you have the Daughter of Memory hear of it?'

Raven looked as if she'd been slapped. Alys had just threatened to report her to Verity and no one had stepped in to disagree, not even Cordelia. Raven nodded slowly to herself and untied the cord around her waist. She lowered her robe to well below her knees and re-tied the cord. Without a word she led the Daughters out of the house and across the terrace, towards the lawns. We stood back and let them pass.

Inside the dining room, Erin sat in splendid isolation at one of the tables. A tired looking Jane Kershaw and a young girl were looking at the barely touched desserts.

'You do not know what you're missing,' said Erin. 'This is delicious.'

'She's got a point,' said Saffron. 'It's been a long day.'

'Not me,' said Mina. 'I am going to take some cheese up to the suite and get my trainers. We're going to take Scout for a walk and then go to bed.' She turned to me. 'Please tell me you are not going to get up before dawn and go riding.'

'Nope.'

When Mina had gone and Saffron had joined Erin at the dessert trough, I did ask Jane Kershaw for a favour.

'Of course I can get you a hip flask,' she said with a wink. 'You deserve it for looking after the Smurf.'

It wasn't Dawn's Blessing, but it would do. It had been a long day. I was looking forward to bed.

34 – Bump in the Night

'Arff! Arff! Arff! HOWWWWWW!'

'Mmm Ugnh?'

'Shh.'

'Arff!'

I don't sleep with a gun under my pillow; I sleep with one next to the bed. I grabbed it and stood up, putting my back to the wall and ready to shoot at anything that threatened Mina. I could already feel a huge wash of Lux around the room. There was a little light from the curtains, and that told me it was still the middle of the night. Outside our room, Scout was still giving it the full Hound of the Baskervilles and I could feel his fear. It was that, more than his barking that had woken me.

The door started to glow, and then Mowbray came through it. Right through it. Or his Spirit did.

'Conrad! What's happening?' said a frightened Mina.

She couldn't see him. 'Take my hand.' I held out my hand and she grabbed it.

'Ohmygod.'

Mowbray was a silver horror – he glowed white without lighting up the room. His eyes were wild and searching for something, then they snapped into focus and locked on me.

'Clarke! They've killed me. I'm dead.'

The voice echoed in my head, directly and with no intervention from my ears.

'Who?'

'In the Lab. I ... No. No. No...'

His eyes locked on something I couldn't see, away to the other side of the room. Then his Spirit sank down through the floor and disappeared. Gone. The room was black again.

I pulled my hand out of Mina's and reached for the light.

'We didn't dream that, did we?'

'No.'

Electric light washed over the room and its disordered contents. Last night's clothes in a mess. The dressing table. No sign of Mowbray. Plenty of noise from outside, though.

'Mina, get up and away from the door.'

She flattened herself against the solid slate wall. Gun still in hand, I opened the door carefully. There was nothing in the sitting room except a psychotic Scout, running round the furniture and barking. I checked left and right and went to catch him. There was a movement behind me: Saffron's door opening, and Saffron appearing with her spiked chain.

'What the fuck?' she said.

I grabbed Scout and held him. I could feel his heart pounding under the fur, racing at a pace no human organ could cope with. 'Easy, boy. Easy.'

Mina had emerged, too. 'We had a visit from the ghost of Mowbray,' she said to Saffron. 'He said that he had been murdered.'

Scout went limp in my arms and spots appeared in front of my eyes. I felt myself sagging over and collapsed on the floor. All the strength in every muscle had gone and my eyes closed of their own accord. A wonderful feeling of weightlessness came over me. Next stop, the International Space Station…

Wet tongue. Wet tongue on my nose. Urgh.

'Come on, Scout, he's waking up. Off you get.'

It was Saffron's voice. I blinked and I could see again. The back of the couch to be exact.

'Conrad? Can you hear me?'

I coughed hard as my lungs kicked back in to action and I had to breathe hard for a few seconds. I felt like I'd just run a marathon. 'Yes. What happened?'

'Familial Dissociation. You're fine now, and so's Scout. Can you get up?'

'Where's Mina and how long was I out?'

'She hauled Erin out of bed and she's getting dressed. You were gone for about two minutes. Nowhere near the danger level. Can you sit up?'

I accepted her hand and dragged myself to a sitting position. Mina appeared, stuffing her feet into trainers. From the bathroom, I heard a groan.

'Is he okay?' said Mina.

'Looks like it.'

I reached out and touched Scout. I felt fear and need. I let him come to me and held him, Lux flowing faster than it would at a distance.

'What shall we do?' said Mina. 'Should Saff and I have gone looking for Mowbray?'

'No. You made the right call. You had a man down and you put the right person on to deal with him. You got Erin up and got ready yourself. Exactly what I'd have done.'

A bleary eyed pale-faced Erin appeared from the bathroom. 'Did I hear you right? Is Mowbray dead?'

Saffron spoke. 'Probably. From what Mina's told me, that was a trauma projection.'

'A what?' I said.

'Sudden death causes a pulling away from the material world. It's a bit like pulling your hand back from a hotplate you didn't know was switched on. Powerful Mages can sometimes keep their Imprint together, and that's what

Mowbray did. Whoever killed him knew this and pulled his Spirit back down to finish the job.'

I let go of Scout and held out both hands. Saffron and Mina helped me get up.

'Oh god I feel sick,' said Erin. 'I didn't know your leg was that bad.'

'Can you function?' I said to her. She pressed her lips together and nodded. 'Good. Mina, I want you to take Erin and go to the Daughters of the Goddess. Round 'em all up and take statements. What time is it?'

'Three forty,' said Saff. 'You don't suspect them, do you?'

'I suspect everyone not in this room. Erin, get dressed. And stick close to Mina. She has the Ancile.'

'Right,' said Erin.

'Saffron, do you think there's any chance that Mowbray is still alive and in need of help?'

'No. He's either past all help or his Spirit escaped and is beyond us.'

'Then we tackle the Mowbrays first. We can examine the scene of crime later. Agreed?'

'Yes. 100%.'

'Good. Quick as you can.'

'I hate to spoil the moment, but I really need to pee before I get dressed.'

'As do I. After you.'

Mina was using the extra minute to put her hair in a ponytail. I handed her my SIG in its holster.

She held it in her hand for a second, then nodded and looked at her tunic and leggings. She grabbed one of my spare belts and her phone. 'I shall go and kick Erin's arse in to gear.'

'All yours,' shouted Saffron. Time to move.

The tour of Pellacombe on our first visit hadn't included the family bedrooms. Saffron and I slipped down the back staircase as quietly as we could and into the only part of the private quarters I knew, the dining room. From there, a solid looking door blocked the way further.

Saff ran her hands over it. 'Locked. Magickally. I can't open it.'

I pulled my lip and gave it some thought. While I did, Saff flicked her torch around and found the light switches. When the lights came up, the answer was staring at me from a side table. I picked up the internal phone and dialled 0.

It rang for so long that I was beginning to panic, and then a sleepy Jane Kershaw answered.

'Hullo?'

'This is Conrad Clarke. Where are you?'

'What?'

226

'Where are you?'

'In the duty bunk, off the main kitchens.'

'There's an emergency. Can you get to the private family dining room without entering the bedroom area?'

'Yes. What's going on?'

'Please, Jane, this really is an emergency. Get here as soon as you can, with your keys, and I'll explain.'

She stumbled into the room less than a minute later, still dressed from last night and clutching a large gold key. She pulled up short when she saw us in uniform.

'Lord Mowbray is dead,' I said. 'He's been murdered in the Lab. We need to tell the family. And check them off.'

'Dead? Mowbray? How? And how do you know? Have you been in the Lab?'

'Mina and I saw his Spirit. We need to get in there.'

Her face had gone white. It now flushed an angry scarlet. 'I can't let you in there. They'll be vulnerable.'

'To what?'

'To … Let me call one of them. Lena and Ethan. Or Eseld.'

'We're not a hit squad, Jane. We're here to help. You know it. Open the door and show us where Eseld's room is.'

She looked at us. She looked at the key in her hand. I don't know what went through her mind at that moment. It might have been trust. It might have been fear of us. It might have been fear of dealing with the situation on her own.

She crossed the room and held up the key. 'This only works on the outer door. Eseld's room is at the far end, as far away from the others as possible. When we get there, she'll have locked it. When the doors are locked by the family, the key only sounds an alarm inside. Like a doorbell.' She checked to see that we'd understood and placed the key against the door. She pushed, and it opened silently on to a corridor that ran right and left. She turned right.

We followed her along a corridor lit by ankle lights and past several unmarked doors, turning left at the end. This new branch was short and ended in a black door, the only surface in the whole space that hadn't been painted light grey.

'She specified black when Pellacombe was being designed,' said Jane nervously. 'A black door: real teenage stuff. It's been repainted twice. You know what she's like.'

'Please,' I said.

Jane pressed the key to the door. She waited and pressed again, and then a third time. She pressed her ear to the door and said, 'She's coming.'

'Good soundproofing,' said Saffron. 'Much better than Cherwell Roost.'

227

'Total,' said Jane. 'You could …' Her imagination wouldn't let her finish that sentence.

With a *whoosh* of air, Eseld flung back the door. 'Where's the fucking fire? Do you … Oh. Conrad?' She was wearing a black silk dressing gown over nothing at all, and instinctively pulled it tighter. She looked at the three of us for a second and stood back to let us in.

'Do you want me?' said Jane.

'Go straight back to the kitchen and put some coffee on,' I replied. 'Lots of coffee.'

'Miss Eseld?' said Jane. 'Shall I go?'

'What? Yeah. Go on.'

Eseld had more than a bedroom, but not much. Behind the door was a small sitting room with a desk against the window. I could see her bedroom off to the left. The room smelled strongly of her scent, bright and zingy, mixed with a waft of stale smoke. She moved quickly, shutting the door to her bedroom and opening the window. She fished for the dressing gown cord and fastened it with her back to us, then turned round.

'Sit down, Eseld,' I said. 'Please.'

She planted herself in the desk chair and swivelled it to face us. Her face was smudged and blurred. Despite wearing less makeup than normal last night, there were still black smears and smudges around her eyes.

'Eseld, I'm so sorry. There's been an incident. We believe that your father has been killed.'

She blinked. 'You are the biggest fucking wind up merchant ever, Conrad.'

Saffron joined in. 'I am so sorry, Eseld. It's true.'

'No. I don't believe you.'

It was my turn again. 'We've seen his Spirit, Eseld. Mina and I. And Scout.'

She slipped off the chair, and before I could do anything, she'd grabbed Scout by the scruff of his neck. She stared at his mismatched eyes. 'Is it true? Have you seen my Daddy?'

He struggled and whined and his claws slipped on the rug. She let go and rocked back and forward for a second. 'How?' She was talking to the empty floor where Scout had been. He was now hiding behind me.

She turned and looked up. 'How? How did he die?' Before I could answer, she sprang up and grabbed her cigarettes. She used a burst of magick to light one and drew in.

I took it slowly. 'He said he was murdered. In the Lab. His Spirit was dragged back down before he could say who had done it. You're the first person we've told over here. Mina and Erin are dealing with the Daughters.'

She smoked for a second, still standing by the desk. With a jerk, she jabbed the cigarette into the ashtray and ran through to her bedroom, leaving the door open and heading into a bathroom.

'Saff?' I said.

'Right.'

Eseld hadn't stubbed her cigarette out properly, and I must confess that I took a few crafty drags while I watched Saffron standing outside the bathroom. She was nearly knocked flying when Eseld emerged, now completely naked.

Eseld started grabbing clothes and struggling into them. Saff stood back and let her get on with it. I'd have done the same.

When she was dressed, Eseld went to an antique painted wardrobe. It was bright red, covered in gold stars and looked like a Victorian stage magician's prop cupboard. She ran her hands over the doors and the lock clicked open.

'What are you doing?' I said.

'Going to find him, and if he really has been murdered, I'm going to gut the bastard who did it.'

'This is ours, Eseld. We need your help, yes, but you have to leave us to it.'

She whirled round. 'Wrong, wrong, wrong. Under the new Deed, regicide and treason are the only crimes reserved from the King's Watch. Ask Cador if you don't believe me.'

Alarm flared in Saffron's eyes.

'What are you going to do?' said Eseld. 'Try to restrain me? Kill me? I wouldn't want to be in your shoes if you did that.' She didn't wait for an answer, and turned back into the cupboard. Now was the moment to stop her, and I couldn't. Her father was the person she cared for most in the world. In many ways he was her world. If someone had tried to stop me avenging Mina's death, they'd be in serious trouble.

She emerged from the cupboard with her leather wristbands in place. She hooked a chain of Artefacts over her neck and zipped a training top over them.

'What are you going to do right now?' I said.

'Go into the Lab. It's me that could use your help, Conrad.'

'You know the Laboratory. I don't.'

'Eh? Laboratory?' She looked at me as if I were mad. '*Lab* isn't short for Laboratory. It's short for *Labyrinth*. He made a bet with Ginnar the Dwarf that he could build a better one. He won the bet.'

'Give me a minute,' I said. 'I'll get my dowsing rod.'

She actually laughed. 'What on earth for?'

'It's how I got round the last Labyrinth I escaped from.'

'I've seen your magickal potential, Conrad. Dad is the greatest Geomancer of the twenty-first century. If you try and dowse your way out of his Labyrinth, you're on your own. You'll never be seen again.'

'Then how?'

She looked at Scout. 'I was going to use magickal smell, but we've got an expert at the real thing here.'

I weighed up my options. A Mage on the rampage is a difficult thing to stop without extreme violence. A bit like a bull on the loose. The best you can hope for is to guide them to somewhere safe and contain them.

'Fine. Have you got a spare key, Eseld?' She nodded. 'Saffron, get everyone up, starting with Kerenza and working down. Before you do, send a quick text to the Boss.'

'It's Saturday,' said Saffron. 'She won't look at it.'

'Yes she will. And this is a direct order: don't let anyone else into the Lab and don't follow us until or unless I contact you. Understood?'

'Yes, sir.'

I nodded to Eseld. She reached into a drawer and chucked a key at Saffron. I followed her back to the dining room and then down a level to the weird lobby with the portraits. I shuddered as we passed the stairs to the cottage and entered the short passage. The portraits now stared at me. One of them blinked. Scout barked.

'Quick as you can, Eseld.'

'Are my relatives creeping you out, Conrad?'

'That would be a yes.'

'I'm just checking for residual traces.'

I turned to the Regency beauty on my right. The jet black hair and piercing blue eyes marked her down as a Mowbray even without the blue ribbon in her bonnet and the wild boar grazing in the background. Was she also a Mage? Yes. Witches in portraits have a serpent ring on their right hand.

I leaned in. 'Who went through the door tonight?' I asked.

Eseld grinned. 'That would be too easy. These are Memorial portraits. One day you can listen to them, if you're interested. The one you're looking at is fascinating.' She stood back from the door. 'No trace of magick used to open the door. The only one of us who *can't* get through on their own is Cador. Are you ready?'

'Yes.'

As Eseld opened the door, I wondered how Mina and Erin were getting on upstairs.

35 – Into the Maze

Behind the door to the Labyrinth was something I've only seen in passing – a fully equipped Mage's workshop. I quickly scanned for threats and found none. Eseld had walked into the middle of the room and either she'd used her Sight or she simply hadn't bothered to check.

The room was square and lit by Lightsticks. I could tell from the layout of the upper floors that we were now properly underground, and during the day this room, like much of Pellacombe, would be lit by daylight. Those great clusters of chimneys I'd seen that first morning were mostly collectors for light tubes. It allowed them to give a natural feel to many of the corridors and save on electricity. I still thought there were too many chimneys, given the lack of open fires. Part of the answer was in here.

All of the left hand wall was given over to forges and furnaces, now cold. Benches were along the back, and the presence of several chairs said that this was a shared space. On the right wall was an arch, and instead of a door, the face of the arch was blackness. Total, light-absorbing magickal blackness. In front of it, Eseld was hesitating.

'Have you been in before?' I asked. 'How does it work?'

'How did Niði's Labyrinth work?' She was delaying. If she didn't make a go for it in a few minutes, I'd be leading her back outside. 'It used magick to move the walls while you weren't looking. It also had some sort of relativity effect. Time slowed down in there.'

'There's one area of magick that Dwarves really aren't good at: Plane Shifting. Dad's Labyrinth moves you seamlessly between different planes of existence. It means the permutations are infinite.'

I gave it some thought. 'Let's start from the obvious. His killer got in there, either with him or on their own. They also got out again. Why would he be in the Labyrinth at three in the morning?'

'He's never been a great sleeper. If he can't sleep, he goes and looks at the flux. This isn't just a maze for the sake of a maze, it's the confluence of every Ley line in Cornwall and the start of the Great West Way.'

'I've heard of that. I thought it started in Glastonbury.'

'It used to. You must have been reading an old book, because Dad re-crafted it. The Great West Way starts here and runs in more or less a straight line through Glastonbury, Oxford, Cambridge, and ends in Norwich. From here, he could examine the load on the whole country.'

I tried to soften my voice. 'How did they do it, Eseld? How did they get in and out?'

She shook her head. 'This was a stupid idea. Only Kenver has the potential to understand what Dad did in there. At least there's no boar here.'

'Boar? You mean there is one somewhere?'

'Yeah. At Kellysporth.'

I pulled at my lip and thought about what must lie beyond the perfect black barrier in the archway. 'Tell me about the history of the Labyrinth in relation to Pellacombe.'

'Why? How will that help?'

'Humour me.'

'It was just before Mum dragged us off to Glastonbury. I can't really remember it, but I've heard the stories so often, it seems like I was there.' She shifted her posture slightly, more confident of what she was doing. 'Dad built Pellacombe by starting with the Labyrinth. There was an old mine just uphill from the original farmhouse, and he built the Labyrinth in there. Ginnar the Dwarf came and tried it out. For a whole week, he was lost in the maze. I was here for that, but I don't really remember it. Not long after that, my mother was offered a place in the Homewood Covens and took it. She also took us away from here. Cador was only a baby.'

I put what I already knew with what Eseld had just told me. 'And that's how legends are born,' I said.

'Sorry?'

'Your real skill is in Wards. Have you had many dealings with Dwarves?'

'I was presented to Ginnar on my eighteenth birthday. By the gods, that was creepy and definitely the worst birthday present *ever*.' She looked back at the arch. 'I haven't been back to Ginnar's Hall since.'

'I've had extensive dealings with the slippery little buggers. They do *not* travel from their Halls to test out mazes. There is no profit in that.'

'What are you saying?'

'That the Labyrinth never existed. Your Dad made it all up. When Ginnar came here, he was digging out whatever's behind that portal. Presumably a cavern for your father's work with Ley lines.'

'No! He wouldn't spin a story like that.'

'Yes, he would. Mowbray had many faults, I'm sure, but he loved all his children. He even loved Kerenza's daughter and spent quality time with her. He would not leave a deadly labyrinth for his children to walk into and get lost. He loved you the most, Eseld. He would never risk his little girl going into a Labyrinth with no escape. What if he were away on a job? And what would it serve? Why have such a thing?'

'But why lie?'

'I'm sure there's *something* in there. Something to offer protection. Something to show off to clients. But no Labyrinth.'

'How could he have kept that up?'

'In the same way that he plotted to become staff king of Cornwall.'

'Kernow.'

I left it there to sink in. The ball was in her court.

'What shall we do. I still want to find him.'

'Go through there and see. And you better be as good at Wards as you say you are.'

'Hunh. Watch me.'

She took a small blue disk from her chain of Artefacts. Mowbray blue. She held it towards the black face of the arch and raised her other hand. The disk shimmered faintly. Then stopped.

She walked over to one of the benches and took a couple of metal tools from a rack. They looked like something a dentist might use to get revenge on a patient who'd eaten garlic before his appointment. She took the disk and the tools over to an anvil and placed the disk on top. In moments, the anvil was glowing with Lux – I could feel it from ten feet away.

She used the tools to tinker with the disk and grunted with satisfaction. She picked it up and crossed the room again. 'Take my hand. And grab Scout.'

I felt the heat of both magick and a sweaty palm. With her other hand, she presented the disk to the arch and the blackness fell away.

'Quick!' she pulled on my hand and we stumbled into an open space. The arch behind us clouded over again, but this time as a mirror.

'Is that a Dodgson's Mirror?' I said. I'd seen one before, in my quest to rescue the Thirteenth Witch.

'Well spotted. It's actually a variant and does a similar job on this side by blocking everything. On the other side, it absorbs everything. It's very energy efficient. I wanted Dad to call it Mowbray's Mirror and share it. He was too modest.'

Beyond the arch, in this new space, we had a simple choice: along the corridor or up the stairs. I knew which I'd chose – the stairs. I looked up and they were blocked off at the top. Bricked up. 'What are these for?' I said.

'Dunno. Changed his mind, probably. Let's go and take it carefully.'

The corridor was definitely Dwarven work, something I pointed out to Eseld. She nodded an acknowledgement and stretched out her arms to check for Wards. I kept quiet and left her to it.

She walked as slowly down the corridor as a Royal Logistics engineer in a minefield. We travelled ten metres and she stopped. 'Nothing.'

She moved faster and we came to a right turn.

'We're going to move to another plane,' I said.

'How do you know?'

'It's that or emerge into the kitchens. They're just down there.'

The only way we knew we were on another plane was that Scout started to glow. Orange. Not a good look on a Border Collie. 'His original Spirit will be enhanced a fraction,' said Eseld. 'He's good. Dad's the best. This is totally seamless.'

The corridor started to turn right again, hard right, and Scout's glow faded. There was an opening ahead, and we found ourselves back in the original

233

room, complete with staircase. The tunnel we'd gone into had disappeared and we'd returned through what had been a brick wall before. I'm sure that if we retraced our steps now, the situation would be reversed.

'The cunning sod,' said Eseld. 'That trip had the subtlest Ward I've ever seen built into it. Somewhere, a bloody great alarm has just gone off. That tunnel acted like a dynamo: the more we moved along, the more noise it generated. What now?'

'Up the stairs. You go on your own. The serious Wards will be up there.'

'It's bricked up!'

'Saffron's cousin, Bertie, has a wall just like that. It hides her workshops from mundane visitors.'

Scout and I retreated, and Eseld did her thing. It took her three minutes (I checked), and she offered no explanation when the brick wall turned into a wooden door.

'Where are we going?' she said.

'Scout! Find Mowbray. Go on.'

He climbed the stairs with more enthusiasm than grace. Eseld opened the door and we followed the pooch into a corridor that was definitely human and which quickly doubled back, around the two rooms below us and then presented another staircase, this time down.

'You were right about the stairs,' said Eseld. 'How come?'

'I knew that they'd take us up, into the foundation levels of the main mansion. Easy to build access there and then cover it up after. And I knew that because wherever we went, it had to lead to a point five metres north of the forges in the workshop, and two metres lower. That's where those stairs will take us.'

'Eh? How do you figure that out?'

'When your father came looking for me, he emerged into the sitting room of the King's Watch suite, which is why Scout got the shock of his life. When they dragged him down from our room, he went at an angle. Those two lines meet down there.'

'Right.' She stopped at the top of the stairs. 'I'm not sure I can face it, Conrad. I've been reaching out and reaching out, and I can't feel him anywhere. Nothing.'

'It's going to be grim. It would be no weakness to wait up here.'

'I need to see. And there might be more Wards.'

'After you.'

We followed her down the stairs, and with every step I got hotter. Even my titanium tibia started to itch. We were coming into the presence of a *lot* of Lux.'

'This should be sealed,' she said. 'We must be coming near to the intersection.'

A small square room at the bottom of the stairs had an open door. The heat of Lux flowed from it like a super-sized sauna.

'They couldn't close the door behind them,' she said. 'Or they were in a hurry. All the Wards are linked to the door being shut. It's safe for you to go in.'

'Excuse me.' I unzipped my combat jacket and put it on the floor. It helped a little.

The cavern beyond was definitely Dwarven. They have a thing for pillars, and this one was stuffed full of them, both structural and ornamental.

It stretched away into the darkness, and on the floor the intersecting Ley lines glowed. Normally they don't, but a good Geomancer will rough the edges in a place like this so he knows where they are. There was so much energy down here that I couldn't work out where I was without a dowsing rod to help me sort things out. I looked around. Nothing. 'Scout?'

He trotted off to the right, into a dark patch. I took Eseld's hand and led her gently forward. There was a little opening, behind a mini-arch. The Ley lines in there were damaged and glowed red, not yellow. At the centre was Lord Mowbray, staff king of Kernow. Mage and father. Eseld broke down and started to cry.

36 – Vigil

We sat by the remains of her father for a while, and I held my arm round her shoulders. He was dressed for a day at the beach – shorts, tee-shirt and deck shoes, which told me that he'd intended to spend some time in here. Just before we'd sat down, I'd pulled his tee-shirt down to cover the hole in his back.

The sobs had stopped for a minute before she spoke. 'Have you brought your fags?' I lit two and passed her one. 'How did they do it? Why is there blood on his back?'

'We're looking for three of them,' I said. 'He trusted one of them. He was facing that person when he was attacked from behind. The second one hid behind a pillar, over there. They used a simple blast to knock a hole in his chest. The third was on hand to drag his Spirit back down. I don't know what they did with it.'

'Why here?'

'So much Lux. Can you sense Scout?'

'Of course.'

I took a treat out of my pocket. 'Close your eyes.' I threw the treat in a random direction and he hared after it. 'Where is he?'

'I lost sight of him after less than three metres.'

'That's why your father was killed here: they could hide and ambush him. And they thought he wouldn't be discovered for a long time. They hadn't reckoned on him raising the alarm. I should go, Eseld. We've been here ages.'

'Time passes slowly in here. Much slower than outside. The opposite of a Dwarven Labyrinth.' She reached out a hand and stroked his fingers. 'Goodbye, Dad. I'll get them. I'll make you proud of me one last time.' She held out a hand. 'Let's go.'

I waited until we were back in the workshop before speaking again, partly out of respect and partly because when I'd touched the body, I'd checked Mowbray's neck for his chain of Artefacts. They were missing, and I didn't want Eseld storming off and trying to search everyone without a warrant. The further I could get away from the scene of crime, the less chance of her asking the question.

When we were on the other side of Mowbray's Mirror, I said, 'What happened after you left the banquet last night?'

'Mega-awkward doesn't even begin to cover it, even by our family's standards.'

I moved myself into a position in front of the door back to the mansion. 'I need to find your father's murderer, Eseld. Tell me.'

'Oh. Right.' Her chin came up and some of the fire returned to her eyes. 'You think it's one of us.'

'I don't think that the Daughters sent an impromptu hit-squad in here last night. At least one of the three killers is from this side of the mansion.'

'Why not me?'

'You loved him most, and after Aisling, he loved you most.'

'Is that it? That simple?'

'As a Watch Captain, yes, it is that simple. As a therapist, that would only be the beginning.'

She blinked, and her voice lost some of its Cornish burr. It also gained a touch of cod-Scandinavian. 'Truly, when the Goddess sent you into the RAF and not psychotherapy, she did the world a favour. Sometimes her ways are not mysterious at all.'

'Yes, Hedda, now tell me about last night.'

'Can't we get some coffee first?'

'Look on it as an incentive. Give me the twenty second version.'

'OK.' She took a breath. 'Dad has broken up the Mowbray Trust into six parts. *Broke*, not broken.' She stumbled over her words. 'Instead of one trust to benefit the family as a whole, it's now six named trusts. Kellysporth and all the north coast lands go to Ethan; Predannack goes to me; Mowbray House in London goes to Cador in one year's time; Nanquidno goes to Kerenza; all the other bits and bobs stay with the Pellacombe Estate and are – were – Dad's for his lifetime. Now that he's gone, they're Kenver's.'

No wonder Rachael had been so keen to talk to me. This would have massive implications for her firm in general and her in particular. There were two obvious questions, so I asked the less important one first. 'Why does Cador have to wait a year?'

'Mowbray House is full of magick, so Cador lives in a mundane flat. Dad was going to make it safe for him to live there.'

It was time for the other question. 'I've got A level maths, Eseld. You only described five trusts and you didn't mention Medbh.'

'That was the second shock. She gets Ethandun. Sort of.'

'What do you mean?'

'Mmm. It's the old palace of the staff kings. Huge castle. Makes Pellacombe look like a holiday cottage. Also mostly in ruins until Dad started work on it three years ago. As a family, we use the lodge in the grounds, and that's gone to Medbh. The castle is in trust to be turned into a research institution. Mowbray College. To explore magick from both the quantum and traditional approaches.'

Scout had been waiting patiently by the door. He stood up and stared at the wood. 'Arff!'

'Someone's tinkering with the door,' said Eseld, running her fingers over it. 'They've stopped. Are we done in here?'

I nodded, and she opened the door. On the other side, Saffron breathed a huge sigh of relief.

'Am I glad to see you,' she said. 'It's all going to kick off soon.'

'What's going on?'

'The Daughters have ordered their coach and locked themselves in to the guest wing. Erin's on watch and Mina's trying to keep the M… your family, Eseld. Mina's trying to stop your family from attacking me or running around the countryside. Medbh's gone.'

'What!' That was Eseld.

Saff flicked her eyes to Eseld but told her story to me. 'I couldn't get into her room. She wouldn't answer the alarm. I had to get Kenver to help me open it. She had given him access. Her bed hasn't been slept in and she's taken all her stuff.'

'What happened next?'

'They were in the family room, trying to take it in. When we found that Medbh had gone, they wanted to get in here, so I had to take guard. Mina's doing her best, but even she has her limits.'

'Any observations?'

She shook her head. 'Everyone has answered the door in their nightwear, which was nothing in some cases. No one was dressed.'

'Well done, Saff.' I looked at Eseld. She was still holding up. 'We found him. Murdered by direct magick. No obvious clues.'

'I … I'd like some time with my family,' said Eseld.

I started walking back to the private quarters. 'There's something you're not telling me, Eseld. Your father broke a promise last night. He promised me he'd make an announcement about Medbh. He bottled it. I can't believe that you and Cador said nothing at the family summit.'

'We didn't get the chance. As soon as we were through the doors, he said that Medbh's story was hers to tell, not ours to ask. He said sorry again. Sorry for lying to us.'

We were outside the door to the family sitting room. I put my hand on the door. 'How did Medbh take it when he told you about the Mowbray College idea.'

'She knew about it. She said, "I'm not ready for that yet," and Dad said, "Nor is the castle. You both will be, in time."'

I opened the door to a room I hadn't seen before. It shared the terrace with the dining room next door, but that was about all it shared. At a guess, I'd say that this was the only room where Kerenza had been allowed to stamp her mark. Unlike almost every other space in Pellacombe where the effect was *furnished*, this one was *designed*. The one room to rival it was the morning room, formerly known as the Aisling Suite.

I didn't have time to take in anything beyond a sense of style and an overwhelming impression of cream. Perched on sofas and chairs around a truly baronial fireplace, the family were directing all their negative energy at the small but immovable figure of Mina.

Someone had lit the fire, and Mina was between the fireplace and the door, with the firelight putting her in silhouette. For a fraction of a second, I thought she had grown an extra pair of arms, truly a scary thought, then she wheeled round and they became the ends of an Indian scarf. When she saw me, she let relief dissolve her face into joy and she didn't care that Eseld and Saffron saw it too.

Her eyes searched my face, then scanned the rest of me. She does that every time I've been further than the garden gate, just to check I've got the requisite number of limbs. Then she turned to Eseld and took in her jodhpurs. 'I suppose you two are the cavalry.'

The Mowbray clan were on their feet and would have mobbed Eseld if Mina weren't in the way. Ethan spoke first. 'Have you found him? Is it true?'

Eseld nodded and tried to speak. Her throat had closed with grief and all that came out was a low moan.

Lena pushed her way past Ethan and dodged Mina with a swerve that any rugby player would be proud of. She stopped in front of Eseld and said, 'I am so sorry. Come. Sit down.' She reached out and took Eseld's hand. A split-second smile creased Eseld's face, and she let herself be led to the sofa where Lena had sat with Ethan.

'Tell me,' said Ethan.

'Lord Mowbray was killed in the junction cavern,' I said, making sure that my voice could be heard by everyone. The only one missing was little Grace. 'It was murder, and obviously the Lab is off limits for now. I'll give you a moment with Eseld while I talk to Ms Desai. Lieutenant Hawkins will be on hand.'

The use of surnames had the effect I'd intended. For all that most of them were grieving, I couldn't afford to lose what little authority we had here. The downside was that I could see them about to close ranks.

'Saff, stand by the main door, will you. I'll go on to the terrace for a minute.'

She nodded and moved into a position where she could block them from the corridor to the Lab and still hear what they said unless they whispered in each other's ears.

I grabbed two mugs of coffee from the large flasks on a side table and followed Mina through the elegant french windows to the terrace. I put the mugs on the balustrade and we held on to each other for a few seconds.

'What was it like?' she said.

I told her about Mowbray and my suspicions. I finished with the news about the division of the Mowbray Estate.

'So that's what they were on about,' said Mina. 'I gathered that Medbh had come into something, and they were starting to speculate about why she'd disappeared until Ethan put his foot down. Ethan looked at me and said, "Medbh has some questions to answer. We should wait until she can speak for herself." As you'd expect, Kenver is convinced of her innocence but he has no idea why or where she's gone.'

'What happened when you roused the Daughters?'

'When we walked through the fire doors, Erin said that we'd triggered a load of alarms. The same thing happened when you were in the Labyrinth. Ethan told me and said not to worry, Eseld knew what she was doing. The obvious implication was that you didn't.'

'The Daughters?'

Mina lifted her nose. 'Sorry. I was worried about you, Conrad.' She stared at me for a second to let me know where her priorities lay, then switched back to the guest wing. 'We could hear movement before we'd even found the light switches.' A strange smile flickered across her face and a glint came into her eyes. 'Shall we just say that a naked Raven is even more striking than a fully dressed one. If she loses her magick, she has a future in niche films. Very niche.'

I tried not to let that image invade my subconscious. 'Go on.'

'Because they were piling out, we waited until they'd all appeared. No one was wearing blood-stained clothing. Will there be blood stains?'

'On whoever was standing in front of him, yes. Covered in blood, tissue, bone. The lot.'

She nodded. 'As soon as I'd told them what we'd seen, Alys took over. She thanked us formally for letting them know and said that it was none of their business and that they were leaving. Alys turned to her sister and said, "Get on the phone and have the coach brought now. Straight away." Where is the coach?'

'In the village. Assuming they can get hold of the driver, it'll be here very soon. Didn't she say anything else?'

'To me? No. She gave some instructions to Isolde and turned away. Erin grabbed me by the hand at that point and started dragging me out of the corridor.'

'What on earth for?'

'Magick. She said they were doing something to lock themselves in, and unless we wanted to join them we should get out.'

'Was Erin okay about standing watch?'

'She was the one who offered. I told her not to do anything stupid and keep me posted. She's messaged a couple of times to see what's going on and tell me that nothing has happened.'

I nodded slowly and wandered along to where Eseld keeps her ashtray.

'What next?' said Mina.

'You know what, love, I have no idea. Eseld seems to have calmed down, but that won't last long. If we do nothing, it will all slip through our fingers. If we get it wrong, more people could easily die.'

She tilted her head. 'Are you normally this indecisive? That's not the impression that Vicky and Saffron give, or what I've seen with my own eyes.'

'I'm like a foxhound: give me the scent of a fox and I'll run it to earth. This is different – we have a whole house full of foxes, but only one of them broke into the hen house.'

She nodded. 'Then we must start by eliminating Medbh.'

'Bit drastic to start with elimination.'

She stuck her head out. 'That was terrible, even by your standards. We will eliminate her from our enquiries. If she's not guilty, she's given the real killer amazing cover.'

I pulled my lip and thought it over. At that moment, Scout emerged from the sitting room, having presumably sniffed everyone and everything inside. 'What do you reckon, eh boy? How do we find Medbh?'

'Arff. Hnnnh.'

'Sounds like a plan to me.'

I walked inside and Mina whispered, 'Tell me you aren't taking advice from a dog.'

'Only when it's useful.'

I checked with Saffron first. She gave me a discreet thumbs-up, and I turned to the youngest Mowbray present, Kenver. 'Give me your phone, please.'

'What for?'

'To check your contacts with Medbh.'

'I've rung her loads and messaged her ten times. Nothing. Straight to voicemail.'

I held out my hand. 'Please.'

'No! She's got nothing to do with this, and it's none of your business.'

'So where is she?' said Eseld.

'I. Don't. Know. OK?'

Eseld sat up straight. She'd been leaning back, next to Lena. 'Then hand over the bloody phone. He's got every right to ask, and I'm telling you to as well.'

'Fine.'

He passed me the phone, and I lobbed it across the room to Mina. She caught it and her thumbs were soon going crazy. The last time we were at Pellacombe, Medbh had arrived with Kenver.

'Has Medbh got a car?' I asked.

'She can't drive,' said Kenver. He stared at Eseld and said, 'Wherever she's been all these years, it was isolated. She's never had to learn. She was going to ask Maggie Pearce for lessons on the estate while she sorts her provisional licence.'

'There is nothing suspicious on here,' said Mina.

'Excuse me,' I said. I retreated from the firing line and called Michael. Being a teenager, he had his phone next to his bed, and answered quickly.

'Sir? Is everything okay?'

'No it isn't, Michael. I need you to get down to the jetty and see if anyone has crossed over from the big house in the skiff during the night. Call me straight back.'

Mina spoke up. 'That reminds me, did Lord Mowbray have his phone with him?'

'He never took it into the Lab,' said Ethan. 'It'll be by his bed.'

'It wasn't,' said Kerenza. 'Was it, Saffron?' She looked at my partner, who shook her head. 'He went into the Lab about one o'clock,' she added. 'He was too wound up to sleep. I was shattered.'

I took a closer look at Kerenza. She'd been crying, and had a bundle of tissues squeezed in her hand. Her voice had trembled when she spoke. Unlike Eseld and Lena, she'd made the effort to take off her makeup before going to sleep, and her face looked freshly washed. Then again, she'd been a model: skincare was as much part of her professional life as shooting practice was mine.

There was a knock at the door, and Saffron opened it. Jane Kershaw stood there, terrified.

'Excuse me, but I've had a call from the Daughters' coach driver. He thinks he's lost. It's the Wards. Unless the Steward lowers them, or I get one of the other staff out of bed, he can't find us or get in.'

'Hang on,' said Eseld. 'I've just had a text.' She checked her phone. 'It's Raven. She says we've got five minutes to get the coach up to the front door or she won't be able to stop the others tearing the Wards down. The driver's been on to them as well.'

I was tempted to force their hand, until I remembered that there were ten of them. Nor would the Mowbrays stand idle while the magick around Pellacombe was dismantled. 'Fine,' I said. 'Text Raven and tell her we can't do it in less than ten minutes, but it will be done. Kerenza, I'm going to have to ask you to comply.'

'I ... I'm not sure,' said Kerenza.

'I will do it,' said Lena. 'Fetch me the badge.'

Kerenza's head jerked back. A woman she clearly looked down on had just ordered her about in the house that she thought was hers to command. No one spoke up for her, and she had to struggle out of the deep armchair with every eye on her. I took the opportunity to drag Jane Kershaw aside and whisper some instructions to her. She left us and got on her phone.

Eseld was about to say something when my phone rang.

'Hello, Michael?'

'Sir. Someone brought the skiff over in the night.'

'Hang on.' I muted his call and asked Saff to put a Silence between me and the room. I picked up the call in the corridor. 'Anything else you can tell me.'

'They weren't an experienced sailor, I can tell you that much, sir.'

'How do you know?'

'They tied it tight to the jetty at full tide. The nose is sticking right up in the air now that the tide's gone down.'

'When was full tide?'

'Between midnight and one.'

'Right. Can you do three things for me? First, wake your father and tell him to get the Smurf ready. I might need her. Then bring the skiff back over here and wait. The third thing is more difficult. This must remain secret until I say otherwise. Lord Mowbray has died.'

There was a stunned silence.

'Really?' he said with a half-squeak. 'Really dead?'

'I'm afraid so, Michael. Tell your father to check with any of the family, or better still to ring Jane Kershaw if he doubts me. No one else. Understand?'

'Yes, sir.' He hesitated. 'Is this anything to do with Mr Kenver leaving?'

'He's here. Why do you think it was him in the boat?'

'He never liked the river, and his car's gone from the Lamorne car park. I checked the cars before I came down here.'

'That's brilliant, Michael. Thank you.'

I disconnected and marched back. Saff hastily cancelled the Silence behind me. 'Kenver, where are your car keys?'

'In the box, like always.'

'What box?'

'At the Ferrymistress's house. If we leave our cars at Lamorne, we leave the keys there in case anyone needs to move them.'

I looked around the group. While I was out, Kerenza had handed the medallion to Lena, who was now checking her watch. Every other eye was on me.

'I now know two things,' I said. 'First, that Medbh was an even more accomplished liar and could drive after all. Either that or she had an accomplice who could drive but got here without bringing their own vehicle. Kenver's car is gone.'

They were wrung out. The only one who reacted was Ethan, the corner of whose mouth gave a twitch.

I continued. 'The second thing I know is that Medbh is innocent. She left the house before one in the morning. Lord Mowbray died at twenty to four. She was long gone by then.'

'I need to lower the Wards,' said Lena. Behind me, Jane Kershaw had slipped back into the room and gave me a nod: mission accomplished.

'Do it. Jane, call the driver if you would.'

Jane waited for Lena to finish concentrating on her magick and left when she got the nod.

While that was going on, Eseld had been doing some thinking. The dangerous light was back in her eyes.

'If it's not Medbh, it can only be one person,' she said. 'The only one that Dad would meet like that, and trust, is Isolde. It must be her.' She stood up. 'I'm going to stop her.'

Part Seven — Dawn's Curse

37 – Daughters, and one mother

She moved quickly. Eseld was half way to the door before the implications of what she'd said had fully sunk in. She was about to take on the Daughters single handed. Saffron reached the same conclusion and put herself in the doorway. She went slightly pale and her hand moved to the spiked chain hanging from her belt.

'Out of my way,' said Eseld.

'That's not going to happen,' I said, belatedly moving to block the way to the terrace.

'Why not?' A different voice. Kenver had stood up and was about to cast his lot in with Eseld now that his full sister was in the clear. 'Isolde's easily capable,' he added.

'Stop them!' It was Cador, and the first time that he'd spoken aloud since I arrived. He was the only Mowbray left who had any time for Isolde, and he made his appeal to Ethan.

Ethan had been standing by the fire. He stood up straight and said, 'Eseld's got a point. Isolde could be in on it. She has questions to answer. What do you suggest, Conrad?'

If I didn't come up with a plan, Ethan would side with Eseld and Kenver, and we'd have a bloodbath on our hands. The moment had come for me to put up or shut up.

'Here's what's going to happen,' I said. 'Eseld, you're going to call Raven and give me the phone. When I've finished, you, Mina and I – and no one else – are going to the front of the house.'

She wavered, so (hate me if you want), I played the dead man's card. 'Your father would want things done properly, Eseld.'

'He would,' she said, 'but that doesn't give you the right to take his name in vain.' Having made her point, she whipped out her phone and pressed the screen. 'Here.'

'What?' said Raven in a hushed voice.

'This is Conrad. I need your help to avoid a catastrophe.'

'Wow. Did Eseld give you her phone or did you kill her and use her lifeless finger to unlock the screen?'

I held the phone away from me. That was a bit extreme. I *have* done something similar, but I didn't kill Surwen just to get her phone.

'Eseld gave me the phone because she's as anxious as I am to investigate her father's murder.'

'No, I'm not,' shouted Eseld. 'I want to avenge him.'

Raven laughed. 'This is shaping up nicely. Sounds fun.'

'Only if you're the Morrigan, Raven, and you're not. I want to talk to Isolde, and I need your help to do it.' I stared at Eseld when I spoke again. 'I will guarantee Isolde's safety if she remains behind, and I'll let Cador advise her.'

Raven chuckled. 'How do you know I'm not the Morrigan? Or her daughter?'

'Because I've met her, and the goddess of war has no child but death.'

'Says the soldier.'

'Airman. You'll probably survive, but do you want to watch Eseld being the first to die?' I left it half a second. 'Thought not. We're on our way.'

I disconnected the call and thrust the phone into Eseld's hand as I walked out. 'Come on if you're coming.'

Mina had already taken a position by the door and fell into step with me. She didn't ask why I'd left Saffron behind, or why I was taking her instead. She knew the answer: Saff would raise the temperature, an unarmed Mina would lower it. They didn't know that she had a handgun under her tunic.

Mina can walk and text as easily as I can fly a helicopter. She checked her phone and said, 'Erin says they're coming out.'

Jane Kershaw was haunting the great hall like a ghost on the threshold, peering from the pitch blackness outside to the dimly lit staircase from the guest wing. She had her phone to her ear and was guiding in the coach driver like a seasoned air traffic controller. 'He'll be here in less than a minute,' she announced. From upstairs, we heard voices.

'Jane, wait outside,' I said, 'and don't come in unless I say so. It may be dangerous.' She nodded and disappeared outside.

I could see white shapes at the top of the staircase. One tried to descend and was elbowed out of the way by a black shadow, and it was Raven who led the Daughters down the stairs. Alys, the one she'd pushed aside followed with a face like thunder and her twin sister at her side.

With her great strides, Raven crossed the hall and pivoted in front of the door to face her fellow Witches.

'There has been a murder here,' said Raven. 'A life taken before its time. We cannot just walk away. Conrad would like to talk to one of us. He is willing to guarantee her safety with his own life.'

They didn't need to ask which of their number I was interested in because Eseld was staring at her mother with pure hatred in her eyes. Isolde was staring at the floor.

Alys moved slightly to the side, with Zoe, and it was Georgia who stepped up to confront Raven. Georgia hadn't spoken to me since the helicopter flight yesterday, and had been placed on an all-female table last night.

'No, Raven,' said Georgia. 'We are not going to hand over one of the Daughters of the Goddess to a Witchfinder and your little tart.'

In the silence of the pre-dawn, the rattle of a diesel engine heralded the arrival of their coach. I scanned the group, looking for threats and to make sure they were all there. They were. Half way down the stairs, Erin was keeping three eyes on the proceedings – her own two and the camera on her phone.

'Grow up and remember who you are,' said Georgia to Raven.

Georgia had been on Raven's side in the battle to replace Hedda. What had changed? Was it Georgia we should be interviewing and not Isolde?

'I'm not going to trade insults with you,' said Raven. 'The days of the Witchfinders are long gone. Let Conrad and Mina do their job. I know who I am.'

The diesel engine outside died, and silence crept back over the hall. Everyone shifted slightly in anticipation of the next move.

Georgia stood taller, and she was only just getting started. 'I beg to differ. You are the 1st of Ash Coven in the Homewood of Glastonbury. It is your job to lead and to protect us, not to kowtow to the Witchfinder and his mundane whore.'

Mina's face remained impassive at this tirade, but her right hand moved first to her left arm and then it hitched up her tunic. She had turned side on so that none of the Daughters could see her gun.

Her first movement had told me that magick was being done even before I felt the temperature rise. Just to show he was still there and on his mettle, Scout gave a low growl. I sighed inside: Raven had done what I asked; it was over to me.

I tried to speak conversationally. 'Isolde, are you going to let this go any further? Eseld could die if you do. Come with us and we can sort this out. Cador can advise you. Mina will watch as an officer of the court.'

The pain on Isolde's face when she looked up was awful to behold. 'I can't leave the Daughters,' she said. 'I can't break my vows.' She turned to Raven. 'Order me, and I will go gladly. Whatever the consequences.'

Every eye turned to Raven. She seemed to grow even larger under the spotlight, relishing the attention and even striking a pose. She fished her Goddess braid from behind her head and stroked the densely bound hair. 'Go, sister. The Goddess will walk by your side.'

I was holding my breath, and I wasn't alone. With simple dignity, Isolde separated herself from the Witches and crossed to stand next to Mina.

Alys let out a venomous hiss of air and moved in front of Georgia, barely an arm's length from Raven. She craned back her head and said, 'It is not for me to question the actions of a First Daughter, but you will answer to the three Covens for what you have done.'

Raven's face seemed to shut down for a second, all life disappearing from her eyes. She blinked, and then she grinned. 'I'll get back to you on that one.

Now off you go, Alys.' She moved away from the door. 'Don't let me stand in your way.'

The Daughters had brought their luggage with them down the staircase, and the principal players had dropped theirs before the drama. Alys left her sister to pick up the bags and walked out of the hall. The others followed her, and only Cordelia stopped to acknowledge Raven. They spoke for a few seconds with Raven's head bent and a neat Silence around them. They clasped hands, and Cordelia left with tears forming in her eyes.

It was only when the engine started up again that Raven realised that they were going without her. She shook herself and drifted away from the door. When she looked around the hall (which she's seen many times), there was an openness in her eyes that spoke of new beginnings.

'Were you filming that, little Enscriber?'

Erin went white and retreated a couple of steps up the staircase. With a shock, I realised that we weren't alone. Three girls and two boys had joined the audience on the gallery. I recognised them as live-in staff. Oh dear. We'd have real problems soon if I wasn't careful.

Erin stopped recording. 'I'm really really sorry. I'll delete it right away.'

'Don't you dare!' boomed Raven in a beautiful contralto. 'Share it with me now.'

'And me,' I added.

Jane Kershaw came back in and looked from Raven to Eseld and then to me. She spoke to all of us at once. 'Forgive me. Please. Several of the household staff were woken by the noise, here and out there. I've told all of them to come to the hall in twenty minutes. I haven't said anything about what's happened.'

I looked up at the gallery. 'Too late for that, but thanks, Jane. Someone will be along to brief them.'

'So no chance of breakfast yet?' said Raven.

'There's coffee in the kitchen,' I replied. I paused to let that sink in, and went up to her. 'Thank you for what you did. I am in your debt. And now, if you'll excuse us...' I put my hand out and felt her power when we shook.

I turned my back on the giant Witch and spoke to Erin. 'Could you get down to the sitting room and brief Saffron. Send Cador to Lord Mowbray's study.'

'Right.'

'Jane, could you lead the way? I suspect the door will be locked.'

I made sure that Isolde was between Mina and myself, away from her daughter, as we followed Jane into the morning room and waited for her to unlock the study door. I could have asked Eseld to do it, but I needed to manoeuvre her into a corner. Not back her into a corner, but lead her gently.

Jane pushed the door open and stood aside. Mina went in, with Isolde following silently. At the last moment, I pivoted and blocked the doorway.

'You and I are going for a smoke,' I said to Eseld. 'While Isolde talks to Cador.'

She looked around and decided not to make a scene here. I could see Raven still standing in the hall, unsure of what to do now she'd made her grand gesture. 'Let's show Raven the way to the kitchen and get some coffee.'

I was glad that it was still cold, or the sweat running down my back would be soaking through my uniform. Since the Spirit of Mowbray had dragged me awake, every step has felt like a tightrope walk, and there's no safety net. In fact, I could distinctly smell brimstone coming up from below.

'This way,' I said to Raven. I took the shortcut through the staff entrance to the kitchens. A couple of the young staff had already migrated down here and started to get food out of the store rooms. I thought that Raven and Eseld might have something to say to each other on the way down. It seems not. Either that or they didn't want to talk in front of Jane Kershaw. I checked my watch: fifteen minutes to the staff briefing.

We stopped by the coffee machines. While I poured, I said to Raven, 'Have you lived all your life in Homewood?'

'Apart from the Rumspringa.'

'Sorry?'

'We borrowed the word from the Amish. Or they borrowed it from us. You have to leave the grove for at least a year between adolescence and taking the cord. I didn't just go to Spain on an exchange visit, I went back for a longer trip. And other places outside Albion. Thanks for the coffee. I think I'll take it down to the dock.'

'If you find Michael or any of his family standing around, tell them to come up to the hall.'

'And where are we going?' said Eseld.

'Outside front. Bit of privacy there.'

It was also cold outside. Very cold in the final pre-dawn darkness. We could barely see each other in the light leaking from a few windows.

'Well?' said Eseld when we'd lit our cigarettes.

'Why did Georgia call you Raven's tart?'

'Is that relevant?'

I didn't answer, and let her decide for herself.

'Same sex relationships are allowed but not encouraged in the Daughters,' she said. 'When I was thirteen, Raven and I exchanged promise rings. It was no promise for me, because I was under age, but Raven promised to wait three years. Three years is a long time when you're seventeen and horny. I left before we consummated anything.'

The mathematics were obvious: Eseld had lost her Familiar and broken with her mother during that period. It was also obvious that some of the Daughters blamed Raven *and* Eseld for what had happened.

I nodded to show that I'd taken what she'd said seriously. 'Mina and I are going to interview Isolde. You can't be there. She may be completely innocent.'

'She may not have killed my father, but she's as guilty as sin, Conrad.'

'What if she *is* innocent of Lord Mowbray's murder? Do you want to let the real culprit off the hook?'

She looked down. 'No.' With her head still bowed, she continued. 'If Isolde took my father's life, you won't stop me taking vengeance.'

'Not on my own, no, but with Saffron and Raven's help I will.'

'Do you think Raven will side with you over me?'

'So long as she wears the cord, yes she will. She's already proved that.'

Eseld looked up and looked away, down towards the dock. 'Perhaps. Probably. We'll see.'

It was good enough.

'Then finish your coffee and go to your family. Tell Ethan to make the announcement to the staff, if he hasn't already started planning for it.'

I left her there and went back into the mansion. Another step taken on the tightrope. If only I could see where it led, it would be a lot easier.

38 – Accidental

Mina was waiting outside Mowbray's study. We held our four hands together for a moment, just to recharge ourselves. Mina held on a little longer because her hands are always colder than mine.

'Do we have to prepare for a siege?' she said.

'Perhaps. Probably not. If Isolde is guilty, I'm not making any announcements unless Raven is standing next to me.'

'That will do wonders for my self-esteem. I have just watched Erin's video, and from that angle, I actually look like a child next to you and Raven. All you can see is my long hair and pink trainers.'

A horrible thought struck me. A truly horrible thought. I called Erin and said, 'Do you want to carry on being my tenant?'

'Eh? What?'

'If you do, then you'll use your skills to edit that video and cover up my bald patch before you send it to the Boss.'

There was a pause. 'Are you being serious?'

'Baldness is not a laughing matter.'

There was another silence. I think Erin may have been talking to Saffron with the mute button pressed. She came back on the line and said, 'Yes it is,' and then she disconnected.

'Do you feel better for that?' said Mina, hands on hips.

I grinned. 'Yes. It's important that the troops know their CO has a sense of humour. Shall we dance with Isolde?'

She nodded her *not yet* nod. 'You forget that I have been interviewed, at length, by trained detectives. You are not a detective, Conrad. Your tactics may not work in there.'

'Are you saying that you want to lead the interview?'

'Mmm. Yes.'

'Then let's get on with it.'

I knocked on the door and pushed it open. Mina had already set things up by putting Cador and Isolde on one side of the conference table with two empty chairs on the other. Mina slid into the chair opposite Isolde and told me to get some paper and a pen.

While I ferreted around in Mowbray's desk, Isolde and Cador looked confused and Mina pushed her hair firmly behind her ears. While they were still off balance, she began.

'Isolde, 9th of Willow, you are being interviewed on suspicion of murder. Were you ever married to Lord Mowbray under mundane law?'

Cador sprang into life. 'My mother would like to make a statement,' he began.

Mina waved her hand in front of him as if she were waving a fly away from her cooking. 'You are not a criminal lawyer, Mr Mowbray, and PACE does not apply here. The sooner your mother answers our questions, the sooner we can move on.'

Mowbray's desk wasn't locked (unlike the cupboard with the crowns in it, I imagine). I had to root around most of the drawers until I found a pen and paper. I judged this the moment to place the stationery in front of Mina and take my seat next to her. That made Cador pause, and it allowed Mina to pick up the pen and say, 'Were you married under mundane law?'

'Yes,' said Isolde.

The flame of pride I have inside me for Mina grew a little brighter. She'd got Isolde to answer on her terms, not Cador's. I tried not to let it show in my face and looked down at the folder I'd also found in Mowbray's desk. While no one was looking at me, I sneaked a look inside.

'And divorced?' said Mina.

'Yes. I had to renounce everything to join the Daughters, including all claims on the Mowbray Estate. My children were written into its terms at birth, so I knew they'd be protected.'

'Thank you. Prior to the conference earlier this month, did you have any contact with Lord Mowbray or any member of his family, or anyone connected to him?'

Isolde shifted in her seat. 'Over what period?'

'This year.'

She shook her head. 'No. Only Cador.' She looked at her son. 'How often?'

'Three times this year,' he said. 'My birthday, your birthday and Mother's Day.'

She looked at her unvarnished fingernails. 'Of course.'

'You are a Guardian,' said Mina. 'Is that your main role in Homewood?'

Isolde shrugged. 'You wouldn't understand.'

'Try me.'

'No, I meant that it's a whole way of life. It would take hours to explain it properly.'

'But you trained in offensive magick?'

Isolde frowned. 'All Mages do. I just took it a bit further, and being a Homewood Guardian is mostly ceremonial, and there's one of us in each Coven. I met Rick James a couple of times. Compared to me, he's like a Terminator.'

That was interesting. In my opinion, anyway. Mina was pursuing a different strategy.

'How did you come to be in Willow Coven?' she said.

'Each Coven chooses its own members. I was told that I'd be looked on favourably when there was a vacancy in Willow.'

Mina had been writing something down. She looked up sharply. 'By whom?'

'It was Zoe, actually. Verity is 1st of Willow, so she made the final decision.'

'I see. And how did you end up in the Daughters' conference party?'

According to Eseld, it had been Hedda's decision. I held my breath while Isolde answered.

She shrugged, a big one that lifted her palms almost to the level of the table. 'I don't know. Georgia was the one who told me, but she didn't make the decisions, and I didn't ask.'

Mina put down her pen. 'And how did you feel?'

Isolde blushed for the first time. 'Like I'd won the lottery. Turns out my ticket was a forgery.'

'Tell me, in as much detail as you can, what happened after you left the house to go to prayers last night.'

Isolde took a moment to gather her thoughts. 'I was at the back, because I stopped to ask Jane if there was any chance of hot chocolate.' Mina thought that was noteworthy. 'We prayed, we made the sacrifice of Lux and we returned to the guest quarters.' She looked at Mina. 'If you didn't know, we always process and return in silence. Jane and one of the boys brought the hot chocolate. We needed it after last night. It wasn't warm out there.'

'Who did you talk to?'

'No one, really. Everyone was still full of what Arthur had done. We all sort-of whispered about who was going to be staff king. I didn't really join in.'

'Why not?'

Isolde put her hands on the table. 'Because I thought I'd missed my chance to see my daughter. I knew that Eseld wouldn't come to wave us off in the morning. I'm fifty-five years old, Miss Desai, and I cried myself to sleep last night. If you can believe that.'

Mina put her head on one side. 'I can believe it. Did you sleep at all?'

'Yes. When I finally dropped off, that was it. The next thing I knew, the Wards had been triggered and you were standing in the corridor with that Enscriber girl.'

'You heard nothing out of the ordinary?'

'Nothing. Not even Raven snoring in the distance.' It was a weak attempt at humour, but it was an attempt. Isolde put her hand on Cador's. 'My children have lost their father. It was nothing to do with me.'

Mina tapped her pen on the table, then looked at me. We locked eyes and both shook our heads by a millimetre: Isolde was innocent. Of this crime, anyway.

'Is there anything you need to know?' Mina asked me.

'Yes. Before Raven blotted her copybook in the main hall, who was winning the race to become Eldest Daughter?'

Isolde frowned. 'Is that important?'

I sat back. Cador knew his mother was off the hook and couldn't help intervening. 'This is the point where the Witchfinder tells you that he decides what's important, Mum. You don't have to answer that.'

Mina pointed her pen at Cador's chest. 'Yes she does, and if you refer to the Watch Captain in that way again, you'll be in trouble. And don't plead irony.'

It was his turn to flush red. 'I might not go riding or have a wardrobe full of fancy dress costumes, but Eseld isn't the only one who's lost their father.'

Mina was about to lose it, so I sat forward again and put my elbow on the table in front of her. 'Isolde? The race for the throne?'

She tried to laugh. 'There is no throne. Before last night, I'd have said Raven had it sewn up. Did you hear our row before we went to prayers.'

'Some of it.'

'Raven was obsessed about the new kingdom of Wessex. She said we should change our statutes to allow one of us to stand. She even hinted that she'd changed her mind about having men in the Covens.'

'And that's why Georgia is Alys's new best friend,' I said.

'Pretty much.' She hesitated. 'Did you know that three of the full Coven members are in long-term relationships with men?' I shook my head and frowned. 'You just can't be married, that's all, and your children have to be educated in single sex streams from eleven.'

I pulled my lip. Mina started to shuffle papers together.

'There's one more thing,' I said. 'I found this in Mowbray's desk.'

I opened the folder and took out a big bundle of envelopes. They were greeting cards, each one addressed to Eseld Mowbray at the Pellacombe cover address.

'Birthday cards,' said Isolde. She reached out reflexively and stroked the envelopes. 'Arthur must have intercepted them.' She looked up at me. 'Eseld must think I've forgotten. That was mean of him.'

'No, mum,' said Cador in a very small voice. 'It was worse. Much worse. Every year, he'd tell her that you'd sent one. He wouldn't let her have it because she destroyed the first four. Burnt them in front of me. He said he was hanging on to them for her.'

Isolde started to cry.

'Can I take those?' said Cador. 'I'll hang on to them like Dad did.'

I slid the pile across to him and said, 'You may want to be with your mother, or you may want to join your family in the main hall. Ethan is addressing the staff. We couldn't keep it from them any longer.'

'Shit,' he said without thinking, and half rose from his seat. 'Erm, Mum…'

'Go,' she said. 'I'll go down to the dock and talk to Raven, if that's okay.'

'We're done,' I said. I stood and let them out of the door back to the morning room.

'Well?' said Mina. 'Where do we go from here? We are sure about Isolde, aren't we?'

'We are. Any woman who still calls Lord Mowbray *Arthur* couldn't stand in front of him and watch his heart blown out of his chest.'

I leaned against the fireplace and did a couple of stretches to try and get the tension out of my leg. Something stirred at the back of my mind and then disappeared when Mina spoke.

'Do all tall people snore, or is it just you and Raven?'

'I wouldn't know, and I don't snore that much.'

'You do sometimes. Now I know why they put her in a room of her own.'

I froze, one leg in the air. 'What did you say?'

'When Erin and I interrupted their beauty sleep, Raven came out first, from the single room nearest the fire doors.'

'Double shit. Ow, my leg hurts. Run after Isolde and stop her, love. Scout! Find Isolde.'

He shot out of the door with Mina in hot pursuit. Mina would have headed for the main hall, but Scout led her into the room that the Daughters had used for the conference, and out of the door in there. I tried to relax my muscles and the thought buried at the back of my head sent me a note. I now knew who had killed Lord Mowbray, and I had a fairly good idea why. I gave my leg a shake and set off after the others.

39 – Teamwork

They hadn't got far. At the far corner of the house, leading down to the docks, Isolde was trying to stop Scout nipping her ankles. Mina caught up with them and pointed to me. I walked steadily, lengthening my stride to get rid of the last of the cramp.

'What's going on?' said Isolde, blinking tears away from her eyes. It was much lighter now, heading towards a bright crisp sunrise.

'Who slept in which room last night, and how did it happen?' I said.

'What?'

'Just tell me. This really is important.'

She blew out her cheeks, thought for a moment and gave a self-deprecating smile. 'When Eseld turned up, just before the banquet, I thought she wanted to see me. I've thought it every time I've seen her, but she grabbed Morning and asked what was going on. I was so proud of her it was devastating.'

She trailed off into silence.

'Why? What did she do?' said Mina, putting her arm round Isolde.

'She didn't put herself first. She thought of Signe, and of how Signe must feel with her mother in hospital. She told us to let Signe have the single room and to stop arguing. Then she just left. She didn't even ignore me, she just left.'

I gave her a moment to get past the worst of the pain. 'What happened next?'

She pulled herself together. 'Because we'd lose face if there was any more arguing, we had to find a solution. Signe said something like, "I wouldn't inflict Raven's snoring on anyone. I'll share with Morning, if that's okay." And then Alys jumped straight in with, "And I shall share with Zoe and Brook." And that was that. We all got on with it.'

'Thank you,' I said. 'Come on, Mina. I wonder if the staff meeting is still going on.'

We hurried along the path. 'What?' said Mina.

'Morning and Signe,' I said. 'They did it. Specifically, Morning did the actual killing and Signe did the Necromancy. They had to be sleeping in a room together for it to work.'

We had arrived at the main entrance. The grand doors had been closed to keep the cold out. I pushed slowly at one and dislodged a rugged man who'd been leaning against them. He jumped away and moved to protect his wife – Leah Kershaw was sitting just inside the hall, cradling her bump. To the right of the doors were Michael, his sisters and his mother. His father was no doubt still checking over the Smurf. There was no sign of Erin, but I could make out Saffron's halo of white hair.

'Keep the door open,' I whispered to Mina.

Half way up the stairs, Ethan and Cador were taking questions. The rest of the Mowbrays were gathered at the bottom. As soon as we entered, the great space fell deathly quiet, and Eseld started to push her way through the crowd. There were a lot of people in there. It must have been every worker and tenant on the estate.

I used my height to peer over the throng, searching for Lena. *Yes!* She was still wearing the Steward's badge. '*Kommen Sie her, bitte. Langsam. Es ist wichtig.*'

Ethan's German had got beyond the very basics, and he understood the first part: *Come here*. Whether he got the rest (*Slowly. It's important*) is another matter.

The crowd was focusing on Eseld's more aggressive progress through their number, and barely noticed Lena join her slipstream. A space appeared in front of the door, and Eseld filled it.

'Well?' she said. 'Have you arrested the bitch, or is she already dead? I can hope.'

The crowd immediately swelled with a murmur of anticipation, and I addressed myself to them, not Eseld. 'Even if we've not spoken, you all know who I am. This is a very difficult time for everyone here, and I know I can rely on your support to find out what happened. Ethan? Have you told them the timescale?'

From the stairs, Ethan said, 'I've asked for anyone who saw or heard anything to speak up. No one did.'

Lena had arrived and had slipped past Eseld to stand with Mina at the open door.

'Then I shall leave you in peace.'

I made one last scan of the room, and there was one face missing. Shit. I walked backwards out of the hall, and when I'd crossed the threshold, I said, 'Close the door, Eseld.'

She slammed it with anger and turned to face us. 'Well?'

'It's not your mother. Call Saffron and tell her to meet us in the King's Watch suite. We'll sort it in there.'

Lena was now looking unsure. The hate and anger in Eseld's eyes would put anyone on their guard. '*Du bist es nicht,*' I said, forgetting for a moment and using the familiar form: *It's not you.* 'Let's take the fire escape route.'

I held my arm for Lena to go first, and she bustled off. Eseld took out her phone and followed behind. I heard her saying, 'No, I don't fucking know what he's up to, but if he doesn't sort it out soon, he'll regret it.'

The first rays of the sun were kissing the top of Lamorne Point across the bay when we got back to the suite. Scout immediately started sniffing around, checking for stray Spirits, I suppose. When he found none, he curled up in his basket. It had already been a long day, and it was barely dawn.

Saffron was there ahead of us.

'Where's Erin?' I said.

'She's helping the staff by keeping an eye on some of the pots in the kitchen. And raiding the fridge, I expect. She's got the munchies after last night.'

'Sit down, everyone,' I said. 'I'm just going to grab something from your bag, love.'

Mina raised her eyebrows, but said nothing. I made the mad dive into Mina's overnight bag and emerged with what I needed. When we were investigating the Flint Hoard, she'd taken to packing a jeweller's loupe along with everything else. Perfect for getting the evidence I knew had to be there.

'Lena, can I have the Steward's badge, please?'

She lifted the heavy metal medallion off her neck and handed it to me by the ribbon. I took it over to the window and peered through the loupe. *There.* She hadn't even tried to wash it off. Probably didn't notice in the rush to get changed and wash herself. I owed it to Eseld to let her see the evidence with her own eyes.

'Take a look at this,' I said.

She got up and joined me at the window. She scanned the badge and ribbon for a second, and then said, 'What am I looking at?'

'Your father's blood. Kerenza wore this to get into the Lab, and she was still wearing it when he died.'

'No! It can't be her.'

'Why not?'

'Because she may be a failed actress, but she's the best thing that's happened to Dad in years. You saw the way he dotes on little Grace.'

'Izzi. With an *i*. Her name's Izzi.'

'Who? Kerenza? I know that's a stage name, but she's had it since she was sixteen.'

'Not Kerenza. Grace. Until her mother met your father, Grace was Isolde. Izzi. Any mother who would make her daughter change her name like that is capable of anything.'

'What? No.'

'I'm afraid so. We could get the ribbon DNA tested. Unless she confesses, we'll have to.'

Eseld was still holding the medallion. She looked at it again, focusing on the metal this time, and not the ribbon. 'You're right. There's organic matter here.' She looked up. 'Why? Why would she?'

'That can wait. We need to get hold of her. Lena, why wasn't Kerenza at the staff meeting?'

'She said she had to wake Grace and tell her what had happened.'

'Does Grace have a separate room?'

'Ja. With bathroom.'

'Then that's where she hid the evidence and got herself cleaned up. Let's go.'

Eseld had finally accepted the truth, and moved on to the next stage. 'Who did she do it with? We're back to square one. It could be anyone.'

'Later,' I said. I took the medallion gently from her hand and gave it to Mina. 'Take the ribbon off and put it in a plastic bag, then give the badge to Lena.' She nodded. 'Where's Kerenza's car?'

'At Lamorne.'

'Let's just hope that she can't get the engine started on the skiff,' I said, knowing full well that she had plenty of time to get away. 'Let's go.'

I ran down the back stairs as fast as I could, with Eseld and Saffron on my heels. When we scooted through the family area, I could hear voices as the staff dispersed from the meeting. We ran into the bedroom corridor and heard frantic pounding from one of the doors to the left.

'Let me,' said Eseld.

She used her key – and a little extra magick – to open the door. A hysterical Grace/Izzi was standing behind it, still in her pony pyjamas, screaming for her mother. She'd been locked in.

I didn't bother trying to ask her any questions, but I did open the laundry basket. Half way down, I found a sopping wet bath towel. 'She used this to dry the shower after she … after she came here.'

Saffron was at the back, and turned to run towards the dock. I paused to say, 'Someone's coming, Izzi. We're going to find your mummy, OK?'

I ran after the others as fast as I could. Nowhere near fast enough. When I emerged into the office, three women were staring open mouthed through the windows. A nightmare vision of Saffron dying to protect Kerenza flooded through my mind. Upstairs, she'd been rational, but Eseld was on a hair trigger. If she attacked Kerenza…

I flung the door open and stopped in my tracks. Eseld was going for Kerenza, but it wasn't Saffron protecting our killer, it was Raven.

The giant Witch was standing by the dock, one hand clamped on Kerenza's shoulder. Kerenza had been forced into a kneeling position and was trying to dislodge Raven's mighty claw. In front of them, Eseld was being restrained by Saffron. Eseld had lifted her left hand, and I could feel the heat of Lux from over here. Raven was grinning, an even scarier look than normal. Scout had got there, too, and as the magick built, he turned and ran to me.

'Enough!' I shouted. 'Eseld, back off.'

She turned to look at me, and Saffron took the opportunity to drag her further away from Raven. When I'd got closer, Saff let go, moving to stand between Eseld and Kerenza.

'Is it true?' said Raven. 'She came out of the cottage, carrying those.'

I hadn't noticed the suitcase a little further down the dock. Next to it was a black bin liner. 'Saff, check them out.'

As well as struggling, Kerenza had been shouting. I only realised when I saw her mouth move in silence. Or Silence. A knee-high Silence. Neat.

'It's true,' I said. 'We have proof.'

Raven's face turned impassive. Whatever she thought of Kerenza's betrayal, it didn't make it to her eyes. 'What shall I do with her?'

'Hold her a second longer.'

I checked Kerenza for Artefacts and removed a small chain of them, far fewer than I'd expected. I took out a cable tie and, when Raven applied a little extra pain, I got Kerenza's arms behind her and secured her hands. 'You can let go now.'

Raven cancelled the Silence and removed her hand. I dragged Kerenza to her feet and said, 'By the powers granted to me, you are under arrest for murder and suspicion of regicide. You will answer to the appropriate court.'

'Sir!' shouted Saffron. The black bag was open at her feet and she held up a low cut top. 'Bloodstains.'

'That's disgusting,' said Eseld.

'What is?' said Raven.

I answered. 'After she killed Lord Mowbray, Kerenza hid her clothes in Grace's room and took a shower in there to wash away the blood. The only thing she couldn't hide was the Steward's badge. We found blood on it. The disgusting part is that she did it with her daughter there.' I turned to our prisoner. 'Did you use magick or tranquilisers to put her out? I'm thinking drugs.'

'I don't know what you're talking about,' said Kerenza. 'I haven't killed anyone.'

Eseld leaned forwards. 'It'll be in your hair. You didn't wash that. I'm going to cut it off. Not for evidence, you understand, but so you won't go to your grave with my father's remains on you.' She paused. Kerenza was just about hanging on. Eseld leaned even closer. 'Did you read the Deed? Regicide is a reserved crime. You'll be tried in Kernow and I'll ask for the death penalty.'

Kerenza looked at me. Her voice trembled. 'Get her away from me.'

'Why should I? What she says is true. I've done my bit. I can get in my car and drive away with my conscience clear. After a good breakfast, of course.'

'You can't!'

I turned to Eseld. 'You will wait until after breakfast to hold the trial, won't you.'

'I'll chain her up in the Labyrinth until after the funeral.'

Kerenza's voice broke completely. 'Stop her. Please.'

'Why should I?'

'Because I didn't kill him!'

'Then explain the blood.'

'They made me. They made me do it.'

'Who did?'

She shook her head.

I turned and shouted to Saffron. 'Anything else of interest?'

'Lots of gold in the suitcase.'

I started to walk towards my partner. From behind me, I heard Eseld whispering something in Kerenza's ear. I got to Saffron and peered down.

'It was Morning,' said Kerenza. 'She killed him! And Signe bottled his Spirit.'

Eseld Grabbed Kerenza's hair and twisted it so violently that the other woman sank to her knees with her neck close to breaking. 'Is his Spirit still intact? Tell me.'

'I don't know. I don't understand. She drew it back down from upstairs. Then we ran. That's all I know.'

Raven moved like lightning, grabbing Eseld's bicep and squeezing.

'Aagh,' said Eseld. She let go of her nearly step-mother and clutched her arm.

Raven slowly put her index finger on Kerenza's chest, right above her heart. 'Say that again.'

'What?'

'Who did it. Who helped you.'

'Morning. And Signe. They called me when I went to check on Grace, after the banquet. They made me let them into the Labyrinth and distract Mowbray.' She looked down at the finger on her chest. Her arms flexed as she tried to break the cable tie. 'They threatened to hurt Grace. I had no choice.'

'Liar,' said Eseld. 'Morning would never hurt a young girl. You were in on it with them. Why did you do it?'

'We can argue about that later,' I said. 'We need to stop that bus before it gets to Glastonbury. And we've got an audience.'

Raven withdrew her finger slowly and we turned to look. Most of the staff had gathered in a semi-circle on the dock, with the family in front. The only person with their back to us was Mina, holding her arms out and using sheer willpower to keep everyone at bay.

'Ethan! Mina! Can you come here? Everyone else stay back. For your own safety.'

Mina stayed facing the crowd. She took a step back, and another, and another. Ethan detached himself and said, 'Please. Stay where you are. Don't let him down.'

The crowd shifted, but stayed where it was. Mina turned to face us and they came up together.

'Is it true?' said Ethan.

'Yes,' said Eseld. 'She lured him to his death and two of the Daughters finished him off. I don't know whether to kill her slowly in private or quickly in public.'

'You'll do neither of those things,' said Ethan. 'You'll let the Watch take her.'

'Make me.'

'Yes, I will.'

Eseld flinched back, and I stepped in. 'Ethan, I'm going to leave Kerenza in Mina's custody. Will you guarantee their safety?'

'Of course. What are you going to do? The Daughters have been gone nearly an hour.'

'He's going to fly,' said Raven. She was already looking at Lamorne Point. 'And I'm going with him.'

'We'll discuss that in a minute. Ethan, can you take Kerenza away and clear the crowd.'

He took Kerenza's arm and moved away. My first thought was for my team. 'Where's Erin?' I said.

Mina smiled. 'Having breakfast with Grace. In Grace's room. She's doing magick with her.'

The crowd slipped away, leaving Ethan and his family.

Lena, Kenver and Cador fell into step behind Ethan, and instead of going through the cottage, he turned and led them up the long slope round to the front of Pellacombe.

40 - Resignation

I looked at Raven. 'Did Isolde come down here before Kerenza?'
'She did. We were talking, and all of a sudden Kerenza emerged with her swag. Isolde told me to ask her what was going on. When she tried to brush me off and get in the boat, I stopped her. Isolde was trying to get someone to answer their phone, then she saw you coming.' She addressed the last remark to Eseld. 'Your mother's in the boathouse.'

'Isolde!' I shouted. 'Come out.'

She emerged, her face haggard in the morning light. 'I've been trying to contact Cordelia,' she said. 'No luck. Did I hear right? Morning and Signe? Why?'

'Medbh,' I said.

'I don't understand. Are you saying that *Medbh* plotted to kill her father and ran off before they could do it?'

Mina went up to Isolde and put her arm round the Witch's waist. 'I think Medbh had a lucky escape,' she said, putting gentle pressure on Isolde's back. They started to move away. 'I think the intended target was Medbh, and I think Mowbray was a last minute substitute. Whether they'll admit it, I don't know.' She led Isolde towards a bench upstream from the dock. 'We'll wait here until we see the helicopter leave'. Mina turned round and looked at me first, then the rest of the crew. 'Take great care, Conrad. I will see you soon.'

'You will.'

I passed my phone to Saffron. 'Get Michael or his mother out here. And food.'

'Shouldn't we get going? They'll be on the motorway soon,' said Eseld.

'No they won't. Not with Maggie Pearce driving.'

'What! How come?'

'I told Jane Kershaw to get Maggie up to the front door and get her to take over from the coach firm's driver. The Daughters were so wound up they wouldn't notice the switch, or suspect a woman. I gave orders for Maggie to take the scenic route from Pellacombe and then stick to the A30. In the dark they wouldn't notice she was taking them in very slow circles.'

Eseld laughed. 'You left orders? I've never known Maggie Pearce to take an order in her life.'

'I left that up to Jane.'

'If we're really lucky,' added Eseld, 'she'll have given them some of her baking. That would slow down a space shuttle.'

There was another bench near the boathouse; we drifted over to it and sat down.

Raven glanced at Mina and Isolde, who were deep in conversation. 'Why didn't Mina object to being left behind? I'd have put my foot down and demanded to be on board.'

I was lighting a cigarette at that moment, and it was Saffron who answered. 'It's because I'm his co-pilot. First priority is guarding the prisoner, and Mina can do that. It's best for the team if I'm in the air and she's on the ground.'

Having satisfied her curiosity, Raven tuned out again. I'd seen her do it a couple of times during the conference, and assumed she was bored. Now I was beginning to think the explanation was a lot deeper.

'Saffron,' I said. 'Did you hear back from the Boss?'

'Oh god, sorry. Yeah. During the staff meeting. She said to carry on and let her know of any major developments.'

Raven tuned back in. 'Is that the Constable you're talking about?' I nodded. 'There's something I need to do before we go,' she said.

'As long as it doesn't take long. Here comes our river pilot and our breakfast.'

The whole clan appeared from the cottage and approached us. The Ferrymistress herself went to start the engines on the big boat, leaving her children to present offerings of bacon rolls and yet more coffee. We fell on the food like starving wolves and started munching. Raven demolished two rolls in quick succession and started doing something with her phone. When we'd staved off starvation, she showed me the screen and said, 'Is that the Loyal Oath of the Invisible College?'

It was actually the mundane Judicial Oath. 'More or less. There's an explicit mention of the statutes of the Occult Council in the magickal version.'

She stared at the screen. 'Is that what all the fuss is about?' She stood up and unfastened the yellow cord around her waist. Her black robes dropped nearly to the ground and she shook them out. She shouted across the dock, 'Isolde! I need you.' She lowered her voice and said to Eseld, 'It's time for a change.'

'Really?' said Eseld. 'You're going through with it?'

'The only thing stopping Witches from spreading the word is that stupid Oath. I'll take it and show them.'

'Paris is worth a mass,' I observed.

'You what?'

'Henri of Navarre said it. He became a Catholic so he could become king of France. Paris is worth a mass.'

Raven grinned. 'I like it. Besides, I'm not the Lady of Shallott.' She gripped the tassels at either end of the cord and turned to face the water. 'Goddess, hear my prayer. I can no longer bind myself as your servant. Do not forsake me on my new path, and guide my footsteps as you ever have. As I bound myself, so I now release myself. So mote it be.'

With her voice barely audible, Eseld echoed her last words.

Raven's fingers moved at the ends of her cord and pulled the knots apart. A breeze blew off the water, and my skin tingled with an extra presence. Isolde, Eseld, Saffron, Mina and I all bowed our heads. Scout hid under the bench.

There was a burst of wind and the gentlest voice of motherhood whispered *I release you*. I looked up, and Raven tossed her hands into the air. The yellow cord shimmered and flashed green before falling to the ground.

Eseld was in awe. 'Why now?' she said.

Raven's massive shoulders lifted in a careless shrug. 'Alys will become Eldest now that I've blotted my copybook with the Daughters. The Homewood is not a place I want to belong to with her in charge. Not when there are new worlds to conquer.' She turned to face Saffron, who had gone very quiet. 'How do I get to be Warden of Salomon's House?'

'I ... err ...'

As ever, Mina stepped into the emotional breach. 'You picked the wrong place to announce yourself,' she said. 'Saffron Hawkins is Heidi Marston's cousin, and Conrad will be Cora Hardisty's security attaché if she is elected.'

Raven threw her head back and roared with laughter. 'Then I'll have to promise a job to Eseld, if she doesn't become staff king of Cornwall.'

Mina's mouth pulled up in a right handed smile. 'In that case you should call Reverend Oldcastle and put your name forward before nominations close.'

'I'll do it today.' She bent down and picked up the slightly singed cord. She tossed it to Isolde and said, 'This needs to go back.' She tried to walk and her robes tangled. 'Anyone got a spare rope? There must be one in the boathouse.'

Mina lifted her tunic and unfastened my belt, removing the SIG pistol. 'This should fit. It's Conrad's'

Isolde was still staring at the lifeless cord. 'Are you sure about this?' she said to Raven. 'You don't know what might happen.'

'Too late now,' said Raven, hitching up her robe and tightening the belt. 'Have you been carrying that gun all the time, Mina? Sneaky. Shall we go?'

Michael jumped to get in position by the ferry and we crossed the river on a rising tide. On the other side, he took us up to the LZ in the buggy. His father was sitting enjoying the sun and announced that everything was ready for us. Scout ran up to check for smells, and I realised that there was no human on this side of the river to leave him with. He'd have to sit at the back and behave himself. I reached into the Smurf and grabbed a map.

'Can you send a message to Maggie Pearce,' I said to Eseld.

'I can, but there's no point. She wouldn't dream of checking her phone while she's driving. Dad once text to amend a trip and she drove for two hours in the wrong direction.'

I ran my fingers over the map and checked my watch. 'Raven, can you sense a bus load of Witches from the air?'

'Only at a very low height. Much lower than you normally fly.'

'No need,' said Eseld. 'Just look for the traffic jam. Even at this hour, there'll be a queue behind the bus.'

It was worth a shot. 'Good. Here's the plan.' I looked at our two new recruits, Eseld and Raven. 'If you're coming along, it has to be with the understanding that the King's Watch is part of the solution, not part of the problem.'

Eseld nodded. Being put in her place by Ethan, with all the family and staff watching her had had an effect.

Raven was different. 'I'm sorry for your loss, Eseld, but I'm just going to see the looks on their faces. If I can catch Alys doing something stupid, so much the better. I shall behave with the dignity appropriate to the next Warden of Salomon's house.'

I could stop Raven coming, but we'd be horribly exposed. I pointed my finger at her and said, 'You are a witness, not a team member. Are we clear?'

She bowed. 'Of course. So what's this plan then?'

Michael was hovering near the helicopter. I looked to his father. 'I could really use your son on this trip. The risk will be minimal, but there's a job that he can do that no one else can try.'

'Please, Dad!'

'Sir?' said Saffron.

'Will it help catch Lord Mowbray's killers?'

'Yes.'

'And you're sure about the risk?'

'As sure as I can be. Hear the plan, and if you're not happy, he stays here.'

'Then go on, boy.'

'Thank you. This is what we'll do.'

41 – By a Roadside in Cornwall

Map reading is a dying art. Things would have gone very differently if Eseld (or Raven) knew their way around an Ordnance Survey map. I'd shown Eseld where we were going, and she'd replied, 'I leave the map stuff to Dad. And Kenver.'

We caught up with the convoy in the middle of Bodmin Moor, Cornwall's contribution to the desolate spaces of the West Country. Eseld had been right about the convoy: although the few cars around at this time in the morning swept past the coach on the outside lane of the dual carriageway, a whole load of lorries were queueing patiently behind Maggie Pearce's stately galleon.

I spotted them from a good height, well above the level where they could hear the engines or detect any magick. 'Saffron?' I said.

'There's a pub in eight kilometres, or a public car park in twelve.'

'We'll avoid the pub. It'll almost certainly have rooms with guests in them. Punch it in, Saff.'

I started losing height straight away, and in a few seconds the autopilot kicked in with an advisory warning – I was too close for a normal landing. That's why we have human pilots.

I didn't land on the car park itself. The rotors would turn that sort of loose surface into a machine-gun, and there could be someone walking nearby. There was a flat piece of grass and, with the dry weather, it was a safe bet for a landing.

Even better, the car park was protected by metal barriers to prevent overnight camping, which meant no civilians. The icing on the cake was a stand of trees at the opposite end. I touched down and waited a few seconds to make sure we weren't sinking, then hit the auto shutdown. A cardinal sin, I know, but sometimes you have to. 'Someone get both barriers open,' I said. 'You know where to go, Michael?'

'Sir.'

'Then let's do it.'

Raven was out first, followed by Michael and then Scout, who squeezed himself past Eseld. Saffron and I looked at each other and she gave me a grin. I unfastened my harness and got ready to scuttle under the rotors.

Raven had already blown the lock off the Entrance gate and was swinging it open. Behind me, Saffron was doing the same to the Exit gate and the Smurf's engines were dying with a splutter. 'Keep out of sight, everyone, until I get a good eye on the coach.'

The car park entrance had been cut through a small embankment, and I scrambled up the dewy grass to get a bit of extra height. I checked that Michael was in position and looked down the road.

'Why does this place look familiar?' said Eseld, more to herself than anyone else.

It was tight. I'd only been on watch for ten seconds when the rich brown front of the executive coach came into view.

'Here they come. Stand at the side of the road.'

I slid down the small bank and joined the others.

'Where is it?' said Raven.

'There. Out we go.' My final order to Maggie Pearce had been to pull in if she saw me.

She didn't just see me, she saw Raven, Saffron, Eseld and Scout, all lined up in the road. A Mercedes overtook the coach and slammed on its brakes when the driver saw the road obstructed. I waved him on and got a look of terror when he saw that two of us were in military uniforms. Meanwhile, Maggie had spotted us and was already indicating to pull in.

'Positions, everyone.'

We jogged back into the car park and waited in the open with the now silent Smurf at our backs. The coach came to a halt in the middle, and I could see one of the Witches remonstrating with Maggie and pointing to the exit. She leaned forward, killed the engine and opened the door. Then she folded her arms mutinously and sat back in her seat.

I activated my Ancile. 'Advance in formation,' I said. 'Slowly.'

We moved towards the coach with Saffron and I at the front, five metres apart. Eseld and Raven walked behind us to take advantage of our Anciles.

The Witches on the coach panicked. Trapped on the bus, they panicked and started to pile out.

'Hold,' I said. 'We need them as far from the vehicle as possible.'

The Daughters milled around for a few seconds, then Alys took control. She wasn't going to get Georgia to fight her battles for her this time, as she had in the main hall at Pellacombe.

I heard Raven move behind me. 'Hold! Scout, away.' My Familiar shot off and started to work his way round the group. My plan hinged on them coming to meet us, and hinged on Alys not wanting to lose face in front of the others.

It worked. She led them towards us at a dignified pace and stopped about ten metres away. They lined up with Alys in the middle and the other seven spread on each side: Zoe, Brook, Georgia, Morning, Kiwa, Signe and Cordelia.

Alys fixed her gaze on me, refusing to look at Raven lurking behind me. 'What is the meaning of this outrage, Mr Clarke? You have no authority to stop us in this way.'

I took the Hammer out of its holster and showed my badge of authority, the symbol of Caledfwlch stamped into the butt. It was also designed to intimidate: they all knew what sort of ammunition it carried.

There was a final purpose. When he saw the gun, Michael emerged from the trees behind them and moved soundlessly towards the bus. I kept my eyes on Alys. 'By the authority of the Constable and the heads of agreement between your Covens and the Occult Council, I am detaining two of your number on suspicion of murder. And regicide.'

Alys had Brook at her right hand. Unlike Alys, Brook hadn't been able to take her eyes off Raven's new belt. Raven had been her 1st, the leader of her Coven. Alys had to speak twice before Brook heard her and answered.

'They need a warrant,' she said. 'Or the permission of the Eldest or of the most senior Daughter. That would be you, now that Raven has forsaken us. What ...'

Alys refused to engage with any discussion of Raven and interrupted her Counsel. 'I deny permission, and I am not scared by your show of force. All you've done is dig yourself a very deep hole, Mr Clarke. You will be suspended for this before we get back to Glastonbury.'

Behind the Witches, there was a sigh like the wind moving through the trees. They ignored it. Michael had got on the bus and Maggie had closed the doors. Then she started the engine.

They all turned round at that.

'What's going on?' shouted Alys.

'I'm impounding that bus to search your belongings for evidence. I don't need a warrant for that. It will be back in an hour or so. It's a nice morning.'

Maggie put the bus in gear and moved slowly towards the exit. Very slowly. Alys looked furious, but not defeated. 'More nonsense,' she said.

Morning pushed Georgia out of the way and got in Alys's face. 'Stop them! Stop them or it's over.'

'I don't know what you mean,' said Alys icily. She was hanging Morning out to dry here, but Morning had other ideas.

She got right in Alys's face and said just one word. 'Fingerprints.'

Morning had looked like a stereotypical librarian when I first met her, mostly because she was the only Mage around who wore glasses – large ones with thick black frames and lenses that made her unblinking eyes even more intense. She was polite to me on the few occasions that we spoke, but I'd always got the impression that I was someone she didn't need to bother making an effort with.

Throughout their time in Pellacombe, most of the Daughters had been friendly or more than friendly. Georgia had made it clear that her flesh crawled in my presence, and that was her loss not mine. Alys clearly had no time for me either, but she'd always respected my place in things.

I knew what Morning had done to Mowbray. I knew she had a core of steel inside, and now Alys was seeing it. Alys turned away. 'Do what you must,' she said to Morning.

Morning and Signe dived towards the bus, and the others looked on appalled. Or determined.

'Scout! Stop her.'

Above all, I had to protect Maggie and Michael on the coach. I raised the Hammer, but I couldn't get a clear shot through the crowd of Witches. Saffron has the speed, and used it, accelerating towards the group with Eseld in her wake.

The bus was level with Morning, and still not accelerating. Maggie's caution could cost her her life, here. Morning raised her arms to blast at the windscreen, and Scout raced across the gravel. He launched himself at her and went for the leg, claws and jaws scrabbling.

Morning staggered when Scout hit her, then tripped and fell on her back. Scout grabbed her ankle and sank his jaws deep into flesh. The coach passed, and Maggie was out of the firing line. I lowered my weapon. Saffron would sort this out. And then everything went very badly wrong.

Signe is a Necromancer. She knows the ways of Spirits, and it turns out that she knows the ways of Familiars. She stooped and grabbed the scruff of Scout's neck with her right hand, and when she'd made contact, she made a violent chopping motion with her left. My heart seized solid with a ... a cardiac cramp. I couldn't breathe and my legs were giving way. I dropped my gun and the last thing I saw before everything went black was Morning firing a deadly blast of magick at Saffron. Then my face hit the gravel and my brain hit the overload button.

Lieutenant Saffron Hawkins

When Signe severed the Familial bond between Sir Conrad and Scout, every Mage in that car park felt it like a hammer blow. I staggered and Eseld screamed behind me. Then, shit, Morning fired a blast of magick. She wasn't aiming for me, she was aiming for Eseld, trying to bypass my Ancile. Stupid cow missed both of us and smashed it into Lemon Faced Georgia.

On the way down, I cut my hands on the gravel. Funny how you notice the little things. Round about, there was a silence. Except for Scout howling. I tried to get to my knees and discovered that I'd also had the breath knocked out of me.

The worst was yet to come. Signe dropped Scout and started to help Morning to her feet. Zoe knelt down to see what had happened to Georgia, and Great Raven bent down to pick up Sir Conrad's gun, the Hammer.

'Stop it, Alys. Put an end to it,' said Raven, pointing the gun at Alys. As bluffs go, that was pretty brave. It didn't work, and Alys bluffed back.

'Who are you?' said Alys. 'I don't take orders from a freak-show attraction.'

I rolled on to my side to get a better look. Eseld was on the ground twitching like she was having a fit. Apart from Zoe, all the other Witches had moved well away. Oh yeah, the coach drew out of the car park. Sir Conrad would be pleased. If he were still alive. And if he is still alive, I might tell him the nickname I gave him. Well, he did get everyone in the Watch to call him *sir*, so it stuck. Scout was trying to crawl over to him; the poor mite had lost the use of his legs or something horrible.

Alys saw that Morning and Signe were on their feet. 'Finish the job,' said Alys. 'We can catch up with the coach in time.' She said it in a Mage's whisper, something I've not seen for a long time. I don't know if anyone but me heard her.

Signe drew a dagger from inside her cloak and came towards me. I fell down again. It wasn't just concentrated air that Morning had tried to hit me with. Something in my nervous system wasn't working properly.

'Stop,' said Raven, pointing the gun.

I tried with every fibre of my being to shout a warning. I really did. A ragged breath came into my lungs, but it was too late. Raven raised the gun, and Alys got what she wanted when Raven pulled the trigger.

I once touched the Hammer. I felt its antagonism to me. It knew me and it hated me because I wasn't Sir Conrad. I left it alone after that. Raven couldn't feel it, because Raven has a hole in her middle: she can't see herself magickally, like having a blind spot. The gun fired and did what it was supposed to when a stranger wielded it.

Conrad's bullets have a Disruption Work built into them. When he fires them at a target they act like magickal nerve agent. When Raven fired the gun, the Work discharged into *her*. I've seen a Fae absorb one of those bullets, but not Raven. A second sun rose over Bodmin Moor as she combusted like an atom bomb made of Lux.

A huge wave of magick washed over me, purging the bad and giving me life. It also helped everyone else, including Morning and Signe.

Signe was coming for me with the dagger, and I was struggling to get my chain sorted out after landing on it. Morning grabbed her arm and said, 'Run. The Barrow.'

They legged it.

Conrad must have trained me well, because I let them go. They could wait: our injured might not have that luxury. My first priority was triage.

Eseld was sitting up, blinking. Not urgent.

Raven was broken and twisted, with Cordelia sobbing on her chest and desperately trying to find some sign of life in her. There was nothing I could do.

Zoe was still looking at Georgia and had been joined by Kiwa. They knew what they were doing, so I left them to it.

Conrad was face down in the gravel with Scout licking him and whimpering. I moved over and touched him. If you've never felt someone's Imprint, it's hard to describe. I mostly sense magick via my ears, like sound but not quite. On a good day, Conrad's Imprint sounds like an old steam locomotive thundering along the track. It doesn't really, but that's all I can give you.

Right now, it was labouring. Hard. I forced myself to tune out the magick and focus on his pulse. Racing, but still strong. He'd get there. I shifted him into the recovery position and checked his airway. I went to touch Scout, but he flinched away and barked like I'd struck him.

I stood up and looked around, and there was only Alys and Brook to look at.

Brook had done more or less the same as me, focusing on Georgia not Conrad. She left her fellow Witch and went up to Alys. 'What have you done?' she said.

'I have done nothing other than protect the Covens,' said Alys. I really think she believed it, too.

'What's happened?' said Eseld, back on her feet but swaying. 'My god, no! Raven?'

I made a grab for her. 'Don't, Ez. She tried to fire the Hammer.'

Eseld bit her hand. 'No. No.' She swung her head around the car park. 'Conrad!'

I gathered her into my arm. 'Easy, Ez. He's alive. Signe broke the bond with Scout.'

'I know she did. I was part-bonded with both of them. Where did the Spirit go?'

When a Familiar loses its master, the Spirit inside loses its life for a final time. Usually. 'What are you saying?' I asked.

'When Signe broke the bond, Conrad pushed all his Lux down the channel, enough for the Spirit to escape. Is Conrad okay?'

'He must by in a hypo-Lux. He'll get there. It doesn't look good for Georgia, though.'

Kiwa stood up. 'She needs an ambulance, and quickly. There's massive internal bleeding and her pelvis is broken.' She wiped her hands and stared at Alys. Whatever else happened after this, Kiwa would not forget or forgive.

Eseld finally caught up with herself. 'Where are they? Morning and Signe. Where are they?'

'Scarpered. That way. Morning said something about a barrow.'

Eseld face palmed. 'Fuck. I knew this place looked familiar. One of the Kernow Ley lines runs through here. Mark's Barrow, it's called, after King Mark.' I gave her a blank look. 'King Mark. Tristan's uncle in *Tristan and Isolde*? Never mind. It's not his grave, really, but it is a Locus Lucis. Why would they go there?'

'Your father. Signe had a big cloak on. I bet the vessel she used to contain your father's Spirit is in her pocket, and she wouldn't discharge it without a lot of power.'

Eseld twisted her neck, like it had a crick in it. I can see why Sir Conrad fancies her (and don't let him tell you otherwise). She's got so much *character* that she puts wallflowers like me in the shade. When she tried to chat me up at Pellacombe, I was flattered but it was like being hit on by your drama teacher.

She went up and touched Brook on the arm, pointing to Conrad. Brook nodded and moved to protect him. 'Who's with me?' she said, turning round the scene.

'What will you do?' said Kiwa. 'I will not be party to slaughter.'

'Nor me,' I said. I tried to think *What would Sir Conrad do*? He'd actually try to protect them. I was about to announce that when Eseld worked it out for herself.

'Protect my father's Spirit, subdue them and hand them over to the Watch,' said Eseld.

She pushed the sleeves of her jacket up again, exposing her Bracers (*not* wristguards; I must tell him that), and then she was off. I followed, and so did Kiwa.

Eseld led us along the footpath from the car park. It was gravelled for a couple of hundred metres, then started to rise up to one of those rocky mounds. *Tors* they call them round here, I think.

'Eseld!' said Kiwa. 'Isn't the Barrow round there, in the dip? I can feel the magick.'

She slowed down. 'Yes. It's also Warded. I know that because I did them myself. The weak point is the steep point. It's a scramble, but we can go down the north side of the tor and burst through.'

It was steep enough going up the tor on the official path. When we got to the top, I could hear distant sirens, 'Ambulance for Georgia,' I said.

Kiwa nodded. 'Thank you for telling me.'

The trail led off to the right; Eseld ignored it and went straight ahead, slowing down and then stopping. We joined her. Bloody hell, that was steep.

A small wood clung to the bottom of the tor, only five or six trees deep. Over the tops, we could make out a haze of Lux. That would be the Wards and Glamour hiding Mark's Barrow from curious mundane archaeologists.

Eseld was looking for a safe way down. I grabbed her arm before she launched herself off. 'We need Silences,' I said. 'Regroup in the trees, if we haven't broken our legs, then I'll lead. I'm still the only one with an Ancile.'

'Fine,' said Eseld. 'Last one to the bottom's a loser.'

She raised a Silence and started down, pumping her legs like she was on a step machine at the gym and letting gravity do most of the work. I made my own Silence and did the same, choosing a different path.

Rocks slipped, I lost my footing and landed on my arse, then slid the last twenty feet. Ow, that was sore. I turned round and saw Kiwa taking it more gently, using one hand on the floor for balance. Eseld was muttering inside her Silence, waving her on. Kiwa kept her eyes down, and slowwwwwly joined us.

I held out my hands to grip theirs and bypass the Silence. 'Stay behind me and use any magick you have to put them off. I'll go for Morning first. Okay?'

'Stop at the last tree,' said Eseld. 'I need to breach the Wards.'

I nodded, and Kiwa said, 'I'm ready.'

I looked down at our joined hands, especially at Kiwa's elegant black fingers. I'd heard she plays a mean harp, and that reminded me. I dug into my thigh pocket and pulled out a couple of restraint ties, giving one each to Kiwa and Eseld.

I dropped my Silence and moved through the trees.

Mark Hayden

42 – A Grave Sight

Signe had the dagger out again. She was standing on top of a long, flat mound of grass, about four feet off the floor of the moor. Morning was facing the path, the way we would have come if we hadn't just risked our necks scrambling down the tor. I stopped and felt Eseld working behind me, a variable, singing pitch of magick.

Up on the barrow, Signe was drawing out a containment circle, using her dagger as a focus. She had already placed a small gold urn on a stone, ready to release the Spirit of Lord Mowbray. The circle would act like a vortex, pushing any magick down and into the ground.

Eseld made a tune out of Lux and the air shimmered in front of me. With a snap, the Wards were down and I was rushing forwards, swinging my chain.

Morning had turned round. She took one look at us and ran up the mound. We were going to hit all together. I headed slightly left, to give more cover and put myself between Morning and Eseld, who was already overtaking me. Morning didn't try anything fancy. She lengthened her stride and launched herself at me. It was now a question of timing.

I braced myself and swung the chain at her. I caught her in the side and knocked her off course. She still hit me, with a charged punch in the face. We collapsed in a heap. I couldn't get my chain hand free and grasped for something with my left, as she wound up to smash me in the face. I scrabbled and caught the end of her Goddess braid. I pulled hard. She rolled her body away from the pressure, and I got my chain from under her. There was already blood pouring out of her side where I'd connected the first time.

I grabbed both ends of the chain and pressed down on her neck. I heard it snap both ways, physically and magickally. Then the backwash of Lux flooded through my arms and I screamed at what I'd done.

I pushed myself away from her and looked around wildly. Instead of a fight in the centre of the Barrow, there was a showdown brewing, because Signe had picked up the golden urn and was threatening both Eseld and Kiwa with her dagger.

Eseld is tough. So is Kiwa. Neither is a fighter, though, and it looked like Signe had used that knife before. I got up and approached them. 'Surrender, Signe,' I said. 'Morning is dead. She was the one who killed Mowbray. Kerenza is in chains at Pellacombe. Let's stop it here.'

'No,' said Signe. 'Not until I've sent him down to Hell. He destroyed my mother's magick, and he'll pay for that. So will that German bitch. I've already had my fun with the Witchfinder, and Raven was a bonus. I'll never forget her blowing up like that.' She finished with a laugh and an extra wave of the dagger in my direction.

'She's trying to open the urn,' said Kiwa steadily.

I'd put my hair in a proper ballet bun this morning. It's easier like that, even if it does make my face look too thin. I'm only telling you because the nape of my neck was exposed and I felt a cold wind of magick blow across it. Suddenly, Signe looked scared. She stared at the bottom of the barrow, ignoring us completely. She could see something we couldn't. And then I didn't need to see it, I could hear it: a low growl.

What the fuck?

A huge dog, blood running red down its flanks and the fires of hell in its eyes appeared on the barrow. *Scout*. Or the Spirit that had merged with the vessel of Scout. The dog leapt at Signe and she dropped the urn, stabbing wildly at the dog. She missed, and the dog knocked her down, plunging its fangs into her face.

I had no idea what to do. I wouldn't say I froze, I just had no idea what to do next. There was no way I was going to attack that dog, because I could feel pure poison running out of the wounds in its side.

There, I've admitted it. I'm not proud of it, but it's true.

Kiwa shied away from the dog, too, but not Eseld. She dived for the urn and her Bracers glowed with power. With a grunt, she broke the seal and her father appeared, shimmering and bright.

Lord Mowbray can't have been sealed very well. He knew what was going on and didn't need time to orient himself. He reached down and grabbed the hound, twisting its neck and pulling it off Signe. At the same time, I could feel my boots throbbing as Mowbray drew power from the Ley lines under the barrow.

He dragged the Spirit away, and suddenly I knew what to do again. I dived on to the grass and grabbed Signe's arm, pinning down the dagger. Kiwa was next to me with the restraint, and between us we disarmed Signe and wrestled her into submission. I think we both tried not to look at her face while we did it. I left Kiwa to fix the restraint and looked up.

Mowbray didn't have a dog in his hands any more. He had a naked man.

'Looks like Conrad had a lucky escape,' said Mowbray. 'This one would have done him no good at all in the long run, no matter how hard you tried to tame him, Eseld. Tell Conrad to look up Lucas of Innerdale.' With a powerful twist of his wrists, aided by decades of Geomancy, Mowbray pulled the other Spirit's arm up its back, and bound it in silver chains of Lux.

Eseld had tears coursing down her face. She took one step towards her father, then another. He came and stood in front of her, still more of a silver shadow than a solid presence. The barrow throbbed even more deeply and Mowbray stretched out his finger. It turned from silver to flesh, and he used it to wipe away some of Eseld's tears. She shivered when the flesh touched her skin.

'A father shouldn't have favourites,' said Mowbray, 'but you were always mine, damn you. I'm so proud of you, girl, it hurts.' He stroked her again, and the finger turned back to silver. He stepped away.

'Dad, what are you doing?'

'Gotta go, girl. Need to shift myself. I want you to do something for me, Eseld.' He started to fade, and spoke rapidly. 'I won't ask you to talk to your mother. You have to do that for yourself. I want you to look out for Kenver. Will you do that for me? He's only a boy.'

'Yes, Dad. Of course.'

She gave her promise to the empty air. Lord Mowbray and Lucas/Scout were gone from here. Mowbray would surface again, somewhere, but whether he'd recognise or acknowledge his daughter when he did so is anyone's guess.

'What are you doing?' said Kiwa to me.

'Calling the Boss. Where there's an ambulance, the police won't be far away.'

'This one should go to hospital,' said a voice near me. It was a local man, so it couldn't be me speaking. That's a stupid thing to say. Perhaps I was hearing Scout's barks as words. The voice had more: 'We need to check him out, but we can't get near him for that dog.'

A great burst of want and need exploded in my chest. I had to get air. I sucked in the biggest lungful I could manage, blew it out and sucked in another.

'That's better. He's breathing more normally now.' This time it was a woman. Definitely not me or Scout.

Scout…

My leg went into spasm and I had to sit up. I opened my eyes and the sun sent the world spinning on its axis. A warm ball of love climbed on to my lap, and my hand moved in its fur. His fur. He was still alive.

I closed my eyes and tried to feel the heat, the Lux, the bond between me and my Familiar Spirit.

Gone.

I opened my eyes again, and the dog sitting on my lap looked back at me with concern but none of my Familiar's human intelligence or canine sarcasm. I brushed his fur. He was still Scout to me.

'Sir?'

Someone was speaking to me, and I hadn't heard a word. The ground had stopped spinning, and it was time to engage with the world again.

A solid male presence blocked the sun but kept shining. Aaah. That didn't make sense. I tried looking again. It was a policeman. The shining sun was his Hi-Viz vest and the solidity was his equipment belt.

'What was that?' I said.

'I asked if you were alright, sir.' He dropped into a squat to make eye contact, keeping clear of Scout. 'Those are some nasty cuts on your face, sir, and you seemed to be unconscious when we arrived.'

'Conrad may have banged his head on the floor when he tried to stop the car,' said a woman. My memory kicked in and I recognised Brook, one of the Daughters, and then it all clicked into place: Signe had severed the bond with

Scout, and I'd fallen flat on my face. The last thing I should do now is talk to the police.

I tried to understand the implications of the situation.

I was alive: good sign.

Saffron and Eseld were missing: bad sign.

The police were here: bad sign.

Brook was here and trying to cover things up: hopeful sign.

In short, things weren't looking good, and I was in no fit state to start jumping about yet.

'I'm sorry,' I said to the officer. 'I can't remember a thing. I don't feel too bad, though. Has anyone got any water?'

There was a crunch of gravel, and a woman police officer, a sergeant appeared. She didn't squat down. 'Are you Squadron Leader Clarke, sir?'

It was on the tip of my tongue to say, *I think so*. That sort of reply has got me in trouble before, so I opted for, 'Yes.'

'Come on, Dave,' said the sergeant. 'We've had orders to leave him in charge. One of the funnies.'

Now that was a good sign. Those orders could only have come via Hannah, and only Saffron could have been in touch to request assistance. Therefore Saffron was alive and had taken over in my absence.

I dumped Scout on to the floor and held out my hand to the male officer. He gave me a smile; his boss was already crunching away towards their squad car. With a big heave, we both stood up, and the world only wobbled rather than span round.

'Take care, sir, and I would get your head checked out.'

I shook hands. 'Bit late for that.'

As they retreated, I did a 360 degree survey of the car park. Brook stood alone. The rest of the space was empty. Completely empty. And why was Brook wearing a summer dress instead of her robes?

Glamour.

Behind where I'd fallen, there was a bloody great illusion of an empty piece of grass. Either that or someone had stolen the Smurf.

My leg ached like crazy, and my hip felt funny. I felt down and found an empty holster. Where the hell was the Hammer?

Brook had been watching me. 'Your weapon is behind the Glamour, but don't try any magick,' she said. 'I'll lead you through the plane of illusion and try to explain. There's water in there, but don't even *think* of smoking for a while.'

'I wish you hadn't said that. Now all I can do is think about it. I need to check my phone first.'

She stepped even closer and put a reassuring hand on my back.

'Was I wobbling?'

'Just a little. You need to sit down soon.'

I got out my phone. There were no missed calls, but the two messages were very reassuring.

Michael: Parked two miles away. Awaiting instructions.

Saffron: RU OK??????

So, Michael and Maggie had escaped unharmed, and Saffron wouldn't have messaged if there was still an emergency going on.

'Come on,' said Brook.

She took my hand and we crossed a blurred line. The magick made me close my eyes at the right moment, and when I opened them, the Smurf was back. And so was Raven, dead on the floor with my gun in her hand. Oh shit.

Cordelia was sitting next to Raven, stroking her hair and staring down. There was no one else in sight. Raven had been moved (by whom? Did they use a truck?) and laid out on the grass.

'What happened?' I said.

Brook pointed to the grass, and I sank into it. She passed me some water and I drank deeply. Then I drank some more.

There was a snuffling and whining as Scout approached. He could smell me, but he couldn't see me anymore. 'Here boy.'

He trotted through the Glamour and went bananas when he saw Raven, Cordy and the Smurf. I called him over and started to calm him down. This was going to take some getting used to.

Brook, her robes restored to their natural look, took a pew next to me and stared towards the moor as if waiting for something to appear from that direction.

'Morning and Signe ran off, hotly pursued by your colleagues and Kiwa. And I'm counting Eseld as one of your colleagues. There was a huge discharge of magick a few minutes later, just as the paramedics were trying to get Georgia into the ambulance.'

'Ambulance?'

'Georgia is on her way to hospital. Morning caught her with a vicious blast and she may not survive. Alys and Zoe have gone with her. We told the paramedics that it was a hit-and-run driver, hence the police presence. I think you know what happened to Raven.'

I couldn't compute how a Mage like Raven had done what she did. It was like a nuclear physicist opening a flask and taking out a rod of plutonium to use as a doorstop. I made eye contact with Brook. 'Was it deliberate? Did she want to take her own life?'

'No. She simply didn't know what she was doing, and everyone who could warn her was out of action. Alys could have, and why she chose not to is one of the many questions she will have to answer.' She took a breath. 'Raven had a hole in her Imprint. It stopped her seeing herself, like having no reflection in a mirror. The magick in your gun was screaming at her to drop it, but she couldn't feel a thing.'

'I am so very sorry.'

'It wasn't your fault.'

I shrugged. It was generous of Brook to say that. I wonder how many will agree with her.

She grimaced and lowered her voice so Cordelia couldn't hear 'We moved Raven out of the way before the ambulance arrived. At that point Alys decided to go in the ambulance with Georgia and drag Zoe along, too. I think Alys wanted to get out of the firing line, as it were.'

I went to rub my face. 'Ow!' There was fresh blood, dried blood and grit on my hand.

'Is there a first aid kit in your helicopter?'

'Under the back seat of the cabin.'

She got up and went to get the kit. There was one job I had to do before she came back.

Getting up was hard. Getting over to Raven and Cordelia was even harder. I knelt down on the grass, facing Cordy, and waited until she looked up. Her face was ravaged with grief.

It's been my lot, over the years, to have seen that face many times. Sometimes the light behind the eyes goes out, sometimes it doesn't. Cordelia's light was still burning.

'I am so very sorry, Cordy. I can't imagine what she meant to you.'

'She was my sun. I was her moon. We used to say that to each other. When we were lovers.' She paused. I could tell from her face that there was going to be more, and I waited. 'I've been thinking it over. While I wait. Nothing else to do. Why did she do it, Conrad?'

'It's beyond me. Brook says she couldn't feel the gun, but…'

Cordy shook her head. Fresh tears were coming. 'Not that. I get that. Why did she leave the Coven? Why did she do it when I wasn't there to stop her?'

I had to pick my words carefully. Raven hadn't given Cordelia a passing thought when she renounced her bond. I decided to fall back on my oldest skill: lying. 'She was going to take you with her. She told me in the buggy. She was going to run for Warden of Salomon's House and you were going to be by her side. Check her phone – she Googled the Loyal Oath.'

'But the prophecy!'

'I'm not with you.'

'When she was delivered to Glastonbury, there was a prophecy that she would die if she left the Grove.'

A memory stirred. 'You know what she said? "I am not the Lady of Shallott." I suppose she thought that life owed her more.'

She looked at something in the distance. Something not in this world. 'You know what? That was Raven all over. Her power was so huge, so bright, she couldn't find ways of toning it down. I think the universe didn't want her let loose. Or the Goddess didn't, and that's something I'm going to have to find out.'

She dropped Raven's braid and patted my hand. 'Thanks, Conrad.'

When I stood up, I put my boot on Raven's arm and dragged my gun from her fingers. Yes, it was as horrible as it sounds. I did put a small Silence over things so that Cordelia didn't have to hear the bones cracking.

43 – Fit

Brook was still clearing blood and grit off my face when a curtain seemed to lift from my brain, like I'd been running on half power since I woke up after the fall. Brook was doing more than first aid.

'I'm not going to dress it,' she said. 'It's clean and it'll stop bleeding soon.'

'Thank you. For everything. That feels a lot better.'

'Good.' She started packing the first aid kit away. 'What are you going to do now?'

He may have lost his magickal senses, but Scout still has all the proper talents of the world's most intelligent (and neurotic) dog breed. He set off barking and scampered towards the moor.

'Hey you,' said Eseld. 'You're a sight for sore eyes.' She bent down and scratched his head. The furious wagging of his tail said that Scout remembered Eseld with affection.

Eseld was ahead of the others and cradled a small gold object. She looked more at peace than she has done since I met her. Kiwa came next, steadying Signe's shoulders with one hand and resting the other hand on a cloth over Signe's face. Saffron brought up the rear.

When Scout smelled Signe, he barked once and ran back to me. I don't blame him.

Eseld went over to Raven and Cordelia. She placed the urn on the grass and joined Cordy in keeping vigil.

'Where's Morning?' I said to Saffron. 'And are you both okay?'

Kiwa answered, addressing Brook as much as me. 'Morning is dead. Lord Mowbray's spirit was released and has departed the mundane world.'

'And Signe?'

'That part's complicated,' said Saff. 'Are there any butterfly strips in that first aid kit?'

There were. I took over and peeled the cloth (part of Morning's robe) away from Signe's horribly mangled face. I made her sit down, and while I did what I could to hold her face together, Saffron and Kiwa told the story.

Throughout, Signe kept quiet. She moaned with pain a few times, but said nothing. Very occasionally, the newspapers print photographs of the victims of dog attacks. It was only one bite, but the Spirit hound had much bigger jaws. While the story was being told, everyone looked away except me.

I finished and put my hands on Signe's shoulders to check my handiwork. Then I squeezed hard on the painful spots in her shoulder blades. She squirmed in the restraints and I squeezed harder. As I said, no one was looking.

'You severed me from my Familiar,' I said. 'You will pay for that, Signe. Not today, but you will meet the blood price one day.' My words had drawn glances, and I released her. I noticed something in her cloak. 'The Goddess wanted you to survive,' I said.

'How do you work that out?' said Eseld.

I pointed to a small hole in her cloak. 'The magick in my gun discharged into Raven, but the mundane bullet still fired. And missed.'

I placed Signe under a Silence and made a phone call to Michael. 'Is there any coffee on that bus?'

'No, but we're in a layby with a chuck wagon.'

'Excellent. Their coffee will be vile, so get six teas and some water.'

Michael lowered his voice. 'I'd get you food, but Mrs Pearce won't let me. She's got rock buns in a Tupperware. Literally rock. Watch out.'

'I shall warn the others. See you soon.'

'We'll have to open the car park,' said Brook. I hadn't noticed that they'd closed it.

During the next hour, we had a lot to sort out. We recovered Lord Mowbray's Artefacts from the bus, along with other incriminating evidence, and we had to make a decision about Signe. My first aid was already starting to give way.

Things started to resolve themselves when Kiwa got a phone call from Verity. The 1st of Willow and Daughter of Memory had been dragged out of Homewood by numerous urgent messages. She was very keen to talk to Alys, who wasn't answering her phone, and I think she instinctively trusted Kiwa's account. Verity gave her undertaking to surrender Signe to the proper authorities in due course. We put Signe on the bus, still restrained, along with Kiwa, Brook and the mortal remains of Morning.

Morning had died a member of the Coven, and I was happy to let them have her. Unfortunately, they wouldn't take Raven.

I had a short talk to Mina, followed by an even shorter one to Hannah, who was at her sister's house. Hannah had got Ruth to answer the phone (it being Shabbos), and she listened carefully when I gave the headlines.

'Do I need to do anything today?' she asked.

'Not in my view, ma'am.'

'Then it can all wait until tomorrow. Ruth, turn this thing off, will you?'

And then there was no more to do. The only question was, could I fly the Smurf?

That question was answered when the Mowbray estate minibus appeared with Lena on board and driven by the original coach driver, who swapped with Maggie and drove off in the hired coach with his much reduced party.

Lena checked me over thoroughly and pronounced me fit to fly, then earned further bonus points by going over to Eseld.

'It's time to go,' said Lena.

'I'm not leaving her,' said Cordelia.

'Me neither,' said Eseld.

'You don't have to. We will take her in the van. All together. Tomorrow she will take the fire boat with Mowbray. All is ready.'

'I'd like that,' said Cordelia.

'Thank you, Lena,' said Eseld. She turned to her former rival for Ethan's affections and put her arms round Lena's shoulders, more like she was clinging on than giving her a hug. 'I'm so sorry.'

Saffron started collecting empty cups. 'I'm coming with you in the Smurf, Conrad.'

'I don't think so.'

'I do. First, I trust you. Second, I can Mayday if there's a problem, and third, you can give me instructions. And if you think Mina would ever forgive me for *not* going with you, you're mistaken.'

I grunted a laugh. 'Fine. Let's get the stretcher.'

We'd already used the portable stretcher to move Morning, and loaded Raven into the back of the minibus with as much dignity as we could. With Lena and Eseld leaving, we also had to lower the Glamour and give some ramblers a nasty shock when a bright blue helicopter appeared next to their car park. Eseld's parting gift was some illusory cones to stop newcomers getting too close to the LZ.

'Ready, Saff?'

She tilted her head on one side. 'I know it's well late, but do you think they'd do breakfast when we get back.'

'They'd bloody well better do. What do you think has kept me going?'

Mina was waiting for us at Lamorne Point, along with Isolde. There had been more developments while we were in the air, as Isolde explained.

'Verity wants me to tell Hedda what's happened, and Mina has offered to come with me. Hedda doesn't know a thing yet. I've heard the headlines, but could you flesh it out for me?'

I gave Isolde the bald facts, leaving nothing out. She knew Hedda much better than I did, and I trusted her to find the right way of putting over the loss of Raven and her daughter's treachery. I'm not sure which was going to hurt most.

Even with the delay to get the Smurf up and running, we were well ahead of the minibus (thanks to Maggie's driving), and the Ferrymistress spoke to me for the first time when we got to the dock.

'Tell me that Michael is okay.'

'He's absolutely fine. He was nowhere near any danger, and he did a great job. You should be proud of him.'

'Hmph. And you got all the Witches who killed Lord Mowbray?'

'We did.'

Ethan, Cador and Kenver had also been busy. With my permission, they had removed Mowbray's body from the Labyrinth and taken it to the boathouse. This might sound a little odd, but Mowbray was going to be cremated on a fireship, and this way they could allow unrestricted access to anyone who wanted to pay their respects.

When the minibus arrived, Maggie drove it down the path to the dock, and Raven was laid out next to Mowbray. When he'd heard what had happened, Ethan had decreed that the Mowbray clan would adopt Raven and give her in death the family she had only had in life from the Daughters. Raven had died trying to avenge Lord Mowbray and protect Eseld. That was good enough for them.

Someone had to watch over the remains, and the family took most of the duties until tea time, when Cordelia took over. Lena had persuaded both Eseld and Cordy to rest for a few hours; Saffron and I needed no persuasion and we crashed out after breakfast.

The last act of the day took place over tea in the family sitting room. Mina had returned from the hospital while I was asleep and told me that Hedda was devastated. Mina hadn't lingered very long, leaving Isolde on her own to be collected later. What did surprise me was that Hedda was coming over tomorrow for the funerals.

Lena had re-arranged the sitting room furniture since our middle-of-the-night crisis (was that today? I suppose it was). We all got to sit on a comfy chair, and two coffee tables were groaning with sandwiches and cakes (none of them made by M Pearce). Ethan was joined on his sofa by Lena, with Kenver next to Eseld, Cador with Saffron and Mina with me. At my insistence, and without too much argument, a chair had been found for Isolde.

Ethan began with an announcement. 'Kenver has asked me to be his guardian. That might sound odd to some of you, but there's a long tradition of it in the world of magick. It will last until he's twenty-one. Lena will stay as Steward while we find a replacement who can handle the magick. Hopefully not long.'

He drank some tea, got ready to eat a sandwich and turned to me. 'You want to talk about Kerenza and Signe?'

'I do. We need to decide what's going to happen to them.'

Cador spoke first, and I expected something legal. No. For him this was personal. 'Why did they do it? Is it something magickal, because I just don't understand. Kerenza took us all in. I really thought she was good for Dad. Have you any ideas, Conrad? I heard that Mina said something about Medbh. Is she connected?'

'Have you heard from Medbh, Kenver?' I asked first.

'Just the once. The one I told you about earlier, where she said *Oh no, I'm sorry. I can't come back yet. Be patient.* That one. She's turned her phone off. I still say that she has *nothing* to do with this. Nothing.'

'You're right and you're wrong, Kenver,' I said. 'Medbh had nothing to do with your father's death and she had everything to do with it. I think if she hadn't turned up, he'd still be alive.'

'Why?' said Eseld. Direct as ever.

I took a deep breath. 'I'll start with Kerenza, if I may.'

'The painted maypole bitch,' said Eseld, just in case we were in any doubt.

'Her. Yes. Try and imagine what she was looking forward to a few weeks ago.'

'Marriage to a billionaire and a secure future for Grace.' Eseld again.

'Yes. Both of those, but don't forget, she may have lived most of her life in the mundane world but she is a Mage. She grew up knowing about the world of magick. She was looking forward to being a staff queen. She was looking forward to Pellacombe, but more than that, she only accepted Mowbray's proposal after he started renovating Ethandun.'

'What?' said Kenver.

Ethan laughed. 'She thought she was going to live in a palace.'

'She did. And then, one by one, all that was taken from her. First the title – no staff queen for her. It's a good job Mowbray kept her out of the negotiations. If she'd heard he was giving that away as part of the deal, it might never have been struck. And then Medbh turns up, and Medbh is *given* Ethandun. You said Kerenza was thinking about living in a palace, Ethan, but it was much more than that. How long has it been since she lived in Cornwall?'

'Not since she was eighteen.'

'Precisely. Ethandun is in Wiltshire, several hours nearer to London, and the London house was going, too. No A list parties for Kerenza. The last two straws were in the new Trust settlement and in his new will.'

'New will?'

Mina took a moment to describe the surprise witnessing of Mowbray's signature while I tucked in to the tea.

'Have you any evidence she knew about the will?'

'Yes. It's in the preamble: a substantial sum of money in trust *for Grace* and any children they might have together. Nothing for Kerenza herself except some personal items. And don't forget the Trust: Kenver gets Pellacombe, Cador gets Mowbray House and she got Nanquidno.'

'Nanquidno is beautiful,' said Lena.

'I'm sure it is. It's also at Land's End. Kerenza had no intention of spending the rest of her life at the end of the world. There's one more thing.' I pointed to the Steward's badge. 'What does it feel like to wear that, Lena?'

'Strange at first. It is like having an invisible accordion on your chest. You have many buttons, and they make sounds. You get used to it.'

'And Kerenza had no intention of sitting here running the estate while her new husband roamed around the country. Not even for a few months. Kerenza was ripe for the plucking, and that's what Morning did.'

'How do you know?' said Cador. 'Where did that come from?'

'From the bond between Mage and Mentor. What little training Kerenza had came from Morning, and they kept in touch. I'll bet Morning went to a few choice parties over the years, or whatever it was that Kerenza had to offer. I'll never prove it, but I think that Morning introduced Kerenza to Mowbray deliberately, for her own reasons.'

'Wouldn't surprise me,' said Eseld. 'I know that Kerenza has leaned on Morning for magickal assistance since the engagement was announced.'

'Why did Morning want Mowbray to die? It was her idea wasn't it?' said Ethan.

'It was,' said Mina. She'd worked out this part, so I let her explain. 'I guessed this, but Hedda confirmed it this afternoon. Education of young Witches is the only reason the Daughters have continued as the biggest collection of Covens. Without the income, the supply of young disciples and the influence, they would seriously lose out.'

'The Mowbray College!' said Kenver. 'Of course. If Medbh got that going, it would seriously undermine the Daughters' education network, and Morning was head of education.'

'Oh yes,' said Mina. 'And that is why Medbh was Morning's first choice as victim. Kerenza had no feelings for Medbh and was happy to go along with the plot. It was only when they discovered that Medbh had gone that Morning decided to get rid of Lord Mowbray. Kerenza says that she was coerced into it. We'll never know.'

'And Signe?' said Eseld.

'Morning needed a Necromancer, and she knew that Signe was vulnerable. She pushed her buttons and convinced her that Mowbray was the main reason that Hedda went to hospital and not back to Homewood.'

'But she would have died!' said Lena. 'That is ... horrible. Terrible.'

Mina nodded. 'Of course it is. Signe couldn't see past her mother being a Mage. I don't know why.

'Which brings us full circle,' I said. 'Do you want to try them for regicide in the Kernow court?'

'No,' said Eseld, with some finality. 'Cador came to see me in the boathouse. He said that because the court doesn't really exist, it could take months or even years to set up. And all the time we wait, Signe gets to live in Homewood. I want her in Blackfriars Undercroft as quickly as possible for as long as possible.'

I looked around. 'Is everyone happy with that?' They nodded or said yes, and I moved on. 'Kerenza is different. As you all know, she isn't much of a Mage, and she will claim coercion. I doubt she'll get off completely free, but the Undercroft won't have the same terror for her. Even a full murder sentence in there is only seven years.'

'Is that all?'

I looked at Eseld. 'Try it. I did a couple of hours in a Limbo Chamber and it was hell. I saw what it did to Keira Faulkner after a few weeks. If she'd gone down for seven years, Keira Faulkner would be long dead by now.'

'So what's the alternative?'

'Hand over Lord Mowbray's remains and I'll make sure she faces mundane justice.'

'No,' said Cador. 'I don't want my father used as a gambling chip. He deserves better.' He looked around, defying his magickal family to disagree.

'He does,' said Ethan.

'Very good. Rick James is on his way down to support Cordelia. I'll get him to take Kerenza away with him on Monday. If you'll excuse me for a second, I'll get Erin.'

Of all the jobs today, Erin's was in many ways the worst. She had taken it on herself to tell Grace that her mummy had been naughty and would be going away. When she told Grace that she might live with Granny in London and go back to her old school, she cheered up.

I found them in Lord Mowbray's study, a riot of calligraphy materials spread over the desk and on to the floor. The exquisite rug would never be the same again. Enscriber's ink is designed to be permanent.

'Tea time,' I said.

'Will mummy be there?' said Grace, hopefully.

''Fraid not, kid,' said Erin. 'She's still on the naughty step. Everyone else is there. Time to show them how hard you've been working.'

Grace picked up a pile of cards and started wandering in the direction of the family wing. I waited until she was ahead and said, 'Are you sure about this, Erin? It's a long term responsibility.'

Someone had to be Grace's magickal guardian until she hit puberty. If she had a Gift, then the guardian would arrange for appropriate steps to be taken.

'Yeah. It's not a big thing. A few visits a year.' She grinned at me. 'And there's a big fee.'

Grace was centre stage in the sitting room. 'I've been helping Erin to make these with her magic ink. Would anyone like to buy a ticket to Mina's sari party?'

The group admired the beautifully drawn handwritten tickets (with some parts coloured in by Grace). They really were magickal. If you gave them a rub of Lux, they shimmered in different colours. One by one, the family admired the tickets and handed them back until Grace got to Eseld.

'How much?' she said.

'Do you want to come or just to make a donation?' said Mina.

'Alcohol. Dressing up. Chance to mingle. What's not to like? If I'm welcome, of course.'

'It would be an honour,' said Mina. 'Forty pounds for entry or eighty with hire of an outfit. Bring a lot more money on the night. There will be an auction, and all proceeds go to support girls in India who haven't had our chances.'

Eseld took two tickets from Grace and said, 'I may just bring a friend.'

'Can I have tea now?' said Grace.

That was our cue to leave. The King's Watch party rose and left the Mowbrays (plus Grace) to take a first step on the road to a new future.

Part Eight — Sunset, Sunrise

44 – Sunset

They came from all over Kernow to say goodbye to their Lord, from Nanquidno to Kellysporth and beyond. There were others, too, mingling with the crowds on the dock or over at Lamorne Point. Ethan and Eseld had been working all day to set up the Glamours and Wards that would keep tourists (and the fire brigade) away from Pellacombe.

The funeral began at sunset, just after seven thirty, when the hastily made raft and its cargo was lowered into the water in the boathouse and then dragged round to the dock. When the raft was in position, a small bonfire was started on the gravel with unlit torches placed in front of it.

The members of the King's Watch party were classed as VIPs, and we had a good place on the northern jetty. The raft was tied to the southern jetty, and that was reserved for the two families, Mowbray's and Raven's.

When it was fully dark, Ethan led them from the cottage. He was wearing a Mowbray blue cloak with a boar embroidered on the back. Morgan, the Witch from Kellysporth had got her way, and Ethan had become the Boar – senior Mage of the Mowbray clan. Cador and Eseld (in a black trouser suit) followed, and then Kenver.

A second party came behind them, led by Lena and consisting of Hedda, Isolde and Cordelia. The two groups made it slowly through the crowds and along the projecting dock. The dais from where Mowbray had revealed the new Deed on the night he died had been placed at the end, and Ethan mounted it. He turned to the crowds and gave the address.

If you are part of the Mowbray estate, you will have been there and will have heard it. If you're not one of Mowbray's people, I won't repeat it here.

He finished by leading the crowd in the largest, most complex shout I've heard outside a sports stadium. When they'd finished, we heard it echoed from Lamorne Point across the water.

Hedda needed Isolde's support to stand on the podium, and some deft magick from Ethan to project her still frail voice across the crowd. What she said was much shorter, and merits repeating. Raven deserves that.

'Children of the Goddess and of many gods, hear me. Yesterday, I lost a daughter in Raven. No ordinary words can fill so vast a void, so help me with your prayers.'

Hedda faltered, and Isolde led the prayers. They finished with one single shout, 'Goddess, receive her.' They stepped down, and it was time.

Every member of the family parties took a torch and either used magick or the bonfire to light it. Michael scurried forward and untied the raft, then one by one they cast their torches on to the raft. Fuel and magick set the logs ablaze, and more magick blew it down the river and out of sight around the bend. When it was gone, Ethan led the family slowly up the path to the upper terraces where the wake would be held.

Scout had been tied to a stanchion during all this, and had waited patiently. I was slowly discovering that he could remember some of his life as a Familiar. He knew the sheep herding commands, for example, but had no idea about vehicles (and avoiding them). As the crowds followed the families up the path, I said to Mina that I'd take him for a walk before joining them.

'You mean you want a smoke. Fine. I shall see you up there. It's too cold out here now.'

I loosened Scout's lead and lit a cigarette. I was staring across the water, thinking, when I heard footsteps and a piercing howl from Scout. I dropped my cigarette, whipped round and reached for my gun.

A tall, giant of a man, taller than Raven, was walking towards me. His cloak billowed around him and he carried a spear. I didn't need to see his face to know that one eye would be missing.

I bowed as low as I dared. 'Allfather.'

I hadn't seen my former patron for some time. I've seen his ravens on a few occasions, but not Odin himself. This was serious, and I had nothing to offer, a point I made while still bowing.

'This is not your home, Conrad. You have no obligation of hospitality here.'

I straightened up before my back broke in two. 'You honour me.'

'I am not here for you. Not primarily. I came to honour my daughter.'

His face was pointing at the water. 'Raven, my lord?'

'Yes.' He turned to face me, and I nearly joined Scout in a whimper.

There was *more* of Odin than I've ever experienced. A feeling of utter terror was nibbling at my side. He bent down and passed his fingers across Scout's back. The little bundle relaxed and flopped onto his tummy. With a great sweep of his cloak, Odin stood up again.

'Raven was the first fruit of that book, the one you call the *Codex Defanatus*. Someone tried to clone a Valkyrie.'

'Clone?'

'It's the closest word to what they did. They took a seed and planted it in a poor young Witch. Mortals aren't designed to carry our children. It ended horribly for the mother, and instead of a Valkyrie, they got Raven.' It's not wise to interrupt the gods. I waited for more. 'To my shame, I saw nothing of this. I was told of it by the Morrigan, putting me again in her debt. When we found Raven – and what was left of her mother – the infant was nearly dead. The Morrigan said we should take her to Homewood, and I agreed. The rest you know.'

'I am always grateful for your wisdom, Allfather.'

The scariest thing about Odin is his face. It came into focus, empty eye socket and all, and then he gave me a smile that made me want to step backwards off the jetty.

'You're wondering why I'm telling you this, Clarke. It's because I want to know when you find who was responsible. I have looked into the future, and you will not find them by looking, but you will know them when you meet. Will you tell me?'

'My lord.'

'Then I shall give you something in return. When you next encounter Medbh Mowbray, and you will, ask her to translate this for you. Her answer should tell you a lot.'

He passed me a long, flat pebble from some beach. It was carefully inscribed with a series of lines. 'Is this Ogham script?'

'It is, though the language it represents is one used by mortals. While you wait for Medbh to return, you can use the stone to weigh down your papers.'

He made that last remark with something closer to a grin than his Valhalla Smile, and there seemed to be an overall change, too. For one thing, I didn't have so much of a crick in my neck looking up. He had more for me.

'Take this piece of charcoal and give it to your Enscriber. Tell her to make ink, and use that ink to write my invitation to your wedding. And only my invitation. Go well, Conrad.'

I accepted the small lump of charcoal. It throbbed with a heartbeat. I did not think it was possible to be scared of a piece of wood.

While I was still feeling the wood, the dock got brighter, because there wasn't a deity standing in front of the lights any more. As I've said, the gods are not big on goodbyes.

45 – Sunrise

I said goodbye to Eseld on top of Mowbray Hill, overlooking the estuary. It was Tuesday morning, bright and early. None of us had been bright or early on Monday: the first staff king of Kernow had a tremendous wake that went on most of Sunday night. The only person who had been bright on Monday was Hannah. I wasn't going to be earning any medals from this trip, but Team Elvenham were the only ones to have come out of the mess with our reputations enhanced. I think that Mina was secretly pleased when both Ethan and Erin formally asked her to act as recorder in the forthcoming elections.

That was the first question I asked Eseld when we dismounted. I looked longingly down the trail for a second, expecting Scout to emerge. I still ached from the loss of his presence. He was down at Pellacombe, being a dog and doing doggy things.

'Do you fancy it?' I said.

'Fancy what? Or should that be who?'

'Knock it off, Eseld.'

'Force of habit. Talking of habits, give us a fag. Are you driving? I've got a hip flask.'

'Just a nip. I wondered if you fancied being staff queen of Kernow.'

I took a nip from the flask and passed it back to her and she lifted it to her lips. They were still purple. Some things didn't change. 'Cheers. There's no chance of me being staff queen. We'll get Kenver elected and Ethan's going to act as local regent until he's twenty-five. We'll let the chips fall where they want over the rest of Wessex.'

We enjoyed the view for a moment. I could just make out the Smurf on Lamorne Point.

Eseld hadn't finished. 'It was all so easy before, Conrad. Follow Dad round the country. Lots of hookups and tasty weekends, then back to Predannack to chill out. That's all gone now. Even if I could recreate it, I wouldn't want to. What do you think I should do? You seem so ... sorted, somehow. Rooted. Happy.'

I blew out smoke. 'Do you want to start a new branch of the Mowbray clan at Predannack? Settle down, have children and make it a stronghold that you'll pass on to them?'

'Hey! Give me a chance. I've only just sworn off one-night stands. I'm not even sure whether I want a wife or a husband. Or both.' She grinned. 'I'll tell you what, though, I'm giving Saffron a free pass.'

'I'm sure she'll be relieved. Have you taken against blondes all of a sudden?'

The grin turned to something drier. Still a smile, but with half a frown thrown in.

'She's like you, Conrad. Hardcore. I couldn't believe it when she broke Morning's neck without thinking and then got up for more. I think you've already figured out that I'm not as tough as I pretend to be.'

'If you don't fancy Cornish domesticity, why not go to London? Get a visiting lectureship at the Invisible College while Kenver is studying with Chris Kelly. You can do that work on Mowbray House for Cador while you're at it.'

She opened her mouth and closed it again. Then she frowned. 'Would I really get a lectureship at Salomon's House?'

'Warding is a very specialised skill. Most of the really good Mages work on their own account. The salary at Salomon's House is pretty rubbish. I can put in a good word for you with the Dean if you like.'

'I like the sound of that. You know, Cador's already asked me to make an offer on the house. He doesn't fancy it, really. It would save me a lot of trouble.' She gave me her sunniest smile. As sunny as it was going to get for a while.

'I owe you, Conrad. I know that Dad paid you well, but this is personal. Would you like the Smurf as a gift? Free and clear. Fly it away today. I'll even pay for a new paint job. I believe that Mina wanted a more royal blue…'

I was so tempted. It was a beautiful, well-maintained and powerful machine. Reluctantly, I shook my head. 'I'm not in your league, Eseld. The Boss would never pay for me to use it on Watch business, and I can't justify it. Thanks, but I'll have to pass. Will you keep it?'

'No. We'll sell it for now. Kenver might get another one when he's ready. And don't worry, we'll keep Leah Kershaw on the payroll as long as she wants.'

'Good to hear.'

I was about ready to re-mount, but Eseld hadn't finished.

'If you won't take the Smurf, please take Evenstar. She was Dad's horse and Kenver doesn't want her. I know you'll look after her. You can have his saddle, too. It's enchanted. And a horsebox to take her home.'

That I could sign up to. The lease on the five acre field behind Elvenham is on a one-month notice. I grinned and held out my hand. 'Uther can have first dibs on covering her,' I said. 'And I'll offer the foal to Izzi.'

'Deal.'

'Deal.'

'There's one more thing I have to say,' I said. 'I know you've lost your father, but you still have one parent.'

'I'll let you off this last once. Mention that woman one more time and I'll never speak to you again. I had a bat for a Familiar and a crush on a freaky monster. So what? She lied and cheated and manipulated Raven – who was only eighteen, don't forget. She twisted Raven into breaking the bond and dobbed her into Hedda. And she's never even tried to admit that what she did was wrong. The most I got was an apology for "hurting me".' She made scare quotes with her fingers. 'If she'd died on Saturday, I wouldn't have visited her grave to spit on it. She's not worth it, okay?'

I held up my hands. When she *really* started missing her father, she might think again.

She sprang onto Uther's back like an uncoiling spring. 'I do have one thing to thank you for. I am going to seriously try to build bridges with Lena.'

I climbed less athletically onto Evenstar and stroked her neck. She truly is a beautiful beast. 'How come that's down to me?'

'You treated her like a normal person. I should have twigged that anyone who could get the loyalty of the staff like that, despite her comedy accent and her jaw, is worth knowing.' Our mounts started ambling down the hill. 'I'll tell the girls to get Evenstar ready. It's a long drive back to Gloucestershire.'

'We're taking a break half way. At Glastonbury.'

Her head whipped up suspiciously. 'Oh?'

'Hedda wants to see us. At Home House. Evenstar can ramble in the woods, and before you ask, I have no idea what she wants.'

What Hedda wanted was a game of bridge. We were escorted into the Lodge of Home House by a young Witch who tried not to get too close to me. Whether that was because I was a man or because I was the man who'd led the raid on the coach is a moot question. Hedda was waiting for us in a *very* chintzy sitting room with Isolde, a card table and two new packs of cards. The young Witch went to get tea and Hedda announced that I was going to be her partner for the game.

'You're looking well, Hedda,' I said. She was. Her speech was now quicker and more natural. She hadn't got up to greet us, though, and a walking stick hung off the back of her chair.

'Thank you, Conrad. I have something I want to say to you, but that can wait. Isolde has made a great sacrifice by agreeing to be my bridge partner. I want her to get some practice.'

Isolde smiled. 'Willow Coven is not flavour of the month at the moment. I am going to have more time on my hands.'

Mina was listening carefully while she opened the cards and shuffled them. 'Why is that?' she asked. 'Not that it's any of our business.'

'It will be all over the world of magick soon enough,' said Isolde. 'Alys has resigned from Willow Coven and left the Homewood to go on a one year retreat.' She nodded at Hedda. 'My new bridge partner has stepped down as 1st of Oak and is now 13th.'

Mina finished shuffling the cards and passed them to me. I cut them and she dealt. 'How's Georgia?' I asked. 'I hear it was touch-and-go in surgery.'

'She'll be in hospital for months, so she's been passed over and Kiwa is the new 1st of Oak. Kiwa's courage on Mark's Barrow has made her favourite to be the new Eldest Daughter. Verity is keeping Raven's place as 1st of Ash vacant, and won't be praying for a new Eldest until the spring at the earliest.'

Hedda sorted her cards and said, 'I doubt you'll be invited to join, Conrad, but I predict mixed covens to be affiliated to us in the near future. One heart.'

I am a poor bridge player; Hedda is very good. Together, Isolde and Mina were much, much better. That didn't stop Hedda pulling Isolde up a few times with a warning. A tiny part of me started to develop a smidgin of sympathy for Signe.

After the excellent afternoon tea, and more bridge, Hedda looked at me. 'I know you've lost a Familiar, but I believe you've gained a horse. Would you like to show me?'

It took a while for Hedda to sort herself out and join me at the edge of the woods. Scout has already made friends with Evenstar. I think he sees her as a mother figure, and he was happily romping round the woods while she moved in search of autumn treats. I was smoking a cigarette when Isolde helped Hedda out of the Lodge.

Once she was down the steps, the old Witch moved more freely, slowly picking up speed. By the time she got to me, she was barely using the stick at all. 'I have ordered Isolde to make me take three walks a day,' she said. 'At least. What I want to show you is on the other side of the trees.'

Neither of the animals followed us any further. I could feel the tingle and warmth of Lux well before we got to open country. I even got a sense that it *wasn't* open country. We were right on the edge of the Homewood, and there was one of its anchor trees: a massive, proud, perfectly shaped oak, its leaves just starting to turn.

Hedda stopped about fifty feet away from the tree and leaned on her stick. 'I will never forgive myself for what Signe did,' she said. 'Not to Mowbray, to you or to the Coven. I wish I knew what I'd done wrong.'

There was no answer to that, nor did she expect any.

'Will she survive the Undercroft?' she asked.

'I don't know. Having something to live for makes a huge difference. I know that much.'

'She has a son, you know. The boy has no magick and is away at school. She barely mentions him to me unless I ask. I'll start by getting him on board.'

'I hope she does survive,' I added.

Hedda stared at me, all her defences down. 'Because you will want the blood price from her. She told me. She also told me who your Familiar was.'

'Lucas of Innerdale. If there was a statue to him anywhere, they'd be pulling it down.'

I had done some research in Mowbray's library yesterday, whilst nursing my hangover and supervising Saffron, who had been ordered by Hannah to write the final report on Pellacombe.

Lucas of Innerdale lived in Lakeland. Innerdale (not to be confused with Ennerdale) was a magickally hidden valley in one of that mountainous region's most inaccessible spots. It was opened up to the mundane world just before the First World War and now goes by a different name. Its last lord was Lucas, a man who tried to revive a long-dead institution: the Pale Horsemen.

Having a Pale Horseman in your ancestry is a bit like having a slave-owner. Not something to shout about. During the middle ages, the Pale Horsemen were licensed by the Catholic Church to hunt down non-humans: Dwarves, Gnomes, the Fae, Elves, the Dual Natured (i.e. Werewolves) and sundry other relics of the ancient past. Their story truly is in the past, and it should have stayed there. Lucas of Innerdale tried to revive them and set up a local chapter in Lakeland.

I only had one account to draw on, and it was written by someone from London (and therefore suspect). She said that Lucas had some success in putting together a posse at first. And then they rode out and were ambushed by a combined party of Gnomes of Clan Skelwith and Fae from the Queen of Keswick. His followers were killed or scattered, but his body was never found, presumed dragged into a sídhe for torture and punishment.

I considered Hedda, and what she wanted. 'I don't doubt that Lucas became my Familiar,' I said. 'What I do doubt is whether Scout and the historical Lucas can be considered the same. I knew him, Hedda. I knew him intimately. I think the Spirit that Mowbray subdued, the Spirit who stopped your daughter attacking Kiwa and Eseld, was Scout, not Lucas. But neither of us was there, were we? I can tell you that I was most definitely there when Signe severed the bond.'

She bowed her head. 'Of course. That was a terrible thing to do.' She looked up again. 'I would like to pay the blood price for her. It is allowed.'

It is. Having told Signe that I would collect it, I couldn't deny Hedda the opportunity to pay. There was one small complication, though: Signe had to agree, or there could be terrible complications down the line. Entire families have been wiped out because of that.

'Is she content?' I asked.

'It was my price. I told her to let me pay, or I could never take her back. She agreed. You have my word.'

'I'm all ears.'

'Go to the tree. You will find my staff inside it. You should have enough magick to reach into the trunk and pull it out.'

'Forgive my total ignorance, but what should I focus on?'

'The opposite of what you feel. I hear C Major and force my brain to conjure C Minor. Or at least I used to. I will need help to shift next time. If there is a next time.'

It was my first taste of Plane Shifting. I approached the tree nervously and felt every nerve tingle. The Homewood Oak was not happy having a man nearby. My skin broke into an acrid sweat that even I could smell, and my hand started to shake when I held it out. I closed my eyes and thought of a weekend just after my twenty-first birthday, when the RAF sent me to Norway for winter training. That was cold. Seriously cold. Especially the exercise.

We were dumped from a chopper in the middle of nowhere, with nothing but a map and compass to get back. We'd been flown there blindfold, just to make it interesting. We were given a radio, yes, but we'd fail if we used it. Any casualties had to be taken with us. The instructor finished his briefing by saying, 'There is no time limit on this exercise. You have until you get back or you die. Whichever comes first.'

Looking back, I think that I either developed my hidden magickal potential as a Navigator on that trip or Odin nipped out from Valhalla to nudge me in the right direction. Perhaps that was when we first met. I focused on the way I'd felt when one of us twisted their ankle and had to be carried. How the cold seeped into me, how the wind razored my face.

I'd stood as tall as I could and I'd said, 'This way or the radio. I'm going this way, and I'll carry James myself, if he'll come.'

James (of the twisted ankle) had said, 'Fuck the radio. I'm with Conrad.'

When my memory served that up, I felt my arm shiver with cold, not heat, and I pushed it forwards, into where the tree existed on the mundane Plane. Nothing. No resistance at all until I bumped my fingers into a staff of wood. I grabbed it and pulled my hand slowly back. Leaving my eyes closed, I took four steps away from the tree.

I took the staff back to Hedda and laid it at her feet. It was about five feet long and still covered in the bark it had worn as a branch. Or sapling, possibly.

'This is my staff of office as 1st of Oak and Eldest Daughter,' she said. 'It is personal. I made it, and Kiwa will make her own in turn. I have until tonight to surrender it. Usually, retired staves are planted in the Homewood, and this is a good time of the year for planting. In the spring, it will grow with new life. I offer it to you. Plant it at your home and you will have a blessing on your family for many, many generations. It will exist on all Planes. Even the gods will see it. That is my offering for the blood price.'

I bowed low and accepted with thanks. I didn't offer any other comments: the blood price isn't a touchy-feely thing. It's the payment of a debt.

Hedda was getting tired when we made it back to the Lodge, and we said goodbye with a hug on the steps. Mina had just emerged from inside as I was leading Evenstar to the horsebox.

'You stink, Conrad,' was her greeting. 'Even more than the horse. What on earth have you been up to?'

'I'll tell you later. I'm looking forward to getting home and really looking forward to Thursday.'

'I hope you haven't got me anything magickal for my birthday.'

I slammed the bolts home and whistled for Scout. He loped up and jumped in the back of the car. We are going to Cheltenham tomorrow to get fitted for our Downton costumes: Myfanwy's birthday present had been a pair of tickets for the dinner special on the steam railway.

'That depends,' I said, 'on whether you choose the green silk dress or the blue one.'

'What do you mean?'

I pulled carefully on to the main road and started the journey home. I had bought her a ruby necklace from a specialist Indian jewellers in Birmingham. It would go very nicely with the green dress she'd been admiring online. After all, Saffron had said that I needed to buy her one for not getting the letters from Merlyn's Tower.

'You'll see. How did it go with Isolde?'

'I'm afraid that I shall have to say no,' she replied.

'To what?'

'To Hedda or Isolde adopting me. I can't say that either of them are good material for mother of the bride.'

I laughed and she pretended to be offended. 'You can use the Bollywood evening to audition. There's bound to be a few candidates on show.'

She ignored that and asked me about Hedda. When I'd told her, she turned round to look over her shoulder. 'If there's one thing I've learnt with you, Conrad, is that you need eyes in the back of your head. Just when you think something's finished with, it comes back to bite you. Looking forward is all very well, but it can be dangerous. We'll be back in Kernow and Old Sarum before you know it.'

'Might not be *we*. If Hannah decides you need an escort, it might be Rick. And there's one part of this adventure that's definitely not over.'

'Medbh?'

'Precisely. I wouldn't put it past her to turn up at the party, like Sofía did at the last one.'

'She wouldn't dare. In fact, I shall contact Eseld and warn her off. Oh, and I've provisionally invited Lena and Ethan to our wedding.'

'Bit ahead of yourself, love.'

She waved a hand. 'Theirs is after ours. I think she wants ideas on how to conduct a mixed magick/mundane affair.'

'And naturally ours will be better.'

'Of course,' she said, lifting her nose in the air like the princess she is.

I've had to reconsider my father since I learnt about his affairs. He never gave me much advice, but what he did give was always excellent, including his advice about women. His first and most important rule was always let the woman have the last word. I was going to stop there, with Mina saying *Of course*, but there was someone else in the car who deserves to have the last word. They've been through a lot recently.

There was a snuffle and a blast of breath on my neck.

'Arff.'

Conrad, Mina and the whole gang's story continues in
The Seventh Star,
The Seventh Book of the King's Watch,
Now available from Paw Press.
You can also find out how Mina secured their engagement in:

Ring of Troth – A King's Watch Story

Turn over for more...

Ring of Troth

The third King's Watch novella is now available to pre-order from Paw Press on Amazon.

Mina is the happiest woman in the world: she has a job, a home and now a fiancé. The only fly in the ointment is a snake called Pramiti.

She owes a debt to Pramiti. A debt that requires her to find, steal and restore the serpent's magickal ruby, last seen in 1903...

This is no job for Conrad, but if there's one thing she's learnt from him, it's this: Get Help.

Find out who signs up for Team Mina in *Ring of Troth*. And then...

Coming Soon

PAW PRESS

The Seventh Star

The Seventh Book of the King's Watch
by

Mark Hayden

One Hell of a Party...

Mina's Bollywood extravaganza is a huge hit – especially when a surprise celebrity makes a dramatic entrance.

While everyone queues for a selfie, Conrad is wondering why a Fae Countess has descended on him.

It turns out she has a problem, and her problem is about to become Conrad's problem: amidst the dark Satanic mills of Lancashire, something is attacking the Fae.

Conrad has to leave his comfort zone in Clerkswell and break in another new partner. It won't be long before he is praying for strength from Kratu, the Seventh Star.

And why not join Conrad's elite group of supporters:

The Merlyn's Tower Irregulars

Visit the Paw Press website and sign up for the Irregulars to receive news of new books, or visit the Facebook page for Mark Hayden Author and Like it.

Author's Note

Thank you for reading this book; I hope you enjoyed it. If you did, please leave a review on Amazon. It doesn't have to be long. Reviews make a huge difference to Indie authors, and an honest review from a genuine customer is worth a great deal. If you've read *all* the books of the King's Watch, please review them, too – even if you're in a hurry to read the next one.

Shakespeare said that *A good wine deserves a good bush*. In other words, a good book deserves a good cover. I'll never be able to prove it, but I strongly believe that *The King's Watch* would not have been the same without the beautiful covers designed by the Awesome **Rachel Lawston**.

It therefore gave me great pleasure to not only dedicate this book to her mother, **Maggie Pearce**, but to include her as a character.

There is an extra *thank you* to add for *Eight Kings*. After the book had been out for a couple of weeks, Shirley Beglinger got in touch to point out that my rendition of Conrad and Lena's German was less than satisfactory. I am very grateful for her help in correcting it!

The *King's Watch* books are a radical departure from my previous five novels, all of which are crime or thrillers, though very much set in the same universe, including the *Operation Jigsaw Trilogy*. Conrad himself refers to it as being part of his history.

You might like to go back the *Jigsaw* trilogy and discover how he came to the Allfather's attention. As I was writing those books, I knew that one day Conrad would have special adventures of his own, and that's why the Phantom makes a couple of guest appearances.

Other than that, it only remains to be said that all the characters in this book are fictional, as are some of the places, but Merlyn's Tower, Pellacombe and Homewood are, of course, all real places, it's just that you can only see them if you have the Gift…

This book could it have been written without love, support, encouragement and sacrifices from my wife, Anne

As ever, Chris Tyler's friendship is a big part of my continued desire to write.

Thanks, Mark Hayden.

Dramatis Personae

Clerkswell

Conrad Clarke	Me.
Mina Desai	My life partner.
Alfred Clarke	My father, now resident in San Vicente nr Valencia, Spain. Retired dealer in antiques.
Mary Clarke	My mother. Still with my father at the time of writing. Retired cryptanalyst for GCHQ.
Rachael Clarke	My younger sister, now resident in Mayfair and a big cheese at a wealth management firm.
Sofía Torres	My half-sister, as of five minutes ago. (We share a father; her mother is Mercedes del Convento, a Tarot reader of San Vicente)
Scout	My Familiar Spirit. A Border Collie.
Myfanwy Lewis	Our resident Druid/Housekeeper. Currently serving a sentence for her involvement in Dragon rearing. A Herbalist and excellent bat for Clerkswell Ladies Cricket Team.
Ben Thewlis	Myfanwy's fiancé. A cereal agronomist and captain of the men's cricket team.
Carole Thewlis	Ben's sister. Works in the oil industry. Very good friend of Rachael's.
Erin Slater	An Enscriber who rents one of my stables. A good friend to Myfanwy. Member of the Arden Foresters Circle of Mages. Superb slip fielder.
Miss Parkes	Former headmistress of the village school. A Formidable Person.
Lloyd Flint	A Gnome. Clan Second to Clan Flint. My magickal blood brother.
Stephen & Juliet Bloxham	Owners of Clerkswell Manor, the Big House. Stephen: developer and chairman of the cricket club. Juliet: housewife and captain of the ladies' team. Hereditary enemies of the Clarkes. Up to a point.
Ross Miller	Young fast bowler.
Emily Ventress	Ditto.
Jack and Erica Robson	Vicky's parents. Normally resident in Newcastle upon Tyne.

London

All of these people feature in the following story, even if only in passing. I've grouped them by association.

The King's Watch

Hannah Rothman	The Peculier Constable, head of the King's Watch. Referred to as the Boss.
Victoria "Vicky" Robson	My former work partner and good friend of all at Clerkswell. A Geordie and proud of it.
Saffron Hawkins	My current work partner. One of the "Oxfordshire Hawkins" and well connected in the world of magick. Second cousin to Heidi Marston.
Rick James	Senior Watch Captain. Also responsible for the Watch of Wessex. Ex-husband of Cordelia (see Glastonbury)
Xavier Metcalfe	Vicky's current work partner.
Tennille Haynes	Hannah's PA. Mother to Desirée Haynes
Iain Drummond	Deputy Constable. Has responsibility for prosecutions in the Cloister Court
Annelise van Kampen	A Watch Officer and assistant lawyer to Iain Drummond. Originally from Holland.

The Invisible College / Salomon's House

Cora Hardisty	Dean of the Invisible College (who wants to be Warden). A consummate politician and an ally rather than a friend.
Dr Francesca Somerton	Keeper of the Queen's Esoteric Library. A wise woman who has not hung up her dancing shoes.
Heidi Marston	Custodian of the Great Work and Master Artificer. A larger than life character in all senses of the word. Saffron's cousin and a member of the Hawkins clan.
Selena Bannister	Mistress of Illusions. Cora Hardisty's best friend
Oighrig Ahearn	The Oracle – senior Sorcerer at Salomon's House. Cora Hardisty's protégé.
Chris Kelly	The Earth Master of Salomon's House – a Geomancer and expert in Ley lines. Almost a friend.
(Tamsin Kelly)	Chris Kelly's wife – for further details see Ring of Troth
Desirée Haynes	A postgraduate student at the College. Vicky Robson's best friend.

The Cloister Court

The Honourable Mrs Justice Bracewell Senior judge in the Cloister Court. May or may not be known as Marcia to her husband.

Stephanie Morgan Deputy Bailiff to the Cloister Court. Wields a mean axe and bakes very nice cakes.

Augusta Faulkner Legendary barrister in the Court. Mostly famous for her work as a defence lawyer. Mother to Keira Faulkner.

Irina Ispabudhan Currently in prison. See the story of the Nine of Wands for full details

Everyone Else

Alain Dupont A Frenchman from a small village in Bordeaux. Founder member of the Merlyn's Tower Irregulars. All his Christmases came at once when he got a job as a paid intern with my sister Rachael at her wealth management firm.

(Mr Joshi) A part-time Hindu priest and retired civil servant. For further details see Ring of Troth

Pellacombe

I could also have called this group *Team Mowbray*. The Mowbrays are above all a family – and every family needs a tree. Theirs is at the front of this book. There is also a full sized copy to look at on the Paw Press Website. Go to Dramatis Personae on the main menu and it's at the bottom.

The Mowbrays in Detail

Lord Mowbray Mage and billionaire. A client of my sister Rachael. Lord and master of Pellacombe in Cornwall (or "Kernow" as he calls it). The most powerful Geomancer in the UK. His first name is Arthur, but no one uses it.

Kerenza	Lord Mowbray's fiancée. A former model/actress and minor Mage.
Eseld Mowbray	Lord Mowbray's oldest child. A powerful Mage specialising in Wards. Daughter to Isolde (see Glastonbury).
Cador Mowbray	Lord Mowbray's second child. Not a Mage at all. A barrister and the one who looks after the Mowbray's non-magickal and legal interests. Has asked Rachael out many times (unsuccessfully). Son to Isolde.
Morwenna Mowbray	Lord Mowbray's third child. Daughter to Aisling Mowbray. Missing believed dead.
Kenver Mowbray.	Lord Mowbray's fourth and youngest child. Son to Aisling. Only eighteen but already named as Mowbray's heir to Pellacombe. A Geomancer of great potential.
(Aisling Mowbray)	Mowbray's second wife, a Witch of Ireland. Died in an accident when Morwenna and Kenver were very young.
Ethan Mowbray	Lord Mowbray's cousin, son of the late Earl of Tintagel. A master of Occulting. Lord of Kellysporth in north Cornwall.
Lena	Ethan's fiancée and Steward of Pellacombe. Originally from the Austrian Tyrol. A Healer.
Grace	Kerenza's eight year old daughter from a previous relationship. Keen on horses.
Leah Kershaw	Lord Mowbray's personal pilot. Former RAF Officer.
Jane Kershaw	Leah's mother and one of the Pellacombe Estate's senior managers.
Maggie Pearce	Lord Mowbray's driver. Legendary for her strict adherence to the Highway Code and for the inedibility of her baking.
The Ferrymistress	Responsible for the crossing of the River Fal between Lamorne Point and Pellacombe.
Her Husband	Senior Estate Engineer with qualifications in helicopter mechanics
Michael	Their son. A natural sailor.
Two Daughters	One older than Michael is just beginning her education as a Mage, and one younger who does what she's told if she knows what's good for her.
Smurf	An Airbus H155 helicopter. Painted bright blue.

Glastonbury

The Daughters of the Goddess at Glastonbury are in one of three covens of Homewood, their Sacred Grove. Each coven (Ash, Oak and Willow) are ranked, and each Witch is known by their place in the Coven ("1st of Ash" or "9th of Oak"). Some of them hold subsidiary titles, as shown below. I've organised them by Coven, with an extra line for Síona. The Hawthorn Coven is based in Highgate, London, and Síona is the most senior Witch outside Homewood.

Oak Coven

Hedda	1st of Oak	Eldest Daughter, leader of all the Daughters. Actual mother to Signe. Originally from Sweden
Georgia	3rd of Oak	Keeper of Homewood. Domestic bursar. Doesn't like men.
Kiwa	4th of Oak	The Traveller. Responsible for liaising / inspecting the many covens around the country who are affiliated to Glastonbury.
Signe	8th of Oak	Page to Ingrid. Actual daughter of Ingrid

Ash Coven

Raven	1st of Ash	Has no formal role because she is the biggest Mage. Literally and metaphorically. Huge talent, very tall.
Brook	7th of Ash	Counsel to the Daughters. Handles legal matters.
Cordelia	11th of Ash	Page to Raven. Ex-wife of Watch Captain Rick James.

Willow Coven

Verity	1st of Willow	Daughter of Memory. Senior priestess and keeper of the memories of the Goddess.
Alys	2nd of Willow	The 'Little Mother' runs the day-to-day business of Homewood. Twin sister to Zoe.
Zoe	5th of Willow	The Pursekeeper. Handles the financial affairs. Twin to Alys.

Morning	6th of Willow	Dame of Homewood. Responsible for all magickal education in the covens.
Isolde	9th of Willow	Guardian of Willow. Ex-wife of Lord Mowbray, mother to Eseld and Cador
Síona	1st of Hawthorn	Sits on the Occult Council and represents Witches in the corridors of power.

Printed in Great Britain
by Amazon

42514525R00187